Themes In Drama

An annual publication

Edited by James Redmond

11

WOMEN IN THEATRE

SUBSCRIPTIONS The subscription price to volume 11, which includes postage, is
£32 (US $63.00 in USA and Canada) for institutions, £18.00 (US $36.00 in USA
and Canada) for individuals ordering direct from the Press and certifying that the
annual is for their personal use. Airmail (orders to Cambridge only) £5.50 extra.
Copies of the annual for subscribers in the USA and Canada are sent by air to New
York to arrive with minimum delay. Orders, which must be accompanied by
payment, may be sent to a bookseller, subscription agent or direct to the publishers:
Cambridge University Press, The Edinburgh Building, Shaftesbury Road, Cambridge CB2 2RU. Payment may be made by any of the following methods: cheque
(payable to Cambridge University Press), UK postal order, bank draft, Post Office
Giro (account no. 571 6055 GB Bootle – advise CUP of payment), international
money order, UNESCO coupons, or any credit card bearing the Interbank symbol.
Orders from the USA and Canada should be sent to Cambridge University Press,
32 East 57th Street, New York, NY 10022

BACK VOLUMES Volumes 1–10 are available from the publisher at £22.00 ($66.00
in USA and Canada)

WOMEN IN THEATRE

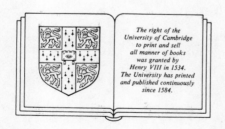

The right of the
University of Cambridge
to print and sell
all manner of books
was granted by
Henry VIII in 1534.
The University has printed
and published continuously
since 1584.

CAMBRIDGE UNIVERSITY PRESS

CAMBRIDGE

NEW YORK   PORT CHESTER   MELBOURNE   SYDNEY

Published by the Press Syndicate of the University of Cambridge
The Pitt Building, Trumpington Street, Cambridge CB2 1RP
32 East 57th Street, New York, NY 10022, USA
10 Stamford Road, Oakleigh, Melbourne 3166, Australia

First published 1989

Printed in Great Britain at The Bath Press, Avon

British Library cataloguing in publication data
Themes in Drama, 11
1. Drama – History and criticism – Periodicals
809.2′005 PN1601

Library of Congress catalogue card number 82–4491

ISSN 0263–676X
ISBN 0 521 37033 7

Contents

Themes in Drama volumes and conferences

Volumes already published in the series

Forthcoming

Themes in Drama *conferences*

Annual conferences are held at the University of London and at the University of California, Riverside. The subjects in 1990 and 1991 will be 'Melodrama' and 'Madness in Drama' respectively, and these subjects have been proposed and accepted for the annual journal *Themes in Drama* (volumes 14 and 15). The subject for the 1992 conferences will be 'National Theatres' and this title will be proposed for publication. Details of the conference held in California may be obtained from: *Themes in Drama* Conference, University of California, Riverside, CA 92521. Details of the conference held in London may be obtained from the Editor.

Potential contributors are asked to correspond with the Editor at an early date. Papers for volumes 14 and 15 should be submitted in final form to the Editor before 1 August 1990 and 1 August 1991 respectively.

James Redmond, Editor, *Themes in Drama*, Westfield College, University of London NW3 7ST.

Contributors

Karen Bassi, *Department of Classics, Syracuse University*

Catherine Boyle, *Department of Modern Languages, University of Strathclyde*

Victor Castellani, *Foreign Languages and Literatures, University of Denver*

Jill Dolan, *Department of Theatre, University of Wisconsin, Madison*

Gail Finney, *Germanic Languages and Literatures, Harvard University*

Robert Gordon, *Department of Drama and Theatre Studies, RHBNC, University of London*

Vera Gottlieb, *Department of Drama, Goldsmiths' College, University of London*

Lorraine Helms, *Department of English, Simmons College, Boston*

Sue Jameson, *Arts Correspondent, London Broadcasting Company*

Sharon D. King, *Program in Comparative Literature, University of California, Los Angeles*

Allen Kuharski, *Department of Dramatic Art, University of California, Berkeley*

Cindy Lutenbacher, *Department of Theatre, Northwestern University*

Cynthia Running-Johnson, *Department of Languages, Western Michigan University, Kalamazoo*

Richard G. Scharine, *Department of Theatre, University of Utah*

Peter Schroeder, *Department of English, California State University, San Bernardino*

Maya Slater, *Department of French, Westfield College, University of London*

Diane Speakman, *writer and editor*

David Wiles, *Department of Drama and Theatre Studies, RHBNC, University of London*

Catherine Wiley, *Department of English, University of Wisconsin, Madison*

Judith Zivanovic, *Department of Spanish, South Dakota State University*

Illustrations

Editor's preface

This is the eleventh volume of *Themes in Drama,* which is published annually. Each volume brings together reviews and articles on the theatrical activity of a wide range of cultures and periods. The papers offer original contributions to their own specialized fields, but they are presented in such a way that their significance may be appreciated readily by non-specialists.

Each volume indicates connections between the various national traditions of theatre by bringing together studies of a theme of central and continuing importance. The annual international conferences (see p. vii) provide an opportunity for scholars, critics and theatrical practitioners to exchange views, and many of the papers in the volumes are revised versions of papers read and discussed at the conferences. The present volume reflects the range and quality of the 1987 conferences on 'Women in Theatre'. Contributions are invited for volumes 14 and 15; they should follow the style of presentation used in this volume, and be sent to

James Redmond
Editor *Themes in Drama*
Westfield College
University of London
London NW3 7ST

The value of a kindly chorus: female choruses in Attic tragedy*

VICTOR CASTELLANI

Whether the 'original' sex of the Dionysiac chorus from which Attic tragedy evolved (or was deliberately created) in the sixth century BC was male, female, or even, conceivably, mixed is not known and may well be unknowable.[1] Yet whether the first choreuts were male and impersonated males (for example, as satyrs), were male and impersonated females (maenad worshippers of the wine god), or were female (literal *bakkhai*, possessed women under the transforming power of the god), when through the extant texts we meet tragedy in the second or third generation of its history at Athens the chorus are male singers and dancers, who routinely play male groups or female, with appropriate masks and attire. In the two earliest surviving plays by Aeschylus, for example, we meet elders of the Persian 'senate' (in the *Persae* of 472 BC) and panicky women of uncertain age (five years later in the *Seven Against Thebes*). All of the great Attic tragedians, Aeschylus, Sophocles, and Euripides, used this chorus of young or not-so-young men freely to represent either men or women who belonged to or, in some cases, accidentally entered, the scenes of their plays.[2] Among these same three playwrights, however, we find striking differences in the frequency and dramatic value of the *female* chorus. This essay will describe those differences, will attempt to explain them, and will illustrate their consequences for Aeschylean, Sophoclean, and especially Euripidean dramaturgy.

First, let us examine the differences themselves. Aeschylus overwhelmingly prefers what may be called a 'cross-sex' chorus – opposite in gender, that is, to the protagonist of his play. In fact, in *every one* of his seven extant tragedies (including *Prometheus Bound* despite some powerful arguments against Aeschylus' authorship of the play we have under this name) this feature occurs.[3] The Persian Queen Atossa in the *Persians* and Queen Clytemnestra in the *Agamemnon* played against male choruses (in both cases, choruses of elders), while in the remaining five plays a *female* chorus occupied the orchestra facing dominant *male* characters (who were:

* A draft of this paper was read at the *Themes in Drama* International Conference held at the University of California, Riverside, in February 1987.

Eteocles in the *Seven,* the Pelasgian king in *Suppliants,* Orestes in both *Libation Bearers* and *Eumenides,* and, in his eponymous play, Prometheus). Furthermore, to the extent that one may judge from titles and fragments of other plays by Aeschylus, and from the literary *testimonia,* among twenty-six where we have either sufficient or at least suggestive information about both chorus and likely protagonist, *fifteen* appear to have had a chorus of women, and no fewer than *twenty* appear to have had cross-sex choruses.[4] The impression we get from the surviving plays therefore does not badly mislead: Aeschylus used female choruses very frequently, rather more so than male ones; and most of the time he set up a potential 'battle of sexes' between his chorus, female or male, and his leading character.

With Sophocles things are very different indeed. Our most solid evidence, of course, lies in his seven complete plays. In them we find two female choruses (in and naming his *Trachinian Women,* and in his *Electra*), five male. In six of the seven the protagonist and chorus are the same sex (for the two female choruses inhabit plays with female protagonists – Deianeira and Electra, respectively); and in the seventh, the *Antigone,* a chorus of Theban citizens are cross sex to the title character, but same sex as her extremely important adversary Creon *with whom they interact more than they do with Antigone.* Sophocles, then, seems to have preferred male choruses, and to have avoided cross-sex dynamics. Our information about the rest of his *oeuvre* seems to confirm both of these tendencies. In Sophocles' case, too, besides the extant seven, twenty-six other 'lost' tragedies are not so far lost that we cannot tell with some degree of certainty who were their leading characters and what their choruses.[5] Sixteen of these had, it seems, a chorus of men, almost all of the sixteen had a male protagonist and *all* must have had at least one centrally important male role, for example, the *Meleagros* and *Tereus,* whose protagonists may have been female, yet whose male title characters must have had a great deal to do, to say, and to suffer.[6] Among the remaining ten Sophoclean plays with (we know or have good reason to think) a chorus of women, all but two appear to have had a major female role. Sophocles, therefore, in contrast with Aeschylus, used same-sex, not cross-sex choruses quite regularly, and somewhat preferred a male presence in the *orkhestra.*

Though he had something in common with Aeschylus, Euripides was really very different from either of his older compatriots in characterizing and deploying his choruses. Seventeen or, if we exclude the 'pro-satyric' tragicomedy *Alcestis,* sixteen of his tragedies survive entire or nearly so.[7] Only *Alcestis,* the *Children of Heracles* and *Heracles Mad* have male choruses. Although Euripides' other tragedies, known of but not extant, have a smaller preponderance of female choruses, they still show a clearly marked preference for them. Nineteen female choruses are known or supposed among the lost plays as against ten, perhaps eleven male ones.[8] The female choruses that this 'most tragic' playwright so clearly favored interacted, however, with the typical Euripidean *set* of leading roles (plural, or at least dual), a phenomenon which thoroughly blurs any same-sex/cross-sex distinction in analyzing his work. For it is often the case in Euripidean drama that the choreuts (in song) and chorus leader (in dialogue) function as *both* same *and* cross sex with respect to different principal characters (for example, same sex as Iolaus, opposite sex to Alcmene in *Children of Heracles*, same sex as Medea, Phaedra, Electra, *et aliae*, and yet opposite to Jason, Hippolytus, Orestes, *et alii*). Euripides' female chorus, therefore, though perhaps related (like many other features of his dramaturgy) to Aeschylean precedent, contributed uniquely to the (social) background of, the (visual) foreground of, and indeed to the *elicitation* of both male and female characters, as this group of women witnessed, reacted emotionally to, and commented upon the sufferings of both men and fellow women.

The differences between Euripides and Sophocles, and between them and their predecessor Aeschylus having been described in general terms, we may now attempt to identify the ideological and/or dramaturgic reasons for which they are likely so to have differed.

Aeschylus, the oldest of the three, operated (to put it simply) *naturally*. This is not to brand him as 'primitive,' since much of his art is anything but![9] It is, however, to acknowledge that he found intrinsic drama both in a moral and political 'battle of the sexes' which goes back to the Homeric poems (whose influence Aeschylus is reported to have professed), and in the mental–emotional contrast between men and women such as he found in his own Athens, such as he found in the heroic and divine myths, but also such as he boldly invented (for example, his memorable 'natural' women Atossa and Electra, his even more memorable *unnatural* Clytemnestra – who so puzzles a chorus of otherwise canny old men in the *Agamemnon*).[10] Masculine and feminine thought and feeling, juxtaposed, produced just the sort of tone and tension that the 'Father of Tragedy' created to give energy and life to his poetry and to his almost dialectical theodicy. Below I shall discuss more precisely how this worked in two very different sorts of play, the *Seven Against Thebes* and the *Eumenides*.

Despite a few grand and not a few subtle female roles in *his* drama, Sophocles seems largely to have agreed with his friend Pericles that women should be little seen, heard, or talked about in comparison with the important actors on the political or the theatrical scene – that is, in comparison with the men.[11] His major female characters are paradoxes, such as Antigone and Electra, contrasted with 'weak sisters', or they are created in response to figures in Euripides' works.[12] On the whole, although Sophocles did pity the Deianeira who was left at home, the Tecmessa who was left alone and alive, it was the hero, the soldier or citizen, the *man* in the context of war or feud or other communal crisis that interested him, not the woman who remained so much behind the scenes, out of sight and out of mind; and to comment and speculate on the man he used *men*. This, too, is reasonable and natural, though quite different from Aeschylus; and it is certainly limited in scope, to reflect socio-political circumstances, rather than comprehensive and humane, to mirror domestic life. Furthermore, a purely technical consideration can also have led Sophocles to eschew the female chorus. Though individual male actors could, it seems, brilliantly impersonate Niobes and Clytemnestras and the rest, a whole *chorus* of a dozen or fifteen men, not merely speaking and gesticulating but rather *singing and dancing as women* might have been more suitable for comedy than for the 'better than life' tragedy at which Sophocles aimed.[13] His preference notwithstanding, the second of the great Attic tragic dramatists did use choruses of women for special and interesting effects in two plays, *Trachinan Women* and *Electra*, to which we shall return later for a closer discussion of his technique.

First, however, we may have a look at Euripides, his younger contemporary and, for nearly half a century, his rival. One reason why Euripides' female choruses (of which 'Aeschylus' makes such delightful fun in the *Frogs*) may have been so numerous is the uniquely Euripidean type of lyricism that Aristophanes mocks so vigorously.[14] There are also, however, three much more important factors, of which one is technical, the others pertaining to content. The technical reason has to do with Euripides' efforts to establish a certain air of realism, or at least of ordinary human probability, for his plays' central events. The younger tragedian, enlightened, perhaps, by the psychological and sociological inquiries of the Sophists, must have been aware how implausible it was for a crowd of bystanders not to intervene in scandalous, often violent events on stage and in their sight, or else just behind the *skene* doors, within their easy hearing. The only expedient, if he wished to make his action believable, was either to remove the chorus from the orchestra entirely (which was possible only infrequently, as during important though non-violent scenes of his *Alcestis* and *Helen*) or else to make the chorus as helpless as possible. It is worth observing in this connection that the only two male choruses in extant Euripides are feeble old men, in *Children of Heracles* and *Heracles*, no more able to intervene against the threats from the villains Eurystheus and Lycus than a similar number of girls or women in the other plays.

The two apparent factors in Euripides' preference for female choruses that pertain to content have to do with audience sympathy for women as uniquely pathetic figures, and with quasi-feminist criticisms of men's behavior in general, of their wars in particular. The choruses of *Medea*, *Ion*, and *Iphigenia at Aulis* will illustrate these features of Euripidean neo-tragedy, after we have looked at the choruses in representative works of Aeschylus and Sophocles.

AESCHYLUS' *SEVEN AGAINST THEBES* (467 BC)

Among his surviving works Aeschylus' sole remaining Theban tragedy will demonstrate the emotional yet also the sensible, rational value possible for a chorus of women. During a crisis for their city Thebes and for their king Eteocles (the protagonist of the play), a group of young women come near panic over the acute danger to both. Stasimon Two, at lines 338–68, includes a graphic description of a city sacked (with special concentration on the fate of its women) that influenced, or at least anticipated, Euripides (including one choral song in the play *Iphigenia at Aulis* discussed below). Indeed, the first five choral sequences are all 'in character' for fearful women, especially their very agitated entrance song (lines 78–180), which not surprisingly draws Eteocles' impatient rebuke; while two of the *kommoi* (lyrical chorus-plus-character sequences) in the *Seven* show them in open conflict with the young king: lines 203–44 and 677–711, the latter continued into iambic dialogue.[15] Their own and their king's positions later become reversed, however; for, although at first it is *he* who urges calmness and courage, eventually *they* try to check his mad determination to confront his brother Polyneices at the seventh gate. In the intervening part of the play, moreover, during a long sequence where Eteocles chooses the first six gates' defenders, the position of the women may be called intermediate, as they come to understand the adequacy of the Theban defense and calm down as a consequence. Only after Eteocles has departed for fratricide and death do they, for a single stasimon, become a 'mere' Aeschylean chorus, without any particular reference or pertinence to their sex meditating (in difficult song, lines 720–91) on the curse of the House of Laius; for, subsequent to this and right to the end of the reliable part of the text, they resume their high emotionalism.[16] They waver between rejoicing (lines 822–6) at the victory of which they had formerly despaired, and lamenting (lines 827–47) over a disaster that has extinguished the royal family of their city. They understand, but they also regret, the curse on Laius' family that has worked through the two previous plays, that has brought this last member of the trilogy to such a distressing conclusion.

AESCHYLUS' *EUMENIDES* (458 BC)

Aeschylus employs very differently the chorus of Furies (or Erinyes) in the play entitled after a euphemism for them meaning '*Kindly Ladies*'. This tragedy was, like the *Seven Against Thebes*, the last part of a trilogy; but, quite unlike the *Seven*, it solved the problem of the preceding plays not destructively, with the extirpation of a royal line, but constructively, with a grand reconciliation of formerly opposed divine blocs. We might call the chorus's role here ideological, since from their entrance (beginning at line 117) to the very end of the play (line 1047) the Erinyes represent one of those blocs as its only direct voice in the trilogy. They take a strong position not only against the matricide Orestes, whom they hound from Delphi to Athens, but also against the 'new' patriarchal Olympian gods and goddesses who have, they protest, overthrown their own ancient female right. They complain to Apollo in their entrance-song (or, rather, their awakening song): 'O son of Zeus, you are a thief; young as you are, you have ridden rough over aged divinities, out of respect for a suppliant [Orestes], a godless man and one bitter to parents. Though a god you have stolen away the matricide. What of this will anyone call justly done? . . . Such things do the younger gods do, ruling the world beyond justice. A throne dripping blood, at the foot, at the head – one may see the earth's navel has taken upon it a hideous stain of blood. Though a prophet he has defiled his place with a visitor's pollution, sped by himself, summoned by himself, honoring mortality against gods' laws, but leaving the ancient portions to perish' (lines 149–54; 162–72). Their chief emotion is indignation, outraged as they are at what they see as the moral collapse of human society (especially in the third stasimon, lines 490–565). They threaten first the man Orestes (in their first three songs, beginning respectively at lines 143, 254, and 307), then the city, Athens, that has received and acquitted him (at lines 778–92 = 808–22, in the first part of their long, eventful *kommos* with Athene). Nevertheless they also have power for good, both to prevent certain types of heinous crime and to promote fertility in the land; and, even more importantly, they have the choice of how to apply that power. Understanding this and understanding them, Athene, through the second part of that *kommos* (beginning at about line 858) persuades them to apply it favorably to her favorite city. Opposed to Orestes, opposed, too, to the god Apollo during the pleadings in the great central episode (lines 574–677), they are nevertheless reconciled with the goddess of Athens and, through her, with the balanced government, by reason, by law, *and* by healthy *fear*, that she intends for her city. We ought, in fact, to compare her remarks on reverence and fear at lines 690–706 with the chorus's at lines 517–25: all these females are agreed upon the necessity and usefulness of what the Greeks seem to have believed was a feminine emotion, and one, as we have seen, that marked the chorus of mortal women in the *Seven*. Perhaps the most important difference between this play and the *Seven* is that in the earlier play the opposition of male protagonist to female chorus does *not* give way before female-to-female interaction; whereas at the end of the Orestean Trilogy just such interaction, of Athene and the not-yet 'Kindly Ladies', leads to a compromise that recognizes *and conspicuously honors* the female role in a male-dominant system. The feminine has, therefore, not merely an ideology that must be heard (acknowledging natural bonds of love, as such as those between son and mother) but a function that must be brought to bear – literally, to *bear* – if human society is to prosper. Ultimately, therefore, Athens must and *will* prosper, as Thebes could not, because of the sort of enlightenment that Aeschylus himself hoped to bring, Athene willing, to his fellow citizens in the Theater of Dionysus.

SOPHOCLES' *TRACHINIAN WOMEN* (PROBABLY C. 430 BC)

Turning to Sophocles we find much less profound, yet psychologically much subtler employment of the female chorus. In the unusual and relatively unfamiliar play *Trachinian Women* the chorus who give it its title play almost all of their role *and sing absolutely all of their hauntingly beautiful songs* before a rapid series of scenes over the last 308 lines of the play that are 'all male' both in speakers and in concerns.[17] The women of this chorus are concerned friends and neighbors of the female protagonist Deianeira, wife of the long absent but soon expected hero Heracles. They make their homes in the central Greek district Trachis, where Heracles' family have awaited either news of the hero or his return for over a year. They arrive upon the scene in the first place to offer their friend sympathy and hope, and, in fact, readily become her confidants. The emotions of their entrance song (lines 94–140) and of two of their 'standing songs' (lines 205–24, a short, cheerful little song-and-dance, and the more sedate but still hopeful lines 633–62) must closely reflect Deianeira's own simultaneous feelings, and another stasimon (the second: lines 497–530) may also be a sort of mirror of her mind, harking back to the marvelous, frightening occasion when Heracles and a metamorphic river god wrestled, with her as the prize. They end this last song with an affecting picture of Heracles' young new wife: 'The pitiful look of the bride, fought over, awaits [the outcome of the battle for her]; and she is gone from her mother, like a strayed and lonely heifer' (lines 527–30). These Trachinian women hear and share her worries, initially over her husband's fate, later over the fate of his and her marriage (gravely threatened by the captive woman Iole, to win whom as his concubine Heracles has just fought a great war), and finally over the dangerous remedy to her love problems that she first believes she has found, but that soon she discovers is no remedy at all (but rather a deadly poison that she has been tricked into using against Heracles by an old enemy of his). A chorus of this nature permits the playwright to explore the female protagonist's confused and developing emotions at a length and with an intimacy otherwise impossible. Euripides' female choruses in works like the *Medea*, to be discussed on pp. 10–11 below, and (depending on the date of *Trach.*) in one or both of the Euripidean Hippolytus-and-Phaedra plays, perhaps also in the *Andromache*, seem likely to have suggested the device to Sophocles. However, since the Trachinian chorus are *young* women, either unmarried or without personal experience of marriage grown 'old', their witness to and vicarious participation in Deianeira's tragedy are especially poignant. Furthermore, we ought not overlook how their youth distances them somewhat from a woman old enough to have a young adult son (Hyllus), even as the concubine Iole's young beauty separates her from Mrs Heracles. Deianeira experiences, in fact, the lonely isolation so typical of Sophoclean protagonists, though here, for once, in a wistful, feminine mode, an isolation that, because there *are* other women who might take her part yet cannot quite do so, is less harsh but even sadder than Tecmessa's among the Greek soldiers in the same playwright's *Ajax*, or than his Antigone's among officers and counselors of state.

SOPHOCLES *ELECTRA* (410S BC)

In the *Electra* of Sophocles the situation is reversed in one sense from that in the play just discussed, though the ultimate effect of his scheme is remarkably similar. For in this piece the chorus of women are distinctly *older* than the female protagonist. Whereas Deianeira could call her chorus *paides*, 'children,' the chorus of Argive matrons can address Electra as *pai*, 'child'.[18] In the later of our two Sophoclean plays, however, the isolation of the young Electra is even more severe. Not only do the women of its chorus differ from the dispossessed and abused princess in age and status (they are not, of course, royal, but *are*, evidently, married – what she cannot now hope to be), they also disapprove not of her mourning but of her behavior (in this resembling the chorus of *male* elders vis-à-vis Sophocles' Antigone). This disapproval these Argive matrons share with *other* females in the cast who are also at odds with Electra: her sister, Chrysothemis, who disagrees about their most helpful policy and even about the very possibility of their happiness, and whom Electra grows to hate; and her mother, Clytemnestra, who is (and has been since long before the action begins) her out-and-out enemy. The *Electra* chorus, moreover, on two occasions (lines 121–250 and 823–70) sing *kommoi* with the agonized princess in which she and they express contrasted emotions, and in which their attempts to console her over her father's murder or to reassure her about the gods' ultimate justice do not merely fail in their desired effect but actually have an effect almost opposite to what the good women intend. Furthermore, their first stasimon, on the eventual advent of Fury and Justice, but also on her family's curse, aggravates rather than pacifies her (lines 472–515, to which she reacts when she also reacts to Clytemnestra's sudden intrusion, at lines 558–609). She finds herself on the defensive, therefore, with women who, like poor young Chrysothemis, mean her no ill, yet who cannot really fathom her feelings. So far as they understand her, they approve. They fully sympathize with her hopes that Agamemnon will be avenged and that Orestes will return to recover his father's throne. On the other hand, the grief and the vindictiveness that shape Electra they cannot fathom, cannot appreciate, especially as her stance becomes increasingly dangerous to her. *She* cannot deliberate with them, cannot open her heart to them, as Deianeira could with her girl-friends; and *they* cannot sympathize with her without reserve, nor admire her without reservation. This is perhaps in major part due to her blighted nature, her Fury-ous temper that makes her something beyond the feminine, beyond the masculine, at least by normal human standards – the standards, that is, which any Sophoclean chorus, male or female, are wont to apply as they interpret and judge the characters who stand beyond them (and a bit above them) on the stage platform.

Electra is utterly unlike the poor wife Deianeira, by past history and by permanent disposition. The Sophoclean Electra is a great-hearted king's great-hearted daughter *and would-be avenger*, while the Sophoclean Deianeira is a super-man's rather meek and timid 'little woman'. Neverthe-less it is important to note that, their differences notwithstanding, in neither of the two plays just discussed does the author offer a thoroughgoing feminine perspective, let alone such advocacy of feminine, of *woman's* claims as we have noted in Aeschylus and as we shall see presently in Euripides. Indeed from Sophocles' stage and orchestra we hear not a moral, not an epistemological, but only a psychological statement by and about the female, and one that contrasts, not interacts, with the male.

As against his two older compatriots, whom his own works deliberately rivaled and sometimes explicitly criticized, Euripides was famous (or notorious) for his portraits of women, of suffering women and, especially, of the 'bad' women whose numbers in Euripidean tragedy a comic poet could laughably remark.[19] Some of these we know from complete surviving plays, the others from reconstructable plots (occasionally with some of the leading ladies' lines preserved). The same poet was also famous, though we have none of the scores, for his lyrics, for both solo songs and *choral* odes and *kommoi* of progressive (some thought it decadent, rather) rhythm, melody, and choreographic movement.[20] Much of this music was clearly more suitable for the high register, whether adult falsetto or scored for boys, that a 'female' tragic chorus must have adopted, and consequently may have influenced the number of tragedies with this type of chorus. There appear, however, to have been other reasons as well (one might even say 'purposes') for the great number of female choruses in Euripides, whether of girls (for example, in the relatively early *Hippolytus* (428 BC) and, twenty years later, in the *Orestes*), of mature or even elderly women (as apparently, in the period between the aforemented two, in *Iphigenia Among the Taurians* and *Helen*), or of women of mixed age or of no ascertainable predominant age (in most other plays with female choruses, especially the several comprising Trojan captives). Among the reasons for the high proportion of these choruses we have already proposed the technical, quasi-realistic fact of women's more plausible helplessness, the ethical value of their perspective on and their criticism of the dynastic, the political, and (especially) the military world of men.

First let us see how having *women* as bystanders gives a technical advantage, using three plays for examples. In *Medea* the playwright has the Corinthian women of the chorus explicitly promise (lines 267–8) not to betray the title character if she should find a way to punish her enemies. Consequently they stand by, though not without protest, when she plans first the death of Jason's fiancée (and incidentally of that young woman's father, the king of Corinth), then that of Medea's and Jason's two little sons. In *Iphigenia at Aulis* Agamemnon does not ask but rather *commands* the chorus (Euboean women who have come across the strait to see the Greek army mustering for Troy) not to say anything to anyone about the sacrifice, now unavoidable, of his daughter Iphigenia. And give it away they do not, although, as in *Medea*, they are not at all happy with what is going on, on the stage just beyond them. In *Ion* the chorus are slaves of the Athenian queen Creusa, whose husband Xuthus orders them, on pain of death, not to tell her of his plan to adopt Ion (whom he believes to be his own bastard son) as heir to her kingdom of Athens. This chorus *do*, however, tell her – and her reaction (an attempt to poison what is actually *her own* long lost son) almost leads to disaster.

For the most part women are relatively helpless to prevent others' action or to initiate much action of their own.[21] Yet even they can foil an intrigue, thereby not only preventing the first intriguers' action but also motivating, perhaps even participating in, counter-intrigue by the intended victims. Because of this Euripides takes care to give his female chorus a strong reason *not* to speak out (for example, the Trojan chorus' sympathy for Hecabe in her campaign against the dastard Polymnestor in *Hecuba*) when an intrigue demands their silence – as it always does, save in so unusual a case as *Ion*. There is also, however, a positive value to the presence of *women* so close to the action as the orchestra brings and keeps them. It is, to put it simply, *plausible* that women, sympathetic, eager to help or at least to console, be around during such intimate scenes as those involving the protagonist alone on stage in *Medea* or, for another example, in the scenes between Phaedra and the Nurse in *Hippolytus*. Therefore one of Euripides' likely purposes in inventing so many female choruses is his partial realism, his dedication to at least superficially plausible action, inaction, or even mere presence of persons to whose potentially embarrassing awareness of events on stage *he* was especially sensitive. But there are other major considerations as well, as our three selected plays will show.

EURIPIDES' *MEDEA* (431 BC)

To the well-known feminism of the title character herself corresponds a salient theme in the choral song of this play: the insistence in the first and fifth stasima that *women* have an answer to make to men's 'music', to men's tales about heroes and heroines. Early in the play, at lines 410–29, they sing: 'The springs of sacred rivers are flowing uphill, justice and everything else is reversed. Men have deceitful counsels, gods' trustworthiness is no longer firm. And report will change, that *my* life has glory; honor is coming for the female sex; no longer will ill-sounding talk beset women. Muses of the ancient poets will cease singing *my* faithlessness. Phoebus, guide of poetry, did not place in our understanding the divine music of the lyre, else I would have sung a counter-song against the race of males. But the long ages have much to say about our and men's lot.' Much later, though they do not entirely approve of Medea's campaign against her enemies, they attempt to understand her in *women's* terms: 'Often I have passed,' they sing in Stasimon Five, 'through subtler tellings and have confronted greater strivings than it is "destined" for the female sex to search into; yet there is a Muse for us, too, who comes to us to impart wisdom – not to all of us, indeed, but you can find a handful among many, and the women's sex is not without music' (lines 1081–9). In general these extraordinary Corinthian women have great pity and much sympathy for the barbarian princess. They nevertheless cannot fully understand her, as much because their sense of her plight is only theoretical as because she comes from across the Black Sea. Medea argues, and they themselves effectively concede in the second stasimon (at lines 643–62), that, since they have their country, their fathers, their husbands, they cannot *know* what she suffers, however carefully they have observed her, however much they try to sympathize – and however bitterly they complain of her mistreatment and of the terrible reaction it has unleashed in her. Indeed they never really condemn her for her unmaternal catastrophe, the slaughter of her own children, in the way they condemn Jason the hero/husband (the same word in Greek: *aner*) for deserting her; but rather they throw up their hands in incomprehension and grope for a precedent in myth to her terrible deed (lines 1282–92). They take, in short, a reasonable, sensitive woman's view of a woman driven beyond human bounds by a reprehensible *man*.

EURIPIDES' *ION* (PROBABLY C. 420 BC)

In the melodramatic *Ion*, written perhaps ten years later, the playwright recurs to the theme of male-betrays-female, in this case raised to a higher level – the Olympian. The protagonist Creusa believes, in the first place, that Apollo has abandoned to death a baby she bore after he raped her; and,

secondly, that the same god intends to foist a bastard son of her non-
Athenian husband upon Athens as her heir and thus as heir to her father's
throne. The chorus, slave women only, yet loyal to the Athenian queen as
her friends *and as her fellow women*, give her husband's plot away, as we have
seen. In Stasimon One they express outrage and pity like hers over what
Apollo has done to a 'friend' of hers (she first has told them the story of her
own rape under a third-person fiction); and then, when they understand
more of the truth, they speak outrage over what the god has done and is
apparently doing to *her*, by imposing (they think) her husband's bastard on
the childless queen. The second stasimon of the play is the key point. 'I see
tears and mournful wailing, the onslaught of groans,' they sing, 'when my
queen sees her husband's good fortune in a son, but she herself is sonless,
destitute of children . . . Friends, shall we tell all this clearly to our mistress?
Her husband in whom she had and shared all her hopes, poor women – she
is ruined by misfortune, yet he prospers!' (lines 676–80; 695–9). The slave
women's indignation causes them to join actively with their mistress in a
murderous plot against the supposed usurper Ion, and to fear that they will
be punished with her when it is discovered. It also causes them, in the third
stasimon, to protest male poets' treatment of women, who only react as best
they can to the abuse of gods and men: 'You see how many of you
[masculine], resorting to poetry, with ill-sounding songs narrate *our* sex and
weddings, of Aphrodite, illicit, unholy; [yet] how much we surpass in
righteousness the unlawful sowing of men! Let tales in reply and ill-
sounding songs about sexual acts come against men. For Zeus' descendant
[sc. Xuthus] shows unmindfulness of sons, by not planting a shared fortune
of children for the house with our mistress; but, settling vain pleasure in
Aphrodite, he got a bastard son' (lines 1091–1105). In fact, Apollo and his
half-siblings Hermes and Athena manage things well enough in the long
run (stupid Xuthus, scandalized Ion, and relieved Creusa live more or less
happily ever *after* the near catastrophe). The criticism of Phoebus' wanton-
ness and his insensitivity nevertheless may yet apply – as the goddess
Athena 'from the machine' allows when she speaks in his behalf, and in his
ashamed absence, at the end (see especially lines 1556–8). Even a reader,
and perhaps much more a viewer, must have the feeling that Creusa and
her maids would not have heeded him if he had dared to show his shining
face, that *they* are somehow vindicated, not he, by the lucky outcome.

EURIPIDES' *IPHIGENIA AT AULIS* (C. 407 BC, PRODUCED
POSTHUMOUSLY IN 406)

Finally we have an unsettling tragedy about the immediate antecedents of
the Greek expedition to Troy, *Iphigenia*, of whose sordid plot and assorted
characters a study appears in volume 7 of *Themes in drama*.[22] The play's

female chorus are interesting in their own right. As mentioned above, they are sight-seers, eager to see Achilles and the other handsome heroes gathering at Aulis for the thousand-ship expedition against Paris and the Trojans. They thus belong to a special class of chorus, distinct from what we might call 'fellow-sufferers' (such as Creusa's slave women, or the captive Trojan women in several of this author's plays), distinct from 'sympathetic neighbors' (as in *Medea*, for example, and in both those plays by Sophocles discussed above). They belong rather to a type that goes back to and doubtless beyond the Oceanids in *Prometheus Bound*. They are, in fact, 'extraneous', having no personal bond at all with the characters on the stage. Euripides used such choruses repeatedly, especially in later plays (for example, in the *Phoenician Women*, which is set in Thebes!). The chorus at Aulis enters only with an 'oh, wow!' excitement about all those glamorous warriors, and with no inkling whatever of impending suffering or tragedy.[23] The poet then brings them into the emotion of his drama by gradually revealing to them not only the terrible facts (that Agamemnon will sacrifice Iphigenia, who *thinks* she has been summoned for her wedding to Achilles) but also personal traits of those who will act or suffer (Agamemnon's cowardice and hypocrisy, his love for Iphigenia and hers for him). These young women's progress toward horror at Iphigenia's doom is fascinating to follow. As already suggested, their first song, as they enter, shows merely a groupie-like glee (note especially lines 192–230, culminating in the description of the 'superstar' Achilles; and lines 294–302 at the end, on how back home they will cherish the memory of all they have seen). Their next song, however, after they have learned Agamemnon's dreadful plan and been told to keep quiet about it, deals with the dangerous power of Eros and Aphrodite, the different virtues of men and women, and the crime of Paris – on whom they lay blame for great woe not yet defined. Then in the second stasimon they vividly imagine the coming great war and the sufferings of the Trojans, especially and in detail of the Trojan women, at and after the sack of their city (lines 779–800). In the next episode they meet the hero Achilles, who resolves to defend Iphigenia from the treachery that has abused his name and her hope; in the ensuing stasimon (Stasimon Three) they envision the glorious wedding of Achilles' parents, hero and goddess, and juxtapose the scene of Iphigenia's imminent slaughter, with bitter reproaches against mortal men (*thnatois, brotois*) who have no shame, no virtue, no lawfulness, and may expect the gods' indignation. Their last 'standing song' is at first a *kommos* in the radical sense of the word, a 'self-beating' song in antiphony with Iphigenia, to mourn her death as she exits to the altar of sacrifice; but it then turns into an ironic prayer to Artemis that she may somehow turn the princess' death to good, giving glory to the rabble of a Greek army and to its craven commander. The girls, indeed, intend no irony, caught up as they are in the grand and pathetic delusion

that has made Agamemnon's daughter a holy martyr in an unholy cause;
but the poet lays it on and the audience picks it up, appropriately through a
group of 'good girls' who come to a military expedition as to a parade – just
like the people of Athens, young and old alike, several years before when an
Athenian armada set out for glorious deeds in western waters.[24] Euripides
exploits their innocence and their error, like that of his title character, to
make an even keener criticism of war than any of his captive women had
done in such plays as *Hecuba* or *Trojan Women*; for these young Greek girls
remain blind to the anguish that awaits their heroes *and* the misery that
awaits their land, thanks to the passions of a Paris and of a Menelaus,
thirsty for his niece's blood, thanks to the abuse and corruption of a Helen
and of a Clytemnestra who will kill her husband the Greek commander.
They *almost* see the truth; yet, patriotic Greek girls that they are (quite
unlike the brutally truthful barbarian women in the chorus of the companion play *Bacchae*), they turn away from it into atrocious propaganda.

We may now review briefly and conclude. We have seen Aeschylus open the
way, technical–theatrical and ideological, for the female chorus in tragedy;
we have seen Sophocles go mainly a different way; and we have seen
Euripides make it a free way for expression of his understanding of male-
female conflict and of his critique of male misbehavior in marriage, in
politics, and in war. Euripides' female chorus would offer to men alternative feeling and thinking, to women sympathy and support, and to all of us
object lessons in meditation, in rage, or in brainwashing.

NOTES

1 On the origins, choral and otherwise, of Attic *tragoidia* see R. P. Winnington-
  Ingram, 'The Origins of Tragedy' in P. E. Easterling and B. M. W. Knox, eds.,
  The Cambridge History of Classical Literature I: Greek Literature (Cambridge Univer-
  sity Press, 1985), pp. 258–63 and 759 (bibliography).
2 Treatments of the chorus and the choral sections in Aeschylus include notably
  Thomas G. Rosenmeyer, *The Art of Aeschylus* (Berkeley, Los Angeles, London:
  University of California Press, 1982), pp. 145–87; and in Euripides, G. M. A.
  Grube, *The Drama of Euripides* (New York: Barnes & Noble, 1961), pp. 99–126.
  The choruses of Sophocles, which have won especial admiration since Aristotle
  (*Poet.* 1456a), have attracted a great deal of attention, in G. M. Kirkwood, *A
  Study of Sophoclean Drama* (Ithaca: Cornell University Press, 1958), pp. 181–214,
  and in two recent monographs: R. W. B. Burton, *The Chorus in Sophocles' Tragedies*
  (Oxford: Clarendon Press, 1980), and Cynthia P. Gardiner, *The Sophoclean
  Chorus: A Study of Character and Function* (Iowa City: University of Iowa Press,
  1987).
3 Perhaps the most powerful case against Aeschylean authorship has been stated
  by Mark Griffith, *The Authenticity of 'Prometheus Bound'* (Cambridge University
  Press, 1977). The earlier defense of Aeschylus' 'claim' to the play by C. J.

Herington in *The Author of the* Prometheus Bound (Austin and London: University of Texas Press, 1970), however, seems to me still adequate (and quite reasonably sustained in the same author's recent *Aeschylus*, New Haven and London: Yale University Press, 1986, pp. 157–77 and 182f.), though the play must be very late and seems to show distinct and somewhat surprising Sophoclean influence – not least in the use of the chorus! See also D. J. Conacher, *Aeschylus'* Prometheus Bound: *A Literary Commentary* (University of Toronto Press, 1980), pp. 21–5.

4 This is no place to argue in detail about the sex of the chorus for each of twenty-six plays (or about that in the 'lost' plays of Sophocles and Euripides I use for similar rough statistics below). Suffice, please, a list of the plays, by (transliterated) titles, by category according to whether there is (a) clear evidence about the chorus, in the very title (frequently naming the chorus), in an ascribed fragment, or in ancient *testimonia*; or (b) ground for reasonable surmise only.

For Aeschylus, then, the list is as follows: female choruses entitle thirteen plays (*Aitnaiai, Argeiai, Bakkhai, Bassarai, Danaides, Heliades, Threissai, Kressai, Nereides, Xantriai, Perrhaibides, Salaminiai,* and, most likely, *Toxotides*), male ones eight (*Aigyptioi, Diktyoulkoi, Eleusinioi, Edonoi, Kares, Myrmidones, Phryges,* and *Mysoi*); we have ancient testimony that the *Hoplon Krisis* (*Award of Arms*) had a chorus of Nereid nymphs, that the *Kabeiroi* had a chorus of Argonauts and the lost Aeschylean *Philoktetes* one of Lemnian men; while a masculine participle in a choral fragment from the *Prometheus Lyomenos* (*Prometheus Unbound*) makes clear the gender (though not the precise identity) of that controversial play's chorus. A reasonable conjecture (by the nineteenth-century scholar Hermann) makes the *Thalamopoioi* a member of the same trilogy as the extant *Suppliant Women*, and assigns it as chorus the cousins and would-be husbands of Danaus' daughters, the 'suppliants' (and the chorus) of that surviving play.

5 The lost plays and the evidence about them may be summarized as follows: six lost Sophoclean tragedies were evidently named for female choruses (*Aikhmalotides, Mykenaiai, Kolkhides, Lakainai, Lemniai,* and *Phthiotides*) nine for male (*Aithiopes, Larissaioi, Dolopes, Kamikoi, Mysoi, Poimenes, Skythai, Skyrioi,* and *Phaiakes*); three others probably also are, but are not certainly, named for their male choruses (*Antenoridai, Epigonoi, Syndeipnoi*); in both *Kreousa* and *Phaidra* choruses are addressed in the feminine gender, the title character in *Nausikaa* was clearly accompanied by a chorus of *Pluntriai*, 'Washing Women', who gave the play an alternative title, and ancient testimony assures us that the otherwise obscure play *Hipponous* had a female chorus; while masculine gender in presumable choral fragments from Sophocles' famous *Tereus*, an ancient scholiast's notice that the chorus of the *Meleagros* consisted of priests, and the likelihood that the choruses of the *Aias Lokros* and the *Helenes Apaitesis* (*Demand for Helen*) were respectively Greek and Trojan men appear to give us the sex of the choruses there.

6 The familiar Aristophanic allusions in the first parts of the *Birds* to Sophocles' *Tereus* and the metamorphosed character of the same name, Aristophanes' 'Epops' or 'Hoopoe', make this clear.

7 Perhaps too much has been made of the non-tragic genre of the *Alcestis*, for it certainly resembles its author's tragedies in most respects. On its unique comic, or at least counter-tragic, features, however, see my 'Notes on the Structure of Euripides' *Alcestis*', *American Journal of Philology*, 100 (1979), 487–96.

I do not reckon the pseudo-Euripidean *Rhesus* among Euripides' tragedies, though coincidentally it contains a 'Euripidean' *female* chorus.

8 The more or less sure conjectures for lost Euripides concern the plays: *Aiolos, Alexandros, Alkmeon 'A', Alkmeon 'B', Andromeda, Auge, Danaë, Diktys, Erekhtheus, Ino, Hippolytos Kalyptomenos, Hypsipyle, Melanippe Desmotis, Meleagros, Peleus, Phaëthon, Phrixos* and *Polyidos* all likely with female chorus; and, with male, *Alope, Antiope, Bellerophontes, Khrysippos, Kresphontes, Kretes, Oineus, Peliades* (which, despite the title *Daughters of Pelias*, had a chorus of youths), *Philoktetes*, and the notorious *Telephos*, whose baby-Orestes-as-hostage scene Aristophanes parodied in his *Acharnians* and again in his *Lysistrata*. Very few of these have title choruses; yet for all a fragment or two spoken by or to or about the chorus and/or a generally plausible reconstruction in, for example, T. B. L. Webster, *The Tragedies of Euripides* (London: Methuen & Co., 1967) gives information enough.

9 On the sometimes gravely underestimated sophistication of his dramatic art see especially Oliver Taplin, *The Stagecraft of Aeschylus* (Oxford: Clarendon Press, 1977), who, however, concentrates on the significant movements and interactions of *characters*, not so much on the chorus.

10 On Aeschylus' understanding of social–sexual issues see especially Michael Gagarin, *Aeschylean Drama* (Berkeley, Los Angeles, London: University of California Press, 1976), pp. 87–118.

11 Thucydides' famous 'Funeral Oration of Pericles' ends with an infamous exhortation to the (bereaved) women of Athens: 'If I must also mention something about the virtue of the women, of all who will now live in widowhood, I shall indicate all in a brief piece of advice. Your great glory is not to be inferior to your natural character, and in each case to be least noted among men for virtue or for blame' (Thuc. II, 45).

This translation, like others to follow, is literal and is my own.

12 Four, possibly five of those ten plays with female chorus and female protagonists from the 'lost' Sophocles discussed in note 5 above correspond to plays/plots by Euripides: *Aikhmalotides, 'Spear-Won Women'*, which was about captives after the Trojan War; *Kolkhides*, a Medea play with inevitable connections to both Euripides' *Medea* and his very early *Peliades; Kreousa*, which resembled the Euripidean *Ion; Phaidra*, which corresponded to the younger playwright's two Hippolytus plays; and possibly the *Phthiotides, 'Women of Phthia'*, about which almost nothing is known, but which could easily correspond to either Euripides' *Andromache* or (perhaps less likely) to his *Peleus*. In any case, *both* Sophocles' surviving plays with female chorus are likely (*Trachinian Women*) or all but certain (*Electra*) to 'answer' the younger playwright (Euripides' *Medea* and *Electra*, respectively).

13 For the report of Sophocles' ambitions concerning the ideal excellence of his characters see Aristotle, *Poet.* 1460b: 'Sophocles himself used to say that *he* made [persons] such as one ought to make, while *Euripides* made such as exist.'

This should refer to aesthetic and ethical qualities at once, and not merely to the moral quality of characters and chorus, but also (given the ancient Greeks' well-known misogyny) to their sex. Certainly Sophocles' grandest characters are either male or explicitly *mannish* females.

14 See Aristophanes *Frogs* 1309–63, which seems to include parody of both monody and choral lyric, in both cases for female voice.

15 For a more detailed discussion of protagonist vs. chorus in this work see Appendix B (= pp. 151–62) in Gagarin's *Aeschylean Drama* (n. 10 above).

16 There is a grave textual problem at the end of this play; for a recent and moderate discussion see the annotated translation of Anthony Hecht and Helen B. Bacon, *Aeschylus: Seven Against Thebes* (Oxford University Press, 1973), pp. 7f. and 83–5; but contrast William G. Thalmann, *Dramatic Art in Aeschylus's* Seven Against Thebes (New Haven and London: Yale University Press, 1978), pp. 137–41, rejecting a great deal of the traditional text's ending.

17 For a sensitive if not in all respects a fully convincing discussion of the chorus in this work see Gardiner, *The Sophoclean Chorus*, pp. 119–38, to which, though earlier written, Burton, *The Chorus in Sophoclean Tragedy*, pp. 41–3 especially, is a gentle corrective. Gardiner exaggerates the distance of feeling between the chorus and Deianeira, mistaking, I think, the fact that they sing relatively little *about* her for an indication of their lack of warm interest *in* her; for they simply reflect her own *quite selfless* thinking about her husband Heracles and about his extraordinary past and hoped-for happy future.

18 This represents a significant difference from Euripides' *Electra*, where the chorus of young married women who invite the unhappy (and, surprisingly, *married*) princess to join their festivities seem to be more or less her agemates as well as her neighbors.

   The wholly admirable discussion of Sophocles' Electra-play and its chorus in Gardiner, *The Sophoclean Chorus*, pp. 139–63, needs no corrective at all, though she may slightly exaggerate the concord between chorus and protagonist.

19 See, for example, the comical, 'generic' plurals in Aristophanes' *Women at the Basket-Feast* (*Thesmophoriazousai*) line 547 ('Melanippes and Phaedras') and in *Frogs* 1043 ('Phaedras and Stheneboeas'). There may be further point in the fact that Euripides wrote the 'same' scandal of Phaedra into two distinct works, the earlier one lost, the later extant as *Hippolytus*; and also composed two *Melanippe* plays, though in this case they presented different episodes in that heroine's eventful history. He seemed unable to let go of a villainess or even of an outrageously clever female character.

20 For a recent description of Euripides' musical progressivism see B. M. W. Knox in the *Cambridge History* (n. 1 above,), pp. 337f.

21 The sole and important exception is the supplication that we find in a number of plays, for example *Suppliants*, of course, and *Andromache* among the earlier plays, *Helen* and *Phoenician Women* among the later.

22 See Victor Castellani, 'Warlords and Women in Euripides' *Iphigenia at Aulis*' in *Themes in Drama*, vol. 7 *Drama, Sex and Politics* (Cambridge University Press, 1985), pp. 1–10.

23 The *Ion* chorus were something like this to begin with, happily admiring the

sights at Delphi during their entrance-song, lines 184–218 in that play, before any trouble appears.

24 See Thucydides VI, chapters 30–2 on the sailing and happy, hopeful send-off of the Athenian 'armada' in summer of 415 BC.

The actor as actress in Euripides' *Alcestis**

KAREN BASSI

The female *persona* in Greek drama constitutes a relatively new (and controversial) field for classicists. In the last several years two general approaches to the subject have emerged. On the one hand, anthropological, sociological or political discussions have compared the dramatized female to her 'real' counterpart, insofar as the archaeological and non-dramatic evidence allows.[1] These studies look at the roles women play on the Attic stage with an eye to the social and biological categories by which women in fifth-century Athens were primarily defined. The second approach is confined, for the most part, to studies of the dramatic texts themselves and to questions of aesthetics and genre theory. This approach deals with the dramatic interpretation of myth and the general conception of the feminine as a mimetic construct in Greek drama.[2] This paper, as will be evident, benefits from both of these approaches. It focuses on one particular and central aspect of the representation of women in Greek drama, namely, the convention of assigning *all* dramatic parts to male actors. This convention presents us with two questions. First, what effect may the male actor in his female role have had upon the script, performance, and ultimately the audience of a play? Second, what are the implications of the absence of women from the Athenian stage?

To answer these questions, I will first summarize what we know about how the actor played his female role, given the evidence provided by vase painting, prose writings dealing with tragedy (Plato and Aristotle) and the dramatic texts in general. Next, I will postulate a theoretical model to describe the possibility for mimetic gender confusion which the convention of male actors in female roles provides. And finally, I will argue that Euripides' *Alcestis* is a text in which this confusion is exploited by the premise of the plot and by the play's gender-confused language. In this play, Euripides exposes the convention of the male actor in a female role and breaks the illusion of the female on stage. This broken illusion not only

* A draft of this paper was read at the *Themes in Drama* International Conference held at the University of California, Riverside, in February 1987.

points to the dramatic convention of the male actor, but also to the socio-political status of women in contemporary Athens.

The dramatic convention is mandated, of course, by the social and professional restraints placed upon women in fifth-century Greek society. Not only were women of this period not actresses, they rarely played any roles other than those of wife, mother, sister, and daughter. Women as *dramatis personae* were women only insofar as the mimetic or imitative capabilities of the stage allowed.

The imitative apparatus of ancient Greek drama included masks and costumes. But unfortunately, even our knowledge about these essential elements in the presentation of female characters is ambiguous. Vase paintings that depict scenes from known dramatic productions often show the female characters *as* females and not as actors wearing the wide-mouthed masks which they are known to have worn.[3] In fact, these 'actors' are sometimes shown with bare breasts – which must be considered impossible even for the most gifted ancient make-up artist.[4] Vase paintings, although perhaps reliable for visualizing the staging of the plays they depict (the placement of props or the grouping of characters, for example), do not offer accurate evidence for the visual impersonation of women.

Our knowledge of female impersonation is also hampered because the texts of the plays do not provide stage directions; nor are there director's notes or actor's notes which might provide evidence for conventional feminine gestures or mannerisms. Although female (as well as male) characters often weep or express intense emotions which would seem best conveyed by bodily movement (the masks make facial expression imposs-ible), we do not know how these emotions were made apparent to the audience. Nor is there any convincing evidence that actors changed their voices to sound like women. Perhaps the best evidence for the possibility of voice imitation is provided by Plato in the *Republic* (393c), where Socrates, talking about poetic imitation (mimesis), mentions the possibility of imitating a person both in voice and in form. As an example of the sort of thing a man must not imitate he mentions 'a woman nagging at her husband or quarreling with gods and boasting' (395d). The sound of the woman's voice is not explicitly given attention, but the fact that Socrates had earlier referred to vocal imitation may mean that the woman's voice (as well as her temper) is imagined as part of his example. There is other, less telling evidence for the imitation of the female voice. But taken together, it is not sufficiently convincing and we must remain sceptical both about the importance and the execution of vocal impersonation (and, in particular, female vocal impersonation) in Greek drama.[5]

Since Aristotle seems to be correct when he says that any one tragedy uses at most three speaking actors, it is conceivable and in fact necessary for

1 Aechylus' *Edonoi*, Lucanian Kalyx-Krater, c. 370 BC

an actor to be called upon to change the gender of his *persona* within a single performance.[6] He may have even been asked to exit playing one gender and to re-enter quite soon after playing the other (for example, the roles of Deineira and Heracles in Sophocles' *Trachiniae* in which the actor playing the wife must re-enter as the husband after 150 lines. But again we have no evidence which describes how he might have prepared himself for such an abrupt switch – other, of course, than the requisite change of mask and costume – or how he might have clearly differentiated himself in voice or gesture from his previous role. Here it must be mentioned that boys did not play the female parts in Attic tragedy, as they did in Renaissance drama. Although Pickard-Cambridge[7] assumes that female characters needed to be played by shorter and slighter actors than did male characters, this seems to be erroneous since, as we have seen, each actor could and often would be called upon to play both genders in a single performance.

The comic poet, Aristophanes, provides an interesting look at men playing women when Agathon, the tragic playwright, and Euripides' cousin, Mnesilochus, dress up in the *Thesmophoriazousae*. But can we trust the comic poet accurately to present tragic convention? Mnesilochus, of course, must be shaved and singed. But the tragic actor, covered by his mask and costume, surely did not need to submit to dipilatory torture to appear more feminine. Euripides enjoins his cousin to 'be a woman with your voice' (*Thes.* 266–8). But this is perhaps less convincing as evidence for female voice imitation in tragedy than it might first appear to be. For Mnesilochus, although he will play the female lead in parodic scenes from Euripides' plays, is not meant to be impersonating an actor on the tragic stage, but rather a woman at the Thesmophoria. Agathon's insistence that a playwright must be womanly when making plays about women (lines 151–2), together with his own androgynous appearance (lines 141–3), may indicate the lengths to which a tragic playwright went to create his female characters. But Aristophanes is making fun of Agathon; we are witnesses to comic hyperbole, not to faithfulness to tragic convention. The *Thesmophoriazousae*, as Zeitlin has shown, *is* concerned with gender representation and its political and aesthetic implications.[8] Yet even though it is tempting to treat Agathon and Mnesilochus as exemplifying tragic practice, we cannot take this temptation too seriously.

Given the kinds of evidence I have just described, we cannot know, other than by means of mask and costume, how the playwright might have used physical or auditory signs to make his male actors into female characters. The significance of this lack of evidence cannot be minimized. For the representation of women was perhaps the greatest task of illusion with which the playwright was confronted. Unlike a male actor playing a god or even an allegorical figure (for example, Might and Violence in Aeschylus' *Prometheus Bound*), a man who is to be perceived as a woman contradicts empirical observation. It is perhaps easier for an audience to suspend its disbelief and to accept as possible something entirely outside of its experience than to accept as possible that which is counter to its perceived knowledge of the world. There are no empirical references by which we can judge as appropriate or not the gestures, mannerisms, or voices of non-human or divine characters in Attic tragedy; we know, on the other hand and in general, how a mortal woman looks and sounds. The costume, mask, speech patterns, and gestures of the male actor playing a female must therefore perform a more arduous task of mimetic deception than those which are meant to transform the male actor into a divine or fantastic personage (whether male or female). The more the female character is meant to be like a mortal woman, the more difficult it is for the male actor to be able to play her role convincingly. Because we have insufficient evidence for the dramatic or illusionary techniques he actually used, we do not know whether the playwright aimed at accuracy or, if he did, how well he achieved it. Therefore, any arguments about how the male actor as female character affects a given tragic text must avoid the temptation to assume knowledge of a mimetic apparatus which operates outside of the text.

Keeping this in mind, we are not prevented from postulating some options theoretically inherent in the presentation of the female *persona*. Because of the double nature of these *personae*, that is, because they are in a sense both men and women simultaneously, two mimetic schemes are possible. In one, the transformation of males into females is not confused in the text and we can take the female characters at face value – as what they unambiguously *seem* to be. In the second scheme, the text allows us in some way to see the male beneath the female mask and costume – it sends us ambiguous signals about the correspondence between gender and character. This second scheme has both dramatic and socio-political implications. On the one hand, it calls attention to the convention of male actors in female roles; on the other hand, it tells us that there are no females on the Greek stage. These points are interrelated, of course, but need to be stressed separately. For when the gender of the female character is somehow undermined by the gender of the male actor, that is, when we can recognize some implicitly inappropriate references which confuse the female character's gender identity, a specific statement is being made about tragic *mimesis* (male actors play female parts) as well as about the social identity of Athenian women (they have no role in the public domain of the theatre).

Euripides' *Alcestis* adopts this second scheme and comments upon the mimetic and socio-political implications of female roles in Attic tragedy in two ways. First, details of its plot point to the general notion of woman as a mimetic construct; as substitute rather than other. The general premise of the play involves the substitution of Alcestis' death (or life) for that of her husband, Admetus. In accordance with an agreement made between Admetus and Apollo, Admetus will be able to prolong his life if he can find someone willing to die for him at the appointed time. Alcestis is the only one who will agree to do so. The play begins on the day appointed for Alcestis' death, includes a prolonged farewell scene between husband and wife, shows us her death and ends with her rescue by Heracles. Outside of Euripides' production, we know few details about the myth of Alcestis, although we do know the skeleton of the story – that she agrees to die for her husband.[9] It might be argued, therefore, that the plot of the drama is a given and that it is unwise to maintain, as I will be doing, that Alcestis' offer to die in her husband's stead has any particular significance in Euripides' production. However, it is equally unwise to maintain that myth is static and necessarily retains the same significance in all of its manifestations (whether in Homer, tragedy or Plato). In the case of Euripides' plays, in particular, such an assumption is explicitly contradicted by clear examples of his reappropriation and subversion of myth, as in the *Helen* and the *Orestes*. But the more general and important point to be made is that just because we know that Euripides is adapting a traditional story, we cannot forget that his play is an entirely new text – that it is an appropriation of traditional material, not a copy of it.

The motif of substitution in the *Alcestis* involves more than the simple story of a noble wife who offers to die for her husband. Substitution is the fundamental element which informs the imitative arts, since the notion of 'imitation' implies the recognition of one thing as it refers to another. Mukarovsky calls the work of art 'merely . . . an external signifier for which in the collective consciousness there is a corresponding signification'.[10] This correspondence in the theatre entails the substitution of actor (signifier) for character (signified), scene painting for place, and dramatic speech (the script) for true discourse. Alcestis' offer to die in place of her husband constitutes an act which is analogous to a mimetic and dramatic performance. She takes on a role and performs a series of acts (including her farewell speech) which, had Apollo not tricked the Fates (line 12), would have been Admetus'. The premise of the *Alcestis*, then, provides a metatheatrical point of reference. The character who is herself only an imitation woman (or a substitute for a woman) plays the role of a substitute who, somewhat ironically, takes the place of a man.

Another and perhaps more explicit metatheatrical point of reference is Admetus' vow to have a statue made of the dead Alcestis, 'fashioned by the skilled hands of craftsmen' (*Alcestis* 348–54). Scholars have called Admetus' desire 'tasteless', or a testament to his 'ardor', or a sign that his 'grief was extreme'.[11] Implicit in his desire, of course, is a belief in the power of art to deceive and, in that deception, to console and to give hope. But the statue also reminds us of Hesiod's description of the first woman, Pandora, whom the poet describes as a work of art (*Erga* 47–105). She is made out of mud by the master craftsman Hephaestus and fashioned to 'look like the immortal goddesses' (*Erga* 62–3). Zeitlin, commenting on this passage, states that, 'Woman is a mimetic creature par excellence, ever since Hesiod's Zeus created her as an imitation with the aid of the other artisan gods and adorned her with a deceptive allure. Woman is perennially under suspicion as the one who acts a part . . .'[12] Alcestis' statue represents an overt reference to the affinity between woman and imitation, as Zeitlin describes it. But it also suggests that in Attic drama the woman is precisely the one who cannot act a part. Like the statue which is a fake woman, the dramatic presence of any woman is also fake. The statue and the actor playing Alcestis have much in common (which is perhaps why the poet suggests the statue as a replacement for the 'dead' character). Alcestis, like a statue, is only a woman by art.

I have suggested some evidence for the *Alcestis'* general concern with imitation and with the dramatic representation of the female. A detailed look at the text will show that the dramatic illusion of the female on stage is broken by the language Alcestis speaks and by the language others use to describe her. The Greek adjective *aristos* means 'most excellent' or 'bravest' or 'most noble', and originally referred to excellence in battle (cf. Homeric 'aristeuo'). It is frequently used of men in Greek literature, but is rarely applied to women. In Homer, when it describes a woman, it always occurs in the phrase 'eidos ariste' (the best in bodily shape or beauty), that is, it is always applied to her external appearance.[13] The only occurrence in which it is not so used is spoken by Hera, Zeus' wife, who calls herself 'theaon ariste', 'most excellent of the goddesses' (Il. 18.364). Neither Pindar nor Aeschylus uses the word to describe a female. Sophocles does so only in three instances. Heracles describes his mother, Alcmene, as 'ariste' (*Trachiniae* 1105). But, like Hera, Alcmene in this play is remote, close to Zeus and more than mortal. Two indirect usages refer to mortal children who happen to be female but who are taking the place of sons in heroic endeavors. The chorus calls Electra a 'most excellent child' (*Electra* 1089) when, because she believes that Orestes is dead, she contemplates avenging her father by herself. In the *Oedipus at Colonus*, Antigone and Ismene, who have performed tasks for their father which his sons ought to have performed (lines 1367–8), are addressed as 'the best of children', 'tek-non arista' (lines 1694–5).

In the *Alcestis*, Euripides uses 'aristē' (in the feminine) emphatically and conspicuously (nine times, including line 324 where Alcestis refers to herself as 'aristē') to describe Alcestis in what seems to be a heroic 'male' sense. The word does not refer to her external beauty but to something like her valor or bravery. He describes her, in other words, by a term which is traditionally applied to males, and which usually is out of place when applied to a mortal female, unless it describes her physical appearance. Indeed, the term 'ariste gunaikos' 'the most noble of women', by which Euripides describes Alcestis, is an oxymoron of sorts, since male heroes but not women are generally described in Greek literature as 'most noble'. This linguistic or rhetorical shift represents an anti-traditional appropriation of heroic language. According to traditional interpretations, this shift simply represents Euripides' re-casting or subversion of Greek epic heroism. This is certainly part of what the playwright is up to. But more important, when he describes Alcestis by a term which traditionally occurs in a locution reserved for women ('ariste eidos'), but which he uses as if he were describing a traditional male hero, he complicates or fragments her 'feminine' identity. While this appropriation of language serves to make Alcestis seem heroic (like a man, in the traditional Greek sense), it simultaneously and emphatically jeopardizes the mimetic presentation, that is, the illusion of the female on the stage.

Alcestis' gender is also compromised in her farewell speech to Admetus. Preceding this speech she is close to death: visions of Charon (line 254) and Hades (line 262) plague her. Then suddenly, in a rather operatic recovery, she addresses Admetus cooly and rationally for forty-five lines.[14] In this speech, she tells Admetus that she need not have offered to die for him and that she could have married again and lived in prosperity (lines 284–6). She emphasizes that she did not spare her youth on his behalf while neither of his aged parents would agree to die nobly to save their only son (lines 290–2). She asks that Admetus not marry again, since a step-mother is hateful to the children of the former wife. And finally she commands Admetus to boast that he had the 'best of wives' (line 324).

Some critics feel that this speech does not present Alcestis sympathetically. They believe that she dwells on her sacrifice in an overly self-congratulatory way and does not show proper love for Admetus. But such a notion is informed by an anachronistically Christian notion of martyrdom and a limited view of 'femininity', rather than by the Greek notion of the heroic ethos which is here appropriated by a female character. Male heroes often boast of their achievements, express disdain for their enemies (as Alcestis does toward her in-laws and the future step-mother) and demand rewards which are worthy of their deeds. In tragedy, Ajax is the outstanding example of these male, heroic prerogatives: he too demands the rewards he believes to be his due and, even on the point of death, continues to hate his enemies (Sophocles' *Ajax* 835–44).

Rosenmeyer finds Alcestis' speech 'most unpleasant' because he does not recognize Euripides' deliberate blurring of traditional male and female roles.[15] Although the speech employs the feminine *topoi* of home and family, it appropriates a masculine and heroic pragmatism which is rooted in self-aggrandizement, expectation of reward and untempered hatred of one's enemies. Alcestis' acceptance of a noble death (as opposed to Admetus' parents who refused to die nobly, 'eukleos thanein', line 292), also means that she must give up the youth in which she found great delight (line 288–9). Lost youth and a death which brings fame ('kleos') are the sine qua non of Homeric masculine heroism.

Alcestis' farewell speech presents a male actor playing a female character who speaks like a man. We can perhaps understand the significance of this more clearly by imagining a female impersonator who speaks as we would expect a man to speak.[16] I would not suggest how each of us might differentiate between male and female speech, nor how a Greek audience would do so outside the context of the literary tradition to which the *Alcestis* belongs. I do suggest that, precisely *because* of that tradition, what she says in her farewell speech compromises her female *persona* in a manner similar to that of the female impersonator described above. Rather than finding that *persona* unsympathetic (presumably because Alcestis does not behave like a proper lady), we should wonder why it is that Euripides creates a discrepancy between the *woman* Alcestis appears to be and the masculine discourse she appropriates; why he invites us to see her as a man in disguise (which, in fact, she is).

Alcestis' role as substitute signifies dramatic mimesis or imitation generally. And the language used to describe her, and which she uses of herself, points to the presence of the male actor behind the female *persona*; of the false image which that *persona* presents. The illusion which, as I have suggested, is perhaps the most difficult for the playwright to create successfully (that of a woman on stage), becomes the means by which Euripides calls attention to the illusionary apparatus of his craft. He undermines the female mask and costume of Alcestis, and in so doing makes us question the tenuous relationship in the theatre between seeing and believing. The actor playing his female role overtly refers to the absence of the actress, and the tragic stage simultaneously becomes a commentary on itself and on the status of the female in fifth-century Athens.

That status is further revealed in Alcestis' final entrance. Heracles brings a veiled woman into the presence of Admetus and we are led to believe that Alcestis has been returned to life. But the identity of the veiled woman is not revealed by Heracles who lies about who she is; nor by the veiled figure herself who remains silent. When Admetus is finally cajoled into lifting the veil and identifying the mystery woman, he is naturally shocked to see his wife returned to life. Anne Burnett comments, 'The trick being played on Admetus creates the peculiar, happy tension of this scene.'[17] Like Burnett, many critics see this as a 'happy ending' in which Admetus' nobility is rewarded.[18] But this so-called 'happy ending' is tempered by the striking fact that Alcestis never utters a happy word; in fact, she never speaks at all –

either before or after she is recognized by Admetus. Heracles explains that she must remain silent for three days – a silence that has not been satisfactorily explained by any known Greek religious practice.[19] Because ritual evidence outside of the text is lacking, critics have attempted to explain Alcestis' silence in other ways. It has been suggested, for example, that the *Alcestis* was meant to be acted by only two speaking actors, leaving no one to speak Alcestis' part at this point. Whitman, however, argues convincingly against this hypothesis and suggests instead that Alcestis is simply mad at Admetus.[20] But if this were so, wouldn't she have a lot to say to him?

We must accept the dramatic necessity of Heracles' explanation, but that explanation, especially since it seems a weak one, does not prevent us from commenting on the striking *effect* which Alcestis' silence has upon us – an effect which has not been taken into account. At the end of her play Alcestis is veiled and speechless. The heroic stance which she had earlier assumed is stripped away. She is led in by one man (who says simply that she is his prize) and is handed over to another (as an ostensible substitute for his dead wife). The final scene suggests that Alcestis is, after all, powerless in a masculine world. We never again see the brave, strong-willed woman whose noble death meant life for her husband, and whose speech constituted the production's only heroic discourse. Throughout the play, ambiguous signals about Alcestis' gender suggested both the political exclusion of women from the tragic stage and the ambiguity of female heroism. In the final scene, that exclusion and ambiguity are made hauntingly explicit in the person of the actor playing a speechless woman. This silent character, like the imagined statue of Alcestis mentioned earlier, speaks of the woman (actress) who has no voice in the tragic theatre and, in addition, of a final inability to maintain even a dramatic pretense of female heroism.

NOTES

1 See, for example, Mary Lefkowitz, *Heroines and Hysterics* (New York: St Martin, 1981); Sally Humphrey, *The Family, Women and Death* (London, Boston, Melbourne, and Henley: Routledge & Kegan Paul, 1983); Helene Foley, ed., *Reflections of Women in Antiquity* (New York: Gordon, 1981); Sarah B. Pomeroy, *Goddesses, Whores, Wives and Slaves: Women in Classical Antiquity* (New York: Schocken, 1975).

2 For example, Froma Zeitlin, 'Playing the Other: Theatre, Theatricality and the Feminine in Greek Drama', *Representations*, 11 (1985), 63–94; and 'Travesties of Gender and Genre in Aristophanes' *Thesmophoriazousae*', *Critical Inquiry*, 8: 2 (1981), 301–27.

3 See Sir Arthur Pickard-Cambridge, *The Dramatic Festivals of Athens*, 2nd edn. (Oxford: Clarendon Press, 1968), fig. 49.

4 See also A. D. Trendall and T. B. L. Webster, *Illustrations of Greek Drama* (London: Phaidon, 1971), plates III.1, 15 and 16.

5 Other evidence in Greek literature for the imitation of the voice includes, the *Homeric Hymn to Delian Apollo* (lines 162–4) in which the Delian maidens are said to know how to 'mimic the voices and chatter of all men'. In tragedy, Aeschylus' *Choephori* (lines 564–5) provides the example of Orestes who proposes to Pylades that they 'imitate the Phocian tongue'. Aeschylus, of course, does not write a Phocian dialect in the *Choephori*. Still, the possibility for dialect imitation cannot be wholly discounted in tragedy and we know that Euripides does employ a kind of dialect imitation for his Phrygian slave at *Orestes* 1237ff. Whether these examples can serve as evidence for the possible imitation of the female voice, however, is uncertain.

6 See Pickard-Cambridge, *Dramatic Festivals of Athens*, pp. 135–40, who finds no objection to an individual actor playing roles which vary greatly in temperament, age or gender in a single performance.

7 Ibid., pp. 135–40.

8 Zeitlin, 'Travesties', *passim*.

9 See Albin Lesky, 'Alkestis, der Mythus und das Drama', *Sitzungsberichte Akademie der Wissenschaften in Wien*, 203.2 (Vienna and Leipzig: Hölder-Pichler-Tempsky A.-G., 1925), 5–86 for a thorough discussion of the legendary antecedants of Euripides' play.

10 Jan Mukarovsky, 'Art as Semiotic Fact' in *The Semiotics of Art* (Cambridge, Mass.: Harvard University Press, 1976, paperback edn 1984), pp. 3–9.

11 The first reading is that of K. Von Fritz, 'The Happy Ending of *Alcestis*', in *Twentieth Century Interpretations of Euripides' Alcestis*, ed. John R. Wilson (Englewood Cliffs, NJ: Prentice-Hall, 1968), pp. 80–4; the second is that of Thomas Rosenmeyer, *The Masks of Tragedy* (Austin: University of Texas Press, 1963), p. 229; the third is from A. M. Dale, ed., *Euripides' Alcestis* (Oxford University Press, 1966). It is also possible, as Ulrich von Wilamowitz-Möllendorff asserts, *Die griechischen Tragödien*, 3 (Berlin: Weidmann, 1906), p. 91, note 1, that Euripides is referring to his own *Protesilaus*. See A. Nauck, *Tragicorum Graecorum Fragmenta*, 2nd edn (Leipzig: Teubner, 1889), p. 563 (= Hyginus fab. 103–104): Laodamia-fecit sumulacrum cereum simile Protesilai coniugis et in thalamis posuit sub simulatione sacrorum et eum colere coepit. See also, Albin Lesky, 'Der angeklagte Admet', *Maske und Kothurn*, 10 (Graz-Köln: Hermann Böhlaus, 1964), 203–16.

12 Zeitlin, 'Playing the Other,' p. 79.

13 It is interesting to note that Hector rebukes Paris by saying that he is 'eidos ariste' at *Iliad* 3.38–45. Paris is a 'girlish' figure in the epic and it is therefore not surprising that this phrase, so often applied to women, is applied to him.

14 A formal explanation for this operatic recovery is given by Dale, *Euripides' Alcestis*, p. 74, who argues that Euripides, according to traditional precedent, has 'simply juxtaposed these two aspects (emotional and rhetorical) of Alcestis' parting from life'. See also, John Gould, 'Dramatic Character and "Human Intelligibility" in Greek Tragedy', *Proceedings of the Cambridge Philological Society*, 204 (1978), 50. I am not concerned with this shift in Alcestis' tone, however, but with what Alcestis says in her 'rhetorical' speech.

15 Rosenmeyer, *Masks of Tragedy*, p. 226.
16 The case of Clytemnestra in Aeschylus' *Agamemnon* is not relevant for this discussion, although it might at first seem to be. In the *Agamemnon*, line 351, the chorus *specifically* comments on the fact that Clytemnestra talks like a man. They consider it to be unusual but, in making explicit reference to it, they diffuse any confusion which her masculine speech might cause. No one in the Euripides play makes explicit reference to Alcestis' 'masculine' speech or behavior. He leaves it up to us to interpret its significance.
17 Anne Pippin Burnett, *Catastrophe Survived, Euripides' Plays of Mixed Reversal* (Oxford University Press, 1971), p. 45.
18 See, for example, G. M. A. Grube, *The Drama of Euripides* (New York: Barnes & Noble, 1961), p. 144; or Rosenmeyer, *Masks of Tragedy*, p. 244, who calls the last scene 'pure fairy tale, to finish the play satisfactorily'.
19 Edna Trammel, 'The Mute Alcestis', *CJ*, 37 (1941–2), pp. 144–50 argues for a ritual whereby the resurrected person is, by means of silence, absolved from the pollution of death. Against this unsupported argument, see Cedric H. Whitman, *Euripides and the Full Cycle of Myth* (Cambridge University Press, 1974), p. 112.
20 Ibid., p. 112.

Marriage and prostitution in classical New Comedy*

DAVID WILES

The idea that a 'comedy' is a narrative which culminates in marriage can be traced back, via the Renaissance, to the Greek dramatist Menander. Though New Comedy was, on the face of it, a realistic form reproducing a specific and contemporary social milieu, it also constituted a kind of myth, a myth which was to satisfy the Graeco-Roman world over several centuries. The myth of romantic heterosexual love had found little place in pre-classical or classical culture, but within the Hellenistic world performances of New Comedy helped this myth to become a common currency.

All works of New Comedy (with one exception) tell the same basic story of how the amorous male tries to overcome the obstacle in his path in order to secure the female of his choosing. The male of the story is usually young, handsome, and free born. The obstacle may be familial, financial or social. For example, the father may object; there may not be enough to pay the brothel-keeper, or the dowry; the couple may be kept apart by the social code that prevented marriage between citizen and non-citizen. These external obstacles may be bound up with psychological considerations. The female of the story, finally, may be at one extreme a virgin bride, at the other a professional prostitute.

A basic concern of New Comedy is the relationship between love and sexuality. Through eliminating the phallic costume and verbal obscenity of 'Old' Greek comedy, the 'New' form set up a dichotomy between body and mind, between actions and feelings. Michel Foucault describes Greek sexual ethics in a way which pinpoints a central preoccupation of New Comedy: Friendship is reciprocal, and sexual relations are not reciprocal: in sexual relations, you can penetrate, or you are penetrated . . . if you have friendship, it is difficult to have sexual relations.[1] If there was no true reciprocity in homosexual relations, which always distinguished 'lover' and 'loved', there was necessarily far less within heterosexual relations in a male-oriented Graeco-Roman world.

* A draft of this paper was read at the *Themes in Drama* International Conference held at the University of London, Westfield College, in March 1987.

With the arrival of Christianity, the concepts of love and marriage become almost indisseverable. At the centre of the sacrament of marriage is a promise that the couple will love each other, and if there is no true love, there is no true marriage. The word 'love' in our culture forges erotic desire and a desire for the lasting companionship and well-being of the other into a conceptual unity. Within classical Greek language, the case is different. *Eros* and *philia* are conceptually distinct. *Eros* is desire, brought on by the arrow shot by the winged son of Aphrodite. *Philia* implies affectionate feelings, as do its synonyms *storgē* (particularly used of parent/child relationships), and *agapē* (the usual New Testament word for love, love which shows itself in external signs of respect). Another word, *hetaireia*, is usually translated as 'companionship': the word implies membership of a common political, social or military grouping. A *hetairos* is a male comrade, but a *hetaira*, because she was present at male social gatherings, is a prostitute.

Within Greek religion we find again no single concept of love. Sexual pleasure falls under the patronage of Aphrodite – homosexual pleasure as much as heterosexual. Marriage is the province of other goddesses: Demeter, goddess of fertility, Artemis, goddess of childbirth, Hera, wife of Zeus. In Athens, a virgin bride dedicated her weavings to Athena, she dedicated her childhood dolls to Artemis before marriage, and sacrificed to Artemis during pregnancy. As a married woman, she joined other married women in the worship of Demeter at the Thesmophoria.[2] Aphrodite had only a transient association with marriage, but was the permanent patroness of courtesans. A *hetaira* dedicated herself to Aphrodite when she embarked upon her profession,[3] worshipped Aphrodite annually at the Adonia, and might give her as a tithe one-tenth of her earnings.[4] Aphrodite Hetaira was one of the cultic names of the deity.[5] We should not conclude that the procreation of children was entirely pleasureless, however. In vases which portray a wedding procession, the bride is shown accompanied by Eros. Aphrodite and marriage connected temporarily on the wedding night.

The Greek distinction between sexuality and marriage has to be understood in its sociological context. Citizen Athenian women were segregated from men. At home they occupied the women's quarters, and did not encounter male guests, who were entertained in the men's quarters. Religious ceremonial provided the one all-important occasion when women were allowed to appear in public and to some extent mingle with free men. Women had no legal or property rights, and were always in the wardship of their husband or closest male relative. A socially approved system of prostitution evolved in response to this segregation of citizen women. In the absence of wives and daughters and sisters, prostitutes were required to enliven private male gatherings. Since men did not normally marry until

their thirties, for unmarried men prostitutes were, apart from close rela-
tives, the only female society available.

Romantic love, with its connotations of strong emotion and voluntary
reciprocity, could not easily flourish between males and females of equal
status. Athenians of the classical period tended to idealize homosexual love
because the passive partner, the free-born youth, gave himself voluntarily
to a mature man who pleased him, and he could not be bought for money.
The mature male expressed dominance through the act of penetration, but
preceded this with rituals of abject submission, and in this sense the
relationship was reciprocal.[6] Free prostitutes were in a rather similar
position. Unlike brothel slaves – *pornai*, 'women for sale' – free *hetairai* gave
their 'companionship' voluntarily, in return for supposedly voluntary gifts
of clothing and jewels. They could withdraw their affections when they
pleased. There might also be a voluntary element in the relationship
between a man and his concubine. A concubine was a non-citizen, she
brought no dowry with her, and could not bear her partner citizen children.
Having no dowry, she had no protection from being discarded. But in every
other sense she was a wife, and the relationship of concubinage carried no
social stigma. Here, where either party was free to withdraw from the
relationship, affection was the principal bond that held the couple
together.[7] These alternatives to legal marriage – homosexuality, *hetaireia*,
concubinage – were a far more natural focus for ideas of romantic
reciprocated love than marriage could be.

The trick performed by Menander's complex plots, with their unexpected revelations of identity, is to make the husband love his legal wife-to-be
while thinking she is, or treating her as, his prostitute or concubine. In all
the extant Greek texts, the plots end with marriage. Aphrodite and
marriage are in a sense reconciled. The idea that sexual attraction properly
and naturally culminates in marriage is something new in Greek culture,
and I shall try to suggest why this new concept emerged.

There is little that we can term romantic love in earlier Greek drama. In
Aeschylus the problematic relationship between Aphrodite and marriage is
confronted in the Danaid trilogy. In the first play of the trilogy, a chorus of
maidens tries to evade marriage. At the end of the play one hemichorus
dedicates itself to Artemis, and prays that no marriage come by compulsion
of Aphrodite, while the other hemichorus acknowledges that Aphrodite is
too powerful not to be honoured (*Suppliants* 1030–42). At the end of the
trilogy, Aphrodite herself appears to argue that she is the basic creative
principle which makes the wet sky choose to mate with the dry earth.[8] This
is basically the same argument as that used by the evil nurse in Euripides'
Hippolytus (lines 447–50) when she persuades Phaedra to surrender to
Aphrodite, and commit incestuous adultery. The chorus, women who have
born children, pray to escape the bolts of Eros and Aphrodite (lines 527–

33). In Sophocles' *Antigone* Haemon may seem to be a prototype romantic lover when he kills himself for love of his betrothed – but again the chorus roundly condemns the destructiveness of Eros. When the bride's eyes are filled with desire, they say, then Aphrodite the unconquerable is at her sport (lines 781–99). We are tempted to sympathize with Haemon because of our own cultural assumptions, but there is no sympathy in the chorus for a young man's infatuation. We find a similar language of love in Aristophanes. 'Aphrodite, why do you drive me mad?' asks the young lover in *The Assembly-Women*. 'Eros, I beg you to free me, and bring her to my bed' (lines 966–8). Love is a species of madness, a powerful external force that must somehow be controlled.

Menander's lovers have no sophisticated language in which to express their new form of love. A vocabulary is lacking. To illustrate the point, I shall quote the opening lines from one of Menander's plays. A mercenary has acquired a girl enslaved in war, has given her a measure of legal freedom and has installed her as his concubine. She refuses to submit voluntarily to his embraces, and he is unwilling to assault her, as a man would normally do in this situation. The speech idiom is borrowed from tragedy, and 'Eros' is the word which I have translated as 'love':

> O Night! you of all the gods have most in common with Aphrodite. *You* are the occasion for most talking about it, most thinking about – love. Have you ever looked on a man more distraught, a lover more doomed? I am standing now before my own doorway, I walk up and down the lane, this way and that, and you are almost half way done. I could be asleep, in possession of the one I love. She is in my house. I could, and I want to, like the maddest of lovers, but I don't do it. This winter weather is preferable, as I stand and shiver, talking to you.
> (*Misoumenos* A1-A14)

Menander's plays give us the actions of lovers, not their verbalizations of feelings. His theatre demonstrates what the lover does – stands about in the rain at night, for instance – not why he does it. The medium of theatre proves well suited to working out a new ethical/emotional orientation which could not as yet be articulated adequately in speech.

Although the soldier in this play has or has had legal power over the woman, he wants something that she can only give voluntarily. Eros could be satisfied with a slave, but the soldier here is looking for free reciprocity. He develops the paradox that although the girl was once his slave, she has now enslaved him (frag.2). The situation is resolved when the girl's father arrives, and her citizen status is established. The hero declares to the girl that he loves her with the verbs 'agapō', 'philō' (line 308). The father asks if the marriage is his daughter's wish (lines 438–9) before bestowing her with the traditional legal formula: 'For the sowing of a legitimate crop, I give my daughter, together with a dowry of two talents' (lines 444-6). Marriage is here accompanied by *agapē* and *philia*, by the free choice of the wife, because of the extraordinary circumstances of the plot – because the hero has already lived with the woman as his slave and as his concubine. The trajectory of the play, from Eros to *philia*, and to a situation which permits the procreation of legitimate children, is a feature of all Menander's extant plays. Menander works out in theatrical terms a problem which the Stoics of the next generation worked out in philosophical terms. Chrysippus the Stoic used this play to support his argument that *eros* is not the result of divine intervention, which is to say irrational, but is the result of *philia*, a wish to do good at the prompting of beauty.[9]

In all Menander's plays, through miraculous coincidences and discoveries of unexpected paternity, the object of erotic desire is fused with the object of matrimony. Menander's plots are all centred on, or triggered by, a rape – that is, by a violent, apparently irrational, satisfaction of Eros. I must point out immediately, in relation to rape, that Greek attitudes were different to our own. For us, rape constitutes unpardonable violence, but in the normal Athenian view rape was less objectionable than seduction. The rapist sucumbs to a momentary weakness, but the seducer, while in full command of his reason, threatens the state through corrupting the mind of a woman destined to be the guardian of a citizen's seed. We can divide Menander's plays conveniently into two groups. In the first group, the hero has at some point in the past raped a girl, without knowing her identity, and this girl, through a chain of circumstances, becomes the rapist's bride. In the second group, a man refrains from sex with a girl who does temporarily lie in his legal power.[10]

Some examples may be helpful. *The Hero* is a play which falls into my first category. A woman before the play begins was raped and gave birth to twins. She disposed of the children and later married the man who raped her. The childen have fallen into debt-slavery, and the daughter, now aged eighteen, has recently been raped by the hero of the play. When the girl's parentage is revealed, the young couple become free to marry. A play which falls between my categories is the *Perikeiromenē*, 'She Who Was Shorn'. A jealous soldier assaults his concubine asexually through cutting off her hair, giving her the mark of a slave. The girl's parentage is revealed, the man sees the error of his ways, and the couple marry. *The Arbitrants* is a play which spans both categories. The hero once raped a girl, and does not know that this is the same girl as the one to whom he has been contracted in marriage. When he finds that his bride has recently given birth, he refuses to consummate the marriage. He hires a slave prostitute, but cannot bring himself to have sex with her. Finally the truth emerges, the hero sees that he has been guilty of double standards, and the marriage is saved.

In these, as in all Menander's other plays, the same inversionary pattern is found. The forbidden woman becomes permitted, the permitted woman becomes forbidden. An arbitrary social code, founded upon the institutions of slavery and endogamous citizen marriage, is magically overturned. At the same time, a new ethical code for interpersonal behaviour seems to be articulated. The man must treat the woman as he would expect to be treated himself: i.e. with respect and understanding.

It would be unwise, however, to regard New Comedy as in some way advocating the cause of women. The interest of the playwright and of his predominantly male Greek audience is centred on the behaviour of the man, not of the woman. No new female role-model is offered, no new system of marriage is envisaged. There is no external evidence to suggest that this theatrical genre coincides with any changes in Greek sexual or marital practices. There are nevertheless important artistic, scientific and political changes which can be correlated with the emergence of New Comedy.

Within the visual arts, the glorification of the naked female body connects very obviously with the cult of romantic love in the theatre. A generation before Menander, sculptures like Praxiteles' *Aphrodite of Knidos* and paintings like Apelles' *Aphrodite Rising from the Sea*[11] established the female rather than the male nude as the idea of erotic beauty. Heterosexual love replaced homosexual love as an aesthetic aspiration. Menander's theatre, like the visual arts, above all celebrated Aphrodite. The salt of his comedies, Plutarch observed, 'springs from the same sea whence Aphrodite rose'.[12] But both art and theatre played down the traditional association between the woman and productive deities like Demeter, goddess of the crops, or Athena, goddess of crafts.

Within the scientific sphere, the new biology of Aristotle is of interest. Popular tradition, enshrined in the teaching of Hippocrates, held that female secretions are seminal, and the female's pleasure in intercourse is linked to her ability to produce children. Aristotle, a generation before Menander, overturned this theory and threw out the idea that female pleasure is linked to procreation. Knowing nothing of ovulation, he portrayed the female as essentially a 'sterile male'.[13] While Hippocratic medicine had traditionally seen pregnancy as an aspect of female health, Aristotle saw it as an affliction.[14] In science as in art, the function of the woman was now not to do but to be done unto, not to look but to be looked at. Aristotle's scientific thought is linked to his political thought. The foundations of the state, for Aristotle, rest upon three natural relationships of authority: the authority of father over son, of master over foreign slave, and of husband over wife.[15]

The role of women in Athens was a function of its system of government, and we can only understand the changing historical position of women in Athenian life in the context of the whole democratic structure. Where the focus of feudal society was the household, the focus of democratic society was the market place, the assembly, the theatre and other public places where women did not belong. Citizenship became both a privilege and a duty, and it was necessary to define with precision who were or were not citizens. If women lived secluded lives, no one could doubt that the children they bore belonged to citizen fathers. The legislation which restricted citizenship to children of citizen mothers as well as fathers was passed in 451 BC and followed naturally upon the triumph of democracy – male democracy as I should rather call it. A related piece of legislation required that an heiress – that is to say, a woman who inherited property for lack of brothers or sons – was obliged to marry her nearest male relative. Two of Menander's plays deal with this law, one focussed upon the plight of the reluctant husband, the other on the reluctant bride.[16] The purpose of this legislation was to prevent the disappearance of a household through marriage, and the concentration of wealth in the hands of an elite. For men as for women, the interests of the state were placed above those of the individual.

Citizen women were secluded, but not simply to preserve their chastity. A woman's participation in public life was restricted also because her appearance was associated with politically unacceptable displays of private wealth in the form of clothes, jewels and chariots. Solon in the early days of Athenian democracy first legislated to minimise female participation in processions, funerals and feasts.[17] Lycurgus' attempts to revitalize Athenian democracy in the generation before Menander involved new restrictions upon women's participation in festivals.[18] Under the Macedonian protectorate in Menander's own day, official 'supervisors of women' were appointed with the task of regulating female conduct in public, in matters of clothing and so forth. One of Menander's plays refers to their covert methods of checking the number of guests at wedding banquets.[19] With this institution, we come to one of the unresolved contradictions in Athenian democracy. These supervisors of women were, on the face of it, a restriction placed upon the rich who wished to be ostentatious. But such officers were equally unacceptable to radical democrats, since the poor were, as Aristotle puts it, forced to use their wives in place of slaves. The wives of the poor could never be secluded like the wives of the prosperous. The freedom of women in the home – 'gynae-cocracy', as he calls it – was seen by Aristotle as a characteristic of fourth-century radical democracy, and a source of its inherent weakness.[20] If Athenian attitudes were confused, non-democratic Sparta was at least available as a clear object lesson. Aristotle shows us why Spartan women were thought in Athens to have too much freedom. Their social freedom encouraged the private display of wealth. Their freedom of movement was a hindrance in time of invasion. The possibility of alienating entire estates through inheritance and over-sized dowries resulted, in the fourth century, in a concentration of wealth, and in a drastic reduction in the manpower of the Spartiate military elite.[21]

It is too simple to see Menander's plays, with their domestic setting and love interest, as clear evidence of *embourgeoisement*, as an assertion of private as opposed to public values – though this is the usual analysis that is made. I cannot accept an approach which suggests that: 'For Menander, contemporary affairs are about as far in the background as the Napoleonic wars are for Jane Austen!'[22] The private and the political were deeply interwoven in Athens. A marriage was not simply – as it might have been for Molière or Jane Austen – a personal and moral fulfilment for the individual. A marriage was a contribution to the strength of the state. In the fourth century, Plato advocated fines for men who did not marry by the age of thirty-five.[23] Philip of Macedon in the third century and Polybius in the second both commented on the weakness of Greek cities in their time through depopulation.[24] The marriages that end Menander's plays are, and this is the definitive distinction between a wife and a concubine, marriages that can provide the city with a new generation of sons. The cult of romantic love in Menander is not a simple reflection of changing interpersonal relations in Athens. The magical trajectory of the plays from erotic desire to marriage permits the reconciliation of many basic oppositions and contradictions in Greek democratic life. I shall describe briefly some of the levels on which the plays work.

There is an opposition between sexual licence and sexual prohibition. On the cosmic level, this can be termed an opposition between Aphrodite and Artemis: the patroness of prostitution on the one hand, the chaste moon goddess on the other who wounds the bride with her bow during childbirth.[25] There is a transition from anarchy to law when the rapist and the raped woman are reunited, when private violence gives way to marriage by contract. The rape usually takes place at a religious festival in honour of a savage deity such as Aphrodite, Artemis or Dionysus.[26] The plays thus bridge god and man, for the wedding is not sacramental but a civil man-made contract. The rape occurs because the god makes a man mad, but the wedding is undertaken through free choice. The human being who acts upon impulse is transformed into the citizen who acts rationally. In the rape, the man is enslaved to emotion, the woman is treated physically as if she were a slave, but in the finale the man and woman become free in both moral and status terms.

Foucault in his *History of Sexuality* requires us to see sexuality not as a drive but rather as a discourse. While Christian sexual ethics are concerned with purity, the main concern of the Greeks, for Foucault, was with self-control: 'The theme of virginity has nearly nothing to do with sexual ethics in Graeco-Roman asceticism. There the problem is a problem of self-domination. It was a virile model of self-domination, and a woman who was temperate was as virile to herself as a man.'[27] This concern with self-domination, so evident in the cult of homosexuality, is scarcely less evident in Menander, where homosexuality is conspicuous by its absence. The discourse is constant in Greek sexual ethics, and only the object of the discourse – the boy, the courtesan, the bride – changes. When the bride becomes the object of the discourse, however, questions of status immediately come into play, for marriage is only possible if the couple are both of legitimate stock. What I wish to suggest is that Menander's plays are a way of talking about self-domination – a necessary positive in the value-system of a slave society, where it matters to be free of soul as well as free of body. And the plays are also a way of talking about social status – about the restrictions which the institutions of the state placed upon people's freedom to act as they wished. It is this second theme that is new. Under the cosmopolitan Macedonian empire, the well-being of the city-state was no longer the ethical imperative that it had been in the classical period. Menander's plays of romantic love provided a discourse capable of dealing with changing relations between the individual and the state.

If we can judge from the papyri that chance has extricated from the Egyptian desert, prostitutes play a relatively small part in Menander's plays. Though the idea of prostitution is important, prostitutes themselves do not dominate the stage. Important helping roles are played by a former *hetaira* turned concubine in *The Samian*, and by a slave *hetaira* in *The Arbitrants*. In two short papyri, the hero is in love with a *hetaira*, in the one case free, in the other a slave in danger of being sold to a nouveau-riche soldier, but we do not know how Menander resolved the plots.[28] In general, young men in Menander undergo a change of character, young women undergo a change of status. The plays locate their heroines in a wide variety of different situations with respect to status, and prostitution is one possibility among many within the complex social system of democratic Greece. I introduce the caveat 'if we can judge from the papyri' because we perceive a very different Menander if we come to him through the eyes of later Graeco-Roman culture. Ovid declared that Menander's work would survive for 'as long as the deceiving slave, the hard father, the shameless bawd, the persuasive prostitute'.[29] Athenaeus preserves for us a large selection of quotations from Menander on the theme of prostitution. And most important of all, Plautus and Terence chose to adapt for the Roman stage plays in which prostitution plays a central part in the plot. If we study Roman New Comedy as an independent form, and not as evidence for reconstructing a Greek form, then we see quickly that the focus of the Greek material upon rape and marriage is replaced by a new focus upon prostitution.

I shall discuss Terence first because, though later than Plautus, his plays are more closely based on Greek texts. Preferring a double plot to the single plots of Menander, Terence in all his plays sets up an opposition between marriage and prostitution. In his first play, *The Andrian*, hero number one marries a rich citizen girl promised to hero number two, while hero number two marries a girl thought at first to be a prostitute's sister. In *The Mother-in-law*, the single hero is torn between a bride whom he has unwittingly raped, and a prostitute. The other four plays all follow the same pattern. Hero number one secures a poor but free-born wife, hero number two secures the favours of the prostitute. In one case, I should add that a marriage is tacked on at the end for number two. The plays of Terence suggest consistently that there is a choice to be made: duty or pleasure, marriage or prostitution. The prostitutes are often attractive and virtuous, and neither choice is inherently right or wrong. A clear choice exists nevertheless. In the pseudo-Greek world of Terence's drama, we find none of the complex nuances of Menander's Athens, where prostitution shades into concubinage, which shades again into marriage. A repressive father may be a problem, the institutions of the state broadly are not.

The plays of Plautus are more numerous, more varied and more obviously Roman. There are four plays in which the hero pursues a prostitute and in the end marries her when she turns out to be free-born. In a large group of nine plays, the hero secures the services of a prostitute without any consideration of marriage. In one of these plays the hero is a slave, in three or four a father decides to share in the sexual pleasures enjoyed by his son. In one the hero is forced into a shotgun marriage, but maintains a private understanding with the prostitute. The remaining plays must be described individually. Several are comedies of middle-aged married life. No prostitute appears in the *Amphitryon*, where the interest lies in the wife's power to terminate the marriage if the husband misbehaves. In *The Brothers Menaechmus* an identical twin is caught in his brother's predicament: how to give no offence either to his wife or to his prostitute. The father in the *Casina* is effectively in the same position, trying to marry off a slave-girl to his trusted slave in order that he will be able to enjoy her sexual favours unbeknown to his wife. Two plays counterpoint youth and age. In the *Stichus* a pair of heroines stay faithful to their bland husbands, while a pair of slaves enjoy a raunchy dance with a fellow-slave who promises her body to both. The father figure opts for the second course, pleasure rather than duty, and bargains with his sons-in-law: since he has given them lavish dowries, they owe him in return the enjoyment of two slave-girls whom they have just imported from the East. In *The Pot of Gold*, the romantic quest of the youth for the miser's daughter is counterpointed against his middle-aged uncle's decision to succumb to social pressure and marry. The uncle decides to take an undowered bride who will not have the economic leverage to make his life miserable. A dowry is also the focus of the *Trinummus* where a reformed wastrel sadly bids farewell to love and decides to take a dowerless bride. The choice lies between love and marriage. Since love is too expensive, he will opt for a life of extreme thrift. The one remaining play in Plautus' oeuvre is an exceptional piece with no female roles, and it need not concern us.[30]

The choice is always the same in Plautus' drama, either marriage, or pleasure. Pleasure is incompatible with the married state. Where the prostitute turns out to be citizen born, the discovery is presented as a means whereby the youth can enjoy the prostitute's favours indefinitely. More often than not, the hero does not contemplate marriage. It will be apparent from this short account of Plautus' plots that the plays are more concerned with being married than with getting married. There is a presumption at every turn that the average married male wants to escape from the clutches of his wife into the arms of a prostitute. We find little trace of this fear of marriage in Menander's writing, and the sociological roots of this fear in the Roman world are not hard to find.

Roman wives did not live the sequestered lives of Athenian women. When guests came to the home, wives were at the centre of the social gathering.[31] When in Plautus' day Cato spoke to oppose the repeal of wartime restrictions on female dress, women took to the streets to oppose him – something that cannot be imagined in Athens except in the fantasy world of Aristophanes. In a speech recorded or reconstructed by Livy, Cato harked back to the old days when women did not speak to other women's husbands, or engage in financial matters, and eastern influences had not given them a taste for luxury.[32] Cato was outvoted, but what is significant for our purposes is his perception of social change. The legal form of marriage was changing fundamentally in Plautus' day. Traditional *manus* marriage – which is to say, marriage giving control to the husband, often through a technical 'sale' of the bride – was vanishing, and the wife was tending to remain under her father's final authority. A marriage was a means of cementing alliances, and if the father retained *manus* over his daughter, then he could dissolve the alliance at any time if dissatisfied with the husband's behaviour. Equally, the husband could terminate the marriage provided he was willing to return the dowry. The effect of the change was to give the wife a certain equality, a power base of her own as it were. After her father's death, though remaining under nominal male 'tutorship', the wife acquired in practice a fair degree of independence.[33] Divorce became increasingly commonplace.[34] There were institutional pressures in Rome to encourage reluctant males to marry. The Censors, in a public ceremony every five years, enquired whether a man had yet taken a legal wife.[35] By the time of the early Empire, drastic measures had to be taken to restore the birthrate.[36]

There is a simple practical reason why Roman New Comedy does not associate marriage with romantic love. Whereas in Greece a girl's marriage took place after puberty, in Rome it commonly took place before. It was believed that intercourse would assist the arrival of menstruation.[37] The

Roman bride was too young to have Eros visit her, and her sexual initiation
was probably not enjoyable. Plutarch explains the rationale for this early
marriage at a time when the girl's mind and body are plainly not ready for
intercourse. Roman marriage was a moral affair, he writes, and the Roman
took his wife when her body and character were undefiled so that she would
learn the right habits.[38] The Roman marriage was an alliance between
families involving a transfer of property, and the wife's consent was not
legally required.[39] The younger the bride, therefore, the less risk there was
that her emotions and wishes would emerge as a complicating factor.[40]

Greek and Roman systems of prostitution also need to be contrasted. In
Athens, state-run brothels were established by Solon.[41] Male and female
slaves were available in brothels at a cheap rate. But men who could afford
it[42] preferred to visit free *hetairai* in their private houses, or to invite women
to entertainments in the men's quarters of their own homes. In Rome,
where the women of the house were not segregated, this last option was not
available, and prostitutes were normally visited in brothels. There is a
semantic distinction between the Greek *hetaira* or companion and the Latin
meretrix who does it for reward. Plautus sometimes translates *hetaira* into
amica, 'friend', but this was not a usage that later Roman writers felt able to
follow.[43] As Fraenkel observed, for Plautus and his audience 'the simple
mention of a *meretrix* automatically evoked the idea of the brothel.'[44] The
Greek distinction between the brothel slave and the free *hetaira* had no
equivalent in Roman life in Plautus' day. Brothels were the norm because
they allowed men to be certain that the women there were licensed
prostitutes. A man could install a free woman in his house as his concubine,
or he could visit a woman who had officially registered herself as a
prostitute and wore the appropriate toga. But if in any other circumstances
he had casual sexual relations with a free woman, then he ran the risk of
prosecution for the crime of *stuprum*,[45] or he might unwittingly be party to
adultery. In Rome, therefore, the home and the brothel are stark alternatives, whereas in Greece we see a spectrum running from marriage through
concubinage and social companionship to slave prostitution, and the lines
of demarcation can be very hazy.

A complex set of problems arises when we try to define whether the
Roman audience was sexually repressed, whether its interest in prostitution
constitutes salacity. One of the easiest ways to read Plautus is to see him as
providing a fantasy world in which taboos are flouted. In a sense Rome was
obviously more repressive than Greece. We know from Polybius, for
example, that in the army masturbation was punishable by the *bastinado*,
effectively a death sentence,[46] and no comparable regulation in Greece is
conceivable. We do not know, however, to what extent it was acceptable for
young men in the decade or more between adolescence and marriage to
frequent prostitutes[47] – and speculation along these lines seems unproduc-

tive. Critics of Roman comedy tend to focus less upon the sexual mores of the time than upon the repressive power of the father. The *paterfamilias* had legal powers of life and death over his sons, who could own no property until their father's death. We know the law, we do not know how people felt. Erich Segal's claim to discern a parricidal urge in Plautus[48] cannot easily be defended when, as happens in several plays, the father, so far from suppressing his son's love affairs, prefers to participate. We may assume that fathers were about as plentiful as sons in Plautus' audience, and there is no reason to doubt that there were also many women in the audience.[49] We have to determine whose repressed impulses are being voiced. If we take repression to be the trigger of the comedy, we quickly become caught up in a circular argument as to whether the plays satisfy repressed frustrations with empty dreams, or whether they constitute subversive assaults upon orthodox morality.

We are on safer ground if we follow Foucault and by-pass what he terms 'the repressive hypothesis': 'I would like to disengage my analysis from the privileges generally accorded the economy of scarcity and the principles of rarefaction, to search instead for instances of discursive production . . . of the production of power . . . of the production of knowledge.'[50] Where do we arrive if we examine *Amor* – love – in Plautus not as an outlet for repressed impulses but as a discursive production?

This Roman discourse is again not concerned with virginity, bodily purity, the great theme of Christian ethics. The central theme, as in the Greek theatre, is dominance – self-dominance versus dominance by an outside force. But Plautus' discourse is more universalist than Menander's, stressing that the same passion is felt by all males. Plautus' discourse of love is on the face of it subversive, vaunting pleasure as the alternative to marriage; but it is, on another level, profoundly solidary, binding all men together as sharers of a single sexual orientation, a single physical practice. While the language used by Menander's soldier to render his experience of Eros points to the particularity of his experience – implying 'no one has felt quite as intensely as I have,' 'I am not behaving as others would do' – the language of Plautus' lovers is very different. Here is the start of the lover's monologue which opens Plautus' play *The Merchant*:

> It is required that I should do two things at once:
> Expound the plot, and expound my love affairs.
> I shall not do the same as others I have seen
> Playing lovers in the theatre, who recount their woes
> To the night or the day, to sun or moon.
> I don't think *they* care much for the complaints
> Of humans, their wants and don't-wants:
> So I shall recount my woes to you.

There is nothing remarkable about the lover's experience that the audience cannot share. There is no cosmic mystery in this earthly experience. The lover's ironic tone continues through the play:

> The flames of love are burning in my breast and in my heart.
> But for the tears in my eyes protecting me, I think my head would have caught fire.

(lines 590–1)

Private emotion is subject for mockery. Deep emotions in Rome should not be private possessions but should be fixed to communal aspirations.

Love in Plautus, then, is a discursive production which binds all men together. Roman society relied upon the solidarity of its male members, who all served long stints in the army in Plautus' time, bound by solemn oath to put the well-being of the state before individual safety. In Menander, where Aphrodite and marriage are reconciled, there is no necessary disjunction between pleasure and virtue. To be good is also to be happy. But in Plautus' world the available discourse of love stresses that pleasure and virtue are incompatible. Moral behaviour can only be understood in terms of abnegation and suffering. The discourse of Plautus' plays is bound up with the power relations of society, and constitutes a form of knowledge.

Plautus' comedies deal with many different types of power relationship. The master has legal or economic power over his slave or parasite, but is powerless without their help. The father has legal and economic power over his son, yet the son's interests are his own. This concern with interpersonal power, this continual tension between dominance and solidarity, can be seen as characteristic of a Roman world cemented together by the institution of clientage. Clientage was the system whereby the poor man gave political loyalty to the rich man in return for legal and financial forms of protection.[51] There was no equivalent infrastructure in Athens, where a man gave his loyalties to his deme, phratry and tribe, and where patronage was politically unacceptable. Since a Roman marriage served to forge an economic and political bond between two heads of families, we can see that the Roman system of marriage is not unconnected to the system of clientage. Given this context, we can begin to see why sexual relations in Plautus are part of a more extensive discourse upon power.

I have suggested that there is a basic opposition in the plays between the home and the brothel, between duty and pleasure. This can also be expressed as an opposition between the prostitute's fee and the dowry. The man without money can be turned away by his prostitute, can be at the mercy of his moneyed wife. Money gives one woman power to buy her freedom from the slave-dealer, another power to buy a malleable husband. Heavily dowered wives are about as common in Plautus as grasping prostitutes.[52] Let me give some examples of how this opposition is expressed. One Plautine hero, overhearing a bawd warn his beloved that heavy perfumes will not attract a man, exclaims to the audience:

> Quite true! as the vast majority of you realise,
> Because of the old women at home, your wives, who've
>   procured you with a dowry.
>
> (*The Haunted House*, lines 280–1)

One father complains that his son's prostitute stands in the way of the dowry that marriage would bring into the family.[53] Another father is pleased that his daughter has been raped because the dowry will now cost him six talents less.[54] In another play, a poor girl without a dowry is disguised as a prostitute and put up for sale[55] – part of a blackmail racket repeated in two other plays where a woman's chastity is given its cash value. In Plautus' world, every woman has a price tag attached to her.

Within the Roman system of marriage, then, the power of the woman in the home is related to her cash value – which is to say, to the power and wealth of her ascendants.[56] The Aristotelian idea that the male is naturally superior by virtue of his masculinity no longer applies in this context. The Roman fascination with prostitution derives, I wish to argue, not so much from sexual repression as from a social context which allocated each woman power equivalent to her price of purchase.

I have tried to follow Foucault in examining Greek and Roman sexuality as a discourse, in deciphering how 'a complex experience is constituted from and around certain forms of behaviour'.[57] The interrelation between theatre and social life outside the theatre is easier to grasp if one thinks in these terms. The theatre provides the physical fact of sexuality with a set of meanings, gives it a language beyond that provided by the semantically inadequate *eros, philia, amor*. New Comedy is not escapism, not a dissipation of mental energies, but an expressive instrument, and an integral part of the power structures of Greek and Roman society.

NOTES

1 'On the Geneaology of Ethics' in *The Foucault Reader,* ed. Paul Rabinow, (Harmondsworth: Penguin: 1986), p.345.

2 A classic exploration of the relationship between Demeter and Aphrodite is Marcel Detienne, *The Gardens of Adonis*, trans. J. Lloyd (Hassocks, Harvester: 1977). For dedications to Athena and Artemis, see the *Palatine Anthology* vi.271, 272, 273, 280, 288, 289.

3 *Palatine Anthology* vi. 285; cf. Plautus *Poenulus* 1132–40.

4 *Palatine Anthology* vi. 285, 290.

5 Athenaeus xiii.559, 571.

6 See K. J. Dover 'Classical Greek Attitudes to Sexual Behaviour in the Ancient World' in *The Arethusa Papers*, ed. John Peradotto and J. P. Sullivan (State

University of New York, 1984, pp.143–57 especially p.150; S. C. Humphreys, *The Family, Women and Death* (London: Routledge & Kegan Paul, 1983), p.57.

7 Humphreys, *The Family, Women and Death*, p.64.

8 The fragment from *The Danaids* is preserved in Athenaeus xiii.600b. In *The Suppliants*, the second hemichorus may be a new chorus of servants.

9 Diogenes Laertius vii. 130.

10 In the first group I place the *Epitrepontes, Georgos, Hero, Kitharistes* (probably), *Plokion, Samia, Synaristosai*, and the *Fabula incerta*; also three plays reconstructed from Terence: the *Adelphoi, Andria* and *Eunouchos*. The heroine of *Phasma* is the product of her mother's rape. A man refrains from taking the girl over whom he has power in *Aspis* (where the uncle is duped to prevent him taking an *epikleros*), in *Dyskolos* (where the hero's power is not legal, but the power of wealth over poverty), the *Epitrepontes, Misoumenos* and *Sikyonios*.

11 The former survives in copies, the second is lost. For the importance of these works, see J. J. Pollitt, *Art and Experience in Classical Greece* (Cambridge University Press, 1972), pp. 157–9; Martin Robertson, *A History of Greek Art* (Cambridge University Press, 1975), vol. 1, pp. 390–4.

12 'A Comparison of Aristophanes and Menander', *Moralia* 854c.

13 Aristotle, *Genesis of Animals* 727a–728b; R. Joly, ed., *Hippocrate*, vol. 11 (Paris: Les Belles Lettres, 1970), p. 17; Aline Rousselle, *Porneia* (Paris: Presses Universitaires de France, 1983), pp. 41–3.

14 Rousselle, *Porneia*, p. 59.

15 *Politics* I.ii–253bff.

16 *Plokion* and *Aspis*. Menander also wrote a play entitled *Epikleros*, 'The Heiress', but we know nothing of the plot.

17 Plutarch, *Solon* 21.

18 Plutarch, *Moralia* 842a.

19 Frag 238 K-T; on the institution of the *gynaikonomoi*, see Claude Vatin, *Recherches sur le mariage et la condition de la femme mariée a l'époque hellénistique* (Paris: Editions E. De Boccard, 1970), pp. 254–61.

20 *Politics* IV.xii.9–1300a; VI.v.13–1323a; V.ix.6–1313b.

21 *Politics* II.vi.5–13–1269b–1270a.

22 E. W. Handley in the *Cambridge History of Classical Literature*, vol. 1 *Greek Literature*, ed. P. E. Easterling and B. M. W. Knox (Cambridge University Press, 1985), p.405.

23 *Laws* 774.

24 Polybius xxxvi.17.5–7. See the discussion by J. K. Davies in the *Cambridge Ancient History*, vol. 7, part 1, *The Hellenistic World*, 2nd edn, ed. F. Wallbank, A. E. Astin, M. W. Frederiksen and R. M. Ogilvie (Cambridge University Press, 1984), pp. 268ff; for the effect of war on population; see also Claire Préaux, *Le monde hellénistique* (Paris: Presses Universitaires de France, 1978), pp. 298–303.

25 The scholiast on Theocritus II.66b records that women in Menander call upon Artemis to forgive them for the loss of their virginity as they are being impregnated. Women in labour call upon Artemis at *Andria* frag.35 K-T and at *Georgos* 112.

26 Aphrodite – *Samia* 39; Artemis – *Epitrepontes* 451, *Kitharistes* 94 and (probably) *Phasma* 98; Dionysus – *Synaristosai* frag.382 K-T.

27 'On the Genealogy of Ethics' in *The Foucault Reader*, p.366.

28 The heroine of the *Dis Exapaton* seems to be free, and Plautus' adaptation is not a safe guide to the finale. The heroine of the *Kolax* earns three *mnai* daily from the mercenary, which leads Sandbach to conclude that the play cannot end in marriage because 'she was actively a *hetaira*' (A. W. Gomme and F. H. Sandbach, *Menander: a Commentary*, Oxford University Press, 1973, p. 421). But this is not a normal sum to pay for a slave: see note 42 below.

29 *Amores* 1.15.

30 In *Captivi* 57 the prologue notes the lack of wicked courtesans as one of the features that make this play different from others.

31 Nepos, *Preface* 6–7.

32 Livy 34.1–8.

33 Keith Hopkins, *Death and Renewal* (Cambridge University Press, 1983), pp.85ff.; Alan Watson *The Law of Persons in the Later Roman Republic* (Oxford University Press, 1967), pp. 19–27 and 66 n.3.

34 The first man to divorce his wife for reasons other than a matrimonial crime was traditionally said to be Carvilius in c.230 BC – see Alan Watson, *Rome of the XII Tables* (Princeton University Press, 1975), pp. 31–2.

35 See Gordon Williams, *Tradition and Originality in Roman Poetry* (Oxford University Press, 1968), pp. 372–3; Alan Watson, *Roman Private Law Around 200 B.C.* (Edinburgh University Press, 1971), p.22.

36 See for instance Jerome Carcopino, *Daily Life in Ancient Rome*, trans. E. O. Lorimer (London: Routledge, 1941), pp.95–100; J. A. Crook, *Law and Life of Rome* (London: Thames & Hudson, 1967), pp.47, 115, 121.

37 Rousselle, *Porneia*, p.47.

38 *Comparison of Lycurgus and Numa* 4.

39 Watson, *Law of Persons*, p.52.

40 I follow Keith Hopkins's argument in 'The Age of Roman Girls at Marriage', *Population Studies*, 18 (1965), 309–27.

41 Nicander of Colophon cited in Athenaeus xiii.569.

42 The fee for a brothel slave was one *obol*: Philemon cited in Athenaeus xiii.569f; Diogenes Laertius vi.4. Market inspectors enforced standard fees. Two *drachmai* was the maximum fee for a music girl (a euphemism in practice for a prostitute) attending a symposium – Aristotle, *Constitution of Athens* 50.2, cf. Suidas *Lexicon* s.v. *diagramma*. Demeas in Menander, *Samia* 392 suggests that ten *drachmai* is the going rate for attending a symposium. (Note: 6 *obols* = 1 *drachma*; 100 *drachmai* = 1 *mna*).

43 See J. N. Adams, 'Words for Prostitute in Latin', *Rheinisches Museum für Philologie*, 136 (1983), 321–58 especially p. 349.

44 E. Fraenkel, *Elementi plautini in Plauto* trans. F. Munari (Florence: La Nuova Italia, 1960), p.144.

45 For a definition of *stuprum*, see P. E. Corbett, *The Roman Law of Marriage* (Oxford University Press, 1930), p.140 n.1; see also Rousselle, *Porneia*, pp.105–7.

46 Polybius vi.37.9.

47 Cicero *Pro Caelio* xx.48 implies that tolerance was traditional. We may be led to the same conclusion by a well-known anecdote told of Cato in which the moralist tells a young man that a visit to a brothel is preferable to lusting for another man's wife – Horace, *Satires* 1.ii.31.

48 *Roman Laughter* (Cambridge, Mass.: Harvard University Press, 1968), p.17.

Segal has reiterated his views in a contribution to *The Conflict of Generations in Ancient Greece and Rome*, ed. S. Bertman (Amsterdam: Gruner, 1976), pp.135–42. David Daube, examining one legal *cause célèbre*, echoes this view: 'It has been argued that a *filiusfamilias* heavily in debt would never commit parricide . . . I wonder how many holders of this view have ever read the plays of Plautus' (*Roman Law: Linguistic, Social and Philosophical Aspects*, Edinburgh University Press, 1969, p.90).

49 The prologue to Plautus, *Poenulus*, envisages nurses, whores and wives as potential spectators.

50 *The History of Sexuality. Volume One* in *The Foucault Reader*, p.300.

51 See for instance Donald Earl, *The Moral and Political Tradition of Rome* (London: Thames & Hudson, 1967), pp.29–33; H. H. Scullard, *Roman Politics 220–150 B.C.* (Oxford University Press, 1973), pp.12–18.

52 See *Amphitryon* 839, *Asinaria* 898, *Menaechmi* 767, *Mercator* 703 etc.

53 *Cistellaria* 305.

54 *Truculentus* 845.

55 *Persa* 329ff. *cf. Bacchides* and *Miles Gloriosus*.

56 So concludes Alan Watson, *Law of Persons*, p.29.

57 Preface to *The History of Sexuality. Volume Two* in *The Foucault Reader*, p.333.

Hroswitha and the feminization of drama*

PETER R. SCHROEDER

Most non-specialists who think about Hroswitha at all tend to think of her largely as a freak of literary history, a kind of duck-billed platypus standing outside the normal flow of evolution – in this case, the evolution of Christian drama in the Middle Ages. Yet our perception of her as a sideshow exhibit – the tenth-century nun who wrote religious plays in imitation of Terence – can prove an obstacle when we come to examine her actual accomplishment: the mere existence of Hroswitha's plays seems odd enough to keep us from finding out if they are anything more than oddities. This paper, ignoring literary history, will take Hroswitha for granted as a phenomenon and focus instead on how, in both her plays and her prefatory comments to the plays, she exploits her own feminine self-consciousness for dramatic and ironic ends.

In the preface and dedicatory epistle to her plays, Hroswitha seems to present herself as an earnestly naive, self-deprecating, artistically insecure but dutifully pious female. She claims that her work, which she calls 'the little work of a weak little woman' ('opusculum vilis mulierculae'), scarcely merits the praise it has received; all credit, rather, is due the giver of the grace which works in her, since her apparent knowledge surpasses her 'muliebre ingenium', her womanly wit.[1] What she has done comes from God, though it would be wrong to deny that with God's help she has acquired a bit of knowledge, since she is a creature capable of learning ('quia sum animal capax disciplinae', p. 236). Indeed, in a sense her works testify more strikingly to God's grace than they would had she been a man, since women are believed to be more intellectually sluggish than men ('quanto muliebris sensus tardior esse creditur', p. 236). The plays themselves, she claims, show how 'feminine fragility conquers and overcomes with confusion the strength of men' (p. 234). These comments suggest that she is acutely conscious of her own position as a woman writer and of her theme as, essentially, a woman's theme.

* A draft of this paper was read at the *Themes in Drama*, International Conference held at the University of California, Riverside, in February 1987.

Though some have taken Hroswitha's demure disclaimers at face value, the tone of the prefatory material is almost certainly ironic. Peter Dronke goes so far as to say that in the preface 'she says little of what she really means, and means almost nothing of what she says'.[2] But while we sense that what Dronke calls her 'weak little woman pose' is indeed a pose, masking considerable self-assurance, her irony is somewhat more complex than would be the case if, for example, Margaret Thatcher were to use a similar ploy to announce a new plan to stamp out the Trades Union Council. Hroswitha's irony is both verbal and dramatic; if on one level she 'means almost nothing of what she says', on another she is forcing us to re-evaluate the very words she is using: seeming weakness becomes strength, as seeming strength reveals its underlying weakness. In this her preface adumbrates, and is illuminated by, the recurrent, ironic overturning of established values in the plays themselves.

Thus, as Dronke shows (particularly in his analysis of *Dulcitius*), the thematic pattern of feminine weakness overcoming masculine strength – the Christian virgins, for example, dismaying their powerful and pompous pagan oppressors – is prefigured in the preface by Hroswitha's own confrontation with Terence.[3] Terence, like the Roman oppressors, is powerful, male, and pagan; Hroswitha is a weak little ill-educated Christian woman. It is interesting how she emphasizes the comparative *weakness* of her own language ('vilitas dictationis', p. 234); all she really has in her favor is a devotion to Christ. Her relationship to Terence encapsulates the same cluster of oppositions which she says her plays exemplify: female–male, Christian–pagan, weakness–strength. And just as her characters, with God's help, succeed against seemingly overwhelming odds, so, by implication, Hroswitha herself manages the unlikely feat of writing plays worthy of comparison with those of her classical predecessor. In her plays, as Dronke says, 'the ultimate victory is a victory of God, but Hroswitha sees it "especially" ('praesertim') as a feminist triumph. Weak women show their power, strong men go under.'[4] Hroswitha seems to see herself participating in an analogous triumph.

Yet in a sense this identification of weakness and femininity is something of a sleight-of-hand trick by Hroswitha. The pervasive pattern is indeed seeming weakness conquering seeming strength, but in only two of the plays – *Dulcitius* and *Sapientia*, the two dramas of virginal martyrdom – do we find the weak, the feminine, and the Christian explicitly united. The others are dramas of conversion in which, I would argue, we are induced to see *fragilitas* as metaphorically feminine even when it manifests itself in men. At the outset of *Gallicanus*, for example, Gallicanus, the leader of the Roman troops, is pagan, masculine, and apparently powerful, yet he is victorious in battle only when, his defeat seemingly assured, he surrenders himself to the True God and his foes, the Scythians, collapse like a punctured tire. Worldly power has given way to worldly weakness (he gives up his position, gives away his wealth, and goes off to become the disciple of a holy man), paganism has given way to Christianity, but his feminization is by association only, as if the offstage prayers of Constantia, Artemia, and Attica had, in a sense, contributed to unmanning him. Returning from his paradoxical victory, he dramatizes this spiritual feminization by renouncing his earlier desire to marry Constantia, Constantine's daughter, and instead embracing her own vows of chastity. In *Callimachus*, Callimachus undergoes an analogous conversion. Appalled by Callimachus' lustful advances, Drusiana – another chaste Christian – altruistically dies in order to spare him the shame of being exposed, and in so doing lays the foundation for his own quasi-posthumous transformation into a chaste Christian. Again the male character triumphs spiritually after losing his worldly power; again the agent of conversion is a woman; again the conversion itself is represented as the substitution of the values embodied in the virtuous woman (chastity, renunciation of the world) for the lust and worldly power more native to the man.

Hroswitha's two remaining plays, *Abraham* and *Pafnutius*, differ from the others in that their central figures are sympathetic, Christian, unworldly men – earnest grizzled hermits – who undertake the salvation of fallen women. Abraham and Pafnutius may be outsiders to the 'masculine' world of the lovers, but they are, ineluctably, men – men, moreover, who from the outset are steadfast in their piety. In a worldly sense they are weak, and their weakness ends up defeating the more obviously powerful worldly lures that have seduced Thaia and Maris, but in what way do these plays illustrate Hroswitha's stated theme of 'feminine fragility' overthrowing the 'strength of men'? The possible answers to this question, though they may be tenuous, nonetheless cast some light on a non-obvious 'feminine' quality in Hroswitha's dramas generally.

On one level, of course, the two hermits can be seen as agents for restoring Thais and Maria to their true natures – the native purity which they have lost as a result of mingling with the world of men. Both women are depicted as essentially good. Maria has endured an oppressively pious upbringing by the holy Abraham and has fallen only after being seduced by a lecher disguised as a monk. Thais professes an unquestioning belief in God; as she burns her ill-gotten treasures she tells her lovers that for the first time in her life she is sane – a sanity misinterpreted as lunacy by those still enamored of the luxury which she is so spectacularly relinquishing. By accepting the false (and, implicitly, masculine) values of the world and the flesh, both heroines have been, in a sense, turncoats to their sex, and the old hermits are vehicles for their refeminization. We might thus regard the triumph in these plays as the triumph of Thais and Maria over a kind of abstracted Idea of the Male – an Idea subsuming, for Hroswitha, sex, glitter, and general spiritual perversion.

But Abraham and Pafnutius are also representative of another quality, so pervasive in Hroswitha's plays that we take it for granted, as a given: the extraordinary subordination of institutionalized rules to a kind of spiritual spontaneity. Her plays are set in the days of the early church not simply to provide her with the opportunity to meet Terence on something like his own ground, nor because that period provided the richest source of hagiographical material; her non-dramatic works show that she could come much closer to contemporaneity. Primitive Christianity seems to appeal to her in large part because she can depict it as a golden age of religious individualism, without ecclesiastical structures or hierarchy, without regulations or rituals (apart from baptism). The abbess in *Pafnutius* is the only real representative of a Christian institution, and she speaks of her 'exiguatatem habitationis' (p. 342), emphasizing her lack of pomp or the trappings of power. When the converted Gallicanus returns triumphantly to Rome he bypasses the pagan shrines and goes instead 'ad domum sancti Petri' (p. 253); this may be a kind of kenning for a church, but it has a decidedly domestic and personal flavor. He then, as we have noted, relinquishes all his earlier institutional ties. Constantine, in the same play, must have posed a problem for Hroswitha: he is at the same time Christian and emperor. But, as we shall see later, he lacks the trappings of power or pomp that Hroswitha gives to her pagan emperors. He pleads rather than commands; his worries – in the face of possible disaster for the Empire – seem largely personal; he makes no effort to impose religious conformity on his pagan general. Conversion, it seems, must come from within; God is available to the willing individual without the need for any formal mediation.

This non-institutionalized view of religion is connected, as well, with Hroswitha's almost proto-Abelardan ethic of intentionality. When, in *Dulcitius*, Sissinius threatens to punish Irena by hauling her off to a brothel, Irena points out that it is better for the body to be besmirched than to worship idols, and that in order to sin it is necessary that the soul consent. When Abraham, casting around for some way to retrieve his fallen niece, tells his fellow hermit Effrem of his plan to seek her out disguised as a potential lover, Effrem asks him what he'll do if meat and wine – which Abraham has vowed to avoid – are put before him. 'I shall by no means refuse, that I may remain unknown', says Abraham, and Effrem assures him that God knows what is in our hearts and understands our intentions ('qua intentione unaquaeque res geratur, intelligit', p. 311). In spite of her surface depravity, Thais is redeemed by her belief in God. And the notion that good intentions count for more than pedantic adherence to rules is applied by Hroswitha, in her preface, to herself: in order to carry out her intentions, Hroswitha admits that it has been necessary for her to write about things 'which are not permitted us to hear', but had she not done so she could not have accomplished her purpose. Although we are right to distrust general claims about what is 'characteristically feminine', I think that, in these plays, we almost subliminally perceive this preference for the relational and the spontaneous over the regulated and the institutionalized as in some sense a 'feminine' characteristic. It certainly forms a fourth element in Hroswitha's central set of oppositions: it is the powerful pagan males who seem obsessed with enforcing their rules, and the weak Christian women whose role, as often as not, is to subvert those rules and institutions. In this sense Abraham and Pafnutius take their place on the feminine side of the opposition.

Now that I've stretched the concept of the feminine beyond what the normal elasticity of the term may be able to tolerate, I'd like to examine in some detail the ironic inversion of expectations in *Sapientia*, the most straightforwardly 'feminist' of Hroswitha's plays and the play in which her central oppositions are most clearly exemplified. *Sapientia* begins with a dialogue between the emperor Hadrian and his flattering lackey Antiochus, who immediately establishes his institutional loyalty and identity ('My Lord Emperor, what desire has your servant but to see you powerful and prosperous? What ambition apart from the welfare and peace and greatness of the state you rule?') and emphasizes his alacrity in calling attention to any dangers which might threaten the state. Hadrian wonders what new dangers have appeared:

> *Hadrian.* Come, if you have discovered some new danger, make it known to me.
> *Antiochus.* A certain alien woman has recently come to this city with her three children.
> *Hadrian.* Of what sex are the children?
> *Antiochus.* They are all girls.
> *Hadrian.* And you think that a handful of women threaten danger to the state?
>
> (p. 358; *Plays*, pp. 133–4)

As readers or audience we surely share Hadrian's surprise at the bizarre disproportion between Antiochus's fawning buildup and the nature of the threat itself, a disproportion that emphasizes Hroswitha's central contrast between worldly power (male, pagan, institutionalized) and seeming weakness (female, Christian, relational). Hadrian's response also echoes the pet word, 'muliercula', by which Hroswitha refers to herself in her preface: 'tantillarum . . . muliercularum aliquid', some very small little women, a double diminutive. The danger to the Roman state comes not simply from females, but from females shrunk to an extreme of insignificance.

Antiochus goes on to justify his fears: this woman is disrupting the concord ('concordiam') of the state with the dissonance ('dissonantia') of her religious practice. And her disruption has been effective: 'Our wives hate us and scorn us to such an extent that they will not deign to eat with us, still less share our beds.' The institutional harmony of the state is being subverted by the sort of threat that Hadrian's pomp and power are completely unsuited to deal with: this one intrusive woman is infecting all the women of Rome, and the result is marital discord. The largely impersonal institution of the state, Hroswitha implies, rests on the largely relational institution of marriage; women, by exercising their power over the latter, can help bring down the former. Christianity is presented as a feminine attack on the male power structure.

The play thus establishes its polarities at the outset, and establishes as well the ironic technique by which Hroswitha undermines our obvious expectations. The first part of the play, in fact, involves a kind of demolition, one after another, of Hadrian's misconceptions about women. He begins by assuming they are weak, but finds that Rome is being threatened by a feminist conspiracy. He goes on to assume that they are easily manipulated. When Sapientia and her daughters are brought before Hadrian, the emperor decides to persuade rather than threaten, and Antiochus agrees: 'the frail sex is easily moved by flattery' ('fragilitas sexus feminea facilius potest blandimentis molliri', p. 359). But as we have seen, Hroswitha has a tendency to use 'fragilitas' ironically, and the women turn out to be triumphantly impervious to flattery. Indeed, Hadrian is far more swayed by Sapientia's fair appearance than Sapientia is swayed by his 'fair speeches'; she seems to have a principled contempt for rhetoric as opposed to truth. But Hadrian, a slow learner, persists in his misconceptions and continues to chat up Sapientia in a greasily avuncular way: what are your children's names? How old are they?

This last question opens the floodgates for Sapientia's brain-teasing response, a long passage of complex numerical gibberish that leaves Hadrian totally mystified. Charity, she begins, 'has lived a diminished evenly even number of years; Hope a number also diminished, but unevenly even; and Faith an augmented number, unevenly even'. When Hadrian says that this answer leaves him in ignorance, Sapientia continues: 'Every number is said to be "diminished" the parts of which when added together give a sum which is less than the number of which they are parts. Such a number is 8. For the half of 8 is 4, the quarter of 8 is 2, and the eighth of 8 is 1; and these added together give 7.' And so on and so on. It has been common to regard this speech as an unfortunate bit of showing off on Hroswitha's part – Christopher St John, in the 1923 translation of the plays from which I have just quoted, apologizes in a footnote: 'It has been my duty to preserve this rather tiresome numerical discourse, which no doubt Roswitha introduced to impress the "learned men" to whom she submitted her work' (*Plays*, pp. 139–40). But a reader more charitably willing to admit that Hroswitha may have known what she was doing can find the passage both amusing and dramatically relevant. Essentially, it strikes me as another undercutting of Hadrian's smug assumptions about women: not only are they weak, harmless, and easily swayed by flattery, they are also stupid and ignorant. But Sapientia's speech leaves Hadrian gasping: 'Your answer leaves me in ignorance.' 'I am not familiar with these terms.' 'Little did I think that a simple question about the age of these children could give rise to such an intricate and unprofitable dissertation.' Sapientia is indeed showing off, but her speech has a double purpose within the play itself: to point Sapientia's own moral – that the exposition reveals God's wisdom in giving human beings the ingenuity to figure out such mathematical formulations – and to point as well the implicit moral that men would be better off not underestimating women. I suspect, in fact, that Hroswitha may have been laughing at the Christopher St Johns among her own circle of learned men.

But Hadrian is too dense to draw the second moral; like the tormentors in *Dulcitius* he is an obdurate buffoon unable to recognize that he is supporting a lost cause. And, like most self-important buffoons, he proves particularly vulnerable to mockery. When, unable to move Sapientia, he turns to bullying her daughters, they jeer at him for his foolishness. This serves to enrage Hadrian, and Antiochus calls them crazy for their insolence. In this he echoes Thais' inversion of seeming lunacy and seeming sanity in *Pafnutius*; it is in fact Hadrian and Antiochus, clinging in spite of everything to their own misguided notion of what works, who emerge as the true lunatics. Their tortures prove no more effective than their blandishments; Faith frisks on a heated gridiron and swims in boiling pitch before joyfully allowing herself to be decapitated; Hope, threatened by scourging, tells Hadrian that the more cruelty he shows 'the greater will be your humiliation'; Charity, the youngest of the lot, continues to make fun of Antiochus' stupidity ('Although I am small, my reason is big enough to put you to shame', p. 371) and mocks the disparity between Hadrian's professions of power and his actual helplessness ('A mighty man! he cannot conquer a child of eight without calling fire to help him!'). After that helplessness has been dramatized by the death of five thousand of Hadrian's men in the fire intended for Hope, she too is beheaded; the play ends with Sapientia, surrounded by matrons, burying her dead daughters and praying for her own death. But, as Hroswitha shows, for this sisterhood of Christians death is victory, and the victory of God is at the same time clearly a 'feminist triumph'.

Sapientia, generally thought to be the last play Hroswitha wrote, is the play which articulates most explicitly her proto-feminist themes: all the women are good, Christian, seemingly weak but really strong, seemingly defeated but really victorious, anti-institutional; all the men are the reverse. The very starkness of the opposition helps us see how, in a play like *Gallicanus*, she can *implicitly* feminize a story in which the moral division between men and women is much less clearcut, and in which the apparently central characters are at the same time powerful men (or men, at least, who hold positions of institutional power) and sympathetic Christians. I'll conclude, then, by looking at the beginning of *Gallicanus* to see how she deals with the character of Constantine, whose dual role as emperor and Christian makes him a particularly interesting challenge.

In the speech with which he opens the play, Constantine sounds, at least, every inch the emperor. Like Julian, Diocletian, and Hadrian – his pagan counterparts – he establishes his role rhetorically, by giving orders: his general, Gallicanus, must hasten off to subdue the Scythians. But Gallicanus balks. Hesitantly, afraid of Constantine's anger, he says that if he is successful in his campaign he wants to marry the emperor's daughter, Constantia. Constantine's answer seems to surprise everyone. He isn't angry – the expected and appropriate imperial response – but says instead that he must first seek his daughter's consent. That is, instead of answering as emperor – his public persona – he answers as father; but as father he once again subverts expectations. Summoned, Constantia approaches with apparent submissiveness:

> *Constantia.* I am here, my lord. Command me.
> *Constantine.* I am in great distress of mind. My heart is heavy.
> *Constantia.* As I came in I saw that you were sad, and without knowing the reason I was troubled.
> *Constantine.* It is on your account.
> *Constantia.* On my account?
> *Constantine.* Yes.
> *Constantia.* You frighten me. What is it, my lord?
> *Constantine.* The fear of grieving you ties my tongue.

(p. 246; *Plays*, p. 6)

In spite of Constantia's continued filial honorifics, these few lines in effect succeed in reversing the relationship between the characters: she arrives expecting to be commanded, but quickly discovers that in fact her father is an inarticulate suppliant. Constantine himself is quite conscious of his problem in reconciling his imperial role with his role as father and Christian: 'For if, as is my duty as your father, I permit you to be faithful to your vow, as a sovereign I shall suffer for it. Yet were I to oppose your resolution – which God forbid – I should deserve eternal punishment' (p. 247).

It is at this point that Constantia comes to the rescue with her own plan: let Gallicanus believe that she agrees to the match, then trust to God to get them out of the dilemma should he happen to defeat the Scythians. Her suggestion is doubly interesting in light of Hroswitha's general thematic patterns. Unable himself to make a wise decision, Constantine has given the real power to direct events to his daughter: his apparent authority is a kind of façade. And Constantia's trickily expedient solution (tell Gallicanus what he wants to hear and worry about the consequences later) contrasts with Constantine's rather blinkered adherence to rules (a vow is a vow; one's word is one's word). We have noted already how Hroswitha seems willing to subordinate rules to intentions, cavalierly disregarding regulations if the cause is good. Moreover, Constantine's faith in God seems mediated by his faith in his daughter, who needs to remind him that God can resolve the apparent impasse he is confronting.

One effect of these opening scenes, then, is to make us redefine our sense of Constantine's character and role. His initial appearance of power ('Go get those Scythians!') has dissolved like a soap bubble in the face of Gallicanus' haggling and Constantia's real authority. In contrast to the Hadrian of *Sapientia*, Constantine shows himself a good Christian in part by showing himself an ineffective emperor – ineffective, that is, according to normal, 'masculine' managerial standards. The opening of *Gallicanus*, like the opening of *Sapientia*, also forces us to re-evaluate the relative importance of the two levels of action, the public and the private. In both plays, the emperors, victims in a sense of their masculine fondness for the institutional, initially misperceive what's going on: Hadrian can't accept that a few women pose a threat to the state, while Constantine thinks that his important conflict is with the Scythians, the external enemy. But where Hadrian fails to learn from the instructive women, and preserves to the end his illusion, or delusion, of being in control, Constantine is touchingly eager to relinquish real authority to his daughter (and, incidentally, to God), and to acknowledge the primacy of the domestic over the political. Ironically, Constantine, whom critics tend to treat with dismissive contempt for his 'weakness', in fact proves far more effective than the 'strong' Hadrian.[5] The feminist-Christian conspiracy, a menace to Hadrian's state, is the salvation of Constantine's.

Hroswitha, then, has reconciled the apparent conflict between Constantine's conflicting roles (powerful emperor and sympathetic Christian) by showing that the imperial role is an empty shell: the 'real' Constantine is the concerned father and worried Christian eager to seek guidance from his wiser and more faithful daughter. He is thus, I would claim, feminized. Not only does he acknowledge the power of women to control events; he also fits into the feminine side of the equation so explicitly delineated in *Sapientia*, and takes his place among those virtuous men whose virtue comes from their rejection of the characteristic set of 'masculine' values (love of power, love of sex, love of rules). The pattern of seeming (and feminine) weakness conquering seeming (and masculine) strength thus encompasses Constantine as it does Sapientia and as, indeed, it does Hroswitha herself.

NOTES

1 *Hrotsvithae Opera,* ed. H. Homeyer (Paderborn: Ferdinand Schöningh, 1970), p. 235. Unattributed parenthetical citations are to this edition. References to *Plays* indicate the translation is from *The Plays of Roswitha,* trans. Christopher St John (New York: Benjamin Blom, 1966).

2 Peter Dronke, *Women Writers of the Middle Ages* (Cambridge University Press, 1984), p. 69. It will be obvious that I agree almost wholly with Dronke's discussion. It should be noted, though, that in this paper I use the more commonly recognizable titles for Hroswitha's plays rather than the fuller and more authentic titles used by Dronke.

3 Ibid., pp. 78–9.

4 Ibid., p. 71.

5 For an example of such dismissive contempt in a recent critic, see A. D. Frankforter, 'Hroswitha of Gandersheim and the Destiny of Women', *The Historian,* 41 (1979), 295–314.

Roaring girls and silent women: the politics of androgyny on the Jacobean stage*

LORRAINE HELMS

When, in 1566, Elizabeth vetoed a petition that she marry, she implied that her right to remain single ultimately depended on her willingness to resist not only political pressure but physical force: 'Though I be a woman, yet I have as good a courage, answerable to my place, as ever my father had. I am your annointed Queen. I will never be by violence constrained to do anything.' When she addressed her troops at Tilbury twenty-two years later, she presented herself as the leader of warriors, implying that of the queen's two bodies, the immortal body politic was appropriately male: 'I know I have the body but of a weak and feeble woman; but I have the heart and stomach of a King, and of a King of England too.'[1]

Like her oratory, Elizabeth's revels and entertainments sometimes reflect a politics of androgyny in representations of women warriors. On progress, the queen travels over highways and through forests to castles and marketplaces; she transforms public places into theatrical arenas where she may display her control of the Tudor 'culture of violence'.[2] In a pageant for Elizabeth's reception at Norwich in 1578, speakers impersonating Deborah, Judith, Esther, and Martia, 'sometime Queene of England', addressed Elizabeth, recounting their martial feats and exhorting Elizabeth to do likewise. Deborah counsels Elizabeth to continue as she has begun, and, as God 'did deliver Sisera into a Woman's hande', Elizabeth too will 'weede out the wicket route' to win lasting fame. Judith recalls the slaying of Holofernes and adds, 'If Widowes hand could vanquish such a Foe: /Then to a Prince of thy surpassing might, /What Tirant lives but thou mayest overthrow?'[3] In the 1592 Sudeley entertainment, Elizabeth's presence transformed an ancient tale of rape, subverting a traditional glorification of male violence. Apollo, 'who calleth himselfe a God (a title among men, when they will commit injuries tearme themselves Gods)', has changed the unwilling Daphne into a laurel, but 'the tree rived, and Daphne issued out . . . running to her Majestie': 'I stay, for whither should Chastety fly for succour, but to the Queene of Chastety' (vol. III, p. 139).

* A draft of this paper was read at the *Themes in Drama* International Conference held at the University of California, Riverside, in February 1987.

Elizabeth's politics of androgyny entered the theatrical traditions of the public playhouse.[4] Like the queen, who cultivated an androgynous persona to diminish the stigma of female vulnerability, Shakespearian heroines disguise themselves as young boys in order to travel safely through mysterious forests and exotic dukedoms. Yet the public world of their androgynous activities is the inverted world of carnival, a saturnalia distanced from the world of contemporary sexual politics.[5] When their cross-dressing places them temporarily on top, they find themselves in situations which reveal their irreducibly feminine essence. This essence is cowardice, an intrinsically female inability to stand and fight. Rosalind admits that no 'gallant curtle-spear upon [her] thigh' nor 'boar-spear in [her] hand' will overcome her 'hidden woman's fear'.[6] She does not, as she remarks later, 'have a doublet and hose in [her] disposition' (iii, ii, 195–6). Viola too must acknowledge her natural timidity. Threatened with a duel against the supposedly ferocious Sir Andrew Aguecheek, she confesses, 'A little thing would make me tell them how much I lack of a man' (*Twelfth Night*, iii, iv, 302–3). Unlike Elizabeth, who 'would never be by violence constrained·to do anything', Rosalind and Viola conspicuously lack the kind of courage Elizabeth takes as the Queen's prerogative. They must, at carnival's end, withdraw from the world of public action. They must accept a husband's protection, for they remain demonstrably vulnerable. Male violence is the bastion of patriarchal power which no Shakespearian heroine can scale.

When James succeeded to the throne in 1603, a new politics of androgyny emerged. The martial-spirited virgin prince ceded her authority to a misogynistic pacifist who described himself as the 'loving nourish-father' of his male favorites. The saying *Rex fuit Elizabeth. Nunc est Jacobus Regina* reflects a contemporary response to James's succession.[7] The theatrical practices of the court also reflect it. Elizabeth, who exempted herself from the restrictions against women's activities, travelled from the court into the countryside on progress; James, who undermined the militarism in Tudor definitions of masculinity, withdrew into Whitehall, where he was enthroned as the chief spectator at the new perspective settings Inigo Jones began to devise for the royal masques.[8] When plays were presented at Elizabeth's court, the queen sat upon the stage. When she received the golden apple in *The Arraignment of Paris* or resolved the contentions of *Every Man Out of His Humour*, Stephen Orgel surmises, she may have done so 'from the stage and as part of the action'. The Elizabethan revels celebrate the theatrical engagement of the monarch. But the perspective settings of Jacobean masques take the source of theatrical energy from the stage to the seated monarch. The Stuart masque celebrates the political power of an apparently passive royal spectator.[9]

The new politics of androgyny did not enfranchise the ladies of the court.

While James's pacifism tended to blur the rigid gender distinctions of 'the culture of violence', his misogyny strengthened the barriers against women's liberty. James celebrated *haec vir*, but he censured *hic mulier*, and especially those fashionable women in men's clothing, who dared to appropriate the 'stilletaes or poinards' which manifested male power. In the court of King James, androgyny became a male prerogative; the image of the Amazonian queen regnant soon dwindled into a wife.

Jonson's and Jones's *The Masque of Queens,* written at Queen Anne's request and produced at Whitehall on 2 February 1609, articulates the Jacobean politics of androgyny in the theatrical language of the Stuart masque. *The Masque of Queens* opens with an antimasque of witches. These witches, performed by professional players, are routed when a sudden 'sound of loud music' signals the appearance of Fame and Virtue, allegorical figures accompanying the queen and her ladies, who are costumed as Bel-anna and such 'wise and warlike' heroines as Penthesileia, Camilla, and Tomyris.[10] Their appearance, enthroned in the House of Fame, magically transforms chaos into cosmos: 'At Fame's loud sound and Virtue's sight/ all dark and envious witchcraft fly the light' (lines 367–8).

Virtue, whom the stage directions further describe as Perseus, or 'Heroic and Masculine Virtue' (line 365) descends from the building to speak. When he does, he claims full credit for the transformation, discounting Fame's auxiliary role: 'I was her parent, and I am her strength' (line 380). Perseus, as Jonathan Goldberg observes, 'acts as a kind of male mother ... The full appropriation of generative powers to the father makes him father and mother at once ... Bel-anna's creativity and activity are continually subordinated to the poetic conceit and political situation.'[11]

The 'poetic conceit and political situation' invert the theatrical dynamic of the Elizabethan image of the Amazonian queen. Elizabeth's role in the entertainments devised for her underscored her political position theatrically: she alone was entitled to improvise. While Deborah, Judith, Daphne, and Paris spoke scripted lines, Elizabeth's response remained the queen's prerogative. Anne's patronage conferred no such privileges. Her Amazons, unlike Shakespeare's Hippolyta, need not be wooed with swords, for they are deracinated and have forgotten their martial origins. In designing his splendid costumes, Stephen Orgel and Roy Strong note, Jones 'strangely' neglected his usual handbook, Vecellio's *Habiti Antichi et Moderni,* ignoring his heroines' national characteristics and mythological attributes. Instead, he selected feminizing shades of pink, peach, crimson, and morrey for bodices, petticoats, and sleeves; he constructed elegant but encumbering crowns for each masquer. Splendidly costumed and silent, Queen Anne and her martial attendants are the objects of the spectators' gaze, as they return to their chariots after the revels:[12]

The first four were drawn with eagles . . . their four torchbearers attending on the chariot sides, and four of the hags bound before them. Then followed the second, drawn by griffins, with their torchbearers and four other hags. Then the last, which was drawn by lions, and more eminent, wherein her majesty was, and had six torchbearers more, peculiar to her, with the like number of hags.

(lines 712–19)

The warrior Queens vanquish the witches; the mythologized ladies of the court rebuke the rowdy, ragged players. The Amazons within the aristocracy, who might have challenged patriarchal authority, have been transformed into phallic women who protect the court from hags and vagabonds.

This Jacobean politics of androgyny also resonates with the theatrical convention of cross-dressing in commercial theatre. Yet the convention varies with the different theatrical venues of Jacobean London. The conservative public playhouses recall the cross-dressed Elizabethan heroine in Moll, the title character of Middleton and Dekker's *The Roaring Girl*, performed at the Fortune in 1610 or 1611, and Bess Bridges, the title character of Heywood's *The Fair Maid of the West*, performed at the Red Bull probably at about the same time.[13] Yet Moll and Bess wear their doublet and hose with a difference. In their exuberance, their resourcefulness, and their wit, they resemble the cross-dressed comic heroines of the 1590s. Yet they are not adventuring aristocrats. Bess is an enterprising tavern wench and Moll, based on the historical figure of Mary Frith, is the notorious 'roaring girl' of the London underworld. These characters are nostalgic reminiscences of Good Queen Bess in a new, plebeian guise; they reformulate the Elizabethan myth of the virgin prince for the popular audiences of the Fortune and the Red Bull.[14] But unlike Shakespearian heroines, Moll and Bess are warriors. Bess beats the braggart Roughman in a fight and engages in hand-to-hand combat with pirates; Moll duels with her would-be seducer Laxton and forces him to beg for his life. Both characters exercise their skills for the good of simple people. In the process, these Jacobean androgynes expand the territory of the cross-dressed Elizabethan heroine, for Moll and Bess are capable of resisting male violence with equal force.

Heywood's Bess Bridges retains more conventional characteristics than Middleton and Dekker's Moll Cutpurse. Bess, like a romantic Shakespearian heroine, ventures through exotic lands and, after her valor and virtue have been fully tested, ends happily married to her Captain Spencer. Middleton and Dekker's *The Roaring Girl* places the convention of the cross-dressed heroine in the new context of Jacobean city comedy. City comedy narrows the arena in which the theatrical action takes place, and in narrowing it, sharpens its focus. Instead of mythical Illyria or the fabulous forest of Arden, the scene is contemporary London. The social disorder on which comic plots depend is no longer cordoned off in a world of holiday adventure, but invades Fleet Street, Holburn, Smithfield, and Grey's Inn Fields.

When the map of London displaces an exotic landscape, the playwright can no longer inscribe *ubi leones* on unexplored territories; the familiar settings of city comedy demand finer discriminations, as Middleton observes in the preface to the 1611 edition:

> The fashion of play-making I can properly compare to nothing so naturally as the alteration in apparel: for in the time of the great crop-doublet, your huge bombasted plays, quilted with mighty words to lean purpose, was only then in fashion. And as the doublet fell, neater inventions began to set up. Now in the time of spruceness, our plays follow the niceness of our garments, single plots, quaint conceits, lecherous jests, dressed up in hanging sleeves.[15]

The Roaring Girl refines on its 'huge bombasted' predecessors by contrasting two cross-dressed female characters. Mary Fitz-allard is the ingenue of the comedy. She appears, like a Shakespearian heroine, romantically disguised in a page boy's costume. This disguise gives Mary safe passage through the troubled seas of a comedy courtship. It does not, however, give her masculine powers or privileges. Whether attired as a gentlewoman or a page boy, Mary rarely speaks and never dissents. The androgynous 'Captain Moll', on the other hand, is a roaring girl of the streets and taverns, who strides about London with a sword and a tobacco pipe, drinking, smoking, and brawling with rogues and cutpurses. Her prototype is the historical figure of Mary Frith, a. k. a. Moll Cutpurse. Moll was a celebrity of the local underworld, 'a notorious bagage', said a witness to her penance at Paul's Cross, 'that used to go in mans apparell and challenged the feild of divers gallants'.[16] Middleton and Dekker acquit their heroine of any crimes the historical Mary Frith may have committed, but both the historical figure and the dramatic character are products of London's popular culture in the first decade of the seventeenth century. Moll Cutpurse is too deeply woven into the texture of contemporary urban life to be appropriated for romantic adventures or pastoral interludes.

The Roaring Girl was produced by Prince Henry's Men; both Mary Fitz-allard the ingenue and Moll the roaring girl were originally played by male actors.[17] To make the theatrical convention of the cross-dressed heroine work in an all-male cast, the actor who plays a woman must first appear in a costume which establishes a female persona. The change to men's clothes must be clearly depicted. Thus before Viola appears as Cesario, she asks the captain to present her 'as an eunuch' to Orsino (I, i, 56). Before Rosalind appears as Ganymede, she announces that she will 'suit [herself] all points like a man' (I, iii, 116).

Establishing Moll's character requires a variant on this technique. The actor who portrays Moll must represent a woman whose persona is habitually masculine. Moll is not a woman disguised as a man, but a creature of 'heroic spirit and masculine womanhood' (II, i, 323–4). So Moll first appears, not in the breeches she will wear for the rest of the play, but in a frieze jerkin and a skirt. This is, as Lisa Jardine notes, the modish masculine attire which earned fashionable women the censure of many preachers and pamphleteers during the early years of the seventeenth century.[18] This costume establishes her sex; her swaggering freedom establishes the costume's appropriateness. Only then does she appear in breeches to duel with Laxton the lecherous misogynist who had offered her gold for a rendezvous at a Brainford inn:

> In thee I defy all men, their worst hates,
> And their best flatteries, all their golden witchcrafts,
> With which they entangle the poor spirits of fools.
> Distressed needlewomen and trade-fallen wives,
> Fish that must needs bite or themselves be bitten,
> Such hungry things as these may soon be took
> With a worm fastened on a golden hook:
> Those are the lecher's food, his prey.
>
> (III, i, 90–6)

Moll's speech, as Linda Woodbridge remarks, exposes the economic structure of the hierarchy of gender.[19] Moll's subsequent action, to duel with Laxton, wound him, and force him to beg for his life, presses further against that hierarchy, for it exposes the violence on which the cultural construction of gender rests. In defending the 'distressed needlewomen and trade-fallen wives' whose hunger makes them 'the lecher's prey', Moll appropriates the protective function which allows men to justify sexual hierarchy. In remaining invulnerable without male protection, she confounds patriarchal distinctions between the fragility of good women and the rebellious autonomy of the bad.

Moll's duel radically reinterprets the convention of the cross-dressed heroine. The male adversaries of other woman warriors discover only after the battle that they have been struggling against a woman.[20] Molls wears men's clothing during her duel with Laxton, but she is not disguised. He knows her identity before he reluctantly begins to fight: 'Draw upon a woman? why, what dost mean, Moll?' (III, i, 69). By forcing Laxton to fight against a woman and yet fight according to the male code of ritual combat, Moll demands the same respect that Laxton would extend to a male adversary. She demands that the assumptions of male supremacy be tested in the relentless meritocracy of the battlefield. This test demonstrates that a woman can not only engage in violence, but control and direct it for social purposes; she can adopt the male virtue of courage to defend the female virtue of chastity, transforming chaste passivity into active autonomy.

Moll is not the first dramatic character to challenge the male monopoly on violence. Middleton and Dekker's innovation lies in the way that challenge is legitimized. Popular drama does acknowledge women's capacity for violence, but it is commonly trivialized in comedy and demonized in tragedy and chronicle. Katherine the shrew will be tamed; Joan of Arc will be burned as a witch. The patriarchal structures of authority stand. But Moll's duel with Laxton does not resemble the erratic and unsanctioned violence of conventional stage shrews and witches. She fights according to the rules of the male code, and her use of violence cannot readily be either trivialized or demonized, even when she fights against patriarchy, defying 'all men' in the person of one would-be seducer. This is not the violence which erupts in terrorist raids and riots, but force sanctioned by a legitimate power to chastise and admonish. It is commensurate with the circumstances and regulated by a code of honor. Moll prepares for the duel with a soldierly braggadocio:

> Would the spirits
> Of all my slanderers were clasped in thine,
> That I might vex an army at one time.
>
> (III, i, 111–13)

She wounds Laxton 'gallantly', as he admits, and spares his life because she 'scorn[s] to strike [him] basely' (III, i, 125,122). 'If I could meet my enemies one by one thus', says Moll with perfect chivalry, 'I might make pretty shift with 'em in time' (III, i, 130).

Moll fights to defend her own autonomy and to vindicate other women. The two motives are interwoven: Moll's autonomy reveals by contrast the source of other women's subordination. Women's economic vulnerability, Moll claims, is the source of their exploitation, yet 'she that has wit and spirit /May scorn /To live beholding to her body for meat' (III, i, 132–4). Moll's economic independence rests on the wit and spirit which grant her the ability to defend herself in combat. Tell the censuring world, she commands the astonished Laxton,

> 'twere base to yield where I have conquered.
> I scorn to prostitute myself to a man,
> I that can prostitute a man to me.
>
> (III, i, 108–10)

Prostitution, which Moll has already removed from the realm of misogynistic moralizing, merges with a language of combat and conquest. Sexual exploitation is identified with physical coercion; defeat equals prostitution. Moll need not yield sexually because she can conquer martially. Her martial art enables her to resist the exploitation most female flesh is heir to; it forces a patriarchal society to acknowledge her autonomy.

It also provides the psychological foundation for that autonomy. A man's

willingness to expose himself to blows, Simone de Beauvoir writes, is his
final recourse against attempts to reduce him to the status of object. It is
'the authentic proof of each one's loyalty to himself, to his passions, to his
own will'.[21] It is this loyalty – then, as now, no more frequent among women
than combat duty – which 'Captain Moll' demonstrates throughout *The
Roaring Girl*. Her willingness to fight constitutes a fierce and active loyalty to
herself. When the comedy ends, she remains unmarried and insubordinate:

> I have no humor to marry . . . a wife you know ought to be obedient, but I fear
> me I am too headstrong to obey, therefore I'll ne'er go about it . . . I have the
> head now of myself, and am man enough for a woman; marriage is but a
> chopping and a changing, where a maiden loses one head and has a worse i' th'
> place.
>
> (II, ii, 35–44)

Moll's belligerent autonomy is not presented as an example for other
women. She is an inexplicable exception to every rule, 'a creature /So
strange in quality, a whole city takes /Note of her name and person' (I, i, 95–
7). Her martial art is an individual strategy for survival, not a program for
general insurrection. The text of *The Roaring Girl* represents a radical
revision of the hierarchy of gender but restricts its benefits to the androgynous heroine whose singularity is assumed. The cultural circumstances
which might create other roaring girls remain hidden. Yet the theatrical
circumstances of *The Roaring Girl*'s original production offer a model the
text alone does not disclose.

The Consistory of London Correction Book for 1611 records Mary
Frith's presence at

> all or most of the disorderly and licentious places in this cittie as namely she
> hath usually in the habit of a man resorted to alehouses taverns tobacco shops
> and also to play houses there to see plaies and proses and namely being at a play
> about three quarters of a yeare since at ye Fortune in man's apparel and in her
> boots and wth a sword at her syde . . . [she] also sat upon the stage in the public
> view of of all the people there present in man's apparel and played upon her lute
> and sange a song.[22]

The play's epilogue corroborates the Consistory record, for it announces
that, should the writers and the actors have failed to satisfy their patrons'
expectations, 'The Roaring Girl herself, some few days hence/ Shall on this
stage give larger recompense' (lines 35–6). The exact meaning of this
announcement remains mysterious, yet legal and literary records concur:
the stage of the Fortune was part of Mary Frith's territory. Since she
appeared there to play her lute and to sit on the stage, she may well have
watched an actor play her greatness and perhaps, as P. A. Mulholland
suggests, she improvised asides and business from her position on stage or
even took the part herself for some portion of the play.[23]

When Middleton and Dekker evoke Moll's historical presence at the

Fortune, they qualify the nature of the entertainment. Like Elizabeth's improvized participation in royal entertainments, Moll's association with the Fortune makes *The Roaring Girl* a festive celebration of a woman's autonomy. In constructing the dramatic character of 'Captain Moll', *The Roaring Girl* confounds gender categories within the world of the play; in evoking Mary Frith's presence on the stage of the Fortune *in propria persona*, *The Roaring Girl* confounds gender categories in the world of the spectators. When Mary Frith created the quasi-theatrical persona of Moll Cutpurse, she transformed playgoing into playacting. No more (but no less) a professional player than Elizabeth, Mary Frith was apparently the first woman to appear on the stage of the public playhouse.

While Mary Frith and Prince Henry's Men reinterpreted Elizabethan androgyny for Jacobean audiences at the Fortune, the private theatres also explored the motif in satirical city comedies. Yet the theatrical values of the private playhouse alter the representation of androgyny. The open stages of the public playhouses, inheriting the *theatrum mundi* of medieval theatre, evoked the mysteries of forests and islands, the rage of sea storms and battlefields, the grandeur of the ancient forum and the bustle of the modern metropolis. The buildings which housed the private playhouses – the singing school at Paul's, the refectories of Blackfriars and Whitefriars – were designed for communal rather than public functions. Their small stages and candlelit halls could recall a Lylian theatrical tradition, with its associations of otiose seclusion and the miniaturized world of childhood.[24]

Jonson incorporated these associations into the domestic setting of *Epicoene, or The Silent Woman*, performed at Whitefriars in 1609. On the open stage of the Fortune, Moll Cutpurse travels through the public places of the city; in the monastic refectory of Whitefriars, the *dyskolos* and his boy bride remain within doors. The Whitefriars setting for Morose's house, with its 'double walls and treble ceilings, the windows close shut and caulked', where he 'lives by candlelight' (I, i, 184–6), is both illusionistic and fully thematized. the *mise-en-scène* is cluttered with the trivialized paraphernalia of private life: cosmetics, crockery, and especially with the continual chatter of women and servants. The fortification itself makes the interior vulnerable to invasion.

By setting his representation of androgyny in these domestic interiors, Jonson reinterprets the theatrical convention of cross-dressing. The setting exerts a centripetal force over the action, pulling the characters into the narrow space of drawing rooms and bedchambers. Shakespeare's, Heywoods', and Middleton's cross-dressed heroines move into the world of public action, but when the collegiate ladies try to appropriate the public space of the masculine world, they must contend with this centripetal force, which leaves them both dislocated and ungendered. They are, Truewit exclaims,

an order between courtiers and country madams, that live from their husbands
and give entertainment to all the Wits and Braveries o' the time, as they call
'em, cry down or up what they like or dislike in a brain or a fashion with most
masculine or rather hermaphroditical authority.

(I, i, 75–80)

While the collegiates venture into traditionally masculine preserves, the
male characters restrict themselves to the world of feminine concerns,
avoiding politics for the *otium* of private life. Morose 'come[s] not to your
public pleadings or your places of noise . . . for the mere avoiding of clamors
and impertinencies of orators that know not how to be silent' (v, iii, 41–6);
and while Morose flees from the hurly-burly of public life into a dark and
silent domesticity, Clerimont 'can melt away his time . . . between his
mistress abroad and his ingle at home' (I, i, 23–5).

Within this feminized space, the entry of the androgynous title character
takes on the significance of espionage. The body of Epicoene is the comedy's
locus of eros and dominance, and its layers of disguise and artifice are
deployed strategically in the battle of the sexes. Epicoene first appears
camouflaged as 'the silent woman', a rare creature whose modesty assures
both her silence and her chastity. She is enclosed and domesticated – the
ideal which the poetaster Daw evokes in his 'ballad, or madrigal of
procreation':[25]

> Silence in woman is like speech in man.
> Deny't who can
> Nor is it a tale that female vice should be a virtue male.
> Or masculine vice, a female virtue be:
> You shall it see
> Prov'd with increase
> I know to speak and she to hold her peace.
>
> (II, iii, 123–4, 126–31)

To equate speech with masculinity and silence with feminine 'increase'
makes women's speech tantamount to abortion. The vociferous collegiates,
who have 'those excellent receipts . . . to keep . . . from bearing of children'
(IV, iii, 57–8), become barren by their own act of violence.

This violence lends new significance to the patriarchal proverb, 'A
woman without a tongue is like a soldier without a weapon.' Words are
indeed women's weapons in *Epicoene*, and conversation becomes a form of
combat. This focus on verbal combat serves ideological ends, for if physical
strength is not the criterion of force, a woman can more readily be
represented as an aggressor who possesses the terrorist's advantage over
the lumbering procedures of duly constituted authority. At the same time,
verbal combat respects the theatrical resources of Whitefriars. The small
stage of the private playhouses cannot easily accommodate the swashbuckling duels in which the Fortune and the Red Bull specialized. Jonson can

afford to parody the bravura swordsmanship of the public playhouse in the
mock duel of Daw and La Foole, for the symbolic violence of women's
speech provides a verbal substitute for theatrical spectacle. Epicoene uses
her tongue as Moll uses her sword: 'Why, did you think you had married a
statue or a motion only?' she exclaims, and, 'I'll have none of this coacted,
unnatural dumbness in my house, in a family where I govern' (III, iv, 37–8,
53–5). Morose's horror at this 'Amazonian impudence' (III, v, 41) measures
his own egotism, for even Truewit must admit, 'she speaks but reason' (III,
v, 42). Yet Morose underscores the comedy's equation of violence and
female self-assertion. Quailing at Epicoene's gubernatorial ambitions,
Morose does not compare her to the shrewish Xantippe, but to the warriors
Semiramis and Penthesileia (III, iv, 57).

Act v exposes another layer of the artifice within which Epicoene's body
is concealed. Dauphine delivers Morose from his marital fiasco by revealing
that his bride is a boy. Neither the modest maiden nor the termagant wife
exists, either within the dramatic fiction or on the Whitefriars stage. The
images of delicate modesty and of aggressive sexuality are both exposed as
male fantasies to which real women are demonstrably irrelevant.

In underscoring the absence of women as characters or players at the
close of *Epicoene*, Jonson's comedy acknowledges that men have created this
theatrical representation of femininity. At the same time, it also denies
women any power to challenge those fantasies. Many playwrights have
created theatrical worlds from which women are absent; Jonson has created
a world in which they are unnecessary. As the body of the male actor
emerges from the fantasized image of the female character, the economics of
patrilineal inheritance emerge from the politics of androgyny. Threatened
with losing his uncle's estate, Dauphine has been 'sick o' th uncle' (I, i, 143),
as Truewit remarks, coining the name of Dauphine's malaise on analogy
with 'mother', a common name for hysteria, or 'womb-sickness'. In
replacing 'mother' with 'uncle', Truewit's metaphor suggests, and the
play's conclusion reveals, that women are superfluous, even in the production of heirs. Dauphine will inherit from his uncle; the estate will derive
through an exclusively male line.

The battle of the sexes has been merely a mock-battle. Beneath the
costume of the shrewish wife is the body of the hired actor; beneath the
battle of the sexes is a struggle between older and younger men for power
and property. In the course of this struggle, the elder is unmanned. First he
confesses impotence in the strategic fiction which he hopes will free him
from his disastrous marriage: 'I am no man, ladies . . . Utterly unabled in
nature, by reason of frigidity, to perform the duties or any the least office of a
husband' (v, iv, 44–7). Then he acknowledges true impotence when he
signs the papers which make Dauphine his heir: 'Come nephew, give me the
pen. I will subscribe to anything, and seal what thou wilt for my

deliverance' (v, iv, 198–200). Dauphine succeeds to the patriarchate, ending the social disorder which licenses unruly women. As Perseus deploys the acquiescent Amazons to rout the boisterous witches, Dauphine employs an actor's artificially feminized body to reinforce patriarchal authority over the coven of collegiate ladies. Morose had quailed at Epicoene's 'Amazonian impudence', but when her status is revealed, and the revelation also exposes Daw's and La Foole's false sexual boasts, Truewit praises Epicoene as an 'Amazon, the champion of the sex' (v, iv, 234–5). But Epicoene's revelation has in fact reinforced the patriarchal distinction between ruled and unruly women. 'You', Truewit tells the exposed braggarts, 'are they that when no merit or fortune can make you hope to enjoy their bodies, will yet lie with their reputations and make their fame suffer. Away you common moths of these and all ladies' honors' (v, iv, 237–40). Like the Amazons of *The Masque of Queens*, Epicoene plays the role of the phallic woman who enforces social restrictions on female sexuality. As she does, the 'hermaphroditical authority' of the collegiates, like the incantatory power of the witches, is lost: 'Madams,' Truewit exults, 'you are mute upon this new metamorphosis' (v, iv, 243–4).

There is still another layer to the artifice in which Epicoene's body is concealed. The Whitefriars production of *Epicoene*, like the Fortune production of *The Roaring Girl*, makes an extra-dramatic comment on its own representation of androgyny. Nathan Field, the leading player of the Children of the Revels and Jonson's protégé, created the role of Epicoene.[26] Field, like Jonson, was the child of a minister who had died within months of his son's birth. When Field was first impressed for the Children of the Chapel, he became Jonson's Latin pupil. He began playing leading roles in Jonson's *Cynthia's Revels* and *The Poetaster*. Within a year of playing Epicoene, Field followed Jonson in the move from player to dramatist. His first comedy, *Woman is a Weathercock*, also produced at Whitefriars, exploits Jonsonian techniques and devices for a misogynistic satire. His next, *Amends for Ladies*, renews Jonson's challenge to the public playhouse representations of androgyny by recharacterizing Moll Cutpurse as a 'lewd impudent' and a monster 'without a sex' (II, i, 32, 36). When such a boy player reveals his identity, the theatrical fiction resonates with the actor's celebrity and his filial relationship to the dramatist. Jonson's comedy *Epicoene* was, in a common metaphor of poetic production, the dramatist's child; his character Epicoene, when played by Nathan Field, was also 'a son of Ben', a product of the paternal relations which form a recurrent motif in Jonson's life and works.[27]

Through the joint enterprises of father and son, playwright and player, Dauphine and Epicoene, James and Perseus, Jonson assimilates androgynous warrior women into patriarchal politics. In *The Roaring Girl*, Middleton and Dekker exploit the swashbuckling traditions of the open stage and the recollection of Moll Frith to extend the theatrical convention of the cross-dressed heroine into a representation of physical violence which challenges the hierarchy of gender. In *Epicoene*, Jonson exploits the feminized space of the enclosed playhouse and the celebrity of Nathan Field to compress the convention into a representation of verbal combat which reinforces the hierarchy of gender. As Moll and Epicoene play the woman's part on their respective stages, they each incorporate new meanings into the theatrical convention of cross-dressing. The conflict between these meanings may remind us that we have not yet concluded whether androgyny will remain a male prerogative.

NOTES

I am indebted to Coppélia Kahn and the members of her UCLA seminar in 'Theatre and Culture in Renaissance England' for engrossing discussions of kings, queens, roaring girls, and boy actors, and to David Riggs for his many contributions to my understanding of *Epicoene* and *The Masque of Queens*.

1 *The Public Speaking of Queen Elizabeth*, ed. George Rice (New York: Columbia University Press, 1951), pp. 81 and 96.
2 The phrase, 'the culture of violence', is Lawrence Stone's in *The Crisis of the Aristocracy* (London: Oxford University Press, 1965).
3 Reprinted in John Nichols, *The Public Progresses and Public Processions of Queen Elizabeth*, 3 vols. (London: John Nichols and Son, 1823), vol. II, p. 147. Subsequent references to this edition will appear in the text.
4 See Leah Marcus, 'Shakespeare's Comic Heroines, Elizabeth I, and the Political Uses of Androgyny' in *Women in the Middle Ages and the Renaissance*, ed. Mary Beth Rose (Syracuse, New York: Syracuse University Press, 1986). On Elizabeth's androgynous self-presentation, see also Wilfried Schleiner, '*Divina Virago*: Queen Elizabeth as an Amazon', *Studies in Philology*, 75 (1978), 163–80; Louis Adrian Montrose, '"Shaping Fantasies": Figurations of Gender and Power in Elizabethan Culture', *Representations*, 1: 2 (1983), 61–94.
5 Natalie Zemon Davis places Shakespearian transvestitism in the tradition of sixteenth-century popular carnival in 'Women on Top' in *Society and Culture in Early Modern France* (Stanford University Press, 1965), pp. 124–51. The ideological implications of cross-dressing on the Shakespearian stage have been differently assessed. See Leah Marcus, cited above; Juliet Dusinberre, *Shakespeare and the Nature of Women* (London: Macmillan, 1975); Clara Claiburne Park, 'As We Like It: How a Girl Can Be Smart and Still Popular' in *The Woman's Part: Feminist Criticism of Shakespeare*, ed. Carolyn Ruth Swift Lenz, Gayle Greene, and Carol Thomas Neely (Urbana: University of Illinois Press, 1980), pp. 100–16; Linda Woodbridge, *Women and the English Renaissance* (Urbana: University of Illinois Press, 1984); Catherine Belsey, 'Disrupting Sexual Difference: Meaning and Gender in the Comedies' in *Alternative Shakespeares*, ed. John Drakakis (London: Methuen, 1985), pp. 166–90; and Phyllis Rackin, 'Androgyny,

Mimesis, and the Marriage of the Boy Heroine on the English Renaissance
Stage', *PMLA*, 102 (1987), 29–41.

6 *As You Like It*, I, iii, 117–18. Quotations from Shakespeare are from *The Riverside Shakespeare* (Boston: Houghton Mifflin, 1974).

7 On the Jacobean politics of androgyny, see Jonathan Goldberg, *James I and the Politics of Literature* (Baltimore: Johns Hopkins University Press, 1983), and Woodbridge, *Women and the English Renaissance*, pp. 143–4 and *passim*.

8 David M. Bergeron notes this shift from Elizabeth's public progresses to James's court entertainments in *English Civic Pageantry 1558–1642* (Columbia, South Carolina: University of South Carolina Press, 1971), p. 65.

9 *The Illusion of Power* (Berkeley: University of California Press, 1975), p. 10.

10 *The Masque of Queens*, line 408. Quotations from Jonson are from Herford and Simpson, *Ben Jonson*, 11 vols. (Oxford: Clarendon, 1925–52). I have modernized spelling and punctuation.

11 Goldberg, *James I*, p. 88.

12 Stephen Orgel and Roy Strong, *Inigo Jones: The Theatre of the Stuart Court*, 2 vols. (Berkeley: University of California Press, 1973), vol. I, p. 43. The surviving sketches for the costume designs for *The Masque of Queens*, with Jones's color notes, are reprinted in vol. I, pp. 139–53.

13 See P. A. Mulholland, 'The Date of *The Roaring Girl*', *Review of English Studies*, ser. 2, vol. 28 (1977), 18–31. I have otherwise followed the dating of Alfred Harbage, *Annals of English Drama 975–1700*, rev. by Samuel Schoenbaum (London: Methuen, 1964).

14 Marcus, 'Shakespeare's Comic Heroines', pp. 149–50.

15 Quotations from *The Roaring Girl* are from the New Mermaids edition, ed. Andor Gomme (New York: Norton, 1976).

16 Quoted in Molholland, 'Date of *The Roaring Girl*', p. 24.

17 In her novel, *Moll Cutpurse* (Ithaca: Firebrand, 1985), based on the life of Mary Frith, Ellen Galford assigns the part of Middleton and Dekker's heroine to 'the biggest, beefiest player in the company, with bellowing loud voice and hands like huge York hams and a manner like a snorting stag – he commonly acts the parts of kings and murderers' (p. 182). This plausible suggestion should remind us that the apprentices did not necessarily monopolize female impersonation. The Ursulas and Mistress Quicklys require different qualities than the Rosalinds and Epicoenes.

18 Lisa Jardine, *Still Harping on Daughters* (Brighton, Sussex: Harvester, 1983), p. 160. Her interpretation of Moll's costume change, however, differs from the one I have offered here. See also Mary Beth Rose, 'Women in Men's Clothing: Apparel and Social Stability in *The Roaring Girl*', *English Literary Renaissance*, 14 (1984), 367–91.

19 Woodbridge, *Women and the English Renaissance*, p. 255.

20 In *Amazons and Women Warriors: Varieties of Feminism in Seventeenth-Century Drama* (New York: St Martin, 1981), Simon Shepherd observes that in Roman poetry, in sixteenth-century Italian *novelle* and in *The Faerie Queene*, a woman warrior's identity is disclosed when her helmet is removed and her long hair revealed: 'With helmets on Bradamante and Britomart look like, and are taken for, male warriors. With helmets off, they are beautiful women' (p. 9).

21 *The Second Sex*, trans. H. M. Parshley (1952; rpt New York, 1974), p. 370.

22 Quoted in Mulholland, 'Date of *The Roaring Girl*', p. 31. I have modernized spelling and punctuation.
23 Ibid., p. 22.
24 For a discussion of the significant differences between Jonson's and Lyly's representations of androgyny, see Rackin, 'Androgyny, Mimesis', p. 30.
25 On the homologies in Renaissance thought among 'the enclosed body, the closed mouth, the locked house', see Peter Stallybrass, 'Patriarchal Territories: The Body Enclosed', in *Rewriting the Renaissance: The Discourses of Sexual Difference in Early Modern Europe*, ed. Margaret W. Ferguson, Maureen Quilligan, and Nancy J. Vickers (University of Chicago Press, 1986), pp. 123–42.
26 On Field's career, see Roberta Florence Brinkley, *Nathan Field, The Actor-Playwight* (1928; rpt, Hamden, Connecticut: Archon, 1973). There is circumstantial evidence that Field played Epicoene: his prominent position in the company assures a leading role, and his own rather epicoene good looks (revealed in the Dulwich portrait, rpt in Edmund Chambers, *William Shakespeare*, 2 vols, Oxford: Clarendon Press, 1930, vol. 1, plate x) reinforce the attribution. There is, however, more definite evidence in Chapman's dedicatory letter to *Woman is a Weathercock*:

> To many formes, as well as many waies,
> Thy Active Muse, turnes like thy Acted woman:
> In which, disprais'd inconstancie, turns praise.

(lines 1–3)

The Plays of Nathan Field, ed. William Peery (Austin: University of Texas Press, 1950). Subsequent references to this edition will appear in the text.
27 See Ian Donaldson, 'Fathers and Sons: Jonson, Dryden, and *MacFlecnoe*', *Southern Review*, 18 (1985), 314–27 and Anne Barton, *Ben Jonson, Dramatist* (Cambridge University Press, 1984), pp. 19–20.

Molière's women – a matter of focus*

MAYA SLATER

Molière's *School for Wives* opened early in 1987 at the National Theatre, directed by Di Trevis. The play concerns Arnolphe, who takes over the education of a four-year-old girl, Agnès (whom he intends to marry when she grows up), with the explicit aim of bringing her up to be as ignorant as possible. Arnolphe's reason is an eccentric fear of being made a cuckold. He thinks that if he fashions for himself a really stupid wife, she will be too dim to play him false. When the play opens Agnès is about eighteen, and her guardian plans to marry her forthwith. What follows is the story of how Arnolphe fails to implement his obsession: he is outwitted by circumstances and by Agnès, who has fallen in love with a much more suitable, younger man; the comedy in the play lies in the guardian's being given all the trump cards and yet failing to outwit the young lovers: the play is an exercise in comic frustration.

However, the programme notes to the Trevis production cast a different light upon the play's meaning.[1] They contain a series of comments on how men view women, and how women allow such views to prevail. The earliest comment dates from about AD 200, the most recent is a remark made by Jane Root in 1984, which sums up the whole angry mood of these pages:

> The majority of porn currently available is about sex as domination, as something which men DO to women.

It goes without saying that these remarks have been included because it is assumed they will help the audience to understand *The School for Wives*. This insistence on a feminist side to Molière's play struck me initially as astonishing: it had always seemed to me that the play was not at all about the appalling degradation of Agnès at the hands of a dominant sexual male ('sex as domination'). Rather, it seemed to be about the folly of Arnolphe.

There is no doubt that Arnolphe is the most important role in the play. It is the part Molière wrote for himself, for as a comic actor he was his own

* A draft of this paper was read at the *Themes in Drama* International Conference held at the University of London, Westfield College, in March 1987.

biggest box-office draw, and performed in almost all his plays. More than this, Arnolphe is the meatiest part in the whole of Molière's theatre, and indeed it is one of the biggest roles in all French theatre: the character is on stage throughout almost the whole play, and his soliloquies alone take up more than 200 lines. I have been told by an actor who has played the part that it is by far the most exhausting of all the demanding roles Molière wrote for himself.

Molière, then, has placed considerable emphasis not on Agnès but on Arnolphe as the central focus of the play. How can a modern director see the play first and foremost as being about women and the way they were exploited by a male-dominated society? And if it is the case that the play is about such exploitation, why did Molière place so much stress on Arnolphe?

An obvious line of approach is to ask what Molière himself thought he was doing with this play; and here we are in the privileged position, almost unique in Molière's theatre, of having his explicit comments on the subject. In his preface to the first published edition of the play, Molière tells us that his views are expressed in dramatic form, in 'a discussion I have written in the form of a dialogue', namely *The School for Wives Criticized, La Critique de l'Ecole des femmes*. Here, through a mouthpiece,[2] Molière explains that he regards the play as illustrating the personality of Arnolphe, and has used Agnès simply as a means towards this end. This fact emerges during a conversation between Dorante, Molière's mouthpiece, and a female character. The conversation is not without interest as regards the question of Molière's attitude to women. The female character, Climène, is a ridiculous précieuse, who has already been a target for mockery earlier in the play. At this stage, she complains about *The School for Wives* because of 'the disobliging satire in it against the ladies'. She adds: 'I don't know how you'll receive the reflections thrown on our sex in a certain part of the piece' (B&M, 1, 308).[3] Dorante retorts that this anti-feminine view is included in the play because it illustrates the character of the speaker, Arnolphe: 'Don't you see 'tis a ridiculous character he makes speak it?' He goes on to stress that the play should be viewed as an examination of the faults of Arnolphe. This, he claims, is Molière's greatest achievement in the play:

> I think it much easier to soar upon grand sentiments, to brave fortune in verse, to accuse the destinies, and reproach the gods, than to enter, as one should do, into the ridicule of men, and to make the faults of all mankind appear agreeable on stage. (B&M, 1, 310)

Dorante adds that the whole plot of the play is geared towards Arnolphe and his misfortune:

> What appears diverting enough to me, is that a man who has sense, and who is warned of everything by an innocent creature who is his mistress . . . cannot with all this escape what happens to him. (B&M, 1, 315)

During the course of *The School for Wives Criticized* Dorante continues to stress the importance of Arnolphe as his target for satire. It seems that to Molière little that Agnès says or does in *The School for Wives* is significant in itself; her actions merely serve to show up the personality of Arnolphe: Molière is concerned not with the rights of women but with the wrongs of men.

Moving on from *The School for Wives* and looking at Molière's plays as a whole, the same holds true. The very elements that could be said to demonstrate Molière's concern for the rights of women could, looked at in another way, be demonstrating just the opposite.

Admittedly, Molière is a didactic writer. We know this not only from what percolates through from his major plays, but also from his writings on the theatre and from his polemic plays. Again and again he refers to his work as corrective. It is however worth noting that he talks of correcting men, not women. He is of course using 'les hommes' to mean men in the sense of 'mankind', not men as opposed to women. But Molière is remarkably systematic in this usage. Every single comment of this kind refers to 'les hommes': he wants 'to correct *men's* vices' ('corriger les vices des hommes'); 'to correct *men* through entertainment' ('corriger les hommes en les divertissant') 'to expose to the full the ridiculous side of *men*' ('entrer comme il faut dans tout le ridicule des hommes'),[4] or this more sustained comment from his polemic play *The Impromptu at Versailles* (*L'Impromptu de Versailles*):

the function of comedy is to paint a general picture of all men's faults, especially those of the men of our century.

(l'affaire de la comédie est de représenter en général tous les défauts des hommes, et principalement des hommes de notre siècle.)[5]

Moreover, if one looks at the subjects of Molière's plays, one can see that in actual fact they are mostly about men and their faults, not about women. Of the plays whose titles indicate a fault in the protagonist (*Le Bourgeois gentilhomme*, *Le Malade imaginaire*, *Le Misanthrope* and so on) twelve titles refer to male characters (played by Molière in most cases), while only two, *Les Précieuses ridicules* and *Les Femmes savantes*, have titles that suggest that women's faults are to be targeted in the play.

Again, consider the range of faults criticized by Molière. Apart from the comments in *The School for Wives Criticized* the most sustained discusion, within a play, of Molière's choice of subjects for satire comes in his polemic play *The Impromptu at Versailles*. This play was written in 1663 as second answer to the many critics of *The School for Wives*. It is an informal piece. Molière shows himself and his troupe in rehearsal. In Molière's day, the members of his troupe all played themselves, and in scene iii Molière used the artifice of naturalness and informality as an opportunity to discuss his targets for satire. Molière himself spoke the lines that concern us here, thereby stressing their importance to the audience. He specifically states that he is aiming at a comprehensive attack on the absurdities of men: he says that at court alone there is a wide range of subjects, and he specifies five types that he feels need the Molière treatment. He singles out for attack men who are polite to your face but derogatory behind your back, fair-weather friends, eternal discontents, helpful men whose kindnesses are motivated by self-interest and finally undiscriminating sycophants.

Where women are concerned, however, even if we take minor female characters into consideration, Molière's plays contain a far more limited range of attacks. He may include the odd incidental dig during the course of a play, but those two plays already mentioned, and which set out primarily to attack the faults of women, address themselves to one question and one question alone: that of preciosity. The programme notes of Trevis's *The School for Wives* describe this social movement that was also a lifestyle as 'an embryo feminist movement'. In the case of *The Ridiculous Précieuses*, which is a very early play, Molière's interest in the movement is evident from the very title. During the course of the play we see Molière dealing with the extreme artificiality and arrogance of two young ladies who regard themselves as quintessential précieuses. Right at the end of his life, with *Les Femmes savantes (The Female Scholars)*, Molière attacks the same sort of faults, though here his target is a group of women whose preciosity is more intellectual or literary than social. Women such as his Philaminte and Bélise are modelled on real-life prototypes, just as were his Ridiculous Précieuses, Cathos and Madelon. Interestingly enough, in *The Impromptu at Versailles*, Molière does reveal an awareness that this women's movement is a legitimate target for satire; but yet again he attacks the over-refinement of the précieuse, in this case her elegancies of speech. At one stage in the play, a female member of the cast acts out the part of a précieuse; and during the course of this play within a play she complains about Molière as follows:

> What? would not the impertinent wretch let women have wit? does he condemn all our elevated expressions, and pretend that we should always talk in a grovelling manner? (B&M, I, 336)

Clearly in *The Impromptu at Versailles* there is an imbalance between Molière's use of men and of women as targets for satire. With men, he is satirizing 'all men's absurdities' ('tout le ridicule des hommes'), while with women (apart from the occasional sly dig at their virtue, as we shall see) he is confining his attack to their use of language. Is the reason for this difference that Molière thought women so perfect that they were more or less beyond criticism? Looking again at *The Impromptu at Versailles*, I note with interest that in the script female members of Molière's troupe are made to express strong views. In response to these, Molière wrote for himself a series of replies which amount to saying, more or less, 'enough of this nonsense'. In short, he does not take the women seriously. At one point, Mlle Béjart, who played parts like Frosine and Dorine in his original productions, becomes indignant on his behalf, and urges him to reply to his critics in the strongest terms. Molière simply replies: 'I'm provoked to hear you talk in this manner, and this is the madness peculiar to you women' (B&M, I, 338) ('vous autres femmes'). At another stage Molière's wife, Armande, who played parts like Célimène and Angélique in *George Dandin*, says that a play should be written justifying women. Molière replies: 'Ahy! laissons cela' ('Well, let that alone!') (B&M, I, 325).

Here, in sum, Molière presents himself as contemptuous and dismissive of what the women in his troupe have to say. Admittedly, the joke is against Molière in that he depicts himself as unable to control the women, despite his blustering; nevertheless I would like to suggest that this dismissive approach is unobtrusively present in Molière's theatre as a whole; Molière's attitude here fits in with the most appropriate slant to give an examination of Molière's female characters in general, which is to regard them as consistently subordinate to the men. They are not subjected to constant scrutiny and repeated attack, they are viewed with indulgent humour, simply because they are not considered worth the trouble of really serious attack.

There are many examples in Molière's plays of female characters who exhibit the same faults as the men; but in the case of the women, these faults are given little prominence. They are included merely to enhance the plot or to shed some light on the character of the male protagonist. For instance, in *Le Tartuffe*, Orgon (the part originally played by Molière) is obsessed with the religious hypocrite Tartuffe, and believes in Tartuffe's ostentatious rejection of the pleasures of the flesh. Much of the plot of the play is concerned with the family's attempts to make Orgon come to his senses and stop his ludicrous hero-worship of Tartuffe. With Orgon we get the impression of a half-crazed individual who has completely lost touch with reality, and is pitting himself single-handed against common sense, represented by all the other members of the family. All, that is, save one. For the play begins with Orgon's mother, Mme Pernelle, taking the family to task for their lax ways. She too has clearly been won over by Tartuffe. She systematically goes through the different aspects of the family's lifestyle of which she disapproves, and seems indeed to have taken Tartuffe's teachings even more to heart than has her son. But whereas the 'deconversion' of Orgon forms the plot of the whole play, Mme Pernelle goes crossly away after the first scene, and we forget her completely.

It comes as a surprise when she reappears in the final act; and it is at this stage that we see Molière exhibiting little interest in her as an individual, but instead using her as a means of showing Orgon up and providing scope for comic effects relating to him. She has been absent during the unmasking of Tartuffe, and she refuses to believe that he is an evil hypocrite. This gives Molière the opportunity of working Orgon into paroxysms of angry frustration (an emotion that Molière seems to have portrayed to perfection on stage); as far as the plot is concerned, the reappearance of Mme Pernelle provides a neat come-uppance for Orgon, who is at last shown how it feels to be confronted with what he himself has just ceased to be: a blind fool who refused to see what was under his very nose. As regards Mme Pernelle herself, there is little discussion of her responses. She merely exclaims (to provide my own irreverent translation):

> I'm all flabberstruck, you could knock me down with a feather! (v, v)

After this we have no further interest in the character, and Molière leaves it at that.[6]

The implication so far is that the same material will be given different treatment according to whether the character involved is male or female. The pattern that is emerging is that the women will be given perfunctory attention, whereas Molière will really concentrate on the male characters.

There is, however, one exceptional circumstance in which the women characters are thrown into relief in Molière's plays. This prominence must next be discussed, though it will become clear that it does nothing to alter the impression that Molière, far from arguing in their favour, consistently belittles women. This circumstance is Molière's treatment of marriage and the married couple. The subject is of great importance in any discussion of Molière's women, because it is inconceivable to consider Molière's women outside the context of marriage. This is not to say, of course, that Molière avoids including unmarried female characters. But his single women are all preoccupied with men. Some of the characters are old maids and unable to attract men; of Arsinoë in *The Misanthrope* we are told: 'she makes every effort / To hook a man, but without success' (III, 2). Bélise in *The Female Scholars*, who is clearly in her fifties and past it, lives in a dream world of languishing lovers and passionate attachments. When a woman is too old to be personally involved with men, she is likely to take a vicarious interest in the loves of younger couples: examples are the old woman who serves as go-between in the *The School for Wives* and Frosine, the matchmaker in *The Miser*. All the other women except the servants, whose love-lives generally seem to be of peripheral interest in Molière, are seriously involved with men. In other words, the status quo in Molière is for women of a certain rank to be depicted in the context of a marriage, or of the sort of serious love-affair that is likely to lead to marriage.

In the light of this truth, let us turn again to *The Impromptu at Versailles* and

to the conversation between Molière and his wife Armande, in which, as
has already been mentioned, she says she would like him to write a play
justifying women. The conversation goes as follows:

> *Molière.* Hold your peace, wife, you are an ass.
> *Mrs Molière.* Thank you, good husband. See how it is; matrimony alters people
> strangely; you would not have said this a year and a half ago.
> *Molière.* Pray hold your tongue.
> *Mrs Molière.* 'Tis a strange thing that a little ceremony should be capable of
> depriving us of all our good qualities; and that a husband and a gallant
> should look upon the same person with such different eyes.
> *Molière.* What a prating is here!
> *Mrs Molière.* I'faith if I were to write a comedy I would write it on this subject. I
> would justify the women in a great many things they are accused of, and I'd
> make the husbands dread the difference there is between their rough
> manners and the civility of gallants.
> *Molière.* Well, let that alone, we are not to prattle now, we have something else
> to do. (B&M, I, 325)

The time has come to discuss an important element previously omitted
when I alluded to this dramatized conversation between Molière and
Armande. Armande is not indulging in idle speculation about what sort of
plays her husband Molière ought to write; her remarks in this extract
constitute a veiled threat. To the student of Molière, it is a commonplace
that the married or about-to-be-married women in his plays threaten to
deceive their husbands if they are thwarted. The most extreme example is
Angélique in *George Dandin*, who threatens her husband George in the
following terms:

> I don't intend to renounce the world, and bury myself alive with a husband . . .
> For my part, who did not tell you that I'd marry you, and whom you took
> without consulting my inclinations, I don't think I'm bound to submit like a
> slave to your will; but will enjoy, by your leave, those happy days which youth
> offers me, make use of such dear liberties as the age permits, see the beau-
> monde a little, and indulge the pleasure of hearing fine things said to me.
> Prepare then for your punishment . . . (B&M, II, 194)

The fact that Molière and his wife took the parts of George and Angélique
must have contributed greatly to the piquancy of the original production.
And clearly one could demonstrate that Molière, under the light-hearted
tone of this speech, was making relevant points here about the status of
women. There may well be implied criticism of the fact that they were
reduced to resorting to such measures because they had no legal redress
against their husbands, who, having married them without consulting their
wishes in the first place, owned them after the marriage as if they were mere
chattels. Others might object that if Molière had serious social criticism in
mind, he would have couched his remarks in somewhat less frivolous terms.
Here I want to look at quite a different angle: what use does Molière make of

threats of infidelity from the point of view of his treatment of female characters?

Molière's techniques are much more blatantly apparent in the farcical comedies, where the humour is, perforce, much cruder than in the high comedies. Several of these farces contain the theme of potential cuckoldry. A good example is the little-known farce *Le Mariage forcé, The Forced Marriage*. This is a short play consisting of nine scenes in which a buffoon called Sganarelle, played by Molière in the original production, decides to get married. In the second scene he meets his betrothed, Dorimène; what she says to him makes him realize that he had much better not marry her after all. The rest of the play shows his despairing and ineffectual manoeuvres to extricate himself. He consults fortune-tellers, tries to persuade her family to let him back out and even attempts to buy his way out. The curtain falls with his realization that he is trapped.

My point derives from a curious feature of this play: Sganarelle is present in every scene of this play, and we become thoroughly acquainted with his despair. But he is placed opposite a partner, Dorimène, who is made much more difficult to understand. She appears in only two scenes; and the odd thing about the way she is presented is her blatant frankness when she talks to her future husband, a frankness for which Molière gives a perfunctory and unconvincing explanation. Her one major speech goes as follows:

> To cut a long story short, my father has been the most boringly strict parent in the world, and has kept me under lock and key. I have been furious for ages because he allows me no freedom. I've been longing for him to marry me off, so as to be able to get rid of him, and be free to do what I want. Thank goodness you turned up in the nick of time. From now on I intend to have fun, and make up for lost time. You're a man of the world, and you know the score. I think we'll make a very happy couple, and you won't be one of those tedious husbands who chain their wives at home like watch-dogs. Because I'm telling you that I couldn't put up with that. I hate sitting at home alone. I like gambling, parties, gatherings, presents, going out, in fact everything frivolous, and you should be delighted to have a wife who feels like me. We'll never quarrel, I'll never intefere in what you do, and I hope that you won't interfere with me. In my opinion, a marriage must be based on mutual trust, and the point of marrying is not to make each other angry. To sum up, once we're married, we'll live like two civilized people. You won't bother your head with jealous suspicions; it's enough for you to be convinced of my fidelity, and I will be persuaded that you're faithful too. But what's wrong with you? Your face looks quite peculiar.[7]

Sganarelle's dismay is so violent that even the thoughtless Dorimène notices he is not his usual self. It is difficult to conceive of a young woman who has reached such a pitch of cynicism, however harshly her father has treated her. Naturally, in the context of farce, we would not expect much in the way of psychological realism; but I believe Dorimène has been made outrageously frank and implausibly cynical for another reason.

In this play Molière studies (if you can call a farcical portrait a study) the state of mind of a character who is in no doubt that he is going to be cuckolded. He is told this by implication by his future wife. So in this play Molière is not concerned with the doubts that may beset the suspicious husband; such doubts are the subjects of other plays like the farcical *Sganarelle or the Imaginary Cuckold* or the more serious *Amphitryon*. Hence the portrayal of Dorimène is determined by that of Sganarelle, and reflects Molière's desire to examine, through the character of Sganarelle, a new variation on the comic theme of cuckoldry. The portrayal of Dorimène is thus purely incidental to the main point of the play; she is scarcely a character, more a mouthpiece for voicing a particular attitude and a foil to the main character.

There are many more examples which reinforce the view that Molière is concentrating on the husband in the marriages he portrays; and it is not necessarily true that he wrote big parts for his husbands merely to give himself a comic role to play. *Amphitryon* is an interesting example of a relatively serious play, based on a Roman original, which examines the subject of infidelity within marriage. The play retells the legend of Jupiter's love for Alcmena, already dramatized by Plautus in his *Amphitruo*, and taken up earlier in the century by Rotrou with his play *Les Sosies*. The story goes that Jupiter, realizing that Alcmena would not consider deceiving her husband Amphitryon, transforms himself into the husband's likeness, so that Alcmena never realizes she is making love to another man. Their affair results in the birth of Hercules. In Molière's play the eponymous hero, a nobleman and warrior-prince, was not the sort of role in which Molière excelled. He probably wrote the part for the actor La Thorillière and he expanded the role of Amphitryon's valet, Sosie, for himself. As a result, we have a different approach to the study of infidelity. And again, we have a curious absence of focus on the wife. We only see Amphitryon's wife, Alcmène, *before* she realizes that she has been, all unknowingly, unfaithful to her husband. Just when it must be becoming clear that there are two Amphitryons, and that something very strange is going on, Alcmène fades from the scene, and we see the perplexity, confusion and misery of the husband only. It could be argued that Molière is showing considerable delicacy here by allowing the wronged wife to draw a veil of dignified oblivion over her own unwitting infidelity. But from the theatrical point of view, it can be seen that he avoids making Alcmène into an interesting, major character: he focuses on the husband, not the wife.

From the standpoint of his plays as a whole, then, Molière's unfaithful (or more often would-be unfaithful) women could be seen as useful devices for providing the male characters with something to worry about. The women introduce the sort of tension or excitement that keeps the plot going and enhances the comic potential of the male character by subjecting him to stress and seeing how he functions.

In making extensive use of the theme of cuckoldry, Molière is drawing on a rich theatrical tradition. He runs through the gamut of deceived husbands, from the clownish Sganarelle figure to the type of the sensible, admirable society gentleman ruefully prepared to make the best of a bad job like Chrysalde in *The School for Wives*. Trevis made Arnolphe upstage Chrysalde during a major speech in which Chrysalde has very serious comments to make on how to be philosophical about infidelity. In my view this was an unpardonable piece of misdirection.

In order to demonstrate the universal nature of this theme and to provide this variety in the husbands Molière draws on an equally varied group of threatening wives. Even a dignified, sensible woman like Henriette in *The Female Scholars* is prepared to use this threat of infidelity as a defence (v, i). The awareness that they hold one trump card emboldens timid characters like Mariane in *Le Tartuffe*, makes women go against everything they have been brought up to value, like Angélique in *George Dandin*. It adds a further farcical dimension to a female clown, like Martine in *The Reluctant Doctor*, and gives extra bite to the rage of a cantankerous character such as Cléanthis in *Amphitryon*.

But the fact that these women are incidental to Molière's main preoccupation is brought home by the realization that if the plot requires it, the woman may have no *intention* even of uttering such a threat, let alone putting it into practice. And yet the cuckold theme may still feature prominently. A good example is the face *Sganarelle or the Imaginary Cuckold*. Sganarelle's wife is a shadowy figure who plays a very minor role. She is included purely as part of a misunderstanding whereby Sganarelle can be led to believe that she is deceiving him. Molière is then able to get down to the farcical centre of the play, which is the ridiculous way Sganarelle expresses his rage and despair at being cuckolded. It must be because of the gusto Molière lent to this role that this farce, rarely performed nowadays, was Louis XIV's personal favourite from among Molière's plays.

Sganarelle's wife, who is not even given a name, sheds a different light on the state of affairs from most Molière plays. Normally the woman *will* threaten to commit adultery; she may even seem likely to do so (Angélique in *George Dandin*);[8] but (and this is an important point) she does not do so during the course of the play. In this respect *Amphitryon*, based as it was on a classical myth, is quite exceptional.

What is implied by the fact that the women's threats are not seen to be executed? It provides the play with a measure of tension without the sinister impact of realization. But as far as the women are concerned, it further lowers their status: already the threats merely serve as a vehicle for varying the approach to the male characters; worse still, the threats themselves are empty, hence derisory. When Molière makes his Arnolphe in *The School for Wives* say complacently, 'It is to show dependence that your sex is here' (II, ii), he is only half-joking.

NOTES

1 The programme was produced by Tim Goodwin.
2 Molière himself states in his preface to the *School for Wives* that Dorante in *The School for Wives Criticized* is a real mouthpiece: we have no such assertion about the *raisonneurs* in any of his other plays.
3 Unless otherwise stated, translations are from the 1739 translation of Molière by the two playwrights H. Baker and J. Miller ('B&M'), published as *Selected Comedies by J. B. Poquelin Molière* (London: J. M. Dent, 1951). The original text
3 Unless otherwise stated, translations are from the 1739 translation of Molière by the two playwrights H. Baker and J. Miller ('B&M'), published as *Selected Comedies by J. B. Poquelin Molière* (London: J. M. Dent, 1951). The original text used is Molière, *Oeuvres complètes*, ed. Robert Jouanny (Paris: Garnier, 1962) ('Garnier').
4 From the preface to *Le Tartuffe*, the first 'Placet' to *Le Tartuffe, The School for Wives Criticized*, scene vi. My translations.
5 Scene iv. B&M, 1, 333, Garnier, 1, 531.
6 The question of Molière's attitude to the women in his plays is further complicated by the fact that Mme Pernelle was played by a man, the actor Louis Béjart, in his own production.
7 Scene ii (Garnier, 1, 553). My translation.
8 This is my interpretation of her remarks and behaviour, though she makes a point of denying that such is her intention.

The 'playgirl' of the western world: feminism, comedy, and Synge's Pegeen Mike*

GAIL FINNEY

Perhaps not surprisingly, most interpretations of *The Playboy of the Western World* (1907) have centered on the title character, Christy Mahon – specifically, on his (ostensible) murder of his father and on the reception of this deed in Mayo. Yet there is much more to the drama than its treatment of the father–son conflict; as Synge himself wrote, 'There are, it may be hinted, several sides to "The Playboy".'[1] As significant as Christy is the character with whom the play begins and ends, Margaret (Pegeen Mike) Flaherty. Indeed the drama can be seen to revolve in part around the tension between her ties to her father and her rebellion against him, a tension microcosmic of an actual clash in many women at the turn of the century: the clash between a sense of duty to the patriarchal establishment, whose power the Victorian era had reinforced enormously, and a desire for autonomy and equality, goals advocated with increasing influence by the contemporary feminist movement. As we shall see, this tension explains both Pegeen's attraction to Christy, who as an (ostensible) father-killer embodies the ideal that she would like to achieve metaphorically, and her ultimate rejection of him.

The contradiction in Pegeen Mike between closeness to her father and the wish to free herself from him stems from the fact that she has been, as she tells Christy, 'my whole life with my father only'.[2] On the one hand, as in so much nineteenth-century fiction, the lack of a mother – typically the primary identity figure for a girl – has caused Pegeen to develop into a woman of unusual independence and strength of will.[3] On the other hand, in assuming joint responsibility for the pub, Pegeen has slipped into the role vis-à-vis her father that her mother would have played, thus realizing the girl's oedipal fantasy as conceived by Freud: 'an affectionate attachment to her father, a need to get rid of her mother as superfluous and to take her place . . .'.[4] Moreover, it is only to be expected that Michael Flaherty, in the absence of his wife, would feel an unusually great tenderness toward his daughter.

* A draft of this paper was read at the *Themes in Drama* International Conference held at the University of California, Riverside, in February 1987.

This dichotomy in Pegeen is reflected even in her name, 'Pegeen' being of course a nickname for 'Margaret', which is a variant of 'Mary', sign of the Mother par excellence, and 'Mike' a man's name and the name of her father. At the outset of the play her submissive side predominates: her first lines list the articles necessary to make the outfit in which she intends to marry the timid but well-to-do Shawn Keogh, her cousin and her father's choice. Having 'no father to kill', i.e. doomed to remain eternally immature, this cowardly 'stereotype of the unmasculine'[5] bows to the paternal authority of Father Reilly, whose precepts he is constantly invoking. In being engaged to Shawn, then, Pegeen Mike is actually under the sway of four fathers: her own, his delegate Shawn, Father Reilly, and the Holy Father whose deputy he is. But the true nature of her feelings for Shawn is indicated by the stage directions designating the tone of her lines to him – 'with rather scornful good humour'; 'with scorn'; 'impatiently' (59, 1).

Insofar as a father's forcing his daughter to marry an unloved man tightens his hold on her, since it insures that she will always love *him* and never really leave him,[6] Michael Flaherty's intentions as the play begins are evident. Also evident, however, is the fact that a young woman like Pegeen, characterized by Michael's crony Jimmy Farrell as a 'fine, hardy girl would knock the head of any two men in the place' (63, 1), cannot subordinate herself to her father's will for long. Her early rhetorical question to Shawn, showing that she is dissatisfied not only with him and her father but with her entire environment, suggests that she is on the verge of a rebellion:

> Where now will you meet the like of Daneen Sullivan knocked the eye from a peeler, or Marcus Quin, God rest him, got six months for maiming ewes, and he a great warrant to tell stories of holy Ireland till he'd have the old women shedding down tears about their feet. Where will you find the like of them, I'm saying? (59, 1)

As if in response to her question, just such a person (or one she imagines to be) arrives. That what Christy represents opposes the world of her father is symbolized by the fact that his encounter with Pegeen is furthered by Michael's absence. The connection between Michael's neglect of Pegeen and Christy's inroads with her is underlined by her repeated complaints about her father's irresponsibility in leaving her alone overnight to attend a wake, e.g. 'If I am a queer daughter, it's a queer father'd be leaving me lonesome these twelve hours of dark, and I piling the turf with the dogs barking, and the calves mooing, and my own teeth rattling with the fear' (63, 1).

With Christy's arrival at the pub and her father's departure, Pegeen's independent side comes increasingly to the fore. To understand the changes in her it is necessary to look closely at her contributions to Christy's identity as a parricide and playboy. Significantly, it is she who first evokes his admission that he murdered his father: when he accuses her of not speaking the truth about him, she responds, 'Not speaking the truth, is it? Would you have me knock the head of you with the butt of the broom?', whereupon he replies, 'Don't strike me . . . I killed my poor father, Tuesday was a week, for doing the like of that' (73, I). Because of this single statement, she proceeds throughout nearly the remainder of the play to build Christy up into a grand figure of heroic proportions. She makes of him, first of all, her protector, as pot-boy: 'if I'd that lad in the house, I wouldn't be fearing the loosèd khaki cut-throats, or the walking dead' (75, I); she then projects royal blood into his veins: 'You should have had great people in your family, I'm thinking, with the little small feet you have, and you with a kind of quality name, the like of what you'd find on the great powers and potentates of France and Spain' (79, I); next she casts him as a ladies' man, replying in response to a compliment of his that 'You've said the like of that, maybe, in every cot and cabin where you've met a young girl on your way' (81, I); and finally she envisions him as a poet – 'I've heard all times it's the poets are your like, fine, fiery fellows with great rages when their temper's roused' (81, I) – a comparison she reiterates during their love scene in the third act.

It is largely through Pegeen's imputation of these identities to Christy that he assumes them; at her suggestion and through her encouragement he really does become courageous, charming, lyrically adept, in short, a true playboy in all senses of the word at the time – consummate role-player, skillful athlete or game-player, and general 'star'. For as we learn in the course of the drama, there is little basis for attributing any of these roles to the son old Mahon characterizes as a 'dirty, stuttering lout', a 'lier on walls, a talker of folly, a man you'd see stretched the half of the day in the brown ferns with his belly to the sun' (121, II), and 'the laughing joke of every female woman where four baronies meet' (123, II). What, then, motivates Pegeen to form this image of Christy?

As Patricia Meyer Spacks has written, Christy's murder of his father represents a 'metaphor of achievement', demonstrating his attainment of the self-confidence and maturity that comes with the release from parental domination.[7] It is little wonder that such an achievement should seem highly desirable to a passionate, strong-willed, imaginative woman like Pegeen, who as a girl 'was tempted often to go sailing the seas' (151, III). Given the conventions of her narrowly provincial society, however, as a woman she can realize this kind of achievement only vicariously. She therefore projects onto Christy, who in killing his father has accomplished what she too wants metaphorically to do, the kinds of characteristics that she would like to possess herself. Having 'given' him these characteristics, she in turn takes back or imitates certain of them, such as the ability to speak like a poet, and no one is more astonished at her transformation than she is: 'And to think it's me is talking sweetly, Christy Mahon, and I the fright of seven townlands for my biting tongue' (151, III).

Christy's function as ideal alter ego for Pegeen is reinforced by parallels

between their fathers and between their relationships with the two men –
parallels that place both old Mahon and Michael Flaherty at something of a
remove from the cliché of the omnipotent father. For example, although
Mahon is cantankerous and Flaherty jovial, both are part of the long-
standing tradition in Irish literature (and life?) of the alcoholic patriarch.
Flaherty gets so drunk at the nocturnal wake that he has to be brought
home in an ass cart, and he chides Christy for not giving his father a wake so
that they could have drunk 'a smart drop to the glory of his soul' (153, III);
his main objection to Christy's murdering Shawn in the pub is that it is
filled with whiskey for the men's drinks that evening. As for Mahon, his past
ravings sound very much like delirium tremens:

> There was one time I seen ten scarlet divils letting on they'd cork my spirit in a
> gallon can; and one time I seen rats as big as badgers sucking the life blood from
> the butt of my lug . . . and I a terrible and fearful case, the way that there I was
> one time screeching in a straitened waistcoat with seven doctors writing out my
> sayings in a printed book.
>
> $$(143; 143–5, III)$$

And yet he has managed to raise Christy on his own, the boy's mother
having died bearing him, just as Flaherty has had sole care of Pegeen.
Similarly, just as Pegeen works for her father in the pub, Christy's life with
Mahon has consisted of 'toiling, moiling, digging, dodging from the dawn
till dusk with never a sight of joy or sport saving only when I'd be abroad in
the dark night poaching rabbits on hills . . .' (83, I). Finally, as Flaherty has
done with Pegeen, Mahon has attempted to coerce his son into marrying an
unloved partner for her money – in Christy's words, 'A walking terror from
beyond the hills, and she two score and five years, and two hundredweights
and five pounds in the weighing scales, with a limping leg on her, and a
blinded eye, and she a woman of noted misbehaviour with the old and
young' (101, II). To Christy the worst of it is the fact that 'she did suckle me
for six weeks when I came into the world' (103, II), and it is of course this
planned match, constituting what has been called 'a kind of inversion of the
Oedipal situation',[8] that incites Christy to 'kill' his father. It is at this point
that the parallels between the two father–child relationships end; as Pegeen
tells Christy, 'I never killed my father. I'd be afeard to do that, except I was
the like of yourself with blind rages tearing me within . . .' (81, I). But
through her glorification of and love for a parracide Pegeen demonstrates
her unconscious desire to do what repels her conscious mind: to rid herself
of the father who has consigned her to a loveless marriage in an environment that is sure to stifle her.

Pegeen's identification with Christy is so strong that she occasionally
exhibits conventionally masculine characteristics, while at the same time
he often displays traditionally feminine traits. Such reversals are typical in
comedy, the humorous effects of which frequently stem from the inversion

of conventional values and norms of behavior. But in a drama where role-playing is as important as in *Playboy*, the reversal of sex roles deserves especially close attention. Carolyn Heilbrun provides a concise summary of conventional gender distinctions:

> According to the conventional view, 'masculine' equals forceful, competent, competitive, controlling, vigorous, unsentimental, and occasionally violent; 'feminine' equals tender, genteel, intuitive rather than rational, passive, unaggressive, readily given to submission. The 'masculine' individual is popularly seen as a maker, the 'feminine' as a nourisher.[9]

Looking at *Playboy* in the light of such categorizations, we find that much about Christy is 'feminine', particularly in the early parts of the play. Before he appears on stage, Shawn says that he has heard him 'groaning out and breaking his heart' (61, I) in a ditch near the pub; Synge's first description characterizes him as a 'slight young man . . . very tired and frightened and dirty', who speaks 'in a small voice' (67, I), and he initially strikes Pegeen as a 'soft lad' (71, I). Furthermore, with his fondness for looking at himself in mirrors and his peacock pride at his appearance in the new clothes Shawn gives him, he displays a kind of vanity sterotypically associated with women. And yet Pegeen is able to overlook all these features in view of his patricide, showing the degree to which she adheres to the conventional notion that the masculine principle is 'predicated on the ability to kill'.[10]

In fact Pegeen often exhibits a hardiness and boldness that render her more of a 'playboy' than Christy. When he seeks to justify his 'oddness' to her by explaining that she has lived 'lonesome in the world' (111, II), she replies that she is not odd, even though she has lived her whole life with her father alone. Similarly, she does not shrink from details of physical suffering, as other girls probably would, but tells Christy for instance how 'Jimmy Farrell hanged his dog from the licence and had it screeching and wriggling three hours at the butt of a string . . .' (73, I). Possessing in Shawn's words 'the divil's own temper' (115, II), she breaks out 'into wild rage' (89, I) when the Widow Quin accuses her of indiscriminate man-chasing, and in menacing Christy with the broom in act I she is the first character in the play to threaten violence. After she returns the next morning from milking to find Christy surrounded by admiring village girls, she treats him with an imperiousness that reduces him to a state of apologetic meekness. Most notably, after Christy's (second) attempted murder of old Mahon, Pegeen is the only one who is 'man' enough to go up to him and slip the noose over his head and, when he twists his legs around the table, to burn him so that he will let go.

One of the central questions posed by *Playboy* is of course that of why Pegeen and the other villagers are so horrified at witnessing precisely that which had enthralled them as a tale, Christy's attempted patricide. Along with the partial explanation that no one loves a good yarn like the Irish but that reality is another matter for them, I am persuaded by Gérard Leblanc's suggestion:

> One may . . . be tempted to see in the *Playboy* another dramatization of a universal model complicated by specific socio-historical circumstances in Ireland, where the son's emancipation was – and is still – delayed much later than in other European countries. Ireland is a fathers' country and the violent liberation of Christy Mahon may pass for the vicarious fulfilment of a deepfelt unsocial wish shared by the villagers of Mayo and perhaps, too, by the Dublin spectators of January 1907 who more or less consciously sensed that the symbolic undertones of parricide might threaten the whole moral and social fabric of their world.[11]

Pegeen's radical turnabout, manifested in her characterization of Christy after she learns his father is alive as 'nothing at all' (161, III) and in her physical cruelty to him, represents a special variation on this model. Her glorification of him as a heroic playboy stems solely from her belief that he has killed his father; it is this fact alone that blinds her to his weaknesses and leads her to project a series of idealized identities onto him. Once this fact is unmasked as a falsehood, then, he truly becomes 'nothing' in her eyes. In her case the 'deepfelt unsocial wish' vicariously fulfilled by Christy is less the overthrow of Ireland's English oppressors than the rebellion against her own personal oppressor, her father. It is likely that in actually witnessing Christy's attempt at patricide (rather than simply hearing about it) she becomes conscious of this wish, whereupon her loyalty to Flaherty and to social convention – evident for example in her earlier willingness to marry an unloved man chosen by her father – again takes over.

Whatever the case, it seems certain that the blurring of gender distinctions culminating in Pegeen's show of violence was as responsible as Christy's notorious mention of 'a drift of chosen females, standing in their shifts' (167, III) for the bewilderment the play met with and the riots occasioned by its first performances in Dublin and the United States. As Synge realized even at the time, the opening of *Playboy* in Dublin's Abbey Theatre was truly 'an event in the history of the Irish stage';[12] indeed few works in the history of *world* drama have caused comparable upheavals. The first performance was accompanied by hissing, the second by shouting, hooting, and trumpet-blowing so loud the actors could not be heard, and things continued in similar fashion for several nights thereafter, with fights ensuing and police brought in to stand guard; the furor moved Yeats to hold a public debate on the freedom of the theater about a week after the première.[13] The play provoked even Joseph Holloway, the architect whose attendance at Abbey productions was so regular that he was virtually regarded as a member of the company and became its diarist, to call Synge 'the evil genius of the Abbey' and 'the dramatist of the dungheap'.[14] Critics railed from all sides against the bawdy language of the play and its apparent celebration of patricide, but a newspaper review of the first performance reveals that what most scandalized audiences was Synge's depiction of women: the review refers to *Playboy* as 'this unmitigated, protracted libel upon Irish peasant men and, worse still, upon Irish peasant girlhood'.[15] Similarly, William and Frank Fay, two of the co-founders of the Abbey Theatre, begged Synge to make Pegeen 'a decent likeable country girl', and a letter to the author from Abbey playwright Padraic Colum includes the following: 'Peggy is a creation distinctly and acted splendidly. Still I think she would have stood by her man when he was attacked by a crowd. The play does not satisfy me.'[16] Such reactions bear out T. R. Henn's claim that by Synge's day the chastity and purity of Irish womanhood had become a national myth.[17]

The degree to which Synge flouted this myth is evident in other works as well. His first completed play, *The Shadow of the Glen* (1904), in which Nora Burke goes in search of other men after she mistakenly thinks her husband has died, was denounced as libelous of Irish women because of its portrayal of her mercenary and 'adulterous' inclinations. In fact the drama shows, through Nora's descriptions of her life with her husband, considerable insight into the frustration and loneliness of a woman married to a much older man for his money and living in an isolated, out-of-the-way place. A similar juxtaposition of sexual realism with an attention to existential questions is found in *The Tinker's Wedding* (1907), in which the tinker Sarah Casey is at first possessed by the desire to legalize her relationship with Michael Byrne in part because she thinks that marriage will ease the pains of aging but is divested of this notion by Michael's lusty, hard-drinking mother Mary. In their strength and tenacity Nora, Sarah, and Mary are comic sisters of the tragic Maurya in *Riders to the Sea* (1903), who bears the successive drownings of her husband, father-in-law, and six sons with monumental stoicism, and of the title character in *Deirdre of the Sorrows* (1910), who is single-minded in her rejection of the much older Conchubor in favor of the young and attractive Naisi even though she knows it will mean death for herself and Naisi. These powerful female figures dominate the reader's/spectator's memory of the dramas; as Saddlemyer writes, 'in nearly all of Synge's plays the women are not only more clearly defined than most of the men but also treated with a sympathetic complexity which frequently determines plot, mood and theme'.[18] The extent to which Synge's women characters cross the conventional gender boundaries of the day suggests that his encounter with feminism through his friendships with liberal-minded women like Hope Rea in Italy and Thérèse Beydon in Paris was more than merely a passing acquaintance.

But nowhere is the blurring of gender roles more evident than in Synge's most well-known female character, Pegeen Mike. Her complex relationship to Christy, alternating as it does between identification and rejection, is further illuminated by contrast with another of Synge's masterful women, and one of his favorite characters,[19] the Widow Quin. Unlike Pegeen she is not restricted by a father and can thus act freely and uninhibitedly. Indeed she stands apart from her entire community both geographically and morally. In her 'little houseen, a perch off on the rising hill' (89, I), she lives at a lofty remove from the other villagers. Her description to Christy of her daily routine is one of the most evocative of the many portrayals of loneliness in Synge's works:

> I'm above many's the day, odd times in great spirits, abroad in the sunshine, darning a stocking or stitching a shift, and odd times again looking out on the schooners, hookers, trawlers is sailing the sea, and I thinking on the gallant hairy fellows are drifting beyond, and myself long years living alone. (127, II)

Her genuine isolation is of an entirely different magnitude from the 'lonesomeness' Pegeen feels on being deserted by her father for a night and underlines the fact that it is the Widow Quin, rather than Pegeen, who belongs like Christy to the world outside the tight social order circumscribed by the Mayo village, as he soon realizes; 'You're like me, so', he responds to the passage quoted above (127, II). Moreover, the moral isolation the Widow experiences because of her accidental murder of her husband prefigures the rejection Christy meets with at the end of the play because of the attempted murder of his father. Michael Flaherty provides an early indication of the village attitude toward the Widow Quin with his rhetorical question to Christy: 'what would the polis want spying on me, and not a decent house within four miles, the way every living Christian is a bona fide saving one widow alone?' (67, I). One of the village girls says to Christy about the Widow Quin that 'all dread her here' (105, II), and Pegeen goes so far as to accuse her of 'rearing a black ram at [her] own breast' (89, I).

In fact the Widow Quin is no witch but rather the most down-to-earth character in the play. As a woman with a good deal of life experience behind her, one who has 'buried her children and destroyed her man' (89, I), she is a hard-bitten, clear-sighted realist. In contrast to the romantic Pegeen Mike she does not seek to escape the world in her imagination, having transcended it in actuality. Unlike Pegeen she does not project onto Christy the roles of heroic parricide, aristocrat, ladykiller, or poet but sees him as he is: 'it'd soften my heart to see you sitting so simple with your cup and cake, and you fitter to be saying your catechism than slaying your da' (87, I). In light of her separate status it is not surprising that the Widow Quin is shocked neither by the revelation that Christy did not succeed in killing his father nor by his renewed attempt to do so. In supporting the father-killer throughout and even helping him escape on several occasions, she distinguishes herself from all the other villagers. And, where Pegeen loves

Christy only conditionally, ultimately rejecting him and returning to the fold of her father's community, the Widow remains attached to him despite the changes in his fortunes, recalling, as Michael Collins has observed, the norm in Shakespeare's Sonnet 116: 'Love is not love / Which alters when it alteration finds.'[20]

In contrast to earlier versions of *Playboy*, in the final one the Widow Quin does not win Christy. Yet the drama's final spotlight is of course not on her loss – she is, after all, 'formed . . . to be living lone' (89, 1) – but rather on Pegeen Mike's. Although both Christy and Pegeen are reunited with their fathers in the end, the play's resolution has very different repercussions for the two of them. Christy undergoes a profound development in the course of the drama, growing into the roles projected onto him by the villagers and above all by Pegeen; his imperious claim to his father near the play's end that he is 'master of all fights from now' (this and all subsequent quotations from the play are from 173, III) shows that through his attempts at patricide he has won old Mahon's respect and has in effect switched places with him. Pegeen, by contrast, remains under the sway of her father and thus unchanged. Where old Mahon reacts 'with a broad smile' to Christy's new-found self-confidence as the two leave behind them these 'fools', Flaherty's last words underline his power over his daughter and the complacent conventionality to which it restricts her: 'By the will of God, we'll have peace now for our drinks. Will you draw the porter, Pegeen?' The crossing of gender boundaries represented by Pegeen's vicarious overthrow of her father through her identification with Christy hence proves to be temporary.

Nowhere is the difference between Christy's development and Pegeen's static nature more evident than in their respective last lines. His departing words are triumphant, announcing his imminent liberation from the narrow-mindedness of communities such as this Mayo village: 'Ten thousand blessings upon all that's here, for you've turned me a likely gaffer in the end of all, the way I'll go romancing through a romping lifetime from this hour to the dawning of the judgment day.' The tone of the famous lines with which Pegeen, putting her shawl over her head, closes the play is altogether different: 'Oh my grief, I've lost him surely. I've lost the only playboy of the western world.' Her words do more than reveal her awareness that Christy, having grown into that which she originally imagined him to be, was worth having after all; symbolically her lamentation points to her loss of that part of herself which might have set her free from her father and from the loveless marriage he has arranged for her. In fact Pegeen is worse off at the play's end than at its beginning, since she has been exposed to Christy, come to know true passion, experienced the liberation brought by identification with the father-killer – and then lost it all.

Thus one of the great comedies of world drama ends in the same dark key as Synge's two tragedies, *Riders to the Sea* and *Deirdre of the Sorrows. Playboy's* conclusion is one of the best examples of what Arthur Ganz has called 'the essential sadness lying beneath even the brightest of Synge's plays".[21] But in view of the fact that a comedy whose title character is a man ends with the words of a grieving woman, more is at stake here, and one is inevitably moved to think about the relationship between comedy and feminism. One of the first to do so was George Meredith, whose essay on comedy (1877) goes so far as to claim that there can be no comedy without sexual equality:

> where women are on the road to an equal footing with men, in attainments and in liberty – in what they have won for themselves, and what has been granted them by a fair civilization – there, and only waiting to be transplanted from life to the stage, or the novel, or the poem, pure comedy flourishes, and is, as it would help them to be, the sweetest of diversions, the wisest of delightful companions.[22]

As its tone might suggest, however, Meredith's analysis fails to take into account the status of female characters at the *end* of a play, novel, etc., and his definition has been modified by recent feminist criticism, notably by work done on Shakespeare. Linda Bamber, for example, writes that the disruption of the social order commonly found in comedy often consists in Shakespeare's plays in the reversal of traditional sexual hierarchies: 'The natural order, the status quo, is for men to rule women. When they fail to do so, we have the exceptional situation, the festive, disruptive, disorderly moment of comedy.' And yet, she continues, 'Whenever Shakespeare's comedies challenge the limits to sexual equality, they end by strenuously reaffirming those limits.'[23] Insofar as the restoration of the social order toward which comedy moves typically includes a traditional, male-dominated marriage, comedy and feminism are in fact usually at odds with each other, Meredith notwithstanding.

The situation is rather different in *Playboy*. Although the drama conforms superficially to the comic pattern, in that the status quo of the Mayo community emerges triumphant and a traditional marriage is in the offing, obviously boy does not get girl, and girl gets the wrong boy; the final focus is on not union but isolation. One is reminded of Synge's own comment that '"The Playboy of the Western World" is not a play with "a purpose" in the modern sense of the word, but although parts of it are, or are meant to be, extravagant comedy, still a great deal that is in it, and a great deal more that is behind it, is perfectly serious, when looked at in a certain light.'[24] One 'serious' aspect is surely Pegeen's fate, which verges on tragedy – not death, as in classical tragedy, but instead the failure of self-realization, symbolized by a union with Christy. In contrast to the comedies of Shakespeare and others, then, in Synge's play comic tone and feminist impulse do not oppose but rather support each other, since Pegeen's liberating identification with Christy is directed, in terms of her development, toward a comic resolution.

Yet the play's final emphasis on the failure of this resolution, highlighting not Christy's comic triumph but Pegeen's tragic lamentations at losing him, produces a stylistic rupture that points ahead formally to post-modern drama while calling attention thematically to the entrapment of Irish women in the conventions of their time.

NOTES

1 'To the Editor, *The Irish Times*', 30 January 1907, *The Collected Letters of John Millington Synge*, ed. Ann Saddlemyer, vol. I (Oxford: Clarendon Press, 1983), p. 286.

2 Synge, *Plays*, book II, vol. IV of *Collected Works*, ed. Ann Saddlemyer (1968; Gerrards Cross: Colin Smythe, 1982), p. 111, act II; subsequent parenthetical references to this edition will include page and act number.

3 Cf. Marianne Hirsch's observation in 'Mothers and Daughters', *Signs*, 7 (Autumn 1981) that 'the powerful and celebrated nineteenth-century mother is so inhibiting a force for her daughter's development that she needs to be removed from the fiction' (p. 216).

4 Sigmund Freud, 'The Development of the Libido and the Sexual Organizations' ('Libidoentwicklung und Sexualorganisation', 1917), *Standard Edition*, vol. XVI, p. 333.

5 Horst Breuer, 'Männlichkeit in J. M. Synges "Playboy of the Western World"', *Germanisch-Romanische Monatsschrift*, 32 (1982), 306.

6 Cf. Shirley Nelson Garner, '*A Midsummer Night's Dream:* "Jack shall have Jill; / Nought shall go ill"', *Women's Studies*, 9 (1981), 55.

7 Patricia Meyer Spacks, 'The Making of the Playboy', in *Twentieth-Century Interpretations of The Playboy of the Western World*, ed. Thomas R. Whitaker (Englewood Cliffs, NJ: Prentice-Hall, 1969), p. 84.

8 Deirdre Laigle, 'The Liberation of Christy Mahon', *Cahiers du Centre d'Etudes Irlandaises*, 2 (1977), 55.

9 Carolyn Heilbrun, *Toward a Recognition of Androgyny* (1964; New York: Norton, 1982), p. xiv.

10 Marilyn French, *Shakespeare's Division of Experience* (New York: Summit Books, 1981), p. 21.

11 Gérard Leblanc, 'The Three Deaths of the Father in *The Playboy of the Western World*', *Cahiers du Centre d'Etudes Irlandaises*, 2 (1977), 33–4.

12 Synge, 'To Molly Allgood', 27 January 1907, *Collected Letters*, p. 285.

13 The fullest account of the riots is by James Kilroy, *The 'Playboy' Riots* (Dublin: Dolmen, 1971). See also the standard biography by David H. Greene and Edward M. Stephens, *J. M. Synge: 1871–1909* (New York: Macmillan, 1959), pp. 234–71, and Richard M. Kain, 'The *Playboy* Riots' in *Sunshine and the Moon's Delight: A Centenary Tribute to John Millington Synge, 1871–1909*, ed. S. B. Bushrui (Gerrard's Cross: Colin Smythe, 1972), pp. 173–88.

14 *Joseph Holloway's Abbey Theatre: A Selection from His Unpublished Journal*, ed. Robert

Hogan and Michael J. O'Neill (Carbondale: Southern Illinois University Press, 1967), pp. 81, 85.

15 'The Abbey Theatre, "The Playboy of the Western World"', *The Freeman's Journal*, 28 January 1907, p. 10, as quoted by Kilroy, *The 'Playboy' Riots*, p. 7.

16 The Fay quotation is found in *My Uncle John: Edward Stephens's Life of J. M. Synge*, ed. Andrew Carpenter (London: Oxford University Press, 1974), p. 188; the Colum passage in Greene and Stephens, *J. M. Synge*, p. 248.

17 *The Plays and Poems of J. M. Synge*, ed. T. R. Henn (London: Methuen, 1963), p. 61.

18 Saddlemyer, 'Synge and the Nature of Woman', in *Woman in Irish Legend, Life and Literature*, ed. S. F. Gallagher (Gerrards Cross: Colin Smythe, 1983), p. 58.

19 Nicholas Grene, *Synge: A Critical Study of the Plays* (London: Macmillan, 1975), p. 140.

20 Michael J. Collins, 'Christy's Binary Vision in *The Playboy of the Western World*', *Canadian Journal of Irish Studies*, 7 (December 1981), 79.

21 Arthur Ganz, *Realms of the Self: Variations on a Theme in Modern Drama* (New York: University Press, 1980), p. 28.

22 George Meredith, 'An Essay on Comedy', in *Comedy*, ed. Wylie Sypher (1956; Baltimore: Johns Hopkins University Press, 1980), p. 32.

23 Linda Bamber, *Comic Women, Tragic Men: A Study of Gender and Genre in Shakespeare* (Stanford University Press, 1982), pp. 29, 32. On the role of women in comedy see also Judith Wilt, 'The Laughter of Maidens, the Cackle of Matriarchs: Notes on the Collision between Comedy and Feminism', *Women and Literature*, 1 (1980), 173–96; several essays in *The Woman's Part: Feminist Criticism of Shakespeare*, ed. Carolyn R. S. Lenz, Gayle Greene, and Carol T. Neely (Urbana: University of Illinois Press, 1980); Marianne Novy, 'Demythologizing Shakespeare', *Women's Studies*, 9 (1981), 17–27; French, *Shakespeare's Division*; Garner, 'A Midsummer Night's Dream'; Susan L. Carlson, 'Comic Textures and Female Communities 1937 and 1977: Clare Boothe and Wendy Wasserstein', *Modern Drama*, 27 (1984), 564–73; and Susan L. Carlson, 'Women in Comedy: Problem, Promise, Paradox' in *Themes in Drama*, vol. 7: *Drama, Sex and Politics*, ed. James Redmond (Cambridge University Press, 1985), pp. 159–71.

24 Synge, 'To the Editor, *The Irish Times*', 30 January 1907, *Collected Letters*, vol. 1, p. 286.

A better Eve: women and robots in Čapek's *R.U.R.* and Pavlovsky's *El Robot**

SHARON D. KING

For centuries it has both terrorized and fascinated humankind. Its name is legion: Golem, homunculus, Frankenstein, Olympia, Gort. It has come to symbolize the threat of technology to escape man's control, to alienate him from his world, to precipitate his loss of humanity. And its reality grows closer every day. Yet have we not, both men and women, made our peace with that artificial creation, the robot? Such would certainly seem to be the case. For although in the 1931 film the betrothed Elizabeth swooned in horror on first sight of the charnel-house composite of Baron Frankenstein, modern audiences have been enchanted by the familial garrulity of C3PO and R2D2 and their companionship with humans. More recently, the 1986 film *Short Circuit* depicts a robot who openly cares for a woman – he makes her breakfast, ogles her 'software', offers her gifts – and she in turn protects him as fiercely as she would one of her many beloved pet animals. Does this image not deny the possibility of considering the robot a threat to women, at least as it now appears in contemporary literature and media?

I suggest that it does not. And I suggest, furthermore, that the robot generally plays a vastly different role when it confronts man than when it deals with woman. This is not to say that both men and women do not feel its often baneful effects. In the Brothers Čapek's futuristic and apocalyptic play *R.U.R.*, for instance, robots destroy all of humankind. In Eduardo Pavlovsky's absurdist one-act drama *El Robot*, both men and women transform briefly into somnolent robotic creatures, symbolizing their dissociation from humanity's ability to feel and care for others. But in both plays women fare quite differently than men do – and are specifically menaced by the spectre and the symbol of the robot. The men in these plays exhibit none of the terror, the revulsion or the anguish when they face the robots that the women do.

To explain this anomaly it is useful to examine a discussion of what has been termed the first science fiction novel, Mary Shelley's *Frankenstein*.

* A draft of this paper was read at the *Themes in Drama* International Conference held at the University of California, Riverside, in February 1987.

According to Ellen Moers, in her essay 'Female Gothic', *Frankenstein* 'is a
birth myth' mirroring Shelley's own horror of birth and its dire consequences and the trauma of the after-birth.[1] Victor Frankenstein shunned
the idea of having children in the usual way (though one life-threatening for
women), rationalizing that he would artificially create 'a new race of man'
in his laboratory that would hail him their creator and lord. Thus, as
George Levine notes, 'in *Frankenstein* we are confronted immediately by the
displacement of God and women from the acts of conception and birth'.[2]
And in fact both plays, *R.U.R.* and *El Robot*, place great emphasis on the
issues of children and childbirth – as well as on their reverse images,
infanticide and sterility – and link them with the appearance of the robots.
These latter are threatening to women because they function as a kind of
'second Eve', designed to perpetuate a kind of life while avoiding the
natural processes of childbearing, nurturing and mothering that have long
been solely woman's sphere. And they were woman's sphere not, of course,
because she had no other capabilities, but because the male-dominated
society has for centuries determined her life. Wife and mother, sex object
and madonna were her roles because she was restricted to them, as both
R.U.R. and *El Robot* make manifestly clear. We shall examine this in more
detail.

There is another reason, however, that the women in these plays appear
menaced by the artificial beings. In his book *Mary Shelley's Monster*, Martin
Tropp observes that Shelley's obvious fear of 'the creation of life by mere
mechanisms' stemmed from her Romantic recognition that 'technology can
never be more than a magnified image of the self'. Thus one can see
Frankenstein's subconscious, hidden desires, his buried self with all its
repressed violence, emerging in his creature, who, according to Tropp,
'does not rebel against his creator but actually accomplishes what the
creator wants'.[3] This is equally true for the robot–woman relationships in
R.U.R. and *El Robot*. The robots attack or restrict women not of themselves
but because they are *male constructs*; they are acting out man's subconscious
desires to control and dominate woman through technology, even as man
has through political, economic and legal institutions. A key term in this
interpretation is 'designed': the women in these plays are 'designed' by
male-dominated society to conform to certain roles, the robots designed by
men to strip what roles women have from them.

R.U.R., or Rossum's Universal Robots, the play which first made use of
the term robot (derived from the Czech word for forced work), centers on
the theme of man dehumanized by his own technology. But its portrait and
treatment of woman make a striking subtheme. The heroine's very name,
Helena, evokes the image of the external, sexual, and deadly Woman who
brought destruction upon an entire nation. This notion of woman as a
passive force of evil and ruin surfaces at the play's end, where she is blamed

for causing the end of the world – a point to which I will later return. For the most part in this play, however, Helena is an idealistic do-gooder, entirely ineffectual in her vague efforts to 'do something' for the robots whom she considers oppressed. Her role as a sex object is stressed from the beginning in her encounter with Domain, the chief of the robots' manufacture. He leers at her, demands that she raise her veil, refuses to let go of her hand, inquires after her age, desires her to remain on the island, and consistently interrupts her, as if he felt her comments of no consequence and in fact distracting, since his real goal is to gaze at her 'in rapture'. Helena is but a step away from being treated like her counterpart in the scene, the 'female' robot Sulla, whom Domain orders to display herself as if she were a prize pig. Throughout the play, although Domain claims to adore Helena, calling her 'life itself', he patronizes her, ridiculing her 'fine idea' of setting the robots free, and keeping her from any real knowledge of the situation in the world or of the robots' production, though they both directly affect her life. Along with his co-workers the scientists, he shelters her as he would a child, leaving her in ignorance until the robots are about to kill them, because they were unwilling to 'frighten her needlessly'. Thus her maid Emma rather disgustedly refers to her as still 'like a baby', even after five years of marriage.

Helena, in turn, having lost what self-reliance and initiative she had had before coming to the island, belittles her own existence. In act II, on the day of her fifth anniversary with Domain, she portrays herself as a 'terrifying young woman' when she first arrived because of her foolishly important notion of setting the robots free:

> Oh, I was fearfully impressed by you all then. I seemed to be a tiny little girl who had lost her way among . . . huge trees. You were all so sure of yourselves, so strong. All my feelings were so trifling, compared with your self-confidence.[4]

She is only too willing to denigrate herself, to find her feelings wanting compared to the bravura of the scientists, with their rational, calculated ideas that contradict her natural intuition. She has become the frail, timid, passive creature, unable to think for herself, that they find so charming; she has fit their mold for her. So well has she, in fact, that, near the end of the play when the robots are about to attack, she sits down at the piano and learns a new piece – the image of a brainless woman-Nero fiddling, unknowing and unconcerned, while her civilization crumbles about her. Like her namesake, the 'lovely but stupid' robot Helena in the play, she is 'simply no good for anything' except for men to look at, for sexual ornamentation.

This point is forcefully brought home by her relationship with the other scientists on the island – five of them besides her husband Domain. In proposing to her – a matter Domain allows Helena only five minutes to consider, demonstrating the purely sexual nature of his interest in her – Domain remarks that if she does not marry him she 'will have to marry one of the other five'. Helena jokingly protests that she cannot marry all six; yet, in a very twisted way, she nearly does. The scientists, like Domain, seem to worship Helena, organizing their feeble talents to cook her her first dinner on the island, praising her great beauty like a chorus, buying her lavish gifts for her fifth wedding anniversary with Domain – and all of them. They view this arrangement of life together with six men 'sharing' one woman in all but the most intimate aspects as perfectly natural. Indeed, when the robots threaten them, they discuss plans, however idealistic, to escape to an Edenic island and found a 'model human colony', where she would rule 'the kingdom of Madam Helena'. This casual acceptance of and wish to perpetuate the status quo appears to the reader, however, as anything but perfect or natural. Their adoration and pedestalization of Helena is in fact charged with the contradiction typical of the madonna/whore complex: how can she 'rule' them if, as Domain insists, she is not to be burdened with too much knowledge for her own good? This bizarre and unnatural ratio reflects more of a fear and horror of woman than an admiration of her, fear that is masked by their 'cult' of Helena. The staging indicates, moreover, that they usually surround her, like wolves eying their prey. Her very femininity, perhaps because it is stereotypically linked with nature, their enemy, threatens them, and they retaliate by objectifying and distancing her. Thus this six-man, one-woman combination is not merely symbolic of man's 'fear of sterility',[5] as one critic has suggested; it stands for man's fear of woman, his need to link up with others of his kind to distance, control and subdue her.

Yet undercutting this sexually charged and symbolically fertile six-to-one ratio is the disturbing fact of Helena's childlessness. Her continuing barrenness, mirrored by that of the entire world around her, confirms her early intuitive fears about the robots and the 'unnatural' inability of his 'sexless throng' to reproduce biologically. Her earthy maid Emma, the peasant woman, characterizes the lack of births as a 'punishment' – Nature punishing the unnatural by shutting itself down. It is significant that only the women in the play show any concern for humankind's loss of the ability to reproduce, which, as a critic has noted, is in the play 'the last thing that distinguishes [man] from the robot'.[6] Even more significantly, Helena links the robots directly with her sterility:

> That children had stopped being born. Harry, that's awful. If the manufacture of the Robots had been continued, there would have been no more children. Emma said that was a punishment. Everybody said that human beings could not be born because so many Robots were being made. And because of that – only because of that – (pp. 82–3)

Helena only too well recognizes the threat the robots pose to her – they will go on and replace humans while she, unable to fulfill her role as childbearer, will watch her kind slowly die out. This alone gives her the impetus to perform her one courageous and active, albeit destructive, action in the play – burning the manuscript for the robots' manufacture.

Helena's attitude towards the robots is thus quite clear. She fears them, distrusts them, pities them – and wishes to change them. Stereotypically linked with nature, with emotion, with intuition, she is horrified at their cold, unnatural rationality. When she does attempt to protect them, she does so as a mother figure, shielding the weak from harm. Her overwhelming compulsion, however, is to change them – to set them free, to give them feelings – in short, to make them 'only a little human'. Thus she persuades Dr Gall to alter the formula for some of them, notably the two that will become human at the end of the play. For as human beings they will take their place beside her rather than take her place. In this desire for humanity she stands alone against the scientists, for even Gall curses himself for 'listening to her' and experimenting with the robots to give them souls. Indeed, the play's humorous first scene, wherein she mistakes the robot Sulla for a woman and the five scientists for robots, reveals how far away they are from humanity: Helena cannot tell them apart because men have already become dehumanized. Helena desires to connect, to integrate, to close the gap between differences. 'It was so terrible that we could not get to understand them properly. There was such a cruel strangeness between us and them' (p. 72), she laments. Though the speed itself refers to the robots, one might interpret it as referring to the gulf of misunderstanding separating man and woman, the cruel myths and restrictive traditions society perpetuates to keep the two sexes far apart.

R.U.R.'s ending is somewhat ambiguous, for while humankind is annihilated, the robots later become human. It is paradoxical as well, since, as the scientist Alquist notes, man has created a new form of life only to have it turn on him and destroy him. Some critics have assigned Helena the full blame, as Domain does, for the robots' destruction: 'Man disappears from the face of the earth because Helena cannot mind her own business.'[7] One can, however, interpret her role as somewhat similar to Eve's in the version of the Fortunate Fall, for the robots are forced, in their struggle to survive 'in terror and pain' to evolve into human beings. The Brothers Čapek apparently saw their play's ending as quite hopeful, stressing, as it does, the importance of procreation for humanity.[8] 'Only human beings can procreate, renew life, increase. Restore. Restore everything as it was' (p. 94), Alquist urges the robots at the end. And in turn they respond 'Teach us to have children so that we may love them' (p. 95). The crux of this play lies in reproduction and childbearing – the main role of woman, the role man would take from her so that he could fully dominate the world, and the one way of giving humanity a future.

R.U.R., therefore, ends on a somewhat hopeful note. Eduardo Pavlovsky's one-act absurdist version of man's dehumanization, with its Brechtian multi-media stage and screen combination, is much less so. The rational grapples with the irrational in this drama: the two main characters, Mr Casoq and Mr Ronald, are literally thrown on stage; they burp and cough and desperately try to interpret these noises, recite long autobiographical monologues, repeat meaningless questions, and even count the number of holes in the ceiling as they vainly endeavor to communicate with each other. But from the beginning of the play there are marked hints of its subtext about woman's private threat of loss. The set itself calls for nothing more than two beds placed squarely in the middle of the stage, symbolic of sex and procreation. Mr Ronald's reminiscences also focus on domestic conflicts with specific sexual implications: he remembers how his cousin Ernest had come 'para comunicarnos que su esposa Janet lo había abandonado. Mi madre trató de consolarlo . . . Pero fue en vano. . . .' ('to tell us that his wife Janet had left him. My mother tried to comfort him . . . But it was in vain . . .')[9] This incident provokes several skeletons to come tumbling out of the family closet, among them that Ernesto's father was impotent and that his real father was an uncle of his mother's. The squabble erupts into a fight and the mother hurls at Ernesto the dreaded epithet 'Cornudo', cuckold (reinforced by the word's projection onto the screen above the stage), evoking the hated and feared symbol of woman, man's property, escaping his control. Meanwhile Casoq reads aloud cards, many of which echo the stereotypical roles women play – as lovers, as objects for sexual gratification: 'A mi querido. Un adiós definitivo de tu mujer. Janet . . . A mi adorado amor. Un abrazo de adiós. Rebeca.' ('To my beloved. A final goodbye from your wife. Janet . . . To my adored love. With all my love, goodbye. Rebecca.' p. 65). Both letters also echo the theme of woman escaping man's restriction. They serve not only to reinforce these ideas but, because they are letters, and letters of farewell, serve to distance and objectify women, as the scientists did to Helena.

Thus the stage is well prepared when a real woman character appears – or rather, like Mr Ronald, is thrown on stage. Like Helena, she is a type, a universal Woman; unlike her, she is never given a name but simply called 'la señora', 'the woman'. Like Helena also, she is well versed in the traditional role of sex object. She plays it so masterfully, in fact, that she needs no supporting male to play it with. When she enters, the men freeze, and she launches into an elaborate soliloquy, at first confessing her crime of murdering her two children. Then, brusquely, her tone changes; she begins to show interest in them as men, fulfilling the stereotype that women see and judge men as potential partners. She flatters them, teases them, and flirts with them, all the while carrying on the conversation as if they were speaking with her, inserting pauses in the appropriate places, reacting with gestures and expressions to their imagined declarations. This is only too manifestly an ironic treatment of traditional male–female relationships: we hear what we want to hear, and we invent if something is lacking. Finally her feigned dialogue with Mr Ronald comes to its inevitable conclusion. She shudders in a imaginary embrace, protests, writhes, pretends to kiss him passionately, lifts her clothes up with one hand and pulls them down with another, and falls on the bed, murmuring (most astutely) 'Todo esto me parece un sueño. Sí, mi amor . . .' ('All of this seems just like a dream. Yes, my love . . .' p. 75). Woman's role as sexual object, willing no matter what the circumstance, is thus firmly established in this play. The subsequent scenes reinforce it. Various combinations of the trio appear in bed together (Casoq and the woman in bed, Ronald in the other bed on stage; Ronald and the woman half in bed, half on the floor, Casoq holding a gun on them, all three in bed together, all holding guns), which emphasizes the motif of sexual control and domination by violence already hinted at in the play. As with the unnatural sexual symbolism of six men to one woman in *R.U.R.*, these scenes offer a perverted view of sexuality and domination.

Due to the very interchangeability of the characters, however, these scenes also suggest their common guilt, the universality of their wrongs. For all are guilty of some heinous crime: the woman of infanticide, Casoq of racist bombings, and Ronald for the rape of a twelve-year-old girl. This latter is especially significant, since rape is the classical crime of anger against women. It is at this point that we first see the robot appear, thrown on stage in exactly the same manner as the humans. Its entrance unleashes in them a storm of rage and hatred which they direct at it, beating it ferociously and blaming it for the crimes they have committed. It is noteworthy that the woman attacks it in precisely the same way she killed her children, by stabbing it over and over again. Her mirror-image infanticide certainly demonstrates her loss of humanity, but it might also suggest her symbolic final rejection of the role of mother. Ronald, too recognizes that his crime stems in part from playing his entire life as he would a role in an absurdist play; in a game:

Me lanzaron a un mundo que nunca pude entender y yo aprendí las reglas de este gran circo horrible, despiadado. Y empecé a jugar a este juego y siempre gané. ¡Aprendí las reglas, Papá! ¡Tu me las enseñaste! . . . ¡Pero solo aprendí las reglas! ¡Y eso no bastaba! ¡Eso no bastaba para entender el resto! En mi juego había sólo una clase de reglas, pero no me enseñaste las otras. ¿Como podía saber yo que dentro del hombre existían todas las posibilidades? (p. 83)

(They threw me into a world that I could never come to understand, and I learned the rules of this horrible, merciless circus called life. And I began to play the game and I always won. I learned all the rules, Papa! You taught them to me! . . . But I only learned the rules of the game – and that wasn't enough! It wasn't enough to let me understand anything else! In my game there was only one set of rules, but you didn't teach me there might be other ones. How was I supposed to know that there were so many possibilities for human beings?)

Pavlovsky thus makes it clear that the roles imposed upon both men and women are mutually confining, damaging, and ultimately fatal. As if to crystallize this idea, all three briefly turn into mechanical dolls, chanting that they indeed have 'perdido la esencia del hombre' ('lost the essence of humanity').

All the more significantly, then, the woman is the only one of the three who cannot evolve back into human status. The two men surround her, menacing her with cruel questions, calling her vicious names, commanding her to speak out and confess her crimes. Equal before in guilt, she is now singled out for punishment. Having lost her voice, she cannot confront the men with their own deeds, and she falls to her knees, desperately gesticulating, groaning, and weeping as they progressively subjugate her. Yet again the very role established for her in the play is taken away from her. The two men do not compel her to go to bed with them but rather force her to use it as a place of refuge: she crawls underneath to hide from their violent threats against her. When the two try to pull her out, there emerges instead a full-sized robot. As with *Frankenstein*, we are privy to another twisted birth myth. But this is much more than simply 'el nacer en un mundo absurdo' ('being born into a world of absurdity'),[10] as one critic has commented. Woman has been displaced in this play, and replaced by a robot, which the two hail as 'el hijo del futuro' ('the child of the future'). They have succeeded in dominating her. Though she was no worse a criminal than they, she remains, as the elaborate scene of her role as sex object made evident, utterly subject to their desires and purposes, and is finally forced to relinquish her existence altogether. The threat of the robot to the woman – and to humanity – is worse than that of *R.U.R.* The final scene, wherein the stage is inundated with robots, suggests the very real fear that if woman does become entirely dominated by man, the robots will indeed take over – for we will have become them.

These two plays, then, deal with modern technology's threat, symbolized by the robot, to dehumanize mankind. But they also present us with a fascinating subtext about women's own private menace: the robot, the improved helpmeet man has created to circumvent nature and the need for woman, so that he may dominate her entirely. Yet, to return to a previous example, the recent film *Short Circuit*, wherein the heroine fights for the survival of the robot, would seemingly present us with a contradiction of this. Upon closer examination, however, this paradox becomes merely the same idea in a different guise. The heroine Stephanie is a classic earth-mother figure – the overwhelming quantity and variety of pets she keeps makes this quite clear. Actively hostile to science, which she sees, like Helena, as barren and destructive, she protects and even embraces the robot 'Number Five' not because it is a robot but because, since it has been magically transformed by a stroke of lightning, it is alive and human – as it demonstrates by its sexual innuendoes and its burgeoning sense of humor. Its evolution into a human of sorts is in fact what motivates the scientists to pursue it, to wrest it from her, and to do everything they can to destroy it. It is no longer their project if it is human; it no longer remains under their control. Its humanity, its link with a woman utterly negate their so-called 'scientific' purposes (and the portrait of modern science in this film, despite the malapropian wit of the Indian scientist, is very black). Hence Number Five fights against the scientists alongside of Stephanie, and just barely escapes. Then, too, the movie's conventional ending, which places Stephanie squarely in the arms of one of the scientists, does nothing to reassure us about the prospects of human existence. Stephanie will remain subject to man's control, just as the women in *R.U.R.* and *El Robot*, though she escapes their fate of falling prey to the new Eve man has created for himself – the robot.

NOTES

1 Ellen Moers, 'Female Gothic', in *The Endurance of Frankenstein: Essays on Mary Shelley's Novel*, ed. George Levine and U. C. Knoepflmacher (Berkeley, Los Angeles and London: University of California Press, 1979), pp. 79–81.

2 George Levine, 'The Ambiguous Heritage of *Frankenstein*', in The Endurance of Frankenstein,p. 8.

3 Martin Tropp, *Mary Shelley's Monster* (Boston, 1976), p. 52, quoted in Levine, 'The Ambiguous Heritage of *Frankenstein*', pp. 16–17.

4 The Brothers Čapek, *R.U.R.*, in *R.U.R. and The Insect Play* (London: Oxford University Press, 1961), p. 37. Further references to the play will be given in parentheses in the text.

5 William Harkins, *Karel Čapek* (New York and London: Columbia University Press, 1962), p. 94.

6 Ibid., p. 85.

7 V. Černý, *Karel Čapek* (Prague, 1936), p. 15, quoted in Harkins, *Karel Čapek*, p. 93.

8 Harkins, *Karel Čapek*, p. 86 and p. 90.

9 Eduardo Pavlovsky, *El Robot*, in *Teatro de vanguardia* (Buenos Aires: Cuadernos de Siroco, 1966), pp. 63–4. Further references will be given in parentheses in the text.

10 George O. Schanzer, ed., in introduction to *El teatro vanguardista de Eduardo Pavlovsky* (Madrid: Gráficas Julián Benita, 1980), p. 14.

The matter with manners: the New Woman and the problem play*

CATHERINE WILEY

If woman, as Shaw asserted, is the product of theatre convention,[1] how can she be acted on stage? Would the effort be redundant; that is, would the formal representation of an entity which depends on the formality of representation for its very existence, its definition, be anything more than the trivial replacement of one substitute for another? The answer to this apparent problem (for what is the Woman Problem but one of appearances?) lies between, or more exactly, outside the comfortable absolutes of yes or no. When Luce Irigaray entitles the first chapter of her feminist revision of western patriarchal ideology 'The Blind Spot of an Old Dream of Symmetry',[2] she is reminding us of Freud's, and by association all his sons' and fathers'', inability to look at woman unless she is represented, a disability mirrored in Shaw's statement. The Victorian woman had the actor's art forced upon her – social acceptance was only guaranteed by the sincere performance of conventional femininity – and thus the woman on stage was a player, a liar, and a fake enacted by another player, liar, and fake. The New Woman phenomenon, which for the purposes of my discussion I will interpret as a feminist-inspired political attack on the double standard of sexual morality, was a reaction against this performative aspect of women's lives, but when the New Woman herself became the object of performance, she fared no better than any woman imagined by conventional men. She could not be conceived by the male playwright, nor subsequently by his audience, until he translated her into what *he* desired the New Woman to be – 'new' enough to revive his own interest in the sexual pursuit of women, but traditional enough to be condemned for 'unfeminine' behaviour. He could not, in fact, see her until he had devised his own image of her and placed it onto that most literal field of representation, the stage.

Theatre, like woman's recognized existence in the world, depends upon convention: the actor substituting him or herself for a fictional character is

* A draft of this paper was read at the *Themes in Drama* International Conference held at the University of California, Riverside, in February 1987.

an act which must be performed with the spectator's consent. If we did not recognize and identify the actor as a person playing a role, we would not enjoy the performance as we do; one reason for our pleasure is the power of naming we exercise on the performer. In the same way, woman is 'enjoyed' only when she is named by man – identified as not-man, or Other, she is safely encased in mystery and thus kept on the periphery of the power-holding community. As soon as the actor began to look like us in terms of dress, gesture, and language, with the rise of naturalism in the late nineteenth-century theatre; or more importantly, like the kind of privileged insider we the audience desired not only to *look* like, but to *be*, the conventions of naming the performer as positively Other began to break down. The problem of distorted representation, however, became more acute as the woman on stage appeared less and less distinguishable from the woman who applauded her; and men, as playwrights, critics, and spectators, continued to see woman – including the New Woman – as they wanted her to be, ascribing to her the behavior and language of passive, pretty, empty femininity. Even when a woman was at the center of the plot, she was not allowed to speak for herself and the spectator's interest in her lay in how she was considered and treated by the men surrounding her. Despite an apparently novel plot focus, the problem play in England offered only a formal, conservative response to the challenges addressing well-established theatre conventions and newly established social conventions, challenges raised by Ibsen on the one hand and by the increasing violence of the suffrage movement on the other. Ibsen's women characters and the suffragettes, both outward aspects of a more general upheaval stemming from industrialization and its attendant social alterations (most notably the rush of women into the factories) precipitated the infamous Woman Question and its answer in the New Woman phenomenon. As noted above, the problem play concerned itself exclusively with this question, and seemed to favor a critical examination of the double standard used as a marker to distinguish the acceptability of male and female behavior. This issue, so central to the suffragettes' demands for women's rights, found itself deprived of political implications in the theatre; instead it was translated into a debate over how much sexuality, either overt or implied, good manners could tolerate. Instead of utilizing either the 'woman with a past' or the New Woman as a tool for pertinent social commentary, playwrights tended to use her to make genteel jokes at the sobriety of social conventions.

Playwrights could not afford, it seems, to offend too overtly the spectators who patronized them. As Raymond Williams points out, because the theatre audience in late-Victorian England was composed of a recently financially empowered middle class aspiring to what it defined as 'Society', theatres had to represent this imagined society favorably, that is, conventionally.

Indeed the general character of the 'questioning' in the problem plays of Society drama is in the end strictly suggestive. The basic reason is that the conventions, alike of the structure of feeling and of the form, are restricted to the uneasy terms of social integration. No sense of any life or any idea beyond the terms of this displayed society can be dramatically established; not even any strictly bourgeois viewpoint, since this is overlaid and compromised by the preoccupation with 'Society' (there is markedly less frankness about money, for example, than even earlier in the century).[3]

If the drama proved squeamish about a topic as impersonal as money, there was little chance that women and their physical and political rights would receive any more of a hearing. As plays dealt less and less with potentially offensive topics, though, more and more middle- and upper-class women were allowed to watch them.[4] What they must have seen were yet further instructions on how to behave, not like women, but ladies, so as to maintain the precarious social position their husbands had bought for them. The New Woman, of course, was hardly respectable in most people's eyes, and thus when she was allowed on stage at all it was, as Shaw so ironically proves with his army of 'unconventional' women characters, in the form of caricature and exaggeration. She was not portrayed as anyone women should aspire to be; she taught instead the lesson of the bad, dangerous, reprehensible example. This conventional treatment of feminism served no more than to mirror popular opinion of suffragettes and other independently-minded women as either immoral, ridiculous, or both – which was (and is) a convenient way to ignore them.

The conservatism of the playgoer, then, tended to uphold the conservatism in the plays he or she went to see, and thus the problem play genre was itself a staged reconstitution of the status quo, as well as a denial of any impact the flesh-and-blood New Woman might be having in the world beyond the theatre. It will be useful to arrange the four plays compared in this paper on a political scale, keeping in mind the political origins of the New Woman movement: Henry Arthur Jones' *Mrs Dane's Defence* (1900) as conservative; Arthur Wing Pinero's *The Second Mrs Tanqueray* (1893) as liberal; Shaw's *Mrs Warren's Profession* (written 1894, privately performed in London 1902) as radical; and finally Elizabeth Robins's *Votes for Women* (1907) as feminist. This scale is convenient if we consider political categories under the ethics of exclusion: conservatives tend to be at the center of power and are the most anxious to maintain their position by reasserting the structure of the status quo – renaming it again and again; liberals are further from the center but agree that it is the most desirable place to be; while radicals and feminists are successively more isolated on the margins, and divided as to whether the center is attractive or not.

The four plays mirror this movement from inside to outside, both in their attitude toward and definition of the 'problem', and in their acquiescence toward conventional stage techniques as a method of expressing this problem. All of the plays are 'well-made' in terms of plot; and their 'conservative ethos', which never exhorts the audience to reform itself and its institutions,[5] is reflected most glaringly (barring Robins's work) in their women characters. The 'woman with a past' stereotype is always the plot vehicle, but because she is used in a drama more concerned with appearance than reality, more interested in manners than the matter behind them, she is subordinated to her predicament. The audience, like the men in the play, is more interested in what she did and does – how she behaves herself – than in who she is, since she is represented as the empty space men perceive women to be in real life. The real-life spectator is also treated differently in each of the four plays; either as a legitimate member of the society on stage, or as an applicant to that society who has retained an unbiased ability to criticize its moral flaws. Jones puts his spectators clearly on the side of Right, the society that creates and upholds unbendable rules, thus placating the middle-class desire for membership in a community defined by the strictness of its standards. Both Pinero and Shaw include their audience in the power structure informing the play while simultaneously demanding whether or not that inclusion is ethically desirable. The irony becomes most evident in the manner of presentation – the metaphorical fourth wall of naturalism so definitively keeping the spectator off stage. Only Robins, by moving out of the drawing-room and into the street, invites the audience to actively comment upon the content of her play. Everyone has access to the suffrage rallies held in open spaces like Trafalgar Square; and this access implies an ethical responsibility of making use of it which is absent from the other plays. *Votes for Women* argues that once women recognize a common enemy in the conventional, power-less non-person men expect them to be, their drawing-rooms and country estates will remain morally uncomfortable places to be. The problem in society drama thus parallels a more urgent social problem; one which early feminists and would-be New Women unmasked and which we are still in the process of, as it were, unmanning: woman's lack of identity will continue to define her until she understands that her very existence, not her actions, not her past, is unacceptable to the man who represents her in his own image.

II

In his preface to *Mrs Dane's Defence*, Michael R. Booth describes Jones as a conservative anti-Ibsenite who often satirized the New Woman and social philanthropy in his plays.[6] His one attempt to dramatize the double standard of morality by pitting an Oedipally obsessed village curate against an independent and dissolute woman in *Michael and His Lost Angel* (1895) was an embarrassment which survived only eleven performances. The conventionality of *Mrs Dane* (1900) proved more popular, which indicates that audiences preferred to see a play reflect society without judging it. The play's setting is Sunningwater, a village whose name suggests the type of idyllic location where the leisured class goes to sun itself, a place inhabited by the kind of people we would like to be. By the second line, in which a Mrs Bulsom-Porter accuses another woman, who is off-stage and unseen, of having a past to keep hidden, we know the kind of play we are to witness. A newcomer to the neighborhood, an outsider trying to invite herself into a favored environment by marrying Sunningwater's most eligible bachelor, is suspected of a scandalous past because someone thinks she looks like someone else. Her appearance, then, even before she appears on stage, is of questionable legitimacy: is she who she says she is and will her manner confirm her words, or is she an imposter, an actress playing a virtuous role?

Like all permissible New Women (permissible because they are only as new as men allow them to be), Mrs Dane's attraction lies in her difference, her 'newness' which distinguishes her from the Mrs Bulsom-Porters of the world – the type of staunch moral watchdog whom everybody both detests and fears. Mrs Dane has a pretty face, soft voice, and charming manner, making her the immediate enemy of all women who must consider their worth in terms of whether or not they can attach themselves to an acceptable man. The Vienna episode, in which Mrs Dane may or may not be implicated, is explained in appropriately theatrical terms: the 'dramatic personae' are the charming and devoted husband, wife, and governess engaged in a conventional scandal whose final curtain falls on the wife's suicide, the husband's insanity, and the governess's mysterious disappearance. The problem exposed in *Mrs Dane's Defence* is that of the invisible woman: can Mrs Dane identify herself as not being the unknown governess; in other words can she perform what is expected of all women – self-naming by denial, by saying not who she is, but who she is not? Her problem is not one of personal history, as Mrs Bulsom-Porter (and the audience) would define it; the truth of whether or not she sinned on the Continent is irrelevant compared to the fact that she has been named a sinner, since her history is really that of all women. Circumstances have forced Mrs Dane to change her identity from scandalous ex-governess with an illegitimate child to respectable widow. She even admits near the end of the play, of the cousin whose name she borrowed, 'I took her name and became her' (p. 394), but this gesture of substitution is common to all women who accept the names – either as old-fashioned or 'new' – men give them.

Mrs Dane is an attractive woman but she is not an attractive character. We suspect her as soon as she speaks to her lover, telling him she is twenty-seven years old while the stage direction preceding her speech informs us that she is at least twenty-eight, or the 'femme de trente ans', a dangerous age for the best of women. Jones shows her to be the kind of woman who says one thing and does another; she is an actress whose manner does not match her intention as she warns her lover, Lionel (Lal) that she may be too old for him and may even not be all she seems.

> *Lal.* You shan't persuade me that you aren't exactly what I want you to be.
> *Mrs Dane.* (*Shows great delight.*) Perhaps my best self isn't very far from that. But then we have so many different selves.
> *Lal.* You have but your own self, and that is the one I know.
>
> (p. 354)

The tainted woman's self-confessed ability to suit her identity to the occasion is the playwright's proof that she is indeed dangerous and reprehensible. But his stage direction belies him: Mrs Dane's delight comes from her realization that she *is* what her lover wants – she appears conventional enough for him to love her, and his desire for a conventional wife makes her that person and gives her an identity.

When Lal turns his back, however, and she is out of his vision, Mrs Dane behaves furtively and exposes herself to us with a gesture of annoyance and despair as the 'truth' of her 'identity' becomes more complicated in her cross-examination by Sir Daniel, the judge who is Mrs Bulsom-Porter's more palatable counterpart as the upholder of society. Sir Daniel is a good man, despite his youthful love for a married woman who gave him up to save her son's life, the son who is incidentally the man Mrs Dane plans to marry. The judge has absolved himself of his amorous indiscretion by adopting Lionel at the boy's parents' death, thus playing the same role of substitute that Mrs Dane is so desperate to succeed at. His role of step-father seems to be more natural than her imitation of a good woman will ever be. They are all actors, all subject to misinterpretation, but because Sir Daniel occupies the center of Sunningwater he can safely judge, and interpret, those who can approach the center and those who must stay on the margins. The parish vicar, Canon Bonsey, enjoys a similar position, although he is blamed for initially introducing, and believing in, Mrs Dane.

> . . . when a delightful lady comes to church, and subscribes regularly to all the parish charities, and has a perfect mastery of the piano, and is evidently a very dear sweet creature in every way, and a gentlewoman, I don't think it's the duty of the clergyman to ask her for references as if she were a housemaid, eh?
>
> (p. 365)

Of course not, it would be bad manners, since Mrs Dane appears to possess Christian piety, money to prove it, ladylike talent, and gentility, just as if she were one of them. But Jones insists that *we* know better; *we* are not duped by the manners which effectively mask her guilt in view of the other characters. We are instructed by society's insiders that to gain admittance to their circle we must behave accordingly, but the best elements of that society, like Sir Daniel, insist that our behavior should show us as we are; it is not enough to act respectably.

Jones uses Sir Daniel's position as judge to validate his role as lawmaker and protector of moral values, but it is his social position as aristocratic landowner which allows him to define the community. He asks of Lady Eastney, who along with Lionel is convinced that Mrs Dane is innocent of the Vienna scandal on the basis of her behavior:

> If you were guilty don't you think you would try to act exactly the same way? And whether you succeeded would depend, not so much upon your guilt or your innocence, as upon your self-control, and how you cultivated the woman's gift for acting.
>
> (p. 369)

Thus women and actors are delegated to the margins as criminals, but theirs is a crime of substitution, of pretence, which depends for its success on their observers' acquiescence. If Mrs Dane's acting has succeeded until the judge unmasks her in act 4 (with an unmannerly, or unmanly lack of composure: 'Woman, you're lying!' (p. 409), it is due less to her skill than to Sunningwater's desire to believe that someone who looks and acts like them is the same as them. Had Jones allowed his audience to believe in Mrs Dane, instead of seeing her as a stereotypically conniving and unfeminine New Woman, her expulsion from the community would have been unsettling, and the play might not have enjoyed its 200-odd performances. Because the playwright's outlook is conservative, he favors the center of society and respects the ambitions of his paying public to be a part of it, and by doing so he must unambiguously condemn the imposter. Mrs Dane's past is not the play's problem; it is rather her attempt to include herself in an exclusive world by performing an act of empowerment which is radically incompatible to the well-mannered woman: naming herself.

As a liberal, the creator of Paula Tanqueray is less liberal with his audience and more lenient with his main character, although her efforts at self-identification are finally thwarted as decisively as Mrs Dane's. Paula's worst fault, one for which others can forgive her even while she cannot forgive herself, is impropriety; and thus unlike Mrs Dane she is a good woman whose bad manners do not accurately reflect what is beneath them. In *The Modern Stage and Other Worlds*, Austin Quigley focuses his suggestive reading of *The Second Mrs Tanqueray* on the incompatibility of Aubrey's effort to make an exception to social conventions for the woman he loves and the play's upholding of those same conventions; in other words, bending the rules should not be confused with changing them.[7] Like Jones, Pinero paints an unflattering portrait of what he thinks the New Woman looks like, because he cannot approve of what he suspects – how independent and threatening – she really is. Mrs Dane's installation in the Sunningwater stronghold would be tantamount to abolishing the assumptions concerning good and bad, who's out and who's in, by which it has established itself; and while Aubrey conscientiously removes his unsuitable wife from his own self-enclosed social circle, he evidently satisfies his conscience without easing hers. Quigley's argument that the well-made structure of Pinero's drama necessitates at the same time a conventional plot resolution and the dismissal of any original treatment of the woman question the characters may have initially invited is a useful one for my own discussion. If forgiveness and the desire to be forgiven perpetuate the social standards dictating what behavior needs absolution, they also solidify the man-made outlines within which women are perceived, by themselves and the rest of the world. Women are admitted into the male perspective only as objects whose limits and limitations are sharply defined. 'A forgiven Paula', in Quigley's words, 'in ongoing need of forgiveness, remains like a splinter under the skin of this society, constantly in the process of being expelled no matter how deeply it inserts itself. Forgiveness is not, and cannot translate into, acceptance.'[8] This is because the act of forgiving is innately hierarchical; the moral person excusing the immoral offender of something they both agree needs to be excused. Nothing changes, however, unless one of the actors removes the moral stigma from whatever has been done and makes forgiveness, and the power of bestowing it, irrelevant.

Paula's suicide must then be seen as a self-defeating act of acquiescence to the social standards she cannot imagine herself living up to; and although it is the opposite of Hedda Gabler's triumphant liberation from those standards,[9] we might echo Judge Brack's condemnation of it: 'People don't do such things.' Not the right kind of people, not the kind of people who renounce melodramatic denouements in favor of more sedate and life-like resolutions to their problems of performance. The untimely deaths of melodrama may be tragic, but they are hardly respectable and thus cannot be taken seriously. It is Paula's refusal to take herself seriously that finally does her in; she acts like a performer in the Music Hall and must play out her role accordingly. Pinero implies, though, that his heroine's frivolity masks not a scornful attitude towards her superiors, but a well-founded fear that she will never be able to alter her position with regards to them; she is fallen and must remain so. She cautions Aubrey to keep her happy at all times:

> I know that I couldn't swallow a second big dose of misery. I know that if I ever felt wretched again – truly wretched – I should take a leaf out of Connie Tirlemont's book. You remember? They found her—(*with a look of horror*).[10]

Women of Paula and Connie Tirlemont's type have no response to real problems other than over-acting; and so while we are expected to pity the woman who has sullied her past, Pinero does not go so far as to ask us to respect her or to see ourselves in her in any credible way. Although one reviewer claimed that Paula is an 'Ibsenitish Hedda Gabler shrew' and wondered why she doesn't get whipped,[11] William Archer's initial praise for the play's 1893 opening was a more popular interpretation of an apparently daring enterprise. As he wrote in *The World* on 31 May:

> Paula's irritability, though partly constitutional no doubt, is embittered and rendered morbid by social slights, isolation, idleness, and the frigid politeness of Ellean – in short, it is not only natural, but almost inevitable, and belongs to the very essence of the situation.[12]

As in all naturalistic drama, then, the character is crucially related to her environment and she behaves badly primarily because she is mistreated by society, a stage society in which, because it is depicted so realistically, we are all implicated.

Archer would later retract his pronouncement of the liberating possibilities of Pinero's work, following Shaw's dismissal of Pinero as a playwright who disguised his moral conventionality with stage naturalism. In an 1895 review of another Pinero success about an ostensibly New Woman, *The Notorious Mrs Ebbsmith,* Shaw wrote:

> His performance as a thinker and social philosopher is simply character acting in the domain of authorship, and can impose only on those who are taken in by character acting on the stage. It is only the make-up of an actor who does not understand his part, but who knows – because he shares – the popular notion of its externals.[13]

And Samuel Hynes reminds us that no one guilty of an honest attempt to disrupt the status quo would be granted a knighthood, as Pinero was in 1909.[14]

Shaw's remarks apply to Paula Tanqueray as well to as Pinero. She does not understand her disadvantage in any terms other than those the envied and unyielding society provides her with, so her problematic existence as a Victorian woman is secondary to her lack of manners and the acts she has performed that separate her from her husband and his daughter. The all-pervasive problem of woman, however, infects the play from beginning to end. Even before Aubrey announces his marriage plans to his astonished friends in the opening scene, he discloses a stereotypical distrust of the wife as intruder; not only his intended, but any wife. 'You know a marriage often cools friendships . . . a worm [begins] to eat its way into those hearty, unreserved, prenuptial friendships; a damnable constraint sets in and acts like a wasting disease . . .' (p. 87). Worm, damnable, wasting disease – familiar misogynist names that eloquently express, even while they attempt to hide, assumptions concerning the emasculating power of the unmanly sex. Cayley Drummle, Aubrey's best friend who has missed the farewell dinner, begs the other men to forgive his bad manners: 'A harsh word from anybody would unman me' (p. 89). Are his manners, and his peers' forgiveness of their lapse, so intimately connected to his manliness? His friends, of course, would not dream of dismantling his masculinity; and as Drummle is unmarried he may never have to face that challenge. Women, especially aspiring New Women, unman men, so men must enforce the manners that keep the sexes in their separate but unequal (and safe) spheres.

Drummle, the self-defined spectator of life, is the raisonneur of the play and the character who, by his own admission ('I'm . . . nothing more than a man at a play' (p. 96)), is closest to Pinero's perception of the audience and our perception of ourselves.[15] Eminently affable, he reasonably sees everybody's point of view while stalwartly protecting his own. He stands midway between Paula, whom he admits to having met on a yacht when she was known as Mrs Jarman, and the priggish Ellean, Aubrey's child who resembles his piously frigid wife and who he hopes will relent and come to live with him; 'come to life, as it were' (p. 93). Both women represent unattractive standards of prescribed womanhood: one unacceptably loose and thus too flagrantly 'new', the other unacceptably restrained, and neither compatible with the other. Because he is a man, and unmarried at that, Drummle is able to enjoy the fun provided by Paula's society while espousing the moral virtues Ellean has artificially adopted while secluded in a convent. He embodies the double standard; to reject it would be to lose his place in the society which has constructed the standard.

All of the characters, in fact, subscribe to this standard, and while Aubrey berates its unfairness, neither he nor the playwright is prepared to change it. Ellean unwittingly articulates the play's real problem, for which, as advocates of the New Woman realized, there was only the glimmer of a solution in the Victorian women's movement, when she tells Paula: 'It's so difficult to be what one is not' (p. 103). It is in fact, as Aubrey learns to his discredit, impossible. Paula cannot become the kind of woman he thought he could make her by improving her surroundings, and her past constantly threatens to sully the kind of woman he thinks his daughter is. He complains of Paula:

> . . . her words, acts even, have almost lost their proper significance for her, and
> seem beyond her control   (p. 102)

and later he tells her,

> You're not mistress any longer of your thoughts or your tongue. Why, how
> often, sitting between you and Ellean, have I seen her cheeks turn scarlet as
> you've rattled off some tale that belongs by right to the club or smoking room!
>   (p. 121)

Paula personifies the actor's nightmare of walking on stage and realizing that the wrong script has been memorized; and thus every line she speaks will be ridiculously inappropriate and out of its anticipated context. She has not, in other words, perfected what Sir Daniel in *Mrs Dane's Defence* called 'the woman's gift for acting'; a histrionic player, she belongs on a lower class of stage, where people like the Orreyds (Cockney (h)orrids) purchase their cheap entertainment.

But by becoming the second, or second-class Mrs Tanqueray, Paula has divorced herself from her former friends. They bore her, she bores them, and since Ellean will not allow her to fulfill the role of loving step-mother, she is left decidedly outside both of the social circles she has tried to incorporate herself into. She learns that real society circles cannot be imitated, even by the most polished of actors. Men, like Cayley Drummle and the soldier Hugh Ardale, seem to be allowed to vascillate comfortably between the circles, and be forgiven, but women do not have this choice. Before she commits the ultimate in bad taste by killing herself, Paula blames Ellean, another woman, for not taking her part: 'She's a regular woman, too. She could forgive *him* [Ardale] easily enough – but me! That's just a woman!' (p. 137). It was not forgiveness that she required from the other woman, but recognition, a recognition that as women they were both unforgivable, and doomed to enact the impossible extremities of perfect virgin or perfect whore. The New Woman (who Paula, of course, never becomes) had to understand this recognition as a prerequisite for independence from the male-defined image of the acceptable woman, but what the first three plays in this paper illustrate is the desirability of maintaining the conventional feminine image. Until Elizabeth Robins produced her own plays, women were not to see a really new representation of themselves on stage, despite the growing social criticism, among both women and men, of the double standard.

The complementarity of the virgin-whore syndrome and the double standard are also central to Shaw's *Mrs Warren's Profession*, and while he implicates his audience in the play's problem to a degree Pinero could not approach, a lack of recognition of the position of women keeps the play from being more than a Shavian revision of the unanswered woman question. The first problem in considering Mrs Warren and her daughter is how to assess Shaw's peculiar brand of feminist theory. According to Margot Peters in *Bernard Shaw and the Actresses*, his New Woman characters are stereotypes of the dominant women (like his mother) he feared rather than admired;[16] but what they are closer to are men in disguise. Vivie Warren may epitomize the ideal 'unwomanly woman' of *The Quintessence of Ibsenism*, but her addiction to the work of calculating numerical figures coupled with the nauseating baby talk in which she and Frank Gardner flirt make her less attractive than her mother. That Shaw attempted to make Vivie the play's hero illustrates his avid distaste for physical passion, a quirk informing 'The Womanly Woman' chapter of *The Quintessence*, in which Shaw's biggest complaint about women seems to be that they are not men. And yet he understood and publicly abhored women's inequality, to a degree. He writes:

> The sum of the matter is that unless Woman repudiate her womanliness, her duty to her husband, to her children, to society, to the law, and to everyone but herself, she cannot emancipate herself. But her duty to herself is no duty at all, since a debt is cancelled when the debtor and creditor are the same person.[17]

What Shaw offers is a superficial remedy to a problem much deeper than he cared to dig; the problem of women's lack of self-recognition which Mrs Warren and her daughter, despite their unconventional appearance, do nothing to alleviate.

Shaw may have successfully sabotaged the conventions of the well-made play with his effort to imitate Ibsen,[18] but characters like Mrs Warren and Vivie appear so conventionally unconventional that we cannot take them seriously. Vivie is described as 'an attractive specimen of the sensible, able, highly-educated young middle-class English woman',[19] surrounded by books and devoid of womanly manners – a perfect candidate for *The Philanderers'* Ibsen Club. Only the men in this play are concerned with correct behavior; they are the unsavory people we are supposed to recognize in ourselves. According to Martin Meisel, Shaw's

> strategy in the Unpleasant Plays is . . . to make audience-surrogates of the most self-righteous and honorable of his characters, those who stand closest to the audience in that their blamelessness seems to give them the right to conventional standards. These are the stage personages whom Shaw overwhelms with taint and sin.[20]

Introduced as a hard-nosed business-woman, Mrs Warren seems to share her daughter's healthy lack of respect for propriety, but as the play progresses she takes refuge in increasingly melodramatic displays of motherly outrage and self-pity. This makes her as tainted and contemptible as Paula Tanqueray in her efforts to be what she is not; her insistence on ingratiating herself into Vivie's 'honorable' company belies her moral conviction about the necessity for convention, for social rules any clever actor can play in order to win acceptance.

But Shaw respects only the women who have dispensed with convention. The following exchange, occurring midway through the play, exemplifies the playwright's ambivalence toward the femininity of his New Woman. Vivie has matured apparently free of any burdens of inheritance; nothing and no one has influenced her except her own choices, and the absence of an identifiable father makes it, fortunately in Shaw's view, impossible for her to marry. In this she is the opposite of her mother, whose adverse childhood circumstances serve as the excuse for her professional alliances – alliances which cannot be named in Vivie's polite society. As an imposter in that society, as the fallen woman who pretends to be someone else to achieve respectability, Mrs Warren reinforces the stereotype of the unidentifiable woman whose real self is best described as absent. Were that self to surface, it would immediately be disowned for the sake of social convention.

> *Mrs Warren. (Again raising her voice angrily)* Do you know who you're speaking to, Miss?
> *Vivie. (Looking across at her without raising her head from her book)* No. Who are you? What are you? . . . Everybody knows my reputation, my social standing, and the profession I intend to pursue. (p. 243)

Mrs Warren's response to this is a conventional one: it is unnatural for my own daughter to behave this way. We cannot sympathize with her, though, because she has behaved no better as a mother than Vivie has as a daughter, and tries to make up for her absence with a barrage of clichés about familiar duty. While Shaw might argue that Vivie is the only 'natural' character in the play because she has no duty to anyone but herself, and indulges in a natural inclination for passionless mathematics, she is hardly credible as a human being. Neither is she plausible, any more than Mrs Dane or Mrs Tanqueray were, as a New Woman.

The closing scene between mother and daughter is troubling not only because the playwright has proven that we are all to blame for Mrs Warren's profession by limiting women's economic choices, but because Vivie, his ideal and ideally free woman, remains so unattractive. She tells her adversary, with whom there is no possibility of reconciliation:

> You attacked me with the conventional authority of a mother: I defended myself with the conventional superiority of a respectable woman . . . People are always blaming their circumstances for what they are. I don't believe in circumstances. The people who get on this world are the people who get up and look for the circumstances they want, and if they can't find them, make them.
> (p. 246)

This speech is unpleasant for a number of reasons. Not only does it resound with social darwinism, but it shows that Vivie is either dishonest or ignorant about the highly favorable economic circumstances in which she has enjoyed her freedom of choice. Her superiority lies not in her repudiation of the false and debilitating femininity other women suffer under, but in her belief that she is no different than a man and can perpetuate the capitalist system (which oppresses women like her mother) as well as any male accountant. She is thus as devoid of identity as her mother, Paula Tanqueray, and Mrs Dane, since she looks like a woman yet is not one; and Shaw's answer to the woman question is unveiled as no answer at all. It is instead a dangerous suggestion that making the problem go away only necessitates making women disappear.

Bernard Shaw's connections with women were problematic at best. His relationship with the American actress responsible for incorporating Ibsen into the London theatre repertoire, Elizabeth Robins, has been well-documented. As Jane Marcus points out in her article 'Art and Anger', although men as prominent as Shaw and Henry James championed Robins when she enacted their ideal of the Ibsen woman, when she began to write and agitate for the rights of women off stage, when she fashioned herself into an actual New Woman, they ignored or belittled her efforts.[21] *Votes for Women*, her 'dramatic tract' as she christened it, spawned hundreds of similar plays before the First World War. While this effect may not attest to the literary or dramatic merits of the play, it does indicate an undeniable political success. Historians like Samuel Hynes dismiss *Votes for Women* and its author as 'a good but forgotten play by an interesting but forgotten woman'[22] without worrying about *why* what they say is true, but if we are to believe playwrights like Shaw who insist that theatre challenge social conventions, Robins and her work must be resurrected. The chivalrous Irishman's response to her firm rebuffs to his incessant flirtation was to dub her alternately St Elizabeth or the Puritan;[23] that she did not need and evidently did not want the amorous attention of better-known men set her apart from most other actresses of the time. But she had made her career as an Ibsen actress, a 'free-thinker', and while this title eventually kept her from getting hired for parts other than Ibsen types, it may have served to propel her off stage and into the political world.

Robins's understanding of women's social priorities, and more importantly her talent in articulating them, can only have come from her experience as an Ibsen actress. As a woman who had to fight, as most did in late-Victorian London, to earn a living in the legitimate theatre, she gained insight into the dishonest representation of women enfranchised by playwrights, actor–managers, and their audiences. The radical Norwegian, introduced to a small London audience with *A Doll's House* in 1889, offered female roles that were significantly different from their British counterparts, as Robins argued in her 'Ibsen and the Actress' lecture to the Royal Society of Arts, published by the Woolfs in 1928. Insisting on well-rehearsed ensemble productions so foreign to the conventional London star system, he was truly an actor's playwright; but even more he was a writer for actresses. Praising the first *Doll's House*, Robins attributed its success to 'the unstagey effect of the whole play . . . [which] made it, to eyes that first saw it in '89, less like a play than like a personal meeting – with people and issues that seized us and held us, and wouldn't let us go.'[24] Her own best-known play, *Votes for Women*, worked toward, and to some degree achieved, a similar effect in terms of presenting women's rights issues not by flamboyantly stereotypical characters, but by comparatively ordinary people, believable New Women among them. Robins modestly concedes her own success as the extraordinary Hedda Gabler and Hilda Wangel to the playwright, who did not ask his actresses to please their spectators, but to play to a potential universal audience with the power to realize, in the off-stage world, the lessons these women were teaching.

Unfortunately for intelligent, politicized actresses like Robins, Ibsen translations did not lead quickly to challenging female roles in the English drama; although Shaw created his own version of the New Woman, his roles went to those who accepted his favors. As Jane Marcus puts it:

> The only way [Robins] could have secured a theater of her own and plays as appealing to women as Ibsen's was to sell her body, as generations of actresses had done before her. When she refused a villa in St John's Wood, she gave up not only her future as an actress of genius, but her achievements, invisible now to the world. To Shaw goes praise for distilling the quintessence of Ibsenism although Elizabeth Robins' acting was the cup he drank it from.[25]

And so a potentially brilliant performer became what an anonymous critic called a 'propagoose', an aptly ironic insult illustrating both the seriousness with which Robins' new profession was taken and the very problem of women's inequality for which she was propagandizing. As a retired actress, Robins freed herself from the necessity of imitating stereotypes so inimical to her beliefs, but she also sacrificed the power, however perverse it may have been, of commanding admiring attention from men.[26]

The interest in *Votes for Women* lies as much in its manipulation of problem play conventions as in the lauded second act Trafalgar Square rally in which those conventions are abandoned altogether. Combining the national issues of the daily headlines with a plot structure borrowed from mainstream melodrama, Robins successfully demonstrated that theatre can be used as a political tool, as well as an effective advertisement for the New Woman ideology. Act 1 begins in a scene reminiscent of the openings of the plays discussed above: a country estate, a butler, the privileged class. The butler, however, 'walks with majestic port',[27] and Lady John has 'gone to fat', indicating that these characters may not be as enviable as they are usually considered to be. The emphasis in this act is concentrated on identifying the separate spheres of men and women: the men discuss politics and the issues of an upcoming election while the women converse on the more 'trivial' topics of marriage, destitute women, and the bad manners of the suffragettes which have finally succeeded in landing them in jail. The men's politics, in fact, concern nothing but who will get elected, as individuals take precedence over issues, while the women's conversation covers a myriad of social topics, all of which the audience would have been familiar with. Spectators also would have recognized the problem play story line: a prominent Conservative MP, Geoffrey Stonor, discovers on the eve of his marriage and a crucial election that the woman he had long ago impregnated and abandoned has invaded his fiancée's social circle at Wynnstay House, and is threatening to educate her about his past. The facts of his past, however, are of less import than their political implications; here the double standard is employed as a tool for the liberation and empowerment of women, not their condemnation.

Vida Levering (modelled after Sylvia Pankhurst), an occasional guest at

Wynnstay House with no real desire to become an insider there, must leave
shortly after her appearance, to give a speech espousing poor women's
housing and sanitation laws. Her response from the men is put best by Mr
Greatorex:

> I protest! Good Lord! What are the women of this country coming to? I *protest*
> against Miss Levering being carried off to discuss anything so revolting. Bless
> my soul! What can a woman like you *know* about it? . . . to be hailed out to talk
> about Public *Sanitation* forsooth! Why, God bless my soul, do you realize that's
> *drains*?   (p. 46)

Invoking the name of the almightiest of fathers, the astonished Greatorex
(big king) can only sputter that nice people don't talk about toilets and a
real woman would not even recognize the word. He infers that Miss
Levering is applying her beauty and charm to an unworthy cause against
her will, but he later asks her, 'If I gave you that much [8,000 pounds] for
your little projects, what would you give me?' (p. 48); in other words she is
too attractive to be credible in any other than a sexual manner. She is
evidently not one of the 'discontented old maids and hungry widows' (p. 47)
who want the vote; she is a 'nice creature' who simply needs a husband.

The house-guest is not, however, as nice as she looks. A fallen woman
carrying the scars of abortion and abandonment, her experience leads her
to the speaker's podium of the second act, where her well-mannered
demeanor is no longer necessary to mask the fury toward men that really
defines her. As Lady John remarks ('her mouth – always . . . as if she were
holding back something by main force', p. 51), appearances should be
deceiving to be political tools and the trick for a woman is learning when to
speak and when to smile. Vida's worst enemies, though, like that of every
New Woman, are not the man and men who oppress her, but the women
who share her inequality and relish it for the security it gives them. At the
end of the first act, Vida begins to teach Jean, the Scottish heiress with the
money and position to institute real parliamentary change, about the
causes behind the suffragettes' failure to improve their standing with the
government. She also implies, for the sake of Jean's ignorance, that winning
the vote might be the first step in keeping 'good' but lower-class girls from
unspeakable degradation at the hands of unscrupulous men. The ladies of
Wynnstay House are suitably shocked:

> *Mrs Heriot. (aside)* How little she minds all these horrors!
> *Lady John.* They turn me cold. Ugh! (*Rising, harassed.*) I wonder if she signed the
>   visitor's book!
>   (p. 51)

Vida's signature, the act of associating herself with the proper residents of
Wynnstay House, would put a name on the dreaded 'sex antagonism'
which ladies like Lady John would rather not identify. Allowing the
problems of poor women to be aired within the safe, expensive walls of

upper-class homes brings these problems, as it were, home. Vida has appealed to the others as women and asked them for a moment to suspend the wealthy woman's privilege to be ignorant and to realize that they are themselves as disenfranchised as those who need, for want of anything better, a public shelter to sleep in.

The public, portrayed as 'a few decent artisans, "beery" out-o'-works, young women of the Strand cashier class, business-like women, middle-class men, and weedy youths' (p. 61) is the focus of the second act. Robins's representation of the suffrage rally was critically admired for its realism: it is actually a compilation of transcripts from the rallies the author attended.[28] The crowd behaves much like a music-hall audience: laughing loudly, interrupting the speakers, hissing, and generally engaging in an honest political debate with the 'performers', who try to convince them that the women's vote will improve the life of the working class. As one 'working woman' speaker says:

> You say we women 'ave got no business servin' on boards and thinkin' about politics. Wot's *politics*?
> (*A derisive roar.*)
> It's just 'ousekeepin' on a big scale. 'Oo among you working men 'as the most comfortable 'omes? Those of you that gives yer wives yer wages.
> (*Loud laughter and jeers.*)
>
> (p. 61)

As Geoffrey Stonor learns, initially to his dismay and finally to his political advantage, women with the right to exercise a choice are not as dangerous as they appear. He even admits that 'However little they want to, women of our class will have to come into line' (p. 75); in other words, if society is not going to be threatened by women voting, the right kind of woman will have to learn the 'right' (Conservative) political line. The play ends on what could be considered a jarring note: Stonor appropriates the 'vote question' for the 'political dynamite' that will bring working-class men (who from the rally appear to favor votes for women) back into the Conservative camp from which they have been wooed, and assure himself of his re-election.

Vida Levering, on the other hand, seems to be left where she started – rankled by the memory of an aborted child to which she was never allowed to give a name. What she has won, of course, is a powerful adversary for the cause of women's rights, not so much in Stonor, but in Jean, a woman who is young enough to learn compassion for women less fortunate than herself and anger at the cause of their misfortune, and old enough to manipulate her husband's vote in parliament. Thus the play's title – '*Votes* for Women' – names a hope and a possibility which would take decades for New Women to realize, but which once named and pasted up and shouted aloud, was not going to disappear. The titles of the three other plays in my discussion stand in direct opposition to the name Robins chose for her work: all are names of married women which identify not them, but their husbands; and in the case of the women with a past, their married names are often literal forgeries like Mrs Dane, Mrs Jarman or Mrs Warren. The titles and names are, in effect, attributions of absence; signs which signify what is not there. Robins's work both on and off stage, like her New Women characters, was an attempt to fill this space of absence with a woman who was new because she had shaken off the manners and 'good name' men assigned her, and determined to name herself.

NOTES

1 The quote is actually: 'Woman, of whom we hear so much, is a stage invention', from a lecture entitled 'The Woman in Bernard Shaw's Plays', given by H. M. Walbrook in 1911 and ghost-written by Shaw. From Michael Holroyd, 'Women and the Body Politic', *The Genius of Shaw: A Symposium*, ed. Michael Holroyd (London: Hodder & Stoughton, 1979), pp. 167–83, quote p. 170.

2 Luce Irigaray, *Speculum of the Other Woman* (Ithaca: Cornell University Press, 1985), in which two long essays on Freud and Plato flank a short essay on Descartes; a 'speculum' shaped view of woman and the female.

3 Raymond Williams, 'Social Environment and Theatrical Environment: The Case of English Naturalism' in *English Drama: Forms and Development*, ed. Raymond Williams and Marie Axton (Cambridge University Press, 1977), p. 220.

4 This is an assertion for which I have no documentation, but it would make an interesting theatre history or sociology dissertation.

5 Joseph Donohue, 'Character, Genre, and Ethos in Nineteenth-Century British Drama', *Yale English Studies*, 9 (1979), 100.

6 Michael R. Booth, ed., *English Plays of the Nineteenth Century* (Oxford: Clarendon Press, 1969), vol. II, p. 344. Future references are to this edition, with page numbers cited in the text.

7 Austin E. Quigley, *The Modern Stage and Other Worlds* (New York and London: Methuen, 1985), pp. 71–2.

8 Ibid., p. 86.

9 Elizabeth Robins's discussion of her portrayal of the first English Hedda Gabler, in *Ibsen and the Actress* (London: Hogarth, 1928), may have been the first critical intepretation of Hedda as a courageous woman whose ability never to compromise herself to her society was due solely to her possession of her father's pistols. She was free to 'get out' when she felt she could bear play-acting no longer; but as Robins points out, 'how should men understand Hedda on the stage when they didn't understand her in the persons of their wives, their daughters, their women friends?' (p. 18).

10 Arthur Wing Pinero, *The Second Mrs Tanqueray* in *English Drama in Transition, 1880–1920*, ed. Henry Frank Salerno (New York: Pegasus, 1968), p. 99. All further references to the play are to this edition.

11 Clement Scott, *The Illustrated London News*, 22 July 1893, cited in the appendix to *The Second Mrs Tanqueray*, in *English Plays of the Nineteenth Century*, ed. Booth, vol. II, p. 339.

12 Cited in ibid., vol. II, p. 336.

13 *Our Theatres in the Nineties* (London: Constable, 1932, reprint 1954), vol. I, p. 60.

14 Samuel Hynes, *The Edwardian Turn of Mind* (Princeton: University Press, 1968), p. 179.

15 Austin Quigley uses Drummle's position as the spectator to full effect in his chapter on *The Second Mrs Tanqueray*, pointing out how often Drummle is described as gazing or staring at something or someone, and how the spectator's gaze is affected by him; in *The Modern Stage and Other Worlds*, pp. 85–8.

16 Margot Peters, *Bernard Shaw and the Actresses* (Garden City, NY: Doubleday, 1980), p. xiii.

17 *The Quintessence of Ibsenism* (New York: Hill & Wang, 3rd edn, 1913), p. 56.

18 Martin Meisel, *Shaw and the Nineteenth-Century Theatre* (Princeton University Press, 1963), p. 70.

19 Bernard Shaw, 'Mrs Warren's Profession; A Play', *Plays Unpleasant* (Baltimore: Penguin, 1961), p. 214. All further references to the play are to this edition.

20 Meisel, *Shaw and the Nineteenth-Century Theatre*, p. 129.

21 'Art and Anger', *Feminist Studies*, 4 (1978), 73.

22 Hynes, *The Edwardian Turn of Mind*, p. 201.

23 Peters, *Bernard Shaw and the Actress*, p. 309.

24 *Ibsen and the Actresses* (London: Hogarth, 1928), p. 10.

25 'Art and Anger', p. 75.

26 For a mention of the ambiguous power actresses exercised in late-Victorian England, see Gay Gibson Cima, 'Elizabeth Robins: The Genesis of an Independent Manageress', *Theatre Survey*, 21 (1980), 145–63.

27 Elizabeth Robins, 'Votes for Women', *How the Vote was Won and Other Suffrage Plays*, ed. Dale Spender and Carole Hayman (New York and London: Methuen, 1985), p. 41. All further references to the play are to this edition.

28 In conversation with Jane Marcus, whose 1974 Northwestern University dissertation is a biography of Elizabeth Robins.

White Marriage and the transcendence of gender*

ALLEN KUHARSKI

Any discussion of the theatrical history and merits of Tadeusz Różewicz's play *White Marriage* must be prefaced by a warning: the play was apparently conceived under the star of paradox and contradiction, a star that has clearly governed its fate ever since. Nevertheless, certain aspects of the play can be introduced with little equivocation. The work of one of Poland's greatest living poets and playwrights, it is arguably the most important new Polish play of the 1970s. Its controversial debut on Polish stages in the mid-1970s has been followed by productions in at least fourteen countries to date,[1] with four productions in the United States alone, a record to my knowledge unequalled by any other Polish play of the period. Within Poland, the play's significance as the first major treatment of a femininst and lesbian theme is not to be underestimated. Outside of Poland, *White Marriage* can be seen as part of a larger European movement of feminist-oriented theatre and drama in the 1970s as exemplified by Dario Fo and Franca Rame's *Female Parts*, Caryl Churchill's *Cloud 9* and Hélène Cixous's *Portrait of Dora*.

In spite of the impressive extent of the play's production history, its critical reception has been highly divided in character. The play's planned world première at Kraków's prestigious Stary Theatre was cancelled in the midst of rehearsals due to the play's sexual explicitness.[2] After productions of the play in New Haven and Los Angeles, however, drama critics in both *Newsweek* and *The Los Angeles Times* described the same work as 'luminous' in character.[3] An anonymous Polish drama critic accused Różewicz of 'playing with his penis' instead of writing a play,[4] yet a few years later American critic Jack Kroll called the play proof of Różewicz's 'beautiful mind', and compared the work favorably to Chekhov and Kleist.[5] Polish critic Michał Misiorny has written that '*White Marriage* is Różewicz's first play which can be dismissed jokingly',[6] yet his compatriot Jan Kott recently hailed the play 'as one of the very best Polish dramas'.[7] An

---

* A draft of this paper was read at the *Themes in Drama* International Conference held at the University of California, Riverside, in February 1987.

excellent summary in English of the early critical response to the play can be found in Halina Filipowicz's unpublished doctoral dissertation entitled 'The Theatre of Tadeusz Różewicz',[8] completed in 1979 at the University of Kansas.

The paradoxical nature of *White Marriage* is such that the critical controversy that has followed the play is likely to continue into the future. The first level of paradox in the play can be seen in its authorship: this dramatic study of feminism and latent lesbianism is, in fact, written by a man. A second level of paradox exists in the play's relationship to its original Polish context: the work stands as both a complex web of allusions, parodies and reworkings of the Polish literary and theatrical tradition, and simultaneously as a bold departure from that tradition. A third, and perhaps most significant, level of paradox can be seen as forming the play's dramatic and thematic core: the heroine's revolutionary quest for a transcendence of gender. While the issue of the validity, or even possibility of a truly feminist work written by a man will be questioned from the start by some, the question can best be answered by a knowledge of the text itself. In order to provide an introduction to either a future reading or theatrical production of the work, I will focus in this discussion on the significance of the play both within its original Polish context and to the drama beyond its native land.

Though written in the early 1970s, the action of *White Marriage* takes place in Austrian Poland at the turn of the century. The setting is the country estate of a prosperous family of the Polish gentry. The play operates simultaneously on a realistic and an expressionistic plane. On one level, it is an Ibsenesque family tragedy of failed marriages, moral hypocrisy and psychological repression, with more than a hint of incest thrown into the brew. On another level, it is an expressionistic dream drama filled with Freudian erotic symbolism. The 'dreamer' in the play is Bianca, the family's hypersensitive adolescent daughter. As in Ibsen, the social and sexual deformation of women within the context of the conventional bourgeois marriages of the time provides the play's dramatic spark. Bianca, in the midst of the family's preparations for a socially appropriate wedding, unexpectedly rebels not only against the prospect of conventional marriage but also against the very act of sex itself. The play is structured as a series of thirteen 'tableaux', and is remarkable for the erotic daring and poetic beauty of both its language and its use of stage imagery. Stylistically, the play is significant as a written embodiment of the strongly visual character of so much of contemporary Polish theatre. Różewicz as a playwright has in this work successfully integrated the bold imagery characteristic of Polish graphic designers and such practitioners of 'image theatre' as Henryk Tomaszewski, Józef Szajna and Tadeusz Kantor with his own poetic gift for language.

The revolutionary nature of *White Marriage* within Polish drama and culture is not to be underestimated. Any relatively complex and sympathetic treatment of either feminism or lesbianism would hardly seem likely to find artistic nourishment in the soil of a country so dominated by the Communist Party on the one hand and the 'loyal opposition' of the Roman Catholic Church on the other. While the unsympathetic attitudes of the Roman Catholic Church regarding both feminism and any expression of homosexuality (particularly under the current Polish-born pontiff) are familiar to the native of the West, the attitudes of the Communist Party on these issues are less well-known.

While, technically, many of the legal rights still sought by Western feminists from their own governments exist as a matter of course in the laws of communist states such as Poland, in practice sexual equality remains merely an ideal as is demonstrated by the almost complete absence of women from top government positions. Any organized feminist movement is seen as unnecessary by the authorities, as equal legal rights already exist in the written law. Acknowledgement of the failure of such laws in practice, however, is also generally seen as 'unnecessary'. The plight of women within Poland's male-dominated communist bureaucracy has perhaps most effectively been dramatized by two films of the Solidarity period of 1980–1: Agnieszka Holland's *A Woman Alone* (which concerns the plight of a single working mother in a contemporary context) and Ryszard Bugajski's *Interrogation* (a study of the brutalization of an innocent woman by the secret police of the Stalinist era). Significantly, neither film has ever been officially released for exhibition by the post-martial-law Polish government. The combination of a direct feminist critique of the communist bureaucracy with the larger ethos of the Solidarity movement clearly proved too volatile for the authorities. The directors of both films now live in emigration; both films have also since 1981 become staples of Poland's flourishing black market in banned video cassettes.[9]

In regard to the issues of homosexuality and lesbianism, Marxist states such as Poland categorically refuse to acknowledge officially the existence of such so-called sexual deviances in the life of the country, defining them as symptomatic of pre-Marxist bourgeois society. Beyond this, the entire profession of therapeutic psychology and counseling found in the West does not exist as we know it in the communist world, where all mental illness (which in their definition includes homosexuality and lesbianism) is again characterized as symptomatic of pre-Marxist bourgeois decadence. Logically, therefore, if one lives under a government that can claim to have systematically eradicated all mental illness, the only possible form of mental illness becomes opposition to that system. Hence, the notorious political applications of Eastern Bloc psychiatric wards. Any dramatic work that however tactfully suggests that either sexism or such sexual

'deviancies' may be part of the emotional and political reality of contemporary Polish life is therefore by definition subversive in the eyes of the
authorities.[10] Given such a cultural and political context, what has made it
possible for the play to have a life on the Polish stage?

While *White Marriage* is certainly the first clearly feminist play by a
contemporary Polish playwright, there is something of a tradition of
feminist writing within Polish literature. Polish playwright Gabriela
Zapolska wrote two plays that survive as minor classics within the Polish
repertory, *Mrs Dulska's Morality* (1907) and *Miss Maliczewska* (1912), which
presented the moral dilemmas of women within Zapolska's contemporary
middle-class milieu in a manner comparable to that of Ibsen in *A Doll's
House* or Shaw in *Mrs Warren's Profession*. Filipowicz in her study of Różewicz
has established that the leading character of Bianca in Różewicz's play is
inspired in part by the life and writings of the turn-of-the-century Polish
poet and feminist, Maria Komornicka.[11] Komornicka, like the play's
heroine, burned her woman's clothing, cut her hair and went about the
streets dressed as a man. Thereafter, Komornicka rechristened herself both
in life and as an author with the male name 'Piotr Włast'. Czesław Miłosz
has described Komornicka's life and thought as:

> . . . unique for the passion and even fanaticism with which she embraced the
> philosophy of Friedrich Nietzsche. Born near Warsaw, she received a good
> education in Poland and then, as a very young girl, went to England to study for
> four years. Her poems, often in free verse or in prose, were quite savage
> vindications of total freedom for the individual, in this case, for a
> superwoman.[12]

The character of Bianca can be seen as a composite of aspects of
Komornicka's life and that of her contemporary, the novelist Zofia
Nałkowska. Bianca's initial narcissism and excessive aestheticism can be
seen as an allusion to the early life of Nałkowska, whose first novels *Women*
(1906) and *Narcissa* (1910) have been characterized by Polish literary
historian Julian Krzyżanowski as 'utterly absorbed with looking into the
refined inner recesses of [Nałkowska's] . . . soul and fascinated by [her]
own physical and spiritual beauty'.[13] In Różewicz's play, Bianca can be
seen to begin as the narcissistic Nałkowska, and end as the Nietzschean
feminist Komornicka.

The undertones of bisexuality and lesbianism in the play have an even
deeper root in Polish literature. Part of Różewicz's initial inspiration for
White Marriage was clearly the life and writings of the nineteenth-century
Polish lesbian novelist, Narcyza Żmichowska, and in particular her novel
The Heathen Woman (*Poganka*, 1846). In a 1970 essay entitled 'Lesbian Love
in a Romantic Disguise', Różewicz has written of his desire at the time to
dramatize Żmichowska's novel, in which the author felt compelled to
portray herself as a man in the love affair that forms the novel's focus. In
Różewicz's words:

I have been thinking of writing an adaptation of *The Heathen Woman* without romantic costumes. I wanted to tell a story of two women who love each other's minds and bodies. That love of Narcyza and Paulina. The catastrophe that must have resulted from their relationship. To attribute the words and actions of Benjamin [Żmichowska's male self-portrait in the novel] to Narcyza. And at the same time, to restore to Narcyza her true nature and the dignity of a brave woman in love. I have not done the adaptation of *The Heathen Woman* yet. The censor inside me tells me that even nowadays lesbian relationships cannot be shown on stage.[14]

While the final form of *White Marriage* is much more than merely a dramatization of the life of Żmichowska, the bisexual triangle of Bianca, her half-sister Pauline and Bianca's fiancé Benjamin that forms the core of the play is clearly indebted to Żmichowska for more than merely the characters' names. While in physical terms, the Bianca/Pauline relationship is never consummated, the emotional bonding of the two characters clearly rivals that of either girl to Benjamin, and clearly precludes any heterosexual consummation for the characters as well. The lesbianism in the play may be essentially latent and adolescent in character, yet the reality of the lesbian dimension in the subtext of the play is undeniable.

Różewicz, by setting *White Marriage* at the turn of the century, has thereby made the play a kind of composite picture of the women who created the first great flowering of Polish feminism and set the play in the politically 'correct' historical context of pre-Marxist Poland in view of the country's theatrical censors. The choice of such a subject in communist Poland in 1975 inevitably raises questions of the contemporay implications of the piece. In effect, the realities of censorship can be seen to have forced *White Marriage* to resemble act I of Churchill's *Cloud 9* (set in a British colony in Victorian times) without act II (set in London in the present). Yet contemporary Polish audiences, trained by forty-five years of continuous theatrical censorship, are well known for their sensitivity to implicit allusions to their contemporary affairs from unlikely theatrical sources. The vitriolic first response of much of the Polish critical establishment can be seen, however, to reflect the true depth of the play's implications beyond the immediate political and social realities of communist Poland. The bitter directness of the play's attacks on the sexism and paternalism of both the Roman Catholic Church and traditional Catholic family life rival those of Dario Fo and Franca Rame in ferocity. Both Bianca and Pauline deliver painfully eloquent speeches attacking the sexism and hypocrisy they see around them in the play.

> *Bianca. (. . . kneeling at the confessional, her face covered with her hand.)* I now see everything as unclean. In the garden, in the meadow, fat frogs mount one another, butterflies open their trembling white wings and raise their abdomens, they fly around coupled, and even flies . . . I don't want to be a girl, I want to be a boy and have a member instead of an opening. I would like to be a soldier when I grow up, and a clergyman now, is that a sin . . .?

They all laugh at me at home. So please tell me why I can't be a priest? Is it because I am a girl and only a man can be a parson? That means everything has been decided once and for all. Is it because I have a womb instead of a male member and a scrotum? Is that why any man may mount me? So anyone with a prick can be . . . Only a bull, a boar, a stallion . . . and us? We are the unclean vessels. They are clean, while those who bleed are unclean. How despicable, how silly this is. Naturally, they all laugh at me. Why can't parsons have bosoms? I don't know where I get these thoughts from. Do I have to chase them away through toil and prayer?[15]

Pauline. Bianca, my dearest, I don't want to offend you but sometimes I get so angry . . . They want to separate us forever, they don't care about our feelings. They are giving you away in marriage, they want to push me out of the house with my studies as an excuse. They order us about as if we were calves or ducklings, but we too are humans. They pretend it's out of love they give away our bodies to the first man who asks for our hand, and it isn't a hand either, Bianca, they talk of hands but have the arse in mind. Our virginity is supposedly revered; they persuade us that the virtue of virginity is the greatest treasure, and then they give away those treasures to the first one that comes. All those saintly virginal martyrs . . . take even those we are staging in our theatre, St Christine or St Agatha; they are fried in oil, they allow their breasts, legs, tongues and heads to be cut off but they won't give up their virginity or their faith. And whenever we hear the word virgin we blush because everyone from Grandpa to Bull-Father makes silly faces when they hear it.

(p. 52)

In her article entitled 'A *White Marriage:* Różewicz's Feminist Drama', Rhonda Blair has presented an intelligent discussion of the play in light of such feminist authors as Germaine Greer and Simone de Beauvoir and provided an insightful analysis of the play's unique position in the history of Polish drama.[16]

Many of the most fascinating aspects of *White Marriage* become apparent only after it is removed from its native Polish context. As already suggested, the play can be seen as a complex reworking and continuation of the tradition of feminist modern drama as initiated by Ibsen and Shaw. It is a characteristically post-modern work, however, in that it is constructed as a form of dramaturgical collage or pastiche employing allusion, reversal and parody of such earlier dramas towards its own expressive ends. Out of the elements of an Ibsenesque or Shavian drama, Różewicz has succeeded in creating both a new form for the work and a new thematic variation on the tradition of modern plays concerning 'the woman question'.

Within the seemingly lyrical and free-form structure of the play, however, exists a thematic symmetry. The heart of the play is the familiar plot of 'the double', as exemplified by such classics as *The Bacchae, Othello, Danton's Death* and *Endgame*. The theatrical archetype of the *Doppelgänger*, as defined initially by Otto Rank, in such works has virtually always been in male form. Followers of Rank such as Otto Weininger have gone so far as to argue that such doubles must be manifested in male form.[17] In *White Marriage*, however, the structure of the *Doppelgänger* plot is retained, but the gender of the protagonists made feminine. The use of such female pairs is relatively rare in world drama, notable examples being Schiller's *Mary Stuart*, Ibsen's *Hedda Gabler*, and O'Neill's *Mourning Becomes Electra*. With his setting of the play at the time of the birth of modern psychoanalysis combined with his portrayal of its two female protagonists, Różewicz undermines the traditional definitions of both the theatrical and psychological models of the 'double'.

Seen as such a symbolic pair, Bianca and Pauline can be understood as two sides of one personality, a personality tragically cut in two like the baby in the Old Testament story of King Solomon. The symbolic and psychological polarities of the Bianca/Pauline relationship in the play, whether taken as polarities within one personality or as two distinct personalities shaped by the opposing forces of their society, together form a balanced whole. Apart, either is fatally unbalanced. Body (Pauline) and Soul (Bianca) must inform and interpenetrate one another, yet society seeks to pull the two apart (through conventional marriage) and considers their full union a perversion (incestuous lesbianism). Thus, the characters exist in an oxymoronic world of ethical and psychological inversions.

The catalyst for the drama is the engagement of Bianca to her fiancé, Benjamin. The possibility of conventional marriage in the male-dominated world of the play is precisely what fills Bianca with dread. Yet Benjamin, it is revealed, is a most unusual fiancé. As an adult male virgin, Benjamin becomes a kind of sexual talisman in the world of the play. He exists in perfect opposition to the degrading order of compulsive, male-dominated sexuality as embodied by the lecherous figures of the Bull-Father and Grandfather. As a man and a virgin, he has as yet been spared the polarization of body and soul already manifest in Pauline and Bianca. As the play's one internally balanced character, Benjamin can be seen as both the exception that proves the rule in the play's male world, and as existing in an unconscious state of natural androgyny. Benjamin's physical desire is aroused by Pauline, his 'other' nature drawn by Bianca. He needs them both and his dilemma is that he must choose between them. Benjamin, like Hippolytus in Greek mythology, represents a seemingly impossible instance of male virtue and is thus intensely pursued by all of the play's sexually abused women.

The creation of a kind of bisexual triangle between Bianca, Pauline and Benjamin results in an unexpected development. Bianca insists as a condition of her engagement to Benjamin that their marriage be a *mariage blanc*: a marriage without sex. Even more surprising is the fact that Benjamin consents. This resolution has both tragic and transcendent aspects. It is tragic in that both Benjamin and Bianca must reject the celebration of physical sexuality represented by Pauline, thus leaving Pauline alone to face the forces of sexual hypocrisy and brutalization that are already stalking her. The transcendent dimension of the choice is also where the play becomes most revolutionary. Through Bianca's refusal to consummate her marriage with Benjamin on their wedding night, not only is her feminist revolution begun in the most fundamental way, but her spiritual marriage with Benjamin is made complete.

> *Bianca.* What did you dream, Benjamin? Your hair was sprinkled with unguents of Araby, your tunic woven from the most delicate Sidon wool. A wreath of roses on your temples and your head propped against a woman's bosom, but not of a mother or a sister, or even of your lover. Benjamin, do you understand that moment in which a woman is not yet a lover, and yet already loves and is loved? As for the woman, have you seen one that is beautiful, powerful in her sensuality, saintly in her spirit, with a forehead that is such a strength of thought that she could direct the fate of Athens, while on her lips such delight, and in her look such warm and piercing attractiveness? Have you dreamt of her? Her eyes, if lowered, are a flame only of hope or memories, they are too dazzling, and therefore shaded, the blush on her cheek, it is life, it is blood which gushes to the outside from the bursting organism, and her love. Believe me, brother, such women there are, you may meet her and you may desire to die in her arms in order not to exist thereafter.
>
> (pp. 66–7)

Bianca's reference to Benjamin as her 'brother' in this speech anticipates the play's curtain line, also addressed to Benjamin, after her Komornicka-like rejection of female dress and conventional middle class marriage. Like Komornicka, Bianca rechristens herself as a man:

> *Bianca.* I am. *(she takes a step towards Benjamin)* I am . . . *(she slopes her shoulders)* . . . your . . . *(in a whisper)* brother   (p. 69)

Benjamin and Bianca paradoxically forge the most genuine marriage to be found within the context of the play.

The symbolic 'death' of Pauline in the midst of Bianca and Benjamin's marriage (signalled by the conspicuous absence of Pauline in the wedding scenes and Różewicz's mixing of funereal elements with those of the nuptials) and the couple's rejection of sex also marks the death of the degrading old patriarchal order and the start of a new era. The nature of Bianca and Benjamin's revolt is three-fold: sexual, political and spiritual. At the end of the play, Różewicz provides his most startling surprises: the play suddenly assumes an unexpected religious dimension, and the embodiment of that dimension is the sexually celibate, spiritually andro-gynous union of Bianca and Benjamin. Against the squalor and tensions of the world around them, Bianca and Benjamin assume a blazing luminosity at the end of the play. Bianca's final removal of her clothes, cutting her hair to a punk-like severity and declaration that she is Benjamin's brother represent her inner transformation and her invitation to him to a new kind of life. Like all complex religious symbols, this final stage image in *White Marriage* is initially confounding in its seeming simplicity, yet it haunts the imagination long after its physical passing.

With this androgynous new 'supercouple', Różewicz challenges not only the duality of male and female but the very principle of dualistic thought. While it is not within the scope of this particular discussion to elaborate on the specifics of the form of Różewicz's drama, which are as complex as they are fascinating, it is important to note that the non-realistic form of the piece – with its slides from dream to reality and its non-linear time structure – represents a most appropriate embodiment of the play's thematic challenge to dualistic philosophical, psychological and political systems.

The star of paradox and contradiction that has governed the play's fate must also be the star of transcendence. Taken on its own terms, the play is remarkably coherent. Placed into a world ruled by sexual, political and religious polemics, the intensity of the divided responses to the work is not at all surprising. In spite of the Nietzschean quest of the play's heroine and Różewicz's own reputation as an absurdist, *White Marriage* is a post-Beckettian play. The precept of a dualistic *either/or* or an absurdist *neither/nor* existential equation is transformed in *White Marriage* to a *both/and* proposition. A feminist play written by a man, a Polish play profoundly critical of Polish culture, a play steeped in Catholic mysticism yet offensive to the Catholic Church, *White Marriage* may indeed prove to have life in no man's land. To date, the play's most loyal advocates are, significantly, theatre artists. The unique theatrical chemistry of *White Marriage* is such that it simultaneously creates a sense of immediacy and mystery. As a work of art, *White Marriage* possesses one of the cardinal virtues: it is first and foremost true to itself.

NOTES

1 According to two authorities on Różewicz's plays, Halina Filipowicz and Maria Dębicz, the countries in which *White Marriage* has been performed to date include: the United States, France, West Germany, Sweden, Norway, Denmark, Greece, Portugal, East Germany, Hungary, Yugoslavia, Mexico, Brazil and Argentina.

2 Halina Filipowicz, 'The Theatre of Tadeusz Różewicz' (dissertation, University of Kansas, 1979), p. 265.

3 Jack Kroll, 'Two Polish Girls', review of *White Marriage* by Tadeusz Różewicz, at the Yale Repertory Theatre, *Newsweek*, 9 May 1977, p. 115; Lawrence Christon, '*White Marriage* at the Odyssey', review of play by Tadeusz Różewicz, *Los Angeles Times*, 7 February 1979, p. 15.

4 NN, '"Love Story" Tadeusza Różewicza', *Teatr*, 29: 1–15 (1974), 7. Quoted in Filipowicz, 'Theatre of Różewicz', p. 269

5 Kroll, 'Two Polish Girls', p. 115

6 Michał Misiorny, 'Nowa sztuka Różewicza', *Trybuna Ludu*, 27 (1976), 8. Quoted in Filipowicz, 'Theatre of Różewicz', p. 270.

7 Jan Kott, colloquium, Department of Dramatic Art, University of California-Berkeley, 21 March 1986.

8 See above, note 2.

9 Judy Stone, 'Banned in Theaters, Film Turns up on Polish VCRs', review of *Interrogation*, film by Ryszard Bugajski, *San Francisco Chronicle*, 17 January 1987.

10 What I describe here held true through the first performances of *White Marriage* in Poland in the 1970s. It is important to note, however, some important changes have taken place since that time. Homosexual activity has now been decriminalized in Poland for several years, and in the summer of 1988 the Polish government passed a law permitting the formation of officially recognized gay and lesbian associations, making Poland the first communist country to do so. This fascinating event was shortly followed, however, by the detainment in a mental asylum of Rural Solidarity activist Gabriel Janowski, suggesting that Soviet-style abuse of psychiatric treatment remains a fact of Polish political life. The legal recognition of such gay and lesbian associations may unfortunately prove more a symbolic political gesture designed to break the virtual monopoly of Solidarity and the Roman Catholic Church in the advocacy of progressive social reform than a sign of true acceptance. The cultural, as opposed to the merely legal or political, background remains the most important issue in making sense of *White Marriage* in its past or present Polish context.

11 Filipowicz, 'Theatre of Różewicz', pp. 234–5.

12 Czesław Miłosz, *The History of Polish Literature* (London: Macmillan, 1969), p. 342.

13 Julian Krzyżanowski, *A History of Polish Literature*, trans. Doris Ronowicz (Warsaw: Państwowe Wydawnictwo Naukowe–Polish Scientific Publishers, 1972), pp. 624–5.

14 Tadeusz Różewicz, 'Miłość lesbijska w romantycznym przebraniu', quoted and translated in Filipowicz, 'Theatre of Różewicz', pp. 235–6.

15 Tadeusz Różewicz, *Mariage Blanc and The Hunger Artist Departs*, trans. Adam Czerniawski (London: Marion Boyars, 1983), p. 20. Future references will be given in parentheses in the text.

16 Rhonda Blair, '*A White Marriage:* Różewicz's Feminist Drama', *Slavic and East European Arts* (Winter/Spring 1985), pp. 13–21.

17 Harry Tucker, Jr, introduction, *The Double*, by Otto Rank (Chapel Hill, NC: University of North Carolina Press, 1971), p. xxi.

'The woman who knows Latin . . .': the portrayal of women in Chilean theatre*

CATHERINE M. BOYLE

'THE WOMAN WHO KNOWS LATIN WILL NEVER WEAR SATIN'

'Mujer que sabe latín' the saying goes, 'no tendrá marido ni buen fin' (literally: 'The woman who knows Latin will find neither a husband nor a good end'). Rosario Castellanos chose this saying as the title of her book about women in Mexican society,[1] as the basic common denominator typifying the archetypal role of women in Latin America. Knowledge of Latin signifies access to education; it implies the move away from the essential female state, since, once woman learns Latin she, willingly or unwillingly, moves out of female terrain and forfeits her claim to the satin, to the husband, to the good end. With regard to notions of the interpretation of the 'good' or 'bad' end to which women are destined I want to look at their portrayal in Chilean theatre.

It is only necessary to look at the most common words applied to women in Latin America to appreciate the conduct expected from the 'good' woman: they describe her 'submission', her 'passivity', her spirit of sacrifice and self-denial (*abnegada*, *sufrida*); the bad woman is described in terms of her individuality, of her adherence to a single state, especially one that falls within the broadly interpreted 'prostitute' category, that of the rejection of motherhood but awareness of sexuality. In fiction she has been attributed devouring abilities, often in connection with supposedly nymphomaniac tendencies and her inability to grasp the most simple moral codes, hence the legendary *devoradora de hombres* (devourer of men) whose men become her pitiful and helpless victims.[2] The worst insults in the Spanish language are violently sexist and 'compliments' passed by men in the street are blatantly intended to degrade more than to flatter. The way women describe themselves underlines the closely defined categories, but the emphasis is different: the words most commonly used refer to enforced submission to men, the woman is 'violated' (*violada*), her place is outside the social order, outside the historical process, she is *desterrada, exiliada*.

* A draft of this paper was read at the *Themes in Drama* International Conference held at the University of London, Westfield College, in March 1987.

Studies of the portrayal of women in Latin American literature inevitably condemn the fact that female characters are created according to broad stereotypes by male writers. This is noted with little surprise and hardly deemed worthy of closer examination given the notoriously patriarchal nature of Latin American society. The counter to that patriarchy is the equally notorious matriarchy within the home, where the female self becomes established and secures a position of stifling dominance. In this paper I shall look at the way in which male dramatists approach the question of woman's subordinate role in society. I have chosen plays with female protagonists written in Chile between the 1920s and the 1960s. This is a period of the consolidation of the middle classes as a vitally important part of the community, it is a period when theatre was developing swiftly, when there was a strong drive for true Chilean expression in the arts, when there was a growth of a notable, if at times apologetic, woman's movement in the country and when women won the vote. The dramas I am going to look at have in common the fact that they recognize an essential fatalistic truth in the 'Woman who knows Latin . . .' wisdom and create female protagonists who undergo a process of emancipation or of enlightenment about their own condition.

TALES FROM A BENIGN PATRIARCHY

'Te admiro porque sabes ser mujer, igual que los hombres cuando saben ser hombres' ('I admire you because you know how to be a woman, just as men when they know how to be men'). Praise of the highest order indeed for the protagonist of Armando Moock's three act play *Natacha*[3] from her wayward love, bohemian poet and unwitting father of her child. Admiration, it is implied, cannot be expressed for a woman who does not, in some way, deny her essential feminity: the baseness of a wholly female condition is not really questioned and woman is worthy of true admiration only once she has assumed the male quality of authenticity. The fact is, however, that the author, aware of the social injustices connected to woman's defined role in society, where beauty and wealth are her only means of playing any role whatsoever, aimed to draw a true portrait of a woman from a female point of view, by divorcing himself fom the social attitudes that prejudge woman according to her external graces and beauty. For this (and perhaps giving himself away) Moock dedicated the play 'A las mujeres que no son bonitas y que han sido mis buenas y cordiales amigas. Agradecido' ('To all those women who are not pretty and who have been my good and cordial friends. With thanks.' p. 31).

The heroine of the drama, Natacha, is an ugly thirty-year-old spinster, dangerously close to being left on the shelf. The dramatic action begins with the discovery that Natacha has rejected the last in a string of suitable mates provided by her equally ugly but married sister, Georgina, one of whose major concerns in life is to 'normalize' Natacha's condition, to free her from the 'disturbing' prospect of becoming an old maid. The play thus opens with the moment of Natacha's enlightenment about her own condition and the role set for her in society. From this moment it is not the fact of being left on the shelf that is disturbing to her sister and brother-in-law, but the fact that she chooses to become a spinster by rejecting marriages of convenience. She renews a friendship with the poet, Gabriel, who shares her belief in the supremacy of the beauty of the soul over socially determined physical beauty and they become lovers, defining their relationship outwith the confines of the traditional marriage. So, when Gabriel feels the urge to travel, he leaves, unaware that Natacha is expecting their child. On his return he is ashamed by his selfish behaviour and tries to make amends by 'normalizing' the family situation, and legitimizing his role as proud father.

Natacha is a complex of devices aimed at revealing the nature of individual imprisonments within the same social order, but it is Natacha, through her decision to live as an outsider in society and hence an intruder in the household, who acts as catalyst to the action within the main dramatic community, composed of her sister and brother-in-law. For, despite the fact that she is married, her sister is not happy. It transpires that Georgina's husband has not only had an affair but that his (beautiful) mistress has given him the child his wife could not provide. Georgina, having learned from Natacha to analyse her life, breaks off all relations with her husband, although he does remain in the house. It must be noted that this is a moneyed family, that the allure of financial security is shown to win over the male heart more easily than the desire to possess a beautiful wife and that, for Natacha and Georgina, access to marriage can be gained through wealth as well as through attractiveness, a recipe for disaster. With this evidence of the marital misery in store for the ugly woman who marries out of love but is married out of interest and is not loved for herself, the focus of the drama changes, and from a dangerous impulse Natacha's decision not to marry is transformed into a rational and comprehensible rejection of the (rich) ugly woman's lot. She rebels against the idea that the ugly woman is essentially denied the right to make such a decision about her marital status ('reason' dictates that she must grab the first opportunity in order to fend off spinsterhood for life), while the pretty woman is implicitly expected to reject certain suitors since her opportunities are infinitely greater and, more importantly, she will inevitably establish a family unit. Natacha's driving force is the desire to conquer the injustice of this unwritten law of her society, one that renders her an outsider: firstly because she is not attractive to men and secondly because she rejects the chance to make a home, the only area in which a woman can develop her self.

Natacha's sister voices opinions learned from her husband; her conversation with him is a constant plea for recognition and love, and at the same time a testimony to submission. Natacha speaks as a man would speak, she has her own opinions, she questions, she makes her own decisions, she is, in the words of Diego, 'una señorita sui generis' (p. 45). Above all her words become actions, so her speech is aligned with male speech, not with the deemed vacuity of female speech. Indeed, Natacha tried to make herself attractive to men by assuming the means of expression of a physically beautiful woman, but she felt like a clown who had violated her own character. She renounces this violence to her self, but cannot easily prevent the daily violation of her character resulting from the male treatment of her as a typical woman and therefore a clown.

The central theme of *Natacha* is that of the battlefield of beauty and the way in which it affects the relationships between the sexes in the bourgeoisie. As the drama unfolds the conflict becomes one between 'apparent and real beauty', real beauty being that of the soul. This notion is lived and expressed throughout by Natacha who, nevertheless, says that Gabriel has 'explained' it to her. Here we have a confusion of issues, for while Gabriel, the poet, speaks of the supremacy of 'real beauty', he betrays his own words and an essential smallness of spirit by leaving the woman who loves him and confessing to affairs with traditional beauties he calls (poetically) 'shadows' of women. Natacha mouths the opinion that she requires Gabriel's words to articulate what she intuitively knows; but the evidence provided in the play belies this idea of Natacha's ideas being second hand, of her inability as a woman to give voice to her own understanding of the world, for it is she who explains her interpretation of beauty throughout, and she is the living expression of inner beauty. By forcing Georgina to think and by imposing the example of inner over external beauty she transforms her sister's marriage, and the couple finish the drama happily married.

In the intellectual plain Natacha is endowed with greater purity of spirit and a huge capacity for idealism. Before Gabriel's return she tells Georgina not to worry about the child being illegitimate, for her lover had spoken poetically to her of the day to come when the state would be parent to all children and the bourgeois family would be destroyed. By the end of the play Moock is tying himself in knots, for Gabriel reveals that this notion was irrelevant idealism: is it that Natacha's idealism could be perfect as a result of her divorce from reality, but that Gabriel, as a man, is aware of the strength of moral codes and of the dangers idealism could cause to their son? Finally 'normality' reigns. In the last scene, Gabriel is seated with his head on her shoulder and she, kissing him, declares, '¡Tengo un hijito más!' ('Another son!'), to which she replies, '¡Mamita!' ('Mummy!') p. 103). By the final scene Moock has managed to contrive a parable for the ugly woman.

From the bourgeois spinster in search of the means to develop her identity I want to turn now to the equally stereotypical *macho* woman, the terror of man, woman and *peón* (farm labourer), the destroyer of egos, the devourer of men. *La viuda de Apablaza (The Widow of Apablaza)* by Germán Luco Cruchaga, first performed in 1928,[4] is generally regarded as the highpoint of Chilean costumbrism. But, as Grinor Rojo has demonstrated, the protagonists are more complex than in the run-of-the-mill costumbrist drama.[5]

The widow of the title is the owner of a ranch left to her by her late husband, Apablaza, whose illegitimate son, Ñico, is the head farmhand. The first act establishes the widow's manly character, her rule of iron over the ranch and her total mastery of the male role of leadership. But towards the end her one weakness is revealed – she feels that she is still young, that part of her life, that of love and affection, is being denied, that she is 'in need of a master'. The second act is one of a confusion of emotions: Ñico is in love and wants to marry, but he reckons without the widow's plans for him to forsake his lover and become her husband and owner of all her land and possessions. The third act takes place two years later as Ñico prepares to bring his lover, the woman he had not been allowed to marry, to live in his home where the widow would rule the roost as mother to them all. But the widow summons her last remnants of willpower and kills herself rather than be further humiliated and morally destroyed.

For our purposes the most important aspect of the play is the development of the character of the widow. In the first act she is playing a man's role, inherited from her husband, with all the power and ability of a man; she is strong, demanding and feared, and is known by all as the 'manly widow'; in the second her 'female weakness' is creeping up on her as she admits her jealousy for Ñico's lover and reveals this as the motivation behind her desire to marry him:

> Por algo tey criao y soy mío. Desde hoy en adelante, vos reemplazai al finao . . .!
> Tuyas son las tierras, la plata . . . la viua. Mandarís más que yo . . . Porqu'ey
> tenío que verte queriendo a otra pa saber que yo te quería como naiden, como
> naiden te podía querer . . . (*Lo abraza estrechamente*). ¡Mi guacho querío! ¡Mi
> guachito lindo!
> (p. 96)

('I've not loved you and looked after you for nothing. From now on you'll take the place of my late husband. The lands, the money . . . the widow are all yours. You'll be more in charge than me . . . Because I had to see that you loved someone else to know that I loved you more than anyone, and more than anyone could love you . . . (*She hugs him tight.*) My dear orphan! My dear darling orphan!)

Her actions in this respect are openly ambivalent in motivation, for on the one hand her marriage to Ñico is a way of perpetuating her love for the late Apablaza, and on the other she is marrying Ñico to mother him, to provide for him and to leave him the wealth of the land she has cultivated. (It is important to note that the widow was unable to provide her husband a son and heir and that, after his death, she inherited the land because he refused to recognize Ñico, and it was the widow who adopted him and reared him.) And, for his part, Ñico is equally mixed up; his role for her in the new household would be as mother to them all, an extension of the role she had always played in his life, for marrying her is a way of legitimizing his position as the heir to lands that should be his by blood, not by marriage.

The third act is one of disintegration: when she becomes Ñico's wife, the transition of the widow to womanliness is complete and her true character is destroyed. Ñico succeeds completely in wiping out the 'viuda hombruna', manly widow, part of her character he says should be forgotten as the manifestation of a 'mistaken life'. Ñico destroys his 'mother' by making her assume her femaleness, her otherness. From a person with a major role to play in the community, she becomes the 'forastera', the outsider. Yet she is aware of her own contribution to her destruction, caused by her submission to an 'unmanly', weak desire for affection through which she had surrendered her self and her power in a vain search for love.[6]

The widow's strength was the product of her access to and mastery of the machinery of power. In her strong scenes she speaks of her 'iron will' and she inspires fear and respect, but at the end, by assuming an attitude of weakness worthy of a woman, she has effectively destroyed herself. She lives in shame and repulsion at the way she has been reduced to 'ánima en pena de la viua de antes' ('only a shadow of the widow of old', p. 104), only physically alive. When she is awakened to the true extent of the suffering brought on by her ambivalent love for Ñico, she commits suicide as the only escape, and it is this act that finally wakens Ñico to the love he has for her, the mother he had loved more than any wife could ever be loved, and he repeats her words: '¡Si'ha matado la viua . . .! ¡Si'ha matado! Y yo la quería más que a mi maire, más que a niaden en el mundo . . .' ('The widow's killed herself! She's killed herself! And I loved her more than my mother, more than anyone else in the world . . .' p. 115). The final words of the play lament the passing of a woman who had been more of a man than any man, '¡Qu'era más rehombre que toos nosotros . . .!' ('She was more of a man than any of us . . .!' p. 116).

Until the period of university theatre in Chile, beginning in 1941, there was a serious depression in dramatic output. Since 1941 there have been new aims in the theatre and, more significantly, female dramatists and prominent actresses. It is interesting to look at the work male dramatists were producing by the mid-1950s and early 1960s, for although they reveal superficial changes in attitude, the question remains as to the real depth of the portrayal of female characters. The overall impression remains of woman trapped within the unfortunate confines of her weak body and psyche, a fact that is brought out not so much by the characterization itself, but by the dramatists' inability to see female characters and create them authentically on stage. The stage is still populated by the prostitute, the mother and the adolescent girl on the road to becoming her predetermined later self.

Mama Rosa by Fernando Debesa (1957)[7] follows the life of a *mama* (wet nurse and nanny) with an aristocratic family in decline over the years 1906–41. When Rosa arrives from the country at the age of sixteen she is naive, simple and happily ignorant of the fact that she has already given her life over to the service of this one family, a fate maliciously described to her by the older *mama*, Mama Chana, as looking after other people's children all her life (p. 38). Initially, Rosa's behaviour is consistent with resistance to her life as a servant, she has occasional escapes and adventures and, as a result of one of these, she has a child who is looked after in the country. In the course of the years that follow she gradually and inevitably assumes the role of the *mama*, changes her manner of speaking, her attitudes, and by the end she is a carbon copy of the old *mama*, gossipy, malicious and very fond of the odd glass of wine. Most importantly, she has fulfilled the prediction that she will look after other people's children all her life while neglecting her own, and finally echoes Mama Chana's words: 'Esa es la suerte'nosotras, pus señora. Querer más a los chiquillos ajenos qui a los propios . . .' ('That's our fate, madam. To love other people's children more than our own', p. 59).

If Mama Rosa follows a slow but inevitable process of entrenchment in her role, then on the outside things are changing. By the time Rosa has been assimilated into the family, laws have been passed to protect servants and she is legally no longer a servant, but an *empleada doméstica* with recognized rights. Yet, while this is noted in the play as a point of social history, the author still presents the praise of the servant who willingly gives up her life for one family, who gladly assumes the moral codes of the class she serves and who perpetuates the status quo by which she is kept in an extremely disadvantaged position. As one commentator has pointed out, there is no real study of the servant's attitude towards her role, nor of her almost inevitable resentment about the sacrifices of a life with a family of her own, nor of the complex system of relationships in the family, through which the servant can, and in the case of Mama Rosa does, exercise a certain amount of power.[8] The author sidesteps the possibility of exploring these issues; the *mama* is a frozen part of the upper-class household and the real implications of the changes in society are ignored.

The rest of the dramatic community is composed of women whose strength keeps together a family populated by a series of congenitally stupid men. Through the three generations changes are reported, but they do not receive any close study. Styles and fashion change, and the younger women are given words that are supposed to bear witness to modernity: 'Se acabó la mujer esclava del hogar, ahogada entre las cacerolas y zurcidos. Ahora la mujer trabaja, lucha, puede ser abogada, doctora, lo que quiera' ('Woman is no longer a slave in the home, buried beneath pots and pans. Now women work, fight, there are female lawyers, doctors, women can do whatever they like', p. 51). Yet the character who tells her mother this, modern aristocrat as she is, with experience of Western European life, betrays herself immediately: 'No pretendo defender las leyes, pero adoro mi época tal como es. Y admiro y envidio a las mujeres que luchan y surgen gracias a su esfuerzo' ('I have no intention of defending the law, but I love my age just the way it is. And I admire and envy women who fight and make their way in the world as a result of their own efforts', p. 52). The deep changes in attitude are to be found in other sectors of society, while this character continues to find her access to the modern world through her marriage and by assuming the new morality that does not frown so much on female sexual freedom. Meanwhile, her sister, Leonor, regarded as an old maid at the age of thirty-one, can only listen and dream with 'bright eyes', forever on the outside. Even her desire to marry a middle-class doctor is interpreted as a desperate attempt to 'normalize' her life by marrying into the despised upstart middle classes. When Leonor becomes pregnant by the doctor, who abandons her, Rosa defends her mistress by pretending that it is she who is pregnant and they both retire to the country to await the event. But the child dies when she is only one week old, which is interpreted as a kind of divine retribution for sinful and unworthy behaviour. The spinster becomes resigned to her fate as an ageing pillar of the family.

As the family wealth declines and changes become inevitable, the dramatist saves himself from exploring the consequences of these changes. Mónica, the matriarch of the third generation, is a modern woman, with modern hair cuts, a car, smoking cigarettes, all of which are external signs of her place in a new age. But she is, over and above that, the reincarnation of her grandmother, Misiá Manuela. In the final scene, the now old Mama Rosa believes that Mónica is Misiá Manuela and the circle is complete as these two stalwarts of the family prove that the order has not changed and that woman is still in her place.

I shall now turn to a play concerned with the 'brutal patriarchy' of Latin American society, *Niñamadre* by Egon Wolff (1962).[9] *Niñamadre* takes place in an old house in a run-down area of Santiago. It is owned by a middle-aged spinster who lives there with her female companion, and a room is let to a painter. In a converted garage at the bottom of the garden live Polla (the 'niñamadre'), and her lover, a bus driver. Polla is pregnant; she tells everyone who is willing to hear about the warmth and love of her relationship and of the family she will create in the future. But the reality is somewhat different, for the father of her child is cruelly blind to Polla's love, he despises her as a prostitute and even lays a trap to put her fidelity to the test. The climax comes when, in a drunken rage at her attempts to please him, and long after Polla's fidelity has been proved, he leaves to drive his bus and has a serious accident. Polla, having suffered the final humiliation before the accident, has determined to look after him until he is well and to learn to type so as to find a real job in order to support her child alone. But, in another twist and a moment of revelation for Pablo, they are united.

It is tempting to see *Niñamadre* (literally: *Child-mother*) as the tale of the golden-hearted prostitute, but this is an injustice both to the character portrayed and the thrust of the play. Polla is really an embodiment of wronged innocence. She is described on her first appearance as being badly dressed, having blonde dyed hair, but also as being essentially innocent and unaware of the depths of her own sensuality, of which she is really ashamed. Although Polla is the central character, we soon find that, in fact, more light is shed on the male characters and how they have been formed by the influence and role of different women in their lives. In this way *Niñamadre* is another example of a play that, while ostensibly being about a female protagonist, is a projection of the author's interpretation of the male in society, confined within boundaries of manliness and role expectations.

One male character is a painter, weedy, failed, resentful of the mummy's boy treatment of his childhood. He remembers the stifling tyranny of his compassionate mother and initially interprets Polla's desire to be a mother as selfishness, as the desire to command entirely one person's affection. But as he begins to appreciate her tenderness, his anger is turned towards the brutality of the male and he begins to wonder at woman's attraction to the violent *macho* type while the considerate man is destined to solitude. Pablo, too, has his grudge against women. On his dressing table he keeps the photograph of the glory of womanhood, a beautiful, submissive and distant woman he claims is the mother he will not allow the unworthy Polla to meet. But this photograph is of an actress, the unreachable perfect woman and the antithesis of the 'woman who called herself my mother', a prostitute who tormented him nightly as a young boy with the sound of her clients in the next room. He imposes this identity on Polla as well, insisting that she is a prostitute, that she is unworthy to be a mother and that she is only having the child 'to save her miserable skin'.

The key to the role of Polla is that for a large part of the play she is nothing, an empty character who becomes the deposit for the resentment and distorted morals of the others. There is no hint that Polla is a prostitute; it is true that she long ago lost her virginity, that she has lived with other men, that once she was forced to sleep with a boss, and that, according to the way she dresses and acts, she is the epitome of the 'loose' woman, synonymous with the prostitute. Her notions about her own life and the role she may be expected to play are tacked together from things she has heard somewhere, sometime: from things the nuns told her; from a priest who says that a woman's role is to make her man's house a home; from Pablo who tells her how she should dress to please him, but who really dresses her as a streetwalker, the victim he wants her to be, the receptable of all his bitterness; and from Paulina, the owner of the house, who preaches a creed of love and purity, of submission and devotion, of accepting woman's fate 'to love until it hurts' (p. 69). She receives all these ideas as a child might, unable to discriminate and make her own decisions, never having learned to do so.

As she lies awake at night Polla feels that she and her baby are intruders into Pablo's life. In essence, her role for a good part of the play is that of an intruder into the household, a misfit, immorality amid fine citizens. This is an important point since Polla is trying to enter legitimate society, but is only in the first stages and is still an outsider. With her child and family she believes she will become wife and mother, a true woman, she will lose the stigma her dyed hair and garish clothes have given her. But as intruder she serves a much clearer function, that of changing the attitudes of other characters. In contact with her innocence and generous goodness, once aware of the love she has to offer and of her real reasons for having a child, the other characters are transformed: the painter finds that he is willing to stand up against the violent *macho* character, and begins to look on himself in a new light, as a true man; Pablo, bedridden and full of remorse, recognizes Polla's true worth and offers to marry her, to finalize the legitimacy of her state. There is no serious development of Polla's character, only a superficial realization that she must find her own worth and strength to survive, but this is not put to the test since her lover comes to his senses and offers to make a real woman of her. The ending is a happy one, brutal patriarchy has had a come-uppance. Of sorts.

Polla is a survivor, saved by her essential innocence and ability to give herself completely through love (she even sees her inability to distinguish between malicious intent and sincere love as a cause of her earlier conduct). She may never have been a prostitute, but her actions put her beyond any doubt in the 'tart' category. Wolff intends Polla's newly won self-respect to be a sign of hope and optimism within the limits possible for such a person.

In *La niña en la palomera* (The Girl in the Attic, 1966),[10] by Fernando Cuadra, the tale is reversed and the decline from innocence to prostitution is traced. The play is based on a newspaper report about a fifteen-year-old girl who was captured by a married man. In the first of the three acts Ana, the leading character, is an innocent teenager from a poor background and a very strict family with a weak, submissive mother and an alcoholic, potentially violent, father. She shares her secret hopes and aspirations with her friend, Gaby, who, at the age of fifteen, has decided to leave school and take to prostitution in order to possess all the things to which their heroine, Marilyn Monroe, seems to have unlimited access.

The second act takes place one year later and the notes tell of a 'subtle change' in Ana. She has become an uneasy mixture of woman and child, while her friend shows a 'disturbing maturity'. With her expulsion from school, Ana is on the verge of making the decision to become a prostitute as well. But her first step is to turn to Manuel, who had moved into the neighbourhood with his wife a year before and, with a mixture of sensuality, fear and violence, she succumbs to his seduction in a frantic game of childish love and affection. Manuel, willing to teach Ana all she wants to know about sex, devises a plan by which she will hide in his attic until it is safe for them to be together.

The third act takes place two weeks later when Ana's disappearance has been well established. Manuel is seen in his *macho* glory, satisfied, fresh, the possessor of the submission of two women, but his wife's return from hospital with the news of her miscarriage changes the position drastically. Ana, having learned a swift and painful lesson about her position, realizes that she will never be more than his plaything and threatens to tell his wife. When he begins to confess, Ana descends from the attic, a fight breaks out and Ana incites Manuel to murder his wife. When the neighbours appear Ana defends herself as the innocent victim and runs home to the protection of her mother, but her father sends her away and in the final scene she is bound for a life of walking the streets as a prostitute.

La niña en la palomera presents a wide array of stereotyped female characters. There is Ana's cowed, obedient and frustrated mother, lonely and unable to make sense of the world around her. She tries to guide her daughter, but fear of her husband and a constant state of timid surprise about the world prohibit her from passing on anything other than a negative model of womanhood. In the final moments she tries to defend and protect her daughter, but the blind alcoholic violence of the father is too much for her. Then there is the *beata*, the overly devout woman, who warns one and all against the sins of the flesh and conjures up ways to quash the *macho* spirit. Manuel's wife, Elsa, under the *beata*'s influence becomes obsequious, falsely flattering and her manner is described as 'enervante' as she learns the old wife's ways of keeping her man. Gaby, from the beginning a potential threat to Ana's innocence, is an archetypal sexually wise child; she is initially 'worried' by her decision to become a prostitute, but is determined, and by the second act is the possessor of a 'disturbing maturity'. In all of these female characters the roles are defined from the outset; they are no more than outlines of characters and there is no room for development. Not so with Ana, who undergoes an unconvincing change in one year.

Gaby's early access to the world of possessions is seen to be the only encouragement Ana needs to become a prostitute. When this decision is made in the second act she embarks on a 'training' with Manuel, telling him that all she wants is to learn, but part of her confusion is that she really wants to take over as his wife. This is, perhaps, a confusion of the author, or it may be a way of having Ana look for an alternative to prostitution, for she has already told Gaby that she wishes someone close to her who cared would tell her not to follow that course. But, by the third act she has lost, and the alternatives have gone; she has surrendered to brutal male domination and the only way to escape is through drastic action, inciting Manuel to murder, playing the role of the innocent victim and even attempting to re-enter her role as the obedient school girl and daughter, which is impossible in the circumstances.

La niña en la palomera takes place in a poor neighbourhood of Santiago where Ana lives within shouting distance of a garage and a gang of young unemployed boys. The whole atmosphere is seen to be one of an almost hopeless future for all the characters. But Ana has a direct counterpart in a teenage boy who works at the garage and whose dream is to win a grant in order to be able to study properly. Both of these characters make a definite decision about their future, Daniel, despite doubts and temptations, is determined to find an exit through education, but Ana has rejected the possibility. In the first act she tells Daniel that she is 'lost', '. . . estoy como perdida, Daniel, porque unas cosas no tienen que ver con las otras' ('I feel as if I am lost, Daniel, it's as if some things have nothing to do with others', p. 130). In this she is a copy of her mother, lost in a man's world. She searches, at this stage, for material wealth, glossy, film-star trinkets because she feels that it is not enough to have people who care for her, she is blinded to their worth by the more powerful reality of poverty, alcoholism and strictness. While Daniel has a legitimate serious alternative, Ana's choice is between motherhood on her mother's model or prostitution; acceptance or rejection of the most visible possibilities open to her. In the final scene Daniel makes a feeble attempt to speak to her and perhaps win her over to his aims in life, but this is only half-hearted and is accompanied by the sound of the 'soft, tender and desperately sad' music of a street barrel-organ. Her fate is decided the moment she puts together the elements of her life and comes up with a whole in which the only exit is through prostitution. The male escape is seen to be through challenging reality, the female escape through entering misformed fantasy.

CONCLUSIONS: UPHOLDING THE PATRIARCHY

Each one of these plays is written in a realist vein. The woman moves in and around the traditional setting and when she has not started in the home she has ended up there, for better or worse. One interesting point about all of these plays is that, despite their realism, action takes place in a social vacuum. Natacha is confined to her home; Mama Rosa and the family live in a world apart and the signs of social change are both superficial and presented as essentially irrelevant to the family, which, despite its decline, holds on to the same old codes; *Niñamadre* is deliberately set apart in the crumbling old house, representative of the state of the individuals, and a device through which the main character can be studied; *La viuda de Apablaza*, costumbrist drama *par excellence*, removes the widow from her 'mistaken' identity as an honorary man and places her in an even more grievously mistaken identity as mother hen; and Ana is locked away in the attic, cut off from her dreams and her future, both of which had been formed as a result of contact with fantasy and evasion of reality.

If we look at the melodrama and the *sainete* (type of farce) of the same period, we will see that the place of woman is more strongly confined outside society. The home is set up as a direct counterpart to society and the mother's role is to build a protective nest where her offspring can return from the corrupting influences outside to a haven of peace, security and the unchanging order of family life. Melodramas and *sainetes* written by women convey this message very strongly, but the emphasis is slightly different. Whereas, in works by male dramatists, the mother or wife will often be a nagging dragon who deserves the beatings and abuse of the tortured husband, female writers would tend towards the exaltation of the suffering, sacrificing, submissive and finally pure mother. Both, in one way or another, reproduce a dated picture with little comment or criticism.[11]

This isolation of woman is, of course, in keeping with the traditional role and place of women in Latin American society and the dramatists studied above do recognize this state as what Octavio Paz has called 'the atrocious female condition in a macho society',[12] for each of the female protagonists is a victim of individual brutality or patriarchy. Yet, despite this sympathy about woman's place in society, there is something unsatisfactory about the plays. Firstly, there is the fact that real changes are not taken into account and the stereotype creeps inevitably to the fore. Apart from, perhaps, *Natacha* and *Niñamadre*, there is little attempt to explore the ways in which women look for escape from their condition, and even in these plays, written forty years apart, the answer lies in assuming with truth and honesty the role of mother, crossing the thin line from total exclusion from society to belonging. Both begin as intruders, both have a strong impact on the immediate dramatic community and both finally conform to the 'good end'. The plays are littered with children, usually born outside marriage, and these, except Leonor's baby who dies in *Mama Rosa*, are all male, as if to perpetuate the notion that, no matter how bad the patriarchy is, it is better to be on the side of the strong, to perpetuate it, rather than to be one of the weak. Polla says she knows that her child will be a boy, for it is Pablo's child: men will breed men. All in all, the plays are projections of the male dramatist's image of women and his (well-intentioned) interpretation of the best way to deal with the female condition, an interpretation which inevitably upholds the patriarchy.

If we look at the portrayal of the male characters it becomes clear the females shine in communities of awful males whose weakness is only shielded by their masculinity and who, in the end, are forced to recognize the superiority of the women. Such is the case in *La viuda de Apablaza* (although she is reinstated as an honorary man after her death), in *Natacha*, in which the ridiculous last scene exalts the mother and wife, regardless of how ugly she may be, and in *Niñamadre* where the men change in contact with Polla's goodness of spirit and the realization that she has what it takes to make the transformation from 'prostitute' to mother. In *La niña en la palomera* Manuel, from the beginning, is presented as a miserable *macho*, lusting after the Lolita-like adolescent, but mankind is redeemed by the character of Daniel, the only person who is capable of fighting circumstances.

This predominance of women in communities of morally weak males is an important point as regards drama about women in Chile. There are still few female playwrights. Of those who appeared in the 1950s – Gabriela Roepke, María Asunción Requena and Isidora Aguirre – only the latter continues to write. Other women dedicate themselves to children's theatre; no one tackles feminist theatre. This is partly to do with the role of feminism in Chilean society, which has been deemed necessary as a way of ensuring woman's legal rights, but has been consistently subordinated to wider social issues with the argument that women are not the only, or the most deprived, sector of the community, and that their struggle should take its place alongside that of workers or peasants. Theatre that is deemed to be feminist has been forgiven on occasion by male critics because it is not 'facile feminism'.[13] That female dramatists are few and far between, often working in collective creations as contributing actresses, is another area to be explored.

Male dramatists on the whole ignore other ways in which woman's role has been changing, and explore legitimate, but narrow and stereotypical escapes from the perceived drudgery of being born a woman. In recent years, however, there have been plays that deal with the changing role of women, but these confirm the impression that women become protagonists on stage when the male community is weakened or proven to be inadequate.[14] Given that Chilean theatre as a whole does not move far from the grounds of realism, this is a true echo of what has been happening in some sectors of the community with high unemployment where the male is losing his traditional role in society. Woman on stage has finally moved into the place that was being prepared for her, as the ultimate symbol of marginality in a demoralized society.

NOTES

1 Rosario Castellanos, *Mujer que sabe latín* . . . (México: Sep Setentas, 1973).

2 Two cases are those of the novels *Doña Bárbara* by the Venezuelan, Rómulo Gallegos, and *La Quintrala* by the Chilean, Magdalena Petit.

3 Armando Moock, *Natacha* in *Armando Moock: Teatro* (Santiago: Editorial Nascimento, 1971), pp. 31–103.

4 German Luco Cruchaga, *La viuda de Apablaza* in *Teatro* (Santiago: Editorial Nascimento, 1979), pp. 59–116.

5 See Grinor Rojo, *Orígenes del teatro hispanoamericano* (Santiago: Ediciones Universitarias de Valparaíso, 1972).

6 See Julio Durán Cerda, 'Luco cruchaga iniciador del realismo crítico en el teatro chileno', *Ideologies and Literature*, 14: 17 (1983), 89.

7 Fernando Debesa, *Mama Rosa* (Santiago: Editorial Universitaria, 1983).

8 See Elena Castedo Ellerman, *El teatro chileno del mediados del siglo XX* (Santiago: Editorial Andrés Bello, 1982), p. 189.

9 Egon Wolff, *Niñamadre* in *Egon Wolff. Teatro* (Santiago: Editorial Nascimento, 1978), pp. 34–140.

10 Fernando Cuadra, *La niña en la palomera* (Santiago: Ediciones Ercilla, 1970).

11 For a study of the *sainete*, including the portrayal of women, see María de la Luz Hurtado, 'Teatro y sociedad en la mitad del siglo xx. El sainete', *Apuntes*, 92 (1984), 3–55.

12 See Octavio Paz, *El laberinto de la soledad* (México: Fondo de la Cultura Económica,1 1969), p. 77.

13 See the comments of Juan Andrés Piña on *Tres Marías y una Rosa* in his 'El tema del trabajo humano en siete obras chilenas durante el autoritarismo', Working Paper, CENECA, Santiago, no date.

14 See my 'Images of Women in Contemporary Chilean Theatre', *Bulletin Of Latin American Research*, 5:2 (1986), 81–96.

Lilian Baylis: paradoxes and contradictions*

VERA GOTTLIEB AND ROBERT GORDON

The title summarizes the aims and limitations of this paper: we are not presenting a thesis, developing an argument, and coming to a reasoned conclusion. Instead, we are raising a series of central questions about Lilian Baylis which throw up contradictory answers and lead, in turn, to more questions. Our interest in the subject is not 'academic', but an aspect of our 'work in progress' in preparing a new play called *Waterloo Road*, scheduled for the Young Vic Theatre in October 1987. Several of the questions which have arisen in the course of research relate to but do not equate with some of the issues which the play will be raising for an audience.

The questions may be divided into several areas. First, what kind of a person was Lilian Baylis? And what is the relevance, if any, of her gender? Second, how did an uneducated female member of the English lower middle class become manager of the Old Vic Theatre from 1912 until her death in 1937, *and* the driving force and manager of Sadler's Wells Opera and Ballet Company from 1931? Third, what is the significance of Baylis's religious belief – of her personal 'hot-line' to God? Then, what kind of manager was she? How far does she provide a kind of stepping-stone between the traditional actor–manager of the English theatre and the Arts Council of today? What was her *role* as manager? Fifth, how far can Baylis's undoubted achievements be seen as a result of her own artistic sensibilities? And, last, what of Baylis's status as an 'amateur' – an amateur who had an uncanny instinct for selecting the professionals who could deliver what she wanted? All of these aspects naturally overlap, but each offers the most immediate contradictions when separately analysed, and several aspects clash with others when considered within the figure of Baylis as a totality. As Dame Peggy Ashcroft put it, Baylis was both 'a power and a joke': the fact that she was both, often simultaneously, suggests complexity of character yet does not explain her importance in, and effect on, the English theatre from 1914 up to the present.

---

* A draft of this paper was read at the *Themes in Drama* International Conference Hall at the University of London, Westfield College, in March 1987.

First, as Harcourt Williams recalled her, 'What sort of woman was Lilian Baylis?'

> It is misleading to say that she was stout. She was thickset, but not fat. She was about five foot four inches high and moved lightly. She had trained as a dancer at one time, and was not a little proud of her lightness of movement. She had pretty, soft brown hair and gentle, rather weak eyes. She always wore spectacles, and all who met her were conscious of her slightly crooked mouth.[1]

Edward Dent has said that 'her voice was about the most disagreeable that I have ever heard issue from female lips', while Tyrone Guthrie gives this description:

> When I came to know this remarkable woman, she was already getting on in years and her extraordinary force of personality as well as her physical energy were beginning to decline. But she was already a legend. She was a thick set, dumpy person. I do not think she ever had been a pretty woman. In later years her features had been twisted a little, the effect, I believe of a slight stroke induced by a swimming accident. As a result she spoke out of the side of her mouth. This, with a marked cockney accent and an extremely individual turn of phrase, made her an all-too-easy mark for impersonation.[2]

And Guthrie also wrote:

> A great personality, as she undoubtedly was, inevitably magnetises a quantity of satellites. Miss Baylis seemed to have more than her share; and, whilst in most respects so shrewd and sharp, she seemed oddly susceptible to flattery. I see now that this was extremely pathetic. She was an intensely affectionate and enthusiastic creature; she had never married; her position as head lady made her isolated. The incense of the adorers was her only substitute for a love and companionship which her eminent, even noble, career, had precluded.[3]

To continue *male* colleagues' views of Baylis, the actor Russell Thorndike (brother of Sybil) wrote:

> Not being a mother herself, she mothered everyone she liked. She was a romantic soul and when she talked of love hinted that she had had many little romances herself. Had she married, however, the husband would have had to take a very second place to the Vic. She would probably have made him pay for his seat, too.[4]

These are *male* views of a woman whom most men respected but found unattractive; and these value judgements of Baylis are essentially those of men for a woman – rather than simply an actor's assessment of his manager, or a director's view of his employer. As such, their assumptions are completely of their time (and by and large still of our time), in that their assessment of Baylis as a person was primarily *gender*-based. This assessment, however, was played up by Baylis herself, perhaps to mask what she felt as her vulnerability as a 'spinster' in charge of men. In 1925 Baylis said:

> The Old Vic is like a child almost grown up and by several sizes grown out of its clothes. The way the child has grown up has been a joy to me, and, though I can only claim it as a foster-child, I may be forgiven for regarding it with motherly love.[5]

Several points arise from this: first, the male assumption that Baylis put all her energies into her work and sublimated personal life for the sake of the Old Vic; second, how far would this be an issue if she had not been a woman? – no 'peculiarity' or 'mystery' is attached to Baylis's male colleagues, Tyrone Guthrie, Ben Greet, Granville Barker, whose commitment to their work was no less than hers. So the question arises: did Baylis, in fact, have to 'de-sex' herself in order to work as an 'honorary man' in a man's world? Is this part of the 'joke'?

Baylis certainly saw herself in conventional terms, and did not publicly identify herself with issues or actions of the Women's Movement. Her aunt, Emma Cons (from whom she took over the Old Vic), had been a Christian Socialist, and as Baylis recollected in her book *The Old Vic* (written with Cicely Hamilton), Emma Cons 'did valuable work in many other directions. I think of her work for Women's Suffrage and of her struggles as one of the three women members of the first LCC.'[6] But although Baylis was acquainted with some of the leading women of her day, she was never a feminist or interested in promoting the cause of women. When asked, for example, if she would employ the gifted and pioneering Edith Craig (the feminist daughter of Ellen Terry and sister of Edward Gordon Craig), Baylis replied: 'We don't want another woman here'.[7] Baylis *was* introduced by her friend Cicely Hamilton, actress, dramatist, critic and feminist, to the Soroptimists, an international federation of women's clubs, first established in California in 1921, which aimed 'for human rights for all people and, in particular, to advance the status of women'. Its motto was 'Best of women, best for women', and it was essentially a women's Rotary Club – women executives working within the Establishment and, generally, uncritical of Establishment values. In this sense, Baylis identified herself as a woman and as a woman executive – but remained 'unpolitical', which is as much as to say that by and large she accepted without question the conventional (predominantly male) values of her day, whether in politics as a whole or the arena of sexual politics. Interestingly, a view of Baylis's aunt, Emma Cons, written by Beatrice Webb in 1885, is relevant to an understanding of Baylis herself:

Not a lady by birth, with the face and manner of a distinguished woman, almost a ruler of men. Absolute absorption in work; strong religious feeling, very little culture or things outside the sphere of her own action . . . To her people she spoke with that peculiar combination of sympathy and authority which characterises the modern type of governing woman . . . A calm enthusiasm in her face, giving her all to others. 'Why withhold any of your time and strength?' seems to be her spirit. All her energy devoted to the practical side of her work. No desire to solve the general questions of the hour. These governing and guiding women may become important factors if they increase as they have done lately; women who give up their lives to the management of men; their whole energy, body and mind, absorbed in it . . . They have the dignity of habitual authority; often they have the narrow-mindedness and social

2 Barr Kinghorn as Lilian Baylis, with projected image of the Old Vic (photo: Carol Baugh)

gaucherie due to complete absorption, physical and verbal, in one set of feelings and ideas.[8]

Baylis, however, unlike Emma Cons, was Christian without being Socialist – her guiding force was always religion, never politics or political change. It is thus essential to see Baylis as a woman working to prove herself in relation to the accepted conservative values of her contemporary society – and never critical of those values. In this, her class background is significant, and there is a relevant comparison to be made with two other eminent theatre women of her day: Lady Gregory, co-founder of the Dublin Abbey Theatre, and Annie Horniman, another founder of the Abbey Theatre, Dublin, and of the Gaiety Theatre, Manchester. Lady Gregory was an aristocrat, a highly cultured and educated woman, a progressive, an artist in her own right as opposed to simply a manager, who also had the added 'protection' of being a widow. Miss Horniman, on the other hand, while a 'spinster' was extremely wealthy, and very well educated. Sybil Thorndike suggests a comparison between Baylis and Horniman in these terms:

> I also quickly began to appreciate the differences between her and another managerial spinster I had acted for – Miss Horniman.
> Now Miss Horniman did splendid work in giving the people of Manchester a theatre. But Miss Horniman was a rich woman and Miss Baylis was a poor one. Miss Horniman was extraordinarily dignified, extremely well-dressed and a bit of a 'do-gooder'. Lil wasn't a bit dignified (except in her innermost spiritual life). She didn't give a damn how she dressed. And she did not do good *to* the people because she was one of the people – a south London cockney whose accent had been slightly darkened by the South African overtones acquired during her adolescence.
> Miss Horniman used to take fearful silent dislikes to people. If Lilian Baylis didn't like you, she'd probably give you a physical or a verbal thump and then it was all over. The biggest difference of all was that Miss Horniman didn't *love* people in the way Lilian Baylis loved them. Nobody would ever dream of calling Miss Horniman 'Annie'; but the Old Vic galleryites were always calling Miss Baylis 'Lil'.[9]

And in a letter to her brother Russell, Sybil Thorndike wrote:

> She's an absolute scream. You remember, Russell, that we always thought Miss Horniman the oddest person we had ever worked for in the theatre and so she was. But not now. Miss Baylis is much odder, she has the oddest criticisms, too, and uses old-fashioned slang words like 'bounder'. I'm sure Shakespeare (whom she treats as a person of the theatre) is roaring at her. She runs the place exactly as we've seen people organise parish rooms. She looks like a church worker and is one. She's High Church, untidy, works like a trojan and counts 'the takings of the house' as a church worker – as if they were the offertory.[10]

This 'rough' side to Baylis should not be interpreted to mean that Baylis *was* 'of the people': up to a point she was democratic in her treatment of people, but she was not 'plebian'. She was not working class, but lower middle class and some critics, such as St John Ervine, have written of her 'small shopkeeper mind'. Like the grocer's daughter from Grantham who has become Britain's first woman Prime Minister, Baylis demonstrated what could be achieved by hard work, commitment, and a ruthless determination to make Establishment values and systems work for her. In this respect, there was neither feminism nor socialism, but a mixture of

Victorian materialism, charity and profit ethics. The struggle to keep the Old Vic open and to re-build Sadler's Wells made Baylis fight not for state subsidy of the arts, but rather for individual charitable contributions.

Baylis's background is crucial to an understanding of both the woman and her work: daughter of a clerk at the Oxford Street store Waring and Gillow, she was one of ten children; her general education was scrappy but from an early age she was given a musical education – as a violinist – and at seventeen she went with her parents, brother William and sister Ethel, to South Africa as a concert party called The Gypsy Revellers to provide touring entertainment for the Gold Rush migrants. Baylis appeared as 'Soprano, Vocalist, Violinist, and acknowledged premier Lady Mandolinist and Banjoist of South Africa'. To some extent, Baylis never lost what has been called her 'ox-waggon mentality', and her stay in South Africa from 1891 to 1897 gave her a South African accent which she retained, and which she combined with a 'public' cockney accent. Again, the question arises: did she play up to her reputation as a 'character' by emphasizing her philistinism and eccentricity? How much was 'role play', and how much was it the real Baylis? As Harcourt Williams has put it: 'There was something of the music hall artist's approach . . . something of the dancing mistress and her concert work in South Africa', while her main biographer, Richard Findlater, writes: 'Playing to the gallery . . . she exaggerated her oddness, homeliness and no-nonsense materialism.'[11] And Norman Marshall has said that Baylis 'invented what was really an elaborate disguise. She became a "character", half comic, half frightening.'[12] In the *Observer* obituary on Baylis, St John Ervine makes it clear that Baylis's conversation gave no indication that she worked in the theatre, even when she was talking about it, and that in fact 'she generally did not know what she was talking about, as far as acting and the drama were concerned'. In the light of Baylis's 'philistinism', it is scarcely surprising that she was immensely proud of the Honorary MA from Oxford which she was awarded in 1924, and the Honorary LLD from Birmingham. From then on, she took every opportunity to wear her cap and gown in public.

Baylis's motivation for the work she did when at the age of twenty-four she took over the Royal Victoria Hall, a Charity run by a Board of Governors, was essentially the same motivation which took Gladys Aylward to China, or Hestor Stanhope to Africa, or Florence Nightingale to the Crimea: a powerful combination of missionary zeal and Victorian commitment to social reform. Baylis's High Church religious belief underlies not merely the work that she did, but also her methods of working: 'She looks like a church worker and is one.' She begged for money to keep the Old Vic open in the same way as others would run the parish fête to aid the Church. One quotation, from Baylis herself, pinpoints her faith, her 'hotline to God', and her peculiar combination of faith and materialism:

In the spring of 1914 my mother lost the sight of one eye and was told her only chance of saving the other was to leave South Africa and return at once to England for a special operation. My parents were greatly troubled financially through the difficulties which followed the Boer War, and I had arranged, with much effort, for them to come and live with my aged aunt and myself.

The strain of re-adjusting my household and the constant burden of Vic work made my eyes so troublesome that I had to consult an oculist. His report was so alarming I felt my sight might fail me quickly. My oculist requested me to take his prescriptions at once to his own chemist near the Queen's Hall. It was exactly a quarter to one and the chemist told me the prescriptions would take half an hour to make up. I was ill and weary and turned into All Saints for twenty minutes while I was waiting.

This was the only time I remember entering a church and not kneeling to pray. I sat and groused to the Almighty. I could hardly shoulder the burden of my aged dear ones with my normal health; my work was bristling with difficulties; my wonderful aunt, who had founded the Vic and had always been such a pillar of strength to me, had passed on some months before. I told God that even the *Daily Telegraph*, which had seldom failed to note my musical programmes, had taken no notice of our last Wagner performance. I had no praise or thanks in my heart – just one hateful grumble.

A few minutes before one o'clock the Editor of the Telegraph rang through to one of his staff, who was keen on my work, telling him to go at once to the Carlton and interview Melba who had just arrived in England, and could be caught there at lunch. Tetrazzini had captured the attention of the English public shortly before, and my friend of the *Daily Telegraph* thought it would be a popular thing if Nellie Melba's first visit on her arrival was to the People's Opera House. He persuaded her to come to the Vic that night where we were playing *Rigoletto*. She was charming to the audience, the cast and the staff – it was like a royal visit. She promised to help my work, and the next day sent me a big cheque. I had longed for a word or two in the *Daily Telegraph*: the following morning I had several columns on Melba's visit to my work. My friend told me later that he was back at the newspaper's office by one thirty – everything having been arranged while I was in our beloved church in anything, I am afraid, but a humble and contrite frame of mind.[13]

Baylis thought of theatre and art as 'doing good'. Emma Cons's original motivation for reopening the Royal Victoria Hall in 1889 (helped by fund-raising from Samuel Morley, a textile manufacturer and MP for Bristol) was to present uplifting entertainment and instruction for the deserving poor of Lambeth, in strict conditions of temperance and respectability: weekly meetings included variety acts, temperance meetings, lectures and some magic lantern shows. The building was used half as a theatre, and half as a working men's College, Morley College. Originally built in 1818 as the Royal Coburg Theatre, it had been used by such performers as Kean, Macready, Phelps, Grimaldi and Madame Vestris and frequently visited by Dickens. It had been closed down in 1879 since both the theatre and the district were considered disreputable; under the Cons and Morley Charity, the building could not be used for political, denominational or sectarian purposes, nor could any alcohol be sold on the premises. From the beginning, the enterprise was charitable, educational and activated by philanthropy, and it is peculiarly English that 'good works' in this case took the form of 'uplifting entertainment': initially the 'pictures' or early cinema which proved profitable enough to finance concerts and, in 1902, the presentation of opera in English.

In the spring of 1914 Rosina Filippi's Shakespeare Company made a guest appearance at the Vic. Inspite of violent antipathy between the two women, Baylis accepted that Shakespeare is 'good for the soul', and from then on his plays were firmly established at the Old Vic; the complete canon, from the First Folio, was performed between 1914 and 1923 – but under Baylis's management, not Filippi's.

The motivation was not 'culture for the people', but spiritual and moral uplift; not 'art' but 'education'. These may be false divisions, but they nonetheless reveal the emphasis she gave her work. Baylis had 'God on her staff', and used him quite shamelessly, as many anecdotes illustrated. For example, an actor pleaded with her for a small rise in salary. 'I shall have to pray for an answer', said Baylis, and left the room for a few minutes. On returning, she said: 'Sorry, dear, God says no.' And effectively on the staff of the theatre was Baylis's confessor and spiritual advisor, the rather strange, Rasputin-like figure of the local parish priest, Father Andrew. As Findlater puts it:

> Father Andrew showed a crusading concern for using theatrical techniques in the service of God, reflecting the turn-of-the-century trend towards the reinstatement of religious drama, and the recognition by the churches of an art long denounced as sinfully profane and still, even at that time, dismissed by some clerics as morally dangerous.[14]

His influence on Baylis was considerable, from censorship of 'rude' words to matters of repertoire and policy, while Edward Dent describes him in these terms:

> He haunted the theatre, and haunted is here indeed the right word, for his tall and sinister-looking figure would sometimes glide silently into the shadows of the Governors' box during a performance . . . suggesting a Grand Inquisitor escaped from the score of some forgotten opera by Mercadante or Donizetti.[15]

Baylis, on the other hand, wrote of him with passionate intensity:

> I believe I never realized God's love so much as when I make my confession to Father Andrew. Though I love him I'm afraid of his tenderness, I never knew loving words could hurt so much. I feel often I'd whip myself for my rotten failings, but one feels aching from head to foot and just as if one had really been scourged all over after his words of loving encouragement. I have practised confession steadily for nineteen years now and have had many dear helpful priests but never one who makes me feel my sins as Father Andrew does, just because of his great loving heart.[16]

Father Andrew was a profoundly unpopular figure backstage, and

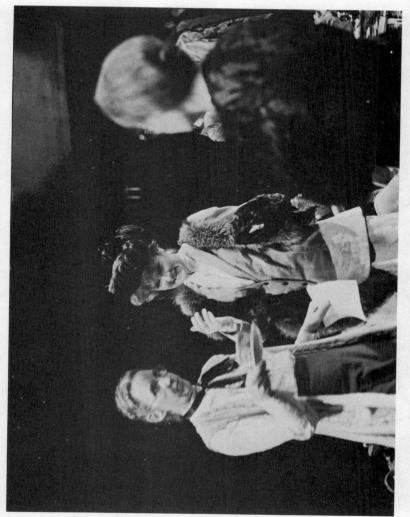

3 Anita Wright as Evelyn Williams, Nina Edwards as Rosina Filippi (photo: Carol Baugh)

4 Barr Kinghorn as Lilian Baylis, Glyn Dilley as Father Andrew (photo: Carol Baugh)

estimates of his influence on Baylis ranged from the sinister to the comic. For many, Baylis's piety was contradicted by her ruthlessness, tactlessness, and meanness. In a sense, Baylis's attitude to the Old Vic was simply an extension of her attitude to other 'good works': Shakespeare became rather akin to God, and directors and actors simply vehicles to do 'God's work'. In the same spirit, Baylis devoted much of her spare time to the support of a leper colony near Chelmsford – and regularly, from 1914 onwards, dragged the actors (as Sybil Thorndike has testified) down to Essex to perform to the patients. As Baylis wrote:

> Tomorrow I hope to take my banjo and sing to each leper who is too ill to get to the common room, and then in the evening we are having a sing-song in the common room . . . One boy played the violin by ear, though almost blind; a sister tells me usually, directly the eyes go the hands start.[17]

So what kind of a manager was she? As a person she was a combination of gauche and bossy, deeply religious and yet pragmatic, uneducated – and yet responsible for the world-renowned Old Vic Shakespeare, *and* the Sadler's Wells Opera and Ballet Companies. George Bernard Shaw, in his Preface to *The Theatrical World of 1894,* wrote:

> Theatrical management in this country is one of the most desperate commercial forms of gambling. You must disturb a man's reason before he will even listen to a proposal to run a playhouse.[18]

But Baylis had two great gifts as a manager: she knew who to employ, and she knew how to get money. As she put it herself: 'I knew nothing about Shakespeare but I went to those who knew nearly everything. I have always done that – gone to those who know.'[19] As Joan Cross, leading soprano at the Vic and Sadler's Wells, reports:

> She really did not have an informed knowledge of music as we would understand it today. What she did have was an enormous *instinct*. She had an instinct for whatever she put her hand to – an instinct for gathering about her just the right people who were going to slave for her, an instinct for getting people to do things just as she wanted them done, an instinct above all for putting her finger on somebody with promising talent . . .
> But the thing about Lilian Baylis was that she knew such a lot of great people and where to go for help.[20]

About the second talent Kathleen Clark has said: 'She was a professional beggar. Rich people used to run at the sight of her – only sometimes they were not able to move fast enough.'[21] On the one hand, as Hugh Willatt (secretary general of the Arts Council in 1974) has described it, there were the begging letters and the church offertory approach and on the other hand, the cheese-paring and the 'make-do-and-mend'.[22]

This was both her 'role' as manager and her method. And her method worked, making Shakespeare at the Old Vic a national institution, and harnessing the talents of Robert Atkins, Ben Greet, Sybil and Russell Thorndike, Lewis Casson, Tyrone Guthrie, Ralph Richardson, Laurence Olivier, John Gielgud, Flora Robson, Edith Evans, Charles Laughton, Alec Guiness, Michael Redgrave, Joan Cross, Adrian Boult, Laurence Collingwood, Edith Coates, Ninette de Valois, Frederick Ashton, Margot Fonteyn, and many others. As Granville Barker summed up, 'Queer woman, Miss Baylis. I don't think that she knows anything about these plays. But she's got something.'[23]

Baylis never really knew anything about drama, or, according to Joan Cross, about opera; about ballet, Ninette de Valois said that 'She recognised good dancing up to a point. That was the point at which it was recognised by the audience.'[24] Her role as manager was that of banker, umpire, supervisor and scapegoat, but she had an instinct for what people wanted to hear and see. Her pragmatism manifested itself in a sound instinct for the commercially successful: when it was pointed out to her that the Old Vic could make money by opening a bar, she immediately applied for a licence and ignored the anti-alcohol origins of the Old Vic; when the success of the Old Vic brought more audiences from the other side of the river than came from the immediate locality of Lambeth, Baylis paid lip-service to the needs of the local community, but watched her theatre become a fashionable and 'trendy' place for the middle and upper classes, whether inpecunious students in the gallery, or the theatre-going elite. History up to a point was to repeat itself when Joan Littlewood's Theatre Workshop became successful enough to start elbowing out the local inhabitants.

Clearly theatre cannot be both an artistic venture *and* a philanthropic institution when dependent on commercial success for its very existence. But Baylis never questioned the need for commercial success – her endless battle to sell tickets, find sponsors, keep the Vic open and raise money for Sadler's Wells was a life's mission. Not once did Baylis move across the divide which separated her from the three most prominent advocates, George Bernard Shaw, Granville Barker and William Archer, in their fight for a *national* and subsidized theatre. Viewed historically, Baylis must be seen as a pragmatist and empiricist, a Victorian in the twentieth century: the conditions and backwardness of the *deserving* poor should be alleviated by individuals working charitably – not by a radical shift in the economic and social organization of the country in the way perceived, for example, by Beatrice Webb or Shaw himself; equally, Baylis did not join in the fight for women's suffrage, or in the fight for a People's Theatre, *or* a National Theatre. In 1937 Baylis stated quite simply: 'When I think of all the work that has been done by our three companies – drama, opera, and ballet – I know *we* are the National Theatre.'[25] And so it became. But her struggle to keep the theatre open was an individual one, not a collective or national one

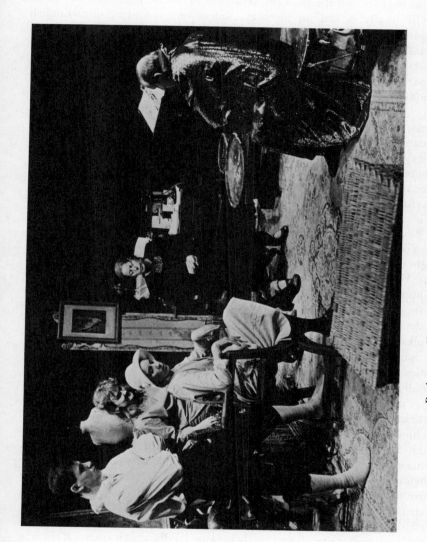

5 Backstage office at the Old Vic (photo: Carol Baugh)

– and this relates to her 'non-political' stance, to her personal missionary
zeal in seeing that a beggar should be fed and clothed, the condition
temporarily alleviated, but no attempt made to change the context which
creates beggars and the political, economic divide between rich and poor.
Baylis totally lacked an ideology, unless one considers ultra-English
empiricism a kind of ideology. She had religious belief, but no developed
social or political ideas. Perhaps as a single and uneducated woman
working in theatre at that time she felt she could not afford it. But this
apparently apolitical stance of Baylis relates also to the kind of people with
whom she felt safe – theatre people, and not intellectuals. She never really
got over her deep suspicion of Tyrone Guthrie and his radical approach and
ideas, and she was always suspicious of directors and designers, if only
because they tended to spend the Vic's money and tended to have 'ideas' in
a way that actors by tradition and convention were not meant to have.
There is, therefore, a link between the English tradition of the actor–
manager and our present-day theatre, and that link *is* partly provided by
Baylis: her theatre propagated actor-orientated Shakespeare, not a theatre
of ideas.

Baylis introduced Shakespeare 'by accident, expediency and the pressures of the time', and as she herself put it in 1914: 'Shakespeare may be all
right in his way, but Opera is entirely right in every way for the success of
the Vic.'[26] One reason for her initially negative response was Rosina
Filippi's claim that *she* was starting a People's Theatre at the Old Vic – a
campaign supported by Sir George Alexander and Sir Herbert Tree at a
special meeting at Drury Lane in April 1914 – a People's Theatre like the
Volksbühne in Germany or the Società Umanitaria in Milan. As Tree
proposed: 'Our People's Society should be extended to the larger provincial
cities: thus we may obtain what is sorely needed, the Municipal Theatre –
finally perhaps the achievement of a National Shakespeare Theatre'.[27] And
here one finds more paradoxes: Baylis remained apart from all campaigns,
whether for a National Theatre or a People's Theatre, and yet the
achievements of the Old Vic *did* lay the foundations of a National Theatre
(though not yet a People's Theatre); her ultimate argument that
Shakespeare is 'good for you' and that 'the people' were discriminating in
their tastes helped to motivate the creation of the Arts Council; she was – to
turn to the last questions raised at the beginning of this paper – neither an
artist nor a professional. Her achievements did *not* result from her own
artistic sensibilities for she had none in a professional sense; the status of the
Old Vic largely came about exactly because Baylis was an amateur: she was
forced to employ professionals, whether Ben Greet or Guthrie, Ninette de
Valois or Laurence Collingwood, and her own lack of education, training,
and professionalism forced her to rely on their talents. She thus provided an
arena, and she helped to create an extraordinarily 'alert, cohesive, and

informed audience[5]. And yet the Old Vic under her management largely ignored the New Drama, the theatre of contemporary ideas: Ibsen, Strindberg, Chekhov and Shaw were largely denied performance at the Old Vic. Her lack of taste made her promote a play by Father Andrew, rather than by George Bernard Shaw. She was partisan in her likes and dislikes, yet lacked any critical concepts or theories; she was an ultra-empiricist, yet possessed of deep religiosity; she was a pragmatist, yet sincerely believed in her 'hot-line to God'; she was a materialist and opportunist, yet devoted to 'good works for others'; she was a single woman working in theatre, still commonly seen as a 'den of iniquity', yet unlike the leading theatre women of her day – Elizabeth Robbins, Edith Craig and a good many others – she did not ever use the theatre to advance the cause of women's suffrage or female equality. She was vulnerable as a woman – and chose to cope with that vulnerability by playing out the various roles of 'woman' which men found acceptable: 'frumpish, eccentric spinster of the parish', mother figure, even a kind of nanny. In this way, unlike Dame Edith Sitwell, or Dame Ethel Smythe or Vita Sackville West, for example, Baylis never really challenged the men around her as a woman. She was essentially right-wing in her uncritical assumptions: she accepted the status quo, with regard to Church, monarchy, class divide, and dependence on Victorian individualist philanthropy; and she was a 'maternalist'.

Perhaps the final word should be given to an ex-secretary general of the Arts Council of Great Britain, Sir Hugh Willatt, who contributed this statement for the Lilian Baylis Centenary Festival brochure in 1974:

> Two points are of special interest to those of us who are involved in what has, since the war, really been a nationwide extension of what she helped to create. The first is the climate in which it grew: late Victorian Philanthropy, adult education (the link with Morley College) and high moral purpose. In a country with no tradition of recognition by state or municipality of the importance of the arts (apart from museums and galleries) and of the performing arts in particular, perhaps this was the correct route to the winning of that recognition. In fact, in a British context, was Miss Baylis' combination of qualities, after all, so unlikely, for the job that had to be done? Even today, the impulse to give voluntary social service is an element in our present method of artistic promotion – the willingness to serve on committees, get something started, or keep it alive. Helped and encouraged by the availability of some public money, this motive has mainly been responsible for the creation of companies, the building of theatres and the development of galleries and arts centres all over the country. The 'do-gooders' may, in time, disappear, in the interests of greater artistic professionalism on the one hand, or municipal participation on the other, but without them much less would have happened, and if they go their contribution will be missed.[28]

It is a sign of *our* times, with Thatcher's expressed wish to see 'a return to Victorian values' and implemented policies, with the Government's unwillingness to maintain proper subsidy through the Arts Council, and with the

6 Mark Ravina as Russell Thorndike, Barr Kinghorn as Lilian Baylis (photo:
Carol Baugh)

renewed struggle of theatres to keep open, that the historical clock could go
backwards and make 'do-gooders like Lilian Baylis' necessary again. Might
it not, however, seem like a negation of theatre history in particular, and
social history in general, if the survival of the arts in this country were to
depend once again on the struggles of individuals in a free-market
economy?

7 Barr Kinghorn as Lilian Baylis (photo: Carol Baugh)

POSTSCRIPT to the production and performance of a play on Lilian Baylis, *Waterloo Road*: critical responses to the play in performance.

Waterloo Road was rehearsed for three weeks before opening at the Young Vic Studio, London, on 30 September 1987. The play was presented for a three-week run by Magna Carta Productions. Lilian Baylis was played by

Barr Kinghorn. The four others members of the cast played fifteen characters: Nina Edwards played Sybil Thorndike, Rosina Filippi, Cecily Hamilton and Annie Powell; Glynn Dilley played Ben Greet, Father Andrew, Robert Atkins and Edward Neville; the roles of Elsie Maynard, Evelyn Williams, Ethel Smythe and Sally Lambert were taken by Anita Wright, and those of Bob Baker, Russell Thorndike and Cedric were played by Mark Ravina.

The action of the play alternated between scenes in the wings and Baylis's office backstage at the Old Vic Theatre, and speeches by her which were directly addressed to the audience as from the Old Vic stage. The shifts from backstage to on stage were simply created by a change from general area lighting to a fixed spotlight on Baylis in the centre of the stage. The action moved in time from the introduction of Shakespeare performances at the Old Vic in 1913 to Baylis's death in 1937.

Strict limitations on the structure and scope of the play were imposed on us as writers and directors by financial considerations, which dictated a cast of no more than five actors and a single set. The irony of the concluding sentence of the conference paper was brought home to us forcefully, partly because we had no form of subsidy but also because this kind of question is one that few theatre critics are prepared to address at the present time.

The play provoked a wide and contradictory range of critical responses from the *Daily Telegraph*'s insistence (3 October 1987) that '*Waterloo Road* turns out to be a cosily old-fashioned biographical drama' to the *Morning Star*'s view that 'It says more about the English theatre than most of the rest of the London scene, South Bank, Barbican, West End, Uncle Tom Cobley and all' (3 October 1987). Both the *Daily Telegraph* and *The Independent* (8 October 1987) rejected the notion that there was anything controversial about the play, yet there was no consensus among critics as to what the play was saying about Baylis's attitude to the theatre and to the community which she claimed to serve. Several of the reviewers justly acknowledged the merits of the set design by Chris Baugh, and costumes by Brian Roberts, but it was surely significant that not one reviewer commented on the many slides of the Old Vic and the surrounding social and physical environment of Lambeth. The slides, taken together with the play's title, clearly invited the audience to view the character of Lilian Baylis within the broader context of the historical and social reality from which the Old Vic, as an institution, was created.

It cannot be accidental that critical attention was focused on either the effectiveness of the character portrayal or the number of anecdotes which were included or omitted, while no reviewer directly confronted the central question of whether the survival of theatre ought to depend on individual enterprise or national subsidy. Oddly enough, it was the *Daily Telegraph* which grasped the implications of the final scene: 'the authors hint at . . .

8 Mark Ravina as Old Bob, Barr Kinghorn as Lilian Baylis (photo: Carol Baugh)

the fact that the Old Vic's success meant an inevitable betrayal of Baylis's earlier idealism towards the people of Lambeth', while the reviewer in *City Limits* (8 October 1987), on the other hand, seemed to miss the point of the scene entirely: 'Whether or not her cavalier, upper-crust despotism was admirable or reprehensible, is left uncommented on.'

Almost everyone who witnessed a performance seemed to have been moved and amused by the play, even when they either wholly disagreed with its point of view, or did not acknowledge that it had one. *Time Out* (7 October 1987) called it 'an entertainment to edify and uplift' while *The*

Independent observed that 'the theatre's young audience laughed right through'.

It is possible that the play did not in fact state the issues with sufficient clarity, and we may have been over-ambitious in attempting to use such a legendary figure as Lilian Baylis to address complex contemporary issues concerning the role and function of the theatre in society. It is also possible, however, to question whether the present climate in British theatre and society is conducive to the presentation of certain kinds of debate. On the one hand, it seems that a point of view may be missed or ignored; on the other hand, any attempt to make an *overt* social and political statement invariably provokes accusations of didacticism, political naivety, or preaching to the converted.

Our experience of the play's production and reception served to reinforce the view of the contemporary situation which first motivated us to create the play. Instead of applauding Baylis's struggles and her eccentric strategies for survival, critics, theatre people and audiences alike might ask themselves whether the notion of 'survival of the fittest' is conducive to the creation of theatre which can offer any significant enhancement of the quality of life.

NOTES

1 Harcourt Williams quoted in *Lilian Baylis Centenary Festival 1974: Lilian Baylis Festival Souvenir Programme*, ed. Peter Roberts (London: Sadler's Wells Foundation, 1974), p. 49.

2 Tyrone Guthrie quoted in *Souvenir Programme*, p. 51.

3 Ibid., p. 53.

4 Russell Thorndike quoted in *Souvenir Programme*, p. 53.

5 Baylis quoted in Richard Findlater, *Lilian Baylis, the Lady of the Vic* (London: Allen Lane, 1975), p. 175.

6 Baylis quoted in *Souvenir Programme*, p. 14.

7 Quoted in Julie Holledge, *Innocent Flowers: Women in the Edwardian Theatre* (London: Virago, 1981), p. 155.

8 Beatrice Webb, *My Apprenticeship*, vol. 2 (Harmondsworth: Penguin, 1938), pp. 315–16.

9 Sybil Thorndike quoted in *Souvenir Programme*, p. 16.

10 Ibid., p. 49.

11 Findlater, *Lilian Baylis*, p. 292.

12 Normal Marshall quoted in Findlater, *Lilian Baylis*, p. 292.

13 Baylis quoted in Findlater, *Lilian Baylis*, p. 109.

14 Findlater, *Lilian Baylis*, pp. 227–8.

15 Edward Dent quoted in Findlater, *Lilian Baylis*, p. 229.

16 Baylis quoted in Findlater, *Lilian Baylis*, p. 231.

17 Ibid., p. 235.

18 George Bernard Shaw, Preface to William Archer, *The Theatrical World of 1894*.

19 Baylis quoted in Findlater, *Lilian Baylis*, p. 113.
20 Joan Cross quoted in *Souvenir Programme*, p. 33.
21 Kathleen Clark quoted in *Souvenir Programme*, p. 49.
22 Sir Hugh Willatt, *Souvenir Programe*, p. 55.
23 Harley Granville Barker, *Souvenir Programme*, p. 50.
24 Ninette de Valois quoted in Findlater, *Lilian Baylis*, p. 259.
25 Baylis quoted in Findlater, *Lilian Baylis*, p. 281.
26 Ibid., p. 106.
27 Sir Herbert Tree quoted in Findlater, *Lilian Baylis*, p. 105.
28 Sir Hugh Willatt, *Souvenir Programme*, p. 54.

Feminine writing and its theatrical 'other'*

CYNTHIA RUNNING-JOHNSON

French author Hélène Cixous has become increasingly involved in theatre during the last ten years. Most recently, she collaborated with director Ariane Mnouchkine to produce the play, *The Terrible and Unfinished Story of Norodam Sihanouk, King of Cambodia*,[1] which opened in September of 1985 in Paris. Considering the direction of Cixous's theoretical work, her interest in writing for the stage is not surprising. For her theory of feminine writing – 'écriture féminine' – which she formulated just as she was beginning to move into theatre, is particularly appropriate to a description of drama. 'Ecriture féminine', with its emphasis upon transformation and profusion and its reference to the corporal, provides a clarifying perspective through which to view performance and the relationship between performance and the written theatrical text. I will begin my discussion of the 'feminine' aspects of drama by presenting Cixous's concept of feminine writing as developed in her 1975 article, 'The Laugh of the Medusa' ('Le Rire de la Méduse') and in her later essay, 'Coming to Writing' ('La Venue à l'écriture').[2]

In 'The Laugh of the Medusa', one of Cixous's most coherent presentations of 'écriture féminine', she describes feminine writing as that which women can do to free themselves from their position as the oppressed in society. By the cultivation of their 'difference' – of inherent libidinal drives which originate in the unconscious – women may subvert oppressive masculine structures. The Medusa figure referred to in the title of Cixous's essay reflects both the traditional position of woman – silenced ('decapitated') – and the New Woman, energized and capable of undoing repressive hierarchical pairings such as active/passive, ruler/ruled and man/woman, through her encouragement of the multiple. The moving, living snakes on the Medusa's head manifest this diverse and profuse force. They incarnate the 'excessiveness' that Cixous associates with feminine writing. Woman, traditionally seen as society's excess – that which is *over-*

---

* A draft of this paper was read at the *Themes in Drama* International Conference held at the University of California, Riverside, in February 1987.

abundant and thus unimportant – can, according to Cixous, turn this characteristic around to undermine the traditionally masculine search for oneness, for the exclusion of that which threatens to disturb control over self and other. The 'feminine', in Cixous's view, does accept the 'other', including the other sex (as represented by the combination of the Medusa's female head and the phallic locks which adorn it); Cixous connects 'écriture féminine' with both literal and metaphorical bisexuality. She further describes the 'feminine economy' as *giving*, and not based, like a masculine one, upon the principle of investment in expectation of a return. Feminine writing both offers and receives, incorporates constant exchange and transformation.

The 'feminine', in its encouragement of growth and change, is a maternal force, procreative and nourishing, bringing to mind a medusa other than the mythological figure: that is, the jellyfish. With its moist, uterine form, it is connected to 'la mer' – the sea, and to 'la mère' – mother. In Cixous's writing, the term 'mother' includes the biological and affective connotations of the word, and also refers to the 'non-dit', the un-said, the space of the pre-symbolic.

Just as the word 'mother' is used in 'The Laugh of the Medusa' on both literal and figurative levels, so is another key term in her presentation of 'écriture féminine': 'voice'. Cixous often uses the word 'voice' to refer to the transforming forces of the unconscious. She describes 'the first voice . . . of love' as 'the chant' from before the imposition of the law.[3] A synonym for 'voice' in Cixous's text is the laughter mentioned in the title of her essay. Laughter, too, can be a manifestation of the unconscious (at least when it erupts spontaneously) and, through the fact that it is unarticulated sound, evidence of the pre-symbolic.

In her description of the 'feminine' as *more* than one in opposition to another, Cixous includes the terms 'inside' and 'outside'. In her article 'Coming to Writing', she describes her own feminine writing as a process that involves both inward and outward movement. Cixous's text is the 'excess' that emerges from this activity. She speaks of 'love' as the outside wellspring ('Source') of her writing, a force that enters to give her text inner life. Her writing is then a projection outward. In Cixous's description, the apparently contradictory concepts of 'inside' and 'outside' take on a different relationship from normal; one contains the other. Writing is not only a movement outward but an exploration of the interior: 'If you write [as a] woman, you know as I do that you write in order to explore, to plunge, to view. Where you write, your body unfolds, your skin tells its hitherto untold legends.'[4] This interior itself contains elements of the 'outside': 'What happens outside happens inside. I am myself the earth, all that happens there, . . . I enter and leave, I am in my body and my body is in me.'[5] Writing becomes a 'reading' of the outside ('History') that is inscribed within the body. The text that emerges from the various inter-penetrations and mutual transformations of inside and outside is called by Cixous a 'third body'. In her description of 'écriture féminine', the domains of body and text, reading and writing, inside and outside, 'History' and 'Literature' appear to cross each other, to become productive of each other, instead of being considered as separate entities.

In 'The Laugh of the Medusa', Cixous urges women to 'write themselves', to create, recreate and explore the possibilities of their body through writing. In her connection of body and text, Cixous makes implicit reference to Jacques Lacan's theories on sexuality and language. According to Lacan in his rereading of Freud, the threat of castration which establishes sexuality is also at work in the acquisition and structure of language. The concept of woman as 'lacking' is connected with both. Cixous, in 'The Laugh' and other writings, takes Lacan's theory as an explanation of the male/female status quo: man possesses the phallus, controls the symbolic realm, while woman has been relegated to the non-symbolic, linked with the body rather than the mind, the unconscious rather than the conscious. Cixous urges women to use their bodily/sexual forces to subvert and change the symbolic as manifested in the linguistic text.

In 'The Laugh' and 'Coming to Writing', then, are presented the main characteristics of feminine writing: its insistence upon movement, profusion, free exchange and transformation, and the importance that it places upon the corporal. All of these traits make Cixous's concept especially suitable to a discussion of theatrical performance. For performance is the reign of the multiple and of transformation. It is the place where fiction and reality interpenetrate. The fiction of a text combines with the reality of a place, the fiction of a role touches the flesh-and-blood reality of the actors and actresses. One mode is constantly changing into (exchanging with) the other.

The importance of the physical in the performance also links it to Cixous's theory. The presence of actors' and actresses' bodies, the visual, auditory and even olfactory and tactile elements of the players' presence (movement, form and color, voice and other sounds), and the actors' and audience's surroundings, including set, light and additional natural and mechanical sounds all constitute this important corporal element.

The phenomenon of 'voice' in Cixous's description of the 'feminine', in particular, finds its parallel in theatrical production. The 'voice' according to Cixous is seemingly, in its most 'feminine' state – that is, closest to the liberating unconscious – an unarticulated, sounded breath rather than a carrier of speech. This first type of voice exists to a certain extent in any play, if only through the characters' nonverbal expression of emotion. In much modern and contemporary drama, the use of nonarticulated voice expands to include humming, chanting, screaming and imitations of other human, animal and mechanical noises. The voice considered in a more general way, to include speech as well is, of course, an element central to most theatre. It provides the closest link between the performance and the written text. In adding the dimension of sound to the written words, in modifying and expanding them through inflection, tone and accent, the voice performs a 'feminine' action of metamorphosis.

The human physical element in theatre, of which the voice is part – the presence of real voices and real bodies – may be seen as an inherently subversive element, just as feminine writing can be characterized as potentially disruptive of the traditional masculine order. For with the involvement of 'live' bodies goes the risk of true action and of consequent change in the real world. Specific texts or drama groups do not in every case consciously declare themselves as desirous of causing change, whether social, political, moral or other. But, through the combination of the openness of the performance to the unknown, and its incorporation of real people (working in a group, no less) and real space and objects, the possibility of transformation of the performance itself is always present. Through its example of openness to change, performed theatre suggests similar possibilities of acceptance of the 'other' in the larger world.

The process of creating a theatrical production may also be seen in light of Cixous's theory, particularly in relation to the maternal characteristics of acceptance and transformation. The staging of a play involves repetition on a number of levels; out of the re-doing, however, the new is always emerging. The performance, for example, is most often a repetition of the written text. But, through rehearsal, the 'other' enters. In the beginning, a basic form is conceived and rehearsed. Within this structure, 'other' gestures, blocking patterns, and intonations are tried out, some developed into more effective forms, some dropped and others added. The final form may no longer physically include these previous stages. But during performance, the memory of previous ways of playing the same piece remains in the minds of the actors, to expand and enhance the result. A more improvisationally-based theatre, or one more tangibly responsive to audience reaction might involve other patterns of repetition. This type of drama would, especially during performance, be more open to entry of the new than would drama that is closer to the written text. But in any case, the repeated performance, because of the elements of time and human presence (chance), constantly produces the possibility of 'other' events and therefore other meanings.

The simultaneously inside and outside movements spoken of earlier in connection with feminine writing also are evident in theatrical creation. The steps in the building of the performance involve both movements: the actors' readings of the written text along with readings of themselves – of the imprint of 'History' upon themselves, combine with their outward projection of characters to produce their performance.

The spectators, too, accomplish both kinds of movement. They first make the effort to go *out* to the theatre. The next step, the perception of the acting going on outside of them, becomes a reading of their own 'inside', as well. In the duality of the actor (his or her 'real' existence in relation to the part he or she is playing), the spectator sees his or her own inherent doubleness, that of the speaking subject made up of self and 'other'. The playwright Jean Genet, for example, described his activity as a spectator in the following way: 'I go to the theatre in order to see myself, on the stage (as a single character, or as a multiple character in the form of a story) as I would not be able – or dare – to see myself or imagine myself, but as I know myself to be.'[6] Though not all audience members would describe their theatrical experience in such a willful way ('I go to the theatre *in order to see myself*'), Genet's statement describes quite well the dual movement involved in the relation between an engaged spectator and the action on the stage.

Certain spectators – drama critics – hold a privileged position in this network of exchange and transformation; or at least they play a somewhat different role than that of the other audience members. Critics occupy an ambiguous – a multiple, 'feminine' place, both inside and outside what is happening before them on stage. They are 'inside' because of their greater knowledge of the technical and poetic sides of theatre than most of the audience. At the same time, and for the same reason, they are 'outside'; their very consciousness of the 'how' and 'why' of the performance puts them at a certain remove from it. The two views merge to produce a 'third body': the critics' writing. The critical text itself potentially possesses an 'other' aspect, also – a performance component, if it is to be spoken on radio or television, or read at a conference, for example. This writing, whether performed or not, is a multiple space, a point where spectators and play meet. Potential spectators may depend upon the critics' opinions to decide whether to see the play or not. And the form or even the continued life of a production may hinge upon the views of these particular play-goers.

Not only the performance, but the connection between it and the written text can be seen in relation to Cixous's ideas. Through production, the written text is crossed by its 'other': by other registers of expression, including the visual and the auditory. These elements exist through the efforts of creators 'other' than the producer of the written text – the director, the actors, and those who manipulate the physical elements of the performance: lighting, set and sound designers and technical crews.

In fact, both the written text and the performance constantly take account of, give to each other. A play is written with a performance in view. Even drama such as that of Musset, whose 'armchair theatre' was meant to

be read and not produced, or Genet's piece, *The Screens*, originally written
with no production in mind – and, appropriately enough, called 'unplay-
able' by director Patrice Chéreau during rehearsals for its most recent
staging in France – shows awareness of a possible production simply
through its form – through the fact that it consists of a dialogue and stage
directions. Similarly, a performance makes reference to a written script. It
may take a written text as its point of departure; conversely, if one considers
rehearsal to be part of performance, the performance can be said to create
the written text. Or, as is most often the case, the performance may involve
both kinds of relationship to the script. Purely improvisational drama, or
drama that includes extensive audience participation may have no – or only
minimal – written text. But, because of the traditional privileged position of
the written text in western theatre, one feels the presence of an 'ideal' script
during any performance. For many of the spectators, if not necessarily for
the actors, 'play' most likely means, first of all, written (literary) drama.

The stage directions become a third term to the double construction
consisting of the script and the performance. They are part of both texts and
yet move outside of them. In a play written to be performed, the stage
directions and the dialogue are written by the same hand and thus display
similar stylistic characteristics. Yet the directions remain 'other' in relation
to the rest because of their prescriptive nature and because they are
normally not meant to be spoken aloud. They are simultaneously integral
to and outside of the performance. They affect the production, whether the
director chooses to follow them or to work in reaction to them. Still, in that
the directions are not as directly translatable on stage as are the characters'
lines, they do not as clearly belong to the performance. They move outside
the double constituted by the written text and the performance, and they
also provide a ground for the interaction of the two.

We have seen that various aspects of the theatrical experience may be
viewed in light of the 'feminine' characteristics of multiplicity, acceptance
and transformation. The implications of this pairing of Cixous and drama
are themselves multiple. Looking at the theatrical genre through Cixous's
theory provides a means of discussing the complexity and liveliness of the
relationship between the performance and the written text, and among the
various players who create the theatrical 'body'. Such a perspective is of
particular value to the literary critic, who, writing about plays primarily
from the standpoint of the written text, may tend to ignore both actual and
potential performances. Discussing theatre in connection with Cixous also
has implications for women – as the word 'feminine' in 'feminine writing'
would imply. As far as Cixous herself is concerned, one certainly may see
her own theatre as part of the project of 'feminine' self-recreation that she
has encouraged in work such as 'The Laugh of the Medusa'. Cixous's
recent writing about drama, in fact, supports this view. She has described

theatre in terms similar to those that she has used to present feminine writing. To her, drama is the reign of 'metamorphosis', of 'beginnings', of creative, maternal movement which can 'give us our true dimensions, our depths, our heights, the foreign lands within us'.[7] May one also, then, go on to posit theatre as capable of giving 'voice' to women in general – to the modern version of the silenced Medusa? The answer to this question depends upon the larger problem of the politics of theatre. If one is to follow Cixous's line of argument in her presentation of 'écriture féminine', women, because of their particularly close connection with the body and the unconscious, are in a privileged position to accomplish self-renewal and eventual societal transformation through drama (an Artaudian dream from a female perspective). But even if such personal change – whether accomplished by women or by men – *is* possible through the physical means that theatre offers, to what extent can it truly affect the larger societal discourse? What exactly are the political consequences of theatrical creation? Cixous has expressed her vision of theatre in the following way: 'In the world of drama, we reacquire what we have lost: . . . our primitive right to hope; the hope that things, which are so implacably programmed by the great social machine, may escape all predetermination, and give themselves up to chance, to the human.'[8] Theatre, as the staging of possibility, at least offers *hope* for change – a dream that is the first step toward the transformation of feminine – and masculine – self and context.

NOTES

1 Hélène Cixous, *L'Histoire terrible mais inachevée de Norodam Sihanouk, roi du Cambodge* (Paris: Théâtre du Soleil, 1985). Cixous's previous work for the stage consisted of *Portrait de Dora* in 1976 (preceded by a radio-play version in 1972), *L'Arrivante* (1977), *Le Nom d'Oedipe: Chant du corps interdit* in 1978, and *La Prise de l'école de Madhubaï* in 1983.

2 Hélène Cixous, 'Le Rire de la Méduse', *L'Arc*, 61 (1975), 39–54. Translated by K. Cohen and P. Cohen as 'The Laugh of the Medusa', *Signs*, 1: 4 (Summer 1976), 875–93; and 'La Venue à l'écriture' in the book of the same name, by Cixous, Madeleine Gagnon, and Annie LeClerc (Paris: Union Générale d'Editions, 1977). See also *La Jeune Née* (Paris: Union Générale d'Editions, 1975), written by Cixous and Catherine Clément, in which ideas presented in 'Le Rire de la Méduse' are further developed.

3 Cixous, 'Le Rire de la Méduse', p. 44. This quote and those that follow in the text are my own translations.

4 Cixous, 'La Venue á l'écriture', p. 48.

5 Ibid., pp. 52–3.

6 Jean Genet, *Les Bonnes et 'Comment jouer "Les Bonnes"'* (Décines, Isère: L'Arbalète, 1963), p. 10.

7 Cixous, 'Le Chemin de la légende' in Hélène Cixous, *Théâtre: 'Portrait de Dora' et 'La Prise de l'école de Madhubaï'* (Paris: Editions des femmes, 1986), pp. 7–9.

8 Cixous, 'Le Chemin', p. 9.

Caste iron bars: Marsha Norman's *Getting Out* as political theatre*

RICHARD G. SCHARINE

Karl Marx once speculated that America's riches might make it immune to the class struggle. Two hundred and ten years into our history, it looks like Marx was right – but not in the way that he thought. Although the United States is beset with social problems, many more are issues of caste than of class.

In his 1937 sociology classic, *Caste and Class in a Southern Town*, John Dollard defines both caste and class designations as means by which social expectations are assigned and social limitations set. But while class limitations are economic dikes vulnerable to cash flow (if not within this generation, at least in the next), caste barriers are biological – and can be no more penetrated than a man can burst out of his own skin.[1]

The advantages of studying America in terms of caste rather than class are obvious. The lower-caste denizen is not like the lower-class citizen, merely inferior in cultural and material attainments. He is an inferior species of humanity. In a sermon entitled *Fair Weather*, Cotton Mather justified the killing of native Americans on the grounds that 'these devils incarnate upon earth . . . had to be made men before they could be made Christians'.[2] On the eve of the United States war with Mexico, Thomas Jefferson Farnham saw annexation of Mexican territory a necessary expression of Anglo-Saxon superiority, 'as the . . . inferior orders of the human family have ever given place to the Caucasian branch'.[3] Probably no more graphic example of a caste designation exists than the US Constitution's description of a black slave as three-fifths of a man.

However, as we have all known since pre-adolescence, there are biological differences other than color. Women are the true invisible caste. Even though they are found in all social classes, one of the most telling phrases of American society is 'women's auxiliary'. Twenty-five years into the latest of a series of 'women's movements' as old as humanity itself, women still occupy the fringes of a male-dominated world. More numerous than men,

---

* A draft of this paper was read at the *Themes in Drama* International Conference held at the University of California, Riverside, in February 1987.

they have only a fraction of the male economic and political power. Furthermore, unlike Blacks, Chicanos, and Indians, women still lack recognition as a social group. To some extent, this is a problem of *self-recognition*. True hegemony in any society lies with the group whose value system is accepted as the standard of the society. For most women in the United States, the standard value system is that of the patriarchy, and they do not recognize that there is any contradiction between its tenets and their rights.

A case in point is that of the characters in Marsha Norman's highly successful 1978 drama, *Getting Out*. Despite its widespread critical acclaim, *Getting Out* is so infrequently described as a political play that a definition of the term becomes essential: political theatre shows public policy, laws, or unquestioned social codes impinging unfairly and destructively upon private lives. Individual though the protagonist may be, what happens to this character is not an example of isolated fate but rather is the result of historically alterable conditions which are inherently unfair to a segment of society. What happens to Arlene Holsclaw could not happen to every woman, but it does happen to many, and because of our laws, policies, and social codes, it is much more likely to happen to women than to men.

Getting Out takes place in a prison within a prison, in a present that is surrounded by – and a reflection of – the past. The setting is a one-room apartment in the slum area of a large Kentucky city. It is bare and dingy, and there are bars on its single window. Its former occupant was a prostitute whose trade paid for her pimp's 'green pants'. Its present occupant, the prostitute's sister, Arlene Holsclaw, has just arrived from Alabama where she has been paroled after serving eight years for a second-degree murder committed during an escape from a prison where she was serving three years for forgery and prostitution.

On a catwalk above the apartment are the locales of a prison – sometimes literal and sometimes figurative – whose chief occupant is Arlie, Arlene as a teenager.

> Arlie is the violent kid Arlene was until her last stretch in prison. In a sense she is Arlene's memory of herself, called up by her fears, needs and simple word cues . . . Arlene is suspicious and guarded, withdrawal is always a possibility. Arlie is unpredictable and incorrigible. The change seen in Arlie during the second act represents a movement toward Arlene, but the transition should never be complete.[4]

The continuous action of *Getting Out* is Arlene's first day in her new home on the 'outside'. At the same time we see flashbacks depicting Arlie's passage from sexually abused child to juvenile delinquent to unwed mother, prostitute, and convict. In the second act, Arlie's behavior is modified – first by a guard's small favors, then by a chaplain's counseling –

9 Jenny Hutchinson as Arlie in *Getting Out* (photo: Alistair Whyte)

10 Jenny Hutchinson as Arlie in *Getting Out* (photo: Alistair Whyte)

until after an emotional crisis which Arlene relives at the climax of the play, she becomes a model prisoner.

Inside or out, Arlene Holsclaw's life has been a succession of unfulfilled promises and withheld opportunities. In the prison announcements that set the tone for each act, the routine is broken only by the suspension of privileges: a library not open, a front lawn and picnic tables off-limits, an exercise class cancelled, a picnic postponed, a visitor mistakenly announced, etc. In spite of inclement weather, however, work details go on. A lost checkerboard suspends all checker playing, and even a gift for a retiring prison volunteer is a required project.

'Completely rehabilitated', Arlene is paroled to Kentucky 'in considera-tion of family residence and appropriate support personnel' (*Getting Out*, I, 11). She has been driven from Alabama by Bennie, her former guard, who confidently expects that Arlene will supply in his retirement years what was missing from his marriage. Here, in her sister's apartment/workplace, she will meet two people from her past – her mother, and Carl, her former pimp, the unaware father of her son, and a current prison escapee – plus Ruby, an ex-con living upstairs. From them Arlene will learn the similarity between her prison and post-prison lives, even as she moves closer to an understand-ing of her past self.

Arlene finds rapprochement with her mother impossible. Ostensibly there to help Arlene move in, her mother cleans in such a way as to eliminate Arlene from the process, then blames her for being lazy. Having never taken time to teach her anything, including cooking or cleaning, Arlene's mother defines her as worthless, denigrating her looks, and assuming she'll return to prostitution. Too uncaring to write her in prison, much less send money, her mother accuses Arlene of turning lesbian tricks or putting out for a guard in order to survive. On the outside, she refuses to have Arlene in her home for fear she'll be a bad example to the children still living at home. She even dismisses Arlene's request to hear about Joey, the baby who was taken from her in prison: 'You never really got attached to him anyway . . . Kids need rules to live by and he'll get em [in the foster home]' (*Getting Out*, I, 26). When she finds Bennie's hat under the bed, it only confirms her assumptions: 'I knowed I shouldn't have come. You ain't changed a bit . . . Same hateful brat' (*Getting Out*, I, 37).

Even a world-class loser like Carl is an improvement over Arlene's mother. A poor white imitation of a black pimp, Carl at least values her as a meal ticket. He even fantasizes for her what she wants most – a lifestyle which would give her something to offer to her son.

Carl. You got your choice, honey. You can do cookin an cleanin or you can do
   somethin that pays good . . . Say it's dishwashin, OK? . . . An you git maybe
   seventy-five a week. Seventy-five for standin over a sinkful of greasy gray
   water, fishin out blobs of bread an lettuce. People puttin pieces of chewed-up

> meat in their napkins and you gotta pick it out. Eight hours a day, six days a
> week, to make seventy-five lousy pictures of Big Daddy George. Now, how
> long it'll take you to make seventy-five workin for me? . . . Two hours maybe.
> Now, it's the same fuckin seventy-five bills . . . You work two hours a night
> for me and how much you got in a week. . . . You come with me an you git
> four-fifty a week. . . .
> *Arlene.* I want to be with [Joey] . . .
> *Carl.* So, fly him up to see you. Take him on that boat they got goes roun the
> island. Take him up to the Empire State Building, let him play King Kong.
> (*Getting Out*, ii, 68–70)

But even as a small-town pimp, Carl was a failure, renting Arlie out to men
who got their kicks causing pain, and being unable to keep her out of jail.
Further out of his depth in New York, wanted for jail breaking, and
carrying a prison-gained drug habit, his promises are as empty as his
future.

As for Bennie, the crude analysis of Arlene's mother is probably accurate:
'No man alive gonna drive a girl five hundred miles for nuthin' (*Getting Out*,
i, 35). But such hopes do not necessarily condemn him. He has been kind to
her in his fashion and he seems in tune with her main interest.

> Wish I had a kid. Life ain't, well, complete without no kids to play ball with an
> take fishin. Dorrie, though, she had them backaches an that neuralgia, day I
> married her to the day she died. (*Getting Out*, i, 43)

However, Bennie, like her mother, presumes to know too much about
Arlene – the way she thinks, what she wants – and thinks his assumed
familiarity and past favors give him rights she has not granted. Like Carl,
Bennie is not interested in letting Arlene choose.

> You don't want me to go. You're jus beginning to git interested. Your ol girlie
> temper's flarin up. I like that in a woman . . . You ain't had a man in a long
> time. And the ones you had been no count . . . Ain't natural goin without it too
> long. Young thing like you. Git all shriveled up. (*Getting Out*, i, 46)

Given her past experience, it is not surprising that Arlene is suspicious of
Ruby who seems to want nothing from her. As an ex-con who has seen more
than one of her own attempts to go straight aborted by trusting the wrong
person, Ruby is sympathetic, but realistic. She even confirms Carl's
assessment of what the straight life will be like if Arlene takes the
dishwashing job opening up where Ruby cooks.

> He tell you you was gonna wear out your hands and knees grubbin for nuthin,
> git old an be broke an never have a nice dress to wear? . . . He tell you nobody's
> gonna wanna be with you cause you done time? . . . He tell you your kid gonna
> be ashamed of you an nobody's gonna believe you if you tell em you changed?
> . . . Then he was right. (*Getting Out*, ii, 72)

The message of the bars over Arlene's apartment window has been delivered. 'Completely rehabilitated', Arlene seems only to have exchanged one prison for another.

What does it mean to 'get out'? At the bitter moment when she discovers just how limited her options for the future are, Arlene tells Ruby, 'outside's where you get to do what you want' (*Getting Out*, II, 73). By this, she primarily means being free of the constrictions placed upon her by her social and economic standing in the community. Arlene has come to believe that by eliminating that part of herself that society has always objected to, the rebellious, anti-authoritarian Arlie, by becoming 'meek', she could 'inherit the earth'. The emphasis is on the tangible fulfillment of her desires. The material benefits that Carl promises – inevitably short-lived because, at worst, breaking parole will send Arlene back to prison, or, at best, because her youth and marketability are fading – are based upon her turning tricks at the customers' demand and primarily for Carl's benefit. The alternative that Bennie offers – however more socially acceptable, potentially enduring, and financially less rewarding – is no alternative in principle at all. It is still sex for pay, with Bennie this time deciding who Arlene is and what she does. If Arlene is to follow Ruby's example, she will in no way have alleviated the extreme financial and social limitations of her life. Within those limitations, however, she will have sovereignty – the power and the responsibility to make her own decisions.

> But when you make two nickels, you can keep both of em . . . You kin always call in sick . . . stay home, and send out for pizza an watch your Johnny Carson on TV . . . or git a bus way out Preston Street an go bowlin. (*Getting Out*, II, 72)

If to 'get out' is to assume sovereignty over one's own life, and if *Getting Out* is a political play, then the factors that mitigate against Arlene taking charge of her life must be seen as flaws in the social system and not as purely personal problems. Therefore, we must study her first as an abused child – and then follow her progress through a sexually discriminating legal system which accurately reflects the economic, social, and educational sexual mores of the country.

Nearly two million wives are beaten annually in the United States. One of every eight children receives serious physical injury at parental hands, and 125,000 new cases of child abuse occur each year. Finally, both abusing mothers and abused children suffer from low self-esteem and poor self-image, frequently leading lives of social isolation lacking in typical friendships and support systems.[5]

In Arlie's case, as in most abusive situations, the damage was psychological as well as physical. Long before she was grown, Arlie came to understand that she was ugly, and that her ugliness was the key to her character and to society's treatment of her.

> Do somethin with your hair. I always thought if you'd looked better you

wouldn't have got in so much trouble. . . . You always was too skinny . . .
Shoulda beat you like your daddy said. Make you eat. (*Getting Out*, I, 28, 23)

As this quote suggests, both beatings and deprecations are usually
couched as being for the child's own welfare. If only he or she had been
'good', the abuse would have been unnecessary. In *Mending Broken Children*,
George and Barbara Henderson remind us that children with unmet needs
cling to their parents, finding excuses even for behavior which harms
them.[6] Arlie does this when she beats up the classmate who accused her
mother of using the family cab for the purposes of prostitution.

Unable to turn her frustration against her mother, Arlie rebels against all
societal authority figures. Transactional analysis terms this reaction: 'I'm
OK, nobody else is OK.' She also has a baby, whom she calls 'Joey' after
the teddy bear with which she consoled herself as a child. Psychoanalyst D.
W. Wennicott notes that children playing with dolls often create what they
perceive as a perfect environment.[7] Abused girls frequently have children
as early as possible in order to get the uncritical love they feel has been
denied them. Unfortunately, that need and the lack of a family role model
leaves them woefully unprepared for the realities of child rearing, and the
sad result is often a new generation of battered children. Arlie sees herself
and her baby in a pact against inadequate authoritarian adults.

> What you gonna be when you grow up, pretty boy baby? You gonna be a
> doctor? You gonna give people medicine and take out they . . . No, don't be no
> doctor . . . be . . . be a preacher . . . Sayin Our Father who is in Heaven . . .
> Heaven, that's where people go when they dies, when doctors can't save em or
> somebody kills em fore they even git a chance to . . . No, don't be no preacher
> neither . . . go to school an learn good . . . so you kin . . . make everybody else
> feel so stupid all the time. Best thing you to be is stay a baby cause nobody beats
> up on babies or hurts them . . . That ain't true, baby. People is mean to babies,
> so you stay right here with me so nobody kin get you an make you cry. An they
> lay one finger on you . . . and I'll beat the screamin shit right out of em. (*Getting
> Out*, I, 44)

When the baby is taken away from her, Arlie loses control. She escapes from
prison, in the process killing a man – a cabdriver like her father and mother
– who tried to assault her. Both child abuse and spouse abuse are cyclical,
returning generation after generation in the same family. The effects of
incest are also cyclical. Arlie was sexually abused by her father who later
paid her to be silent. Recent studies indicate that what has been called the
'last taboo' may be broken in one American family in ten. In cases of father–
daughter incest, the mother may well be a 'silent partner' in the act – not
condoning it, but failing to protest because (a) she wishes to hold the family
together; (b) she is totally dependent on her husband financially; or (c) she
lacks the self-esteem to challenge her husband even in so basic an area. The
daughter herself is victimized by both her father's psychological coercion

and her mother's lack of support. She may crave her father's affection and approval and/or fear his anger. She has every reason to expect that a complaint from her would trigger denials from all the power figures in her life, and that, even if she is believed, both she and the father, whom she nevertheless loves, are likelier to be punished than helped.

Always, the natural response is intense, but unreleasable, anger. Arlie attempted to poison her father by substituting toothpaste for mayonnaise in his sandwich and received yet another mother-condoned beating. The rest of Arlie's world pays dearly for that thwarted impulse.

But the incest cycle is not merely generational. One of the tragedies of incest is the likelihood that its female victim will pass from the home to still other coercive sexual relationships. According to Nancy Gilpatrick of Salt Lake City's Phoenix Institute, 90 per cent of the Utah State prison women inmates whom she counsels are from incestuous homes.[8] The histories of incest victims abound with self-destructive choices. Their self-concepts, typically, are weak and they are drawn to men whose personality type and behavior pattern are similar to those of their fathers. In many cases, this is because their home situation while they were growing up isolated them from the rest of society. Their emotional development tends to be arrested at the point of violation and they associate affection with exploitation. Arlie's tie to Carl, who is her pimp as well as her lover, is a common, rather than an unusual, situation. Bennie is drawn to Arlene at least partially because her reputation as 'damaged goods' excites him, and because it gives him as her 'moral superior' the right to determine how those goods will be distributed. Bennie has been Arlie's keeper and, to retain this role, he will presume knowledge of feelings she has not revealed, use elements of her past to keep her in her place, and invade her body even as he has invaded her privacy. Significantly, Bennie does not even recognize his actions as rape until Arlene points it out to him. And why should he? He has simply traded small kindnesses for complete power over her – the same power exercised by her father and Carl before him, the same power every school and prison Arlie was ever in has demanded over her (as evidenced by the requirement of Alabama State Women's Prison that she transmigrate into Arlene the 'meek' before she can 'get out'). In taking advantage of Arlene's low self-esteem to make her do something she doesn't want, Bennie reflects the rule of the system, not its exception.

It is her final rejection of self that causes the prison to decide Arlie is rehabilitated. The shell she has developed to hostility and neglect is vulnerable to kindess and attention. In prison she comes to rely on the chaplain who renames her Arlene, teaching her that Arlie was her evil side that God would help her destroy. The destruction of Arlie was God's will, so that Arlene might join the meek that inherit the earth. Then, without telling Arlene before he left, the chaplain was transferred away.

They said it was three whole nights at first, me screamin to God to come git Arlie an kill her. They give me this medicine an thought I's better . . . Then that night it happened, the officer was in the dorm doin count . . . and they didn't hear nuthin but they come back out where I was an I'm standin there tellin em to come see, real quiet I'm tellin em, but there's all this blood all over my shirt an I got this fork I'm holdin real tight in my hand . . . an there's all these holes all over me where I been stabbin myself an I'm sayin Arlie is dead for what she done to me, Arlie is dead an it's God's will. I didn't scream it, I was jus sayin it over an over . . . Arlie is dead, Arlie is dead . . . they couldn't git that fork outta my hand til . . . I woke up in the infirmary an they said I almost died. (*Getting Out*, II, 74–5)

What is still alive is Arlene, knitter of sweaters, the best housekeeper in the dorm, honor cottage assignee, and early parole material. The final exploitation has occurred. Arlene has been perfectly socialized. She has been institutionalized from an adversary into a defenceless victim.

In its treatment of young female victims, society is a chronic offender. Arlie's mother told her principal to have Arlie 'put away somewhere' and later blames the prison for not knowing 'how to teach kids right. They should git you up at the crack of dawn an set you to scrubbin the floor' (*Getting Out*, I, 31). As state senator Barbara Lorman noted in her comments on the 'Profile of Young Women in Wisconsin's Juvenile Justice System', the operative slogan in the legal system's handling of young girls has been to 'punish the victim'.

Over three-quarters of the incarcerated females studied had suffered physical abuse resulting in injuries, about one-third had been sexually abused and about one-half had been sexually assaulted. Over half had attempted suicide more than once and almost all had problems with school . . . Females were four times more likely to be locked up than male runaways. Over one-half of the young women were locked up for status offenses (related only to their youth) or public order offenses, as compared to one-fifth of the young men. Misdemeanors were the most serious offense committed by over one-fifth of the females placed in secured correctional facilities. It takes an average of only 20 months from the first offense to correctional placement for young women, while young men average 31 months.[9]

Given that commonality of Arlie's experience, it may be extraneous to mention that it is she who serves time for prostitution, not Carl or her clients – even those whose specialty is beating her up; or that Arlie was imprisoned for killing the cabdriver with his own gun in self-defense; or that her state of mind at the time of the killing was scarcely stable. The depth of the state's concern for Arlene is probably best represented by its program for her rehabilitation and release. In prison she is trained as a beautician.

Mother. Said you was gonna work.
Arlene. They got a law here. Ex-cons can't get a license.
Mother. Shoulda stayed in Alabama, then. Worked there.
Arlene. They got a law there, too. (*Getting Out*, I, 29)

She is then paroled to Kentucky 'in consideration of family residence and appropriate support personnel' (*Getting Out*, I, II), presumably her mother and siblings.

> I ain't hateful, how come I got so many hateful kids? Poor dumb-as-hell Pat, stealin them wigs, Candy screwin since day one, Pete cuttin up ol Mac down at the grocery, June sellin dope like it was Girl Scout cookies and you . . . Thank God I can't remember it all. (*Getting Out*, I, 31)

As Carl succinctly puts it: 'Who you know ain't a "con-vict"?' (*Getting Out*, II, 67).

In addition to its other values, *Getting Out* is an economic primer for American women. Even if society had acted out of character and allowed Arlene to practice the trade she learned in prison, it would have placed limits on what she could have earned. If she had achieved her heart's desire, the custody of Joey, they would have joined the 325,000 American families affected since 1981 by reductions in benefits for Aid to Families with Dependent Children. The 'Feminization of Poverty' is a generalization inductively reasoned from appalling statistics. Female-headed families make up less than one-fifth of all families with children under the age of eighteen, yet comprise nearly half of all poor families. Possibly one out of every five unemployed women is so because she cannot find child care, and there are six or seven million 'latch-key' children caring for themselves while their parents work. This is not a problem time will cure. There are roughly as many working women as men, but their numbers are increasing at twice the rate of men. They are earning three-fifths as much as men, and 80 per cent of them are without pension plans. Therefore, when a working woman retires, she is three times as likely to be poor as her male counterpart.[10]

The obvious answer is to pay women on a comparable basis to men. The questions are how to determine a formula for action and how to find the funds to carry it out. Over twenty states have recently enacted laws containing comparable-worth language. In a typical case, Wisconsin found the work of legal secretaries (100 per cent female, $14,800 yearly) to be of comparable worth to public defender investigators (92 per cent male, $20,600 annually).[11] The effect of correcting this injustice on the tax base of an agricultural state during a period of depressed farm economy has not been calculated, but the Washington-based Bureau of National Affairs says the cost to employers of the proposed Comparable-Worth plans could reach $320 billion nationally and result in an annual inflation rate increase of 9.7 per cent.[12]

What is the origin of an inequity so expensive to redress and, more important, how has it maintained such an unequestioned hegemony?

Feminists give the answer as patriarchy, but the extent and implications of this concept are by no means easy to discern. By definition, patriarchy is a system of tribal government in which the leader is male, and family authority, identity, and property are passed on to the male heirs. Female descendants in this system have no sustaining family identity of their own, but rather take the name of their current male protector. Under patriarchy, women are held as property and marriage is seen as a transfer of deed. If the property is valued, the groom must purchase it with a bride-price. If it is not, the father must add a dowry to the transaction. This concept of property is seen in English law which until the time of Elizabeth I defined rape as the theft of a woman, an economic loss to the male head of her family.[13]

It is plain that this state of affairs has not always existed, and that it has required more than physical strength and legal precedent to maintain it. Even as it was the chaplain's counsel that quelled the rebelliousness in Arlie, it is religion that has been used through the ages to justify woman's subordinate place. Every patriarchal culture has as part of its mythology an incident which establishes the right of male dominance. In ancient Greece, it was *theomachy* – the war between the gods in which the sky gods, led by Father Zeus, conquered the titans of Gaia, the Earth Mother. In the Judeo-Christian culture, it is the sin of Eve (the source of Evil) and her influence on Adam which condemned her to child-bearing and evicted them from the Garden of Eden. From Pandora's Box to the chronicles of St Augustine, the problems of mankind have been laid at the door of women. Psychiatry, that religion of the twentieth century, with its 'uterine biology as psychology' theories, is one in principle with the Elizabethans who accounted for woman's lower place in the Chain of Being through her moral corruptability, resulting from the thinness of blood emanating from a heart further left in her body than that of her brother.

This historical interpretation accepted, it is clear that changes in women's social status involve challenges to established legal, economic, religious, scientific, and familial structures. It is also not surprising that in the recent history of the Women's Movement, those groups which would completely transform the legal system are merely called 'reformist', while those who would alter the basic male/female relationship are termed 'radical'.[14] As we have seen with Arlie and her parents, even codes of law seldom penetrate into the family unit. On the eve of the July 1985 Nairobi Conference marking the end of the United Nations Decade for Women, the Justice Department suspended a $625,000 grant to the National Coalition Against Domestic Violence, which supports most of the 900 American shelters for battered women and children; the stated justification for withdrawing funds was that the Coalition is a 'pro-lesbian, pro-abortion, anti-Reagan radical feminist group'. Since, as columnist Ellen Goodman pointed out, the grant itself was earmarked for a public-awareness campaign, a national referral plan and a program to train police workers, the charge was clearly specious.

Indeed, the subtext of the attack was much more important: the familiar charge that shelters are the subversive creation of anti-family types who are really out to break up homes.[15]

It would appear that even self-protection is a sign to some Americans of a threatening feminine independence.

Given then the magnitude of this problem (and we have not even considered the added plight of women who are also members of racial or sexual minorities), how is it to be approached politically?

The key to keeping any lower caste 'in its place' is to keep it divided against itself, and to deny it a history which reinforces its group pride and affirms its rights in society. The West African slave traders deliberately separated members of the same tribe on board ship, and forced the new slaves to learn to communicate in English – the language controlled by the masters. Many social factors have separated women from one another, including religious systems which have dogmatized their baseness and their need to be redeemed by 'God the Father', legal systems which recognize them only in relation to a man, and economic systems which force them to compete against one another for a man's protection or his employment residue.

Arlene comes to trust Ruby's political analysis and accept her friendship because Ruby is able to validate Arlene's experience by showing its similarity to her own. The acceptance by another of her views is to Arlene in miniature the beginning of the end of her alienation, her awakening to a history of which she is a part, and the subsequent strengthening of her self-concept. When Arlene describes her suicide attempt, the 'murder' of Arlie, it is Ruby who convinces her that 'you can still love people that's gone' (*Getting Out*, II, 75). The play ends with Arlene and Arlie sharing a pleasant memory – an acceptance by Arlene of her past and of the qualities in Arlie without which the battle for the future will be lost.

Meanwhile, the bars on Arlene's window remain. Men have placed them there – Bennie insists – 'to keep folks from breakin' in'. Perhaps – in some men's eyes – this is true. When will the bars be removed? Perhaps when men realize that keeping a caste in its place is as socially limiting to the confiner as to the confined. Perhaps when women recognize that they're there.

NOTES

1 John Dollard, *Caste and Class in a Southern Town* (Garden City, New York: Doubleday, 1937), p. 63.
2 Quoted by David Levin, *Cotton Mather: The Young Life of the Lord Remembrancer, 1663–1703* (Cambridge, Mass.: Harvard University Press, 1978), p. 186.
3 Quoted by David Leary, 'Race and Regeneration' in *The Mexican-Americans: An Awakening Minority* (Beverley Hills: Glencoe Press, 1970), p. 25.

4 Marsha Norman, *Getting Out* (New York: Avon Books, 1980), Preface, p. 5.

5 Frances Summerell Hinchey, 'Parenting and Behavioral Patterns in Mothers from Violent Homes' (unpublished Ph.D. dissertation, Department of Educational Psychology, University of Utah, 1982), pp. 6–9.

6 George and Barbara Beard Henderson, *Mending Broken Children* (Springfield, Illinois: Charles C. Thomas, 1984), p. 36.

7 Nancy Friday, *My Mother/My Self* (New York: Dell Publishing Co., 1977), p. 27.

8 Author's interview with Nancy Gilpatrick, Phoenix Institute (Salt Lake City, Utah), August 1983.

9 Barbara Lorman, 'Capitol Comments', Whitewater (Wisconsin) *Register*, 25 November 1982, n.p.

10 Ruth Messinger, 'Feminization of Poverty Is Detailed in Report', *Nation's Cities Weekly*, 7 (12 November 1984), p. 7.

11 Robert J. Samuelson, 'The Myths of Comparable Worth', *Newsweek*, 22 April 1985, p. 57.

12 Linda R. Woodhouse, 'Report on Comparable Worth Issue', *Nation's Cities Weekly*, 7 (1 October, 1984), p. 5.

13 Nazife Bashar, 'Rape in England between 1550 and 1700', in *the Sexual Dynamics of History*, ed. London Feminist History Group (London: Pluto Press, 1983), p. 30.

14 Jo Freeman, 'The Origins of the Movement', in *Women and the Politics of Culture* (New York: Longman, 1983), p. 401.

15 Ellen Goodman, 'Domestic Violence Transcends Politics', *The Janesville (Wisconsin) Daily Gazette*, 16 July 1985, p. 6A.

Feminists, lesbians, and other women in theatre: thoughts on the politics of performance*

JILL DOLAN

In 1982, when the founding editors of *Women & Performance Journal* were casting about for what to call our fledgling publication, the issue of politics arose. We knew the journal was to take a feminist perspective, but we hesitated to put the word feminism in the title. As the first publication to focus on women in the performing arts, we felt the journal should be all things to all people. Since we knew some women in theatre object to political labels, we hoped the feminism would seep into our journal by accretion instead of by proclamation. We felt we could not afford to alienate people by pointing out, right from the start, that according to feminist tenets, women and performance is really a contradiction in terms. So, like many of those people called 'women in theatre', the founding editors of *Women & Performance* relegated feminism to a subtitle – *A Journal of Feminist Theory*.

As one of the journal's five founding editors, I accepted our name and our inclusive, if ambiguous, editorial concept. But three or four years into publication, I began to grow uneasy with the lack of distinctions we were making among our subject matter. I privately felt that our journal was contributing to the confusion of terms I found detrimental to a serious consideration of women in theatre.

When I took a leave of absence from *Women & Performance* a year-and-a-half ago, I'd come to feel that our editorial policy was really a subterfuge for not taking a stand. By not editorializing on the differences among our readership and the women whose work we published, the journal implies at once that women – in theatre and outside of it – are a homogeneous, single-minded group, and that feminism is something to think about, not something to, as it were, act out. By soft-pedalling the politics, I think we failed to stand by what we believed – that a feminist perspective on performance is subversive enough to crack the theatrical mirror held up to nature.[1]

There have never really been women in theatre. On the earliest Greek

* A draft of this paper was read at the *Themes of Drama* International Conference held at the University of California, Riverside, in February 1987.

stages, women were played by men. On recent Broadway stages, in plays by
David Mamet and David Rabe, for instance, women are only projections of
male desire. Women have never participated actively in theatrical
representation. There are feminist theorists, in fact, who suggest that the
whole exchange between performers and spectators fundamentally privileges the male perspective and makes it impossible for women to be
represented on stage at all. Some theorists argue that the new generation of
female playwrights, directors, and producers is really just aping male
models, and that even good, strong female characters are undermined by
their position behind the proscenium arch.

These writers argue that the critical tradition that shapes spectators'
expectations of theatre allows no way to see women – except through the
historically male gaze. They suggest that women have appeared in
representation only as a mythological, idealized notion created to serve the
dominant ideological order. These writers say that the enforced passivity of
women is built into the performer/spectator/stage apparatus, and that
nothing short of a radical restructuring will allow women's active subjectivity to be represented in theatre.[2]

While women have been cheated both on stage and as spectators in the
dominant culture's theatre, women creating alternative theatre have also
been stifled. The mainstream media, for example, have neutralized feminist
perspectives in theatre by categorizing the diverse movement only in terms
of its difference from the mostly male standard. The convenient label
'women in theatre' is a misnomer that has obscured the political and
aesthetic differences among the variety of people lumped under its aegis.
But the same expedient, ambiguous labelling, has marred feminist critical
efforts as well, as even we who care about these issues struggle to define our
ideology and aesthetics in relation to the dominant culture and to each
other. Feminist academics and popular press critics over the last few years
have begun to realize the importance of sorting out the variety of work
produced from different 'women's' perspectives. If nothing else, it has
become clear that no one is fooled by subterfuge, and that politics really is
the issue.

The political era that provided the impetus for the new feminism has
been replaced by a new conservatism. The rightward shift of the country's
political mood has produced a trickle-down effect on the resources of any
group that describes itself as different from the popular, vehemently
conservative – or at least staunchly apolitical – majority. When *Women &
Performance* was applying for money two years ago, we were warned that
federal funding groups like the National Endowment for the Arts are
disinclined to offer grants to political projects.

For many groups in New York, the struggle to maintain a space in which
to produce precludes discussion of the producing organization's political or

ideological agenda. Margo Lewitin, artistic director of the Interart Center in Manhattan, said in an interview with *Backstage* last year that people are retreating from feminism in order 'not to limit their work'.[3] While Interart began as a place to display primarily women's theatre and fine arts, its purpose has clearly shifted. With Manhattan real estate development schemes threatening to re-zone Interart out of business, aesthetic and certainly ideological considerations must now seem extraneous.

But that very subtle, staunchly defended shift in focus is part of the reason feminist women who have maintained their ideological concerns in theatre are now getting such bad press. The funding crunch has exacerbated the tension between the several camps of women who work in theatre. It's dangerous these days to be branded a feminist, so many women try to disassociate themselves from the term. Julia Miles, director of the Women's Project at the American Place Theatre, denies that there are any ideological or political underpinnings to her group and publicly dismisses feminism as a threat to mainstream success. In the same *Backstage* article, Miles insisted the Women's Project wasn't founded on 'feminist notions'.[4]

Feminism is a touchy subject. But in order to describe the variety of women in theatre more precisely it is important to identify the different kinds of feminist ideology – like it or not – that underlie our efforts. It is useful to make two general points: first, that feminism is not an ideological monolith with prescriptive notions about theatre; and second, that different types of feminism are responsible for the variety of feminist theatrical forms and critical expressions. Women in theatre can generally be grouped according to the three distinct strains in feminist rhetoric: liberal, cultural or radical, and materialist.

Briefly, liberal feminists strive to achieve economic and political parity with men by working within existing government and social systems. Cultural, or radical, feminists propose a separate sphere of social and political activity comprised solely of women, whose values they see as innately superior to men's. Materialist feminists regard social relations in the context of material conditions, that change through history and are influenced by race, class, and sexual identification as well as by gender.[5] These distinctions offer a way to look more clearly at women in theatre.

From a purely sociological point of view, the theatre profession has allowed very few women to be placed in positions of influence as writers, directors, producers, or designers. Yet there are women working in theatre who insist that if their hands were holding the mirror, women would assume their rightful places beside men in the profession and see themselves reflected there.

Although many of them hesitate to accept the feminist label, these women are allied ideologically with liberal feminism. Many are affiliated with advocacy groups like the League of Professional Women in Theatre, the Women in Theatre Network, and the Women's Project, all based in New York, which define the issue as a problem with equal opportunity, not as one endemic to the medium. They are uneasy with the fact that the ghetto of women's groups is a place to draw attention to themselves before they can join the mainstream. Women who want to work in professional theatre need to prove that their abilities are equal to men's, so advocacy groups provide opportunities for their constituents to display their work in showcase productions and staged readings.

At issue here is the desire for validation. Telling safe stories of unsung women in history has become the signature production style generated by this attitude. As *Village Voice* critic Alisa Solomon pointed out in her review, the Women's Project 1986 'Women Heroes' series is a case in point. The one-woman show – or the several-women revue – in which dramatic moments from women's history are essentially read or enacted, is the perfect vehicle for women seeking validation from the culture at large.[6] The form testifies to women's worth – in the past tense, no less – without threatening anyone. Who can argue with the fact that historical figures like Emma Goldman were heroes? *A . . . My Name Is Alice*, an all-women revue that started at the Women's Project and has since become popular on the regional theatre circuit, is also an example of theatre that carefully avoids presenting a political threat while attempting to glorify women's experiences.[7]

The increasing visibility of this kind of work, and of women playwrights and to a certain extent directors, is a triumph of the liberal feminist endeavor. Ironically, however, many working women playwrights hesitate to accept the feminist label because for playwrights to survive economically, their plays must be produced widely in commercial venues, and overt politics is seen as threatening to theatre's 'universal' stance.

But is theatre really universal? There would be no need for distinguishing terms like women in theatre, Blacks in theatre, or Asians in theatre *if* the theatre was the melting pot of aesthetic and social tradition that it purports to be. The need for such terms is insidious proof that politics and ideology pump through the heart of what we call *the* theatre. To distinguish women in theatre at all is to reveal the lie of universality framed by the proscenium arch. The theatre has always specially been addressed to the privileged, visible, speaking 'majority' widely known as white, middle-class, and male: they are the 'universal' spectators.

The radical feminist movement of the late 1960s and early 1970s made an issue of this male gerrymandering of aesthetic forums. Many women working in experimental theatre groups at that time splintered off into radical feminist collectives that determined to mix ideology with aesthetics.[8] For feminist groups, such as the Women's Experimental Theatre in New York and At the Foot of the Mountain in Minneapolis, the goal became to bring feminist content into theatre and in the process to explore the possibilities of an alternative, distinctly female form. Women's experience and their intuitive, spiritual connection – with each other and with the natural world – took a hallowed place as the content of the new feminist theatre. A *female* universal standard was being born.

Guided by radical feminist ideology, feminist theatres wrestled with the issue of a female aesthetic. The traditional theatre hierarchy was rejected and the playwright as a single authoritative voice was cast out. Linear, well-made plays were discarded. Naturalistic plots were exchanged for myths, and realism disappeared with the return to ritual forms. The female aesthetic evolved as a strict anti-aesthetic; whatever was acceptable to patriarchal culture was unacceptable to the new women's counter-culture. By the mid-1980s 'radical feminist' as a distinguishing term was replaced by the phrase 'cultural feminist', since it more closely characterized those who believe that a separate women's culture can and should be created.[9]

The model for cultural feminist theatre's evolving form became extra-theatrical. Consciousness-raising – the social ritual of sharing previously unexpressed experiences – became its political and aesthetic cornerstone. Following the structure of consciousness-raising in one of their first acts of theatrical subversion, the Women's Experimental Theatre – or WET – appropriated a classic male text to be re-told from a female point of view. WET reclaimed *The Oresteia* by making its central question 'What happened to the women?' The narrative of the House of Atreus became *The Daughter's Cycle Trilogy*, the story of family told from the daughter's perspective. WET challenged the position of the universal male spectator by considering its spectators female witnesses to the stories of women's experiences they told. With the new stories came a new style – expository, improvisatory, testimonial, informal – geared to produce the shock of recognition in the new audience.

Consciousness-raising groups faded in the late 1970s as the movement grew more complex and varied. Differences among women over race, class, and sexual preference began to disrupt the celebrations about their commonality. But cultural feminism continues to promote sameness among women based on their common difference from men. As a result, the cultural feminist theatrical model has certain limitations and dangers.

The Daughter's Cycle Trilogy, for example, is based on the premise that all women share the experience of being daughters. By speaking to what they thought of as a transcendent idea of 'woman', however, WET began to unintentionally alienate members of their audience who could not fit themselves into the narrowly, universally drawn term. At the 1984 Modern Languages Association conference in New York, WET member Sondra Segal said that as a feminist performer, she is women's representative on stage. While the statement was meant to be inclusive and positive, as all of

WET's productions intend, it ends by being politically and theoretically naive. Only under the dictates of cultural feminism can any one woman represent all women. In theatrical terms, it also sounds a lot like the tragically flawed, universal man with whom we were all magically to identify, once upon a time.

Ironically, a lot of cultural feminist theatre production continues to refer to women in terms of men. WET fell into the trap of being obsessed about the nuclear family it wanted to leave. *Electra Speaks* – the last play in WET's *Daughter's* trilogy – ends with Electra stepping out of the patriarchal father's house. But WET never examined what was on the other side of that threshold. As a result, it remained trapped in the dramatic mirror that it thought would reflect women for the first time in cultural history. The group remained frozen in that theatrical and feminist historical moment because it never went beyond its concern with reflecting an undistorted image of woman – itself questionable – that was impossible in the mirror it held up. WET remained on the doorstep, while feminism moved on.

Where cultural feminist theatre gets tripped up by its desire to recast the universal spectator as a female, the materialist feminist perspective sets out to debunk the myth of universality. It suggests that femaleness – and maleness – is not a transcendent state of being, but a subject position that changes through history and is influenced by considerations of race, class, and sexual preference as well as gender. Materialist feminism suggests that since social relations and identities are constructed and manipulated for the benefit of those who control the society, these constructs can be exposed and changed.

The materialist feminist point, on the issue of representation, is that traditional theatrical forms are not inherently oppressive, but the ideology that governs them has promulgated dangerous assumptions about social relations. The theatre, as a cultural forum, has been used to promote the dominant culture's economic and political ends. The materialist method is to refashion the theatre's forms and content by changing the ideology that guides them.

The women in theatre doing the most exciting work in this area bend both gender and genre, and many of them are lesbians. The WOW Cafe in Manhattan's East Village offers a place for lesbian performers who play with gender issues to work on the margins of more legitimate theatre. They advertise mostly within the lesbian community; they don't apply for government grants; they are seldom reviewed in the mainstream press; and they enjoy their status as social and theatrical outlaws. As a result, they are free from the dominant culture's judgements, which hamper the mix of art and politics sought – or denied – by more fiscally accountable feminist groups.

The WOW Cafe set up shop in 1982 in a narrow storefront on East 11th

Street, and now leases space from the city in a nearly-abandoned ware-house building on East 4th.[10] Although it shares the block with LaMama and other legitimate alternative theatres, WOW has no aspirations to legitimacy. In 1984, when other more punk, apolitical East Village clubs were drawing enormous media attention, WOW remained neglected on the sidelines. A lesbian performance club just was not as chic to the uptown slummers who popularized the others. WOW could not be co-opted by fashion because lesbianism is still too threatening. After all, the folks at WOW are pushing against the polarization of gender, on which heterosexual culture is founded.

The strict, socially sanctioned construction of both male and female gender is parodied in every WOW performance. Performers dress in male and female drag while maintaining lesbian identities, so that the performances become not about men, and not about women, but about lesbians. WOW is socially and theatrically subversive because it represents women to women within the performer/spectator/stage apparatus – something the feminist theorists said could not be done.

Basing their work in theatre conventions like situation comedies, detective thrillers, and variety shows allows these performers to comment on and manipulate the traditional workings of the performance apparatus. Lesbianism is always assumed as the standard in WOW Cafe performances. When it replaces the historically heterosexual male axis of categorization, the way theatre communicates its ideological meanings between performers and spectators is thrown into high relief.[11]

One of the most popular WOW performers is Carmelita Tropicana, who is played by Alina Troyano. From her own Cuban ethnicity and her lesbian sexuality, Troyano has created a performance persona which is an amalgam of ethnic satire and male and female drag, all performed from a lesbian perspective. Carmelita is a flamboyant, Carmen Miranda-style talk-show host, costumed in a long gown, a feather boa, and heavy make-up that exaggerates the acceptable trappings of the feminine role. At other moments in her performances, Carmelita is costumed in male drag to parody the social construction of the male gender role.[12] Most of the lesbian performances at WOW use gender impersonation to overturn spectator expectations about both gender and performance. For example, a WOW production last spring called *Fear of Laughing* parodied 1950s television with a large cast of men and women, all played by women. The ideological assumptions of pieces of Americana like *Father Knows Best* become very clear when father is a lesbian and the middle-class living room is reconstructed in a low-budget theatre. The production ended with an abrupt interruption by a man (that is, a real man) in a firefighter's coat and hat who burst into the space yelling about the fire permit. His pre-emptive authority was so totally out of place that, for a moment, his threat seemed real. His intrusion stood as an uneasy reminder that representing lesbian sexuality to lesbian spectators is still a political act.

By maintaining its roots in a lesbian community for whom the performances are both entertaining and self-validating, WOW never waffles about who it serves or the politics of its project. WOW is community theatre, but ironically, because it is so specific, it has wide appeal. By appropriating familiar forms and injecting their genderized conventions with lesbian content, WOW catches the lie of universality these forms once proclaimed. The WOW performers stand so far outside sex opposition and gender polarization – and the limitations of the traditional theatrical mirror – that they seem to include every one in the specificity of their address. Not everyone is a lesbian, certainly, but the point is that not everyone is a white, middle-class, heterosexual male or universal female, either.

There is still really no such thing as women in theatre, but in little pockets of activity like the WOW Cafe, there are women diligently creating new messages from old mediums. That's why it's important to keep the different kinds of women in theatre straight, so to speak. Perhaps *Women & Performance* isn't specific enough for anyone to relate to. *Feminism and Performance: A Journal of Aesthetic Activism* might be more like it.

NOTES

1 For an analysis of the theatre-as-social-mirror analogy in terms of feminist theory on gender roles, see my 'Gender Impersonation Onstage: Destroying or Maintaining the Mirror of Gender Roles', *Women & Performance Journal*, 2: 2 (1985), 3–11.

2 See E. Ann Kaplan, *Women & Film: Both Sides of the Camera* (New York: Methuen, 1983), particularly her chapter 'Is the Gaze Male?', pp. 23–35; Laura Mulvey, 'Visual Pleasure and Narrative Cinema', *Screen*, 16: 3 (1975), 6–18; and Teresa de Lauretis, *Alice Doesn't: Feminism, Semiotics, Cinema* (Bloomington: Indiana University Press, 1984) for theoretical work on women in representation.

3 Francesca Primus, 'Women's Theatres Around Town: Feminist or Contemporary?' *Backstage*, 6 December 1985.

4 Ibid.; see also Julie Malnig, 'The Women's Project: A Profile', *Women & Performance Journal*, 1: 1 (1983), 71–3, in which Miles states that the ideal would be to phase out the Women's Project as women in theatre achieve the goal of parity with men.

5 See Alison Jaggar, *Feminist Politics and Human Nature* (Totowa, NJ: Rowman & Allanheld, 1983) for an investigation of feminist epistemology in relation to these terms; Zillah R. Eisenstein, *The Radical Future of Liberal Feminism* (New York: Longman, 1981) for an analysis of the potential radicalism of liberal feminism; Alice Echols, 'The New Feminism of Yin and Yang', in Ann Snitow, Christine Stansell, and Sharon Thompson, eds., *Powers of Desire: The Politics of Sexuality*

(New York: Monthly Review Press, 1983), pp. 439–59, for an explication of cultural feminism; and Judith Newton and Deborah Rosenfelt, eds., *Feminist Criticism and Social Change: Sex, Class and Race in Literature and Culture* (New York and London: Methuen, 1985), particularly their introduction, for a description of materialist feminism in relation to literary criticism that has helpful correlations to performance criticism.

I do not mean to imply a hierarchical progression in my placement and subsequent discussion of these terms. The continuum from liberal through materialist feminism is evolutionary, more than hierarchical. One does not replace the others; these separate movements continually inform each other. While I tend to subscribe, at the moment, to a materialist perspective, I do not mean to make judgements about liberal and cultural feminism except to point out that their distinctions illuminate a discussion of feminist theatre.

6 There is also an economic factor in the prevalence of one-woman shows in feminist theatre. As K. Kendall pointed out to me at the Riverside conference, these plays are easy to produce and to tour, and they often provide a means of income for women who need the flexibility and freedom of working for themselves. While I do not mean to condemn the form, I do feel it tends to have limited potential for expressing feminist knowledge and for experimenting with feminine formal inventions.

7 See Kate Davy's review of *A . . . My Name Is Alice* in *Women & Performance Journal*, 2: 1 (1984), 85–8.

8 For a history of the feminist theatre movement in the 1970s, see Janet Brown, *Feminist Drama: Definitions and Critical Analysis* (Metuchen, NJ: Scarecrow Press, 1980); Dinah Leavitt, *Feminist Theatre Groups* (Jefferson, NC: McFarland & Co., 1980); Elizabeth J. Natalle, *Feminist Theatre: A Study in Persuasion* (Metuchen, NJ: Scarecrow Press, 1985); and Helene Keyssar, *Feminist Theatre* (New York: Grove Press, 1985), particularly her chapter 'Roots and Contexts', pp. 1–21.

9 Alice Echols, in 'The New Feminism of Yin and Yang', writes, '*cultural feminism* . . . equates women's liberation with the development and preservation of a female counter-culture. The phrase *radical feminism* [is] used to describe the earlier antecedent of this movement' (p. 441, italics hers).

10 See Alisa Solomon, 'The WOW Cafe', *The Drama Review T105*, 29: 1 (Spring 1985), 92–101 for a history of the WOW Cafe. Kate Davy's '*Heart of the Scorpion* at the WOW Cafe', pp. 52–6, describes one of the WOW performances.

11 See Monique Wittig, 'The Point of View: Universal or Particular?', *Feminist Issues*, 3: 2 (1983), 63–9, for a relevant discussion of the 'axis of categorization'. See Kate Davy, 'Constructing the Spectator: Reception, Context, and Address in Lesbian Performance', *Performing Arts Journal 29*, 10:2 (1986), 43–52 for a description of Holly Hughes's *Lady Dick* that illustrates how the use of popular culture forms can foreground theatre conventions in terms of their gender bias.

12 For a full description of one of Carmelita's earliest performances, see my '*Carmelita Tropicana Chats* at the Club Chandalier', *The Drama Review T105*, 29:1 (Spring 1985), 26–32.

The rhetorical and political foundations of women's collaborative theatre*

JUDITH ZIVANOVIC

In 1973, Karlyn Kors Campbell wrote an article examining the 'rhetoric' of women's liberation. In that article, she discussed the characteristics of style involved in this rhetoric. She found that the primary purpose of this rhetoric was 'consciousness raising' directed toward other women and that traditional concepts of the rhetorical process were rejected – persuasion of the many by a leader who adapts to the audience needs and leads them to specific commitment or group action. She noted that these traditional means, designed to encourage passivity and acceptance in an audience, were at odds with the goals of women's liberation, especially the fundamental goal of self-determination. In addition, the rhetors had to deal with the situation that their audience, women, were traditionally divided from one another by almost all sources of identification: ranges of age, ethnic origin, income, even geography. Also, it was discovered that women, living in a male-oriented society, had rather undynamic self-concepts. Thus, rhetoric addressed to women had 'to transcend alienation and create "sisterhood", modify self-concepts to create a sense of autonomy and speak to women in terms of private, concrete individual experience, because women have little, if any, publicly shared experience.'[1] She goes on to state that such 'consciousness raising' involves, in the first place, meetings of small, leaderless groups in which each person can express herself and all are considered expert. The goal is to take the experience at the personal level and make it political – the participants are encouraged to understand and interpret their lives as women; generally each must decide which action is suitable for her.[2] The second major component of this type of rhetorical situation is the use of audience participation in this sharing – 'the goal of the work is a process, not a particular belief or policy'.[3] Thirdly, women's liberation rhetoric, according to Campbell, is characterized by 'the use of confrontative non-adjustive strategies designed to "violate the reality structure"'.[4] Thus, she concludes, 'women's liberation rhetoric is a DIALEC-

* A draft of this paper was read at the *Themes in Drama* International Conference held at the University of California, Riverside, in February 1987.

TIC between courses that deal with PUBLIC, structural problems and particularly significant statements of PERSONAL experience . . .'[5]

It may seem beside the point to begin a discussion of women's collaborative theatre with a summary of the components peculiar to feminist rhetoric. It is, however, the contention of this paper that such an overview is precisely to the point – that the process of women's collaborative theatre is largely geared to feminist concerns and has at its foundation these bases of feminist rhetorical and political theory. In fact, in 1978, Patti Gillespie published a paper entitled 'Feminist Theatre: A Rhetorical Phenomenon'. She argues that 'all feminist theatres are rhetorical enterprises; their primary aim is action, not art. Each group is using theatre to promote the identities of women, to increase awareness of the issues of feminism, or to advocate corrective change.'[6] This writer has been involved with women's collaborative performance as a performer, discussion leader, researcher and audience member. Through each capacity and contact with various groups, it has become clear that, despite the diversity of specific concerns, women's collaborative theatre has this rhetorical and political basis, which governs all action, from the very decision to utilize a collective form of production development, to the determination of theme and style, to the decisions concerning financial support.

In large measure, women choose to form a collaborative theatre group because of the special rhetorical capacity of theatre and because they have decided that the traditional (determined as male-dominated) theatre has not fulfilled their artistic needs. Eleanor Johnson, the co-founder of Emmatroupe, recognized that she would always be excluded from traditional theatre because of her vision of the avant-garde and 'because I was a woman with a woman-centered sensibility and commitment. The knowledge that I had worked so very hard to acquire would never be honored because my vision was antithetical to male values. As a result my aesthetic achievements are simply invisible . . .'[7] Yet, theatre has the special capacity to speak, in a collective voice, of collective, human concerns. As Dolores Brandon, founder of the New Cycle Theatre states, 'Yes, the theatre is a political agent. Relationships created on stage reinforce social relationships . . . it is the world we create on our stages which must be true to the collective essence of humankind.'[8]

Gillespie's examination confirms the choice of theatre due to its inherent capacity as a vehicle for a feminist rhetoric and politics. She affirms Campbell's view of feminist rhetoric as unlike typical public address forms and suggests that theatre provides special advantages: There is no obligation to provide systematic arguments – the women's theatre group can present its own vision of 'reality' with all of its complexity and contradictions. While public speaking can only assert connections, drama can embody them, presenting them in all their intricacies and incongruities.[9]

Women recognized this capacity of theatre but until the late 1960s and the 1970s, they had remained primarily within the ranks of traditional theatre, many of them holding Eleanor Johnson's view of the invisibility of their special vision. Rosemary Curb asserts that it was the 'second wave of the women's movement' which provided the impetus for women to remove themselves from traditional theatre and to begin to form groups on their own.[10] These groups would be devoted to women's concerns in both content and organization. For many of the groups this meant working in a collaborative fashion, rather than the traditional development of a perform-ance from established script, under the direction of one director. Mickie Massimino, a founding member of the Circle of the Witch Theatre, explains one reason for this decision:

> It has been my experience that working with men demands that the group must deal with the questions of power on an entirely different level, due to the fact that men are accustomed to holding some power, while women are not. Of course, not all women are loving, cooperative, non-competitive or willing to work and share skills. But since women are not used to exerting large amounts of power, either over themselves, or over others, they are not used to situations that demand that they give up power to others.[11]

My experience with such companies, both in person and through research, confirms that the determining force for development of not simply a women's theatre but a collaborative women's theatre was the desire to share skills and ideas without engaging in a power struggle – to affirm the goals of the women's movement not only in content of performance but in the co-operative sharing of the company members. These groups determined to work collaboratively, in a non-traditional mode, in order that they themselves and the audiences with whom they shared the experience would be broadened in their perceptions of relationships in society and women's identity in that society. Most groups would agree with Lucy Winer that the companies had a dual commitment to politics and to theatre; that the balance with many companies leaned more toward the political and the impetus was 'the excitement of an active community of women working together, outside the system, trying to create a new culture entirely our own'.[12] Many women's theatres have tended to fit this definition – they are a collective without a designated leader, engaging in largely non-traditional presentations which involve collaboration among the members, society, and the audience before, during, and after the presentations. The productions are, then, frequently in a state of flux; dynamic, both personal and political; non-realistic. The companies today continue the collaboration, experimenting and searching for forms that fit their specific purpose, 'for masterpieces are not single and solitary births; they are the outcome of many years of thinking in common, of thinking by the body of people, so that the experience of the mass is behind the single voice'.[13]

There are two kinds of collaboration: among the artists and between the artists and the audience prior to a performance or during a performance.[14] An examination of these processes of collaboration reveals most strongly the foundation of feminist rhetoric and politics within such companies.

1. AMONG THE ARTISTS

Women's theatres tend to be collective, started and maintained typically by between three and seven women.[15] They work together, largely without hierarchies and preferably without competition, taking duties which rely on their primary talents, and bringing their own perspectives on the themes and the art. As Dinah Leavitt states, 'No other experimental/political theatre has so extensively relied on collective playwriting.'[16] Theatres such as It's All Right to Be a Woman perform pieces which are entirely personal with the company, based on past experiences or dreams. These evolve through improvisation and theatre games until they are perfected into the performance piece. This type of effort is ongoing. While some companies have consistently benefited from this method of working, others have diverged from this course. For some theatres, this method permitted a more universal political voice emanating from very personal matters while, at the same time, permitting an equal voice for all members. Megan Terry, on the other hand, has found the method of improvisation time-consuming for the amount of material which ultimately finds its way into the script. For her method, in which the company collaborates to form a final script written by herself, a variety of means – from discussions with experts prior to performance, through expert and company reaction to written scenes – is more productive than improvisation from scratch.[17] Nonetheless, all collaborative companies utilize some form of ongoing sharing and winnowing. As playwright Karen Malpede stated: 'I have always felt that none of my plays could have been written were it not for the close working relationships I have had with the actors and directors of the previous play.'[18]

Most of the collective theatres are working toward a freedom from past strictures in order to make their particular comment. The Foot of the Mountain Theatre brochure can speak for many:

> We struggle to relinquish traditions such as non-participatory ritual and seek to reveal theatre that is circular, intuitive, personal, involving.[19]

2. ARTISTS AND THE AUDIENCE

To create this ritual, theatres not only use their own company members but frequently the collaboration extends to the audience in a variety of forms. It may be part of the creative process or it may occur, with participation or discussion, as part of the performance. Many feminist theatres collaborate in some way with the audience prior to the performance in order to present the themes in which they are interested and to bring forward each person's separate experiences toward a more universal political statement. For instance, Omaha Magic Theatre gathered numerous humanists and experts on language to discuss sexist language before they took the ideas and developed them into *American King's English for Queens*. They gathered experts on family abuse – sociologists, psychologists, law enforcement officials, etc. to discuss the problems of family abuse and then wrote the black comic *Goona Goona*, a Punch and Judy show of cyclical family abuse. They visited prisons and talked to prisoners before they wrote *Babes in the Bighouse*. They gathered from many people and sources stories of the plains area before writing *100,001 Horror Stories of the Plains*.[20] The stories, concerns and fears of several teachers in our summer workshop for teachers are included in the play *Kegger* because this was the method utilized by the company at the time Megan Terry participated in the workshop on our campus. In the case of this particular theatre, the final writing is generally done by Megan Terry or Jo Ann Schmidman. Ultimately turning to one writer is done by some of the theatres for several reasons: they are attempting to be more artistic and have a unified voice; they believe there is a time for creative anarchy and a time for some authoritarianism; publishers are not very interested in publishing the group efforts – they want a discernible, preferably recognizable, name.

Few of the plays done by the Foot of the Mountain Theatre in Minneapolis have been published in the recent past. In the early days, they improvised much like the early work of the Omaha Magic Theatre. Martha Boesing, their resident playwright, wrote the final play they would do. For instance, *Antigone Too* by Boesing was formulated when the collective worked together with twenty-one student actors who joined the theatre for the summer to create the play and learn feminist acting technique.[21] Lately, they have been collaborating as a group of actors or with the community and have all done part of the writing. This latest writing has not been published. Two productions with which I am familiar are a case in point: *Ladies Who Lunch* and *Neurotic Erotic Exotics* which was created in collaboration with the Spiderwoman Theatre, a Native American feminist theatre group from New York. The former production began as a workshop project to do acting exercises with older women. The women developed the story line – a tea room in which the ladies like to take tea and talk is to be torn down and they strive to save it, in the course of which they relate past experiences there which are important to their lives. The older women then did the production. In *Neurotic Erotic Exotics*, the company auditioned from the community and then worked in the method of the Spiderwoman Theatre which is to bring in stories and tell them in narrative form and do a number of improvisations associated with this. The group then sifts

through and decides on the best stories and tries to help the narrator/
actress to strengthen the story.[22] This collective method with no one
playwright can be interesting and bring out highly emotional reactions if
the women dig deeply, but the method has also been criticized when it
became what the critics viewed as inconsistent and amateurish. It is said
that It's All Right to Be a Woman Theatre, which performs pieces based
primarily on the performers' experiences, sometimes has situations in
which the cast is so involved and choked that they cannot go on; other times
they are stunning; other times they are very inconsistent in quality.[23]

The work of the Circle of the Witch Theatre during its four years of
existence fairly consistently followed a favored pattern in its relationship to
its audience. The group would decide upon a theme of interest and make a
preliminary outline of concerns. Then research of printed material would
be undertaken. Since the group was concerned with the relationship of the
particular problem to the immediate Minneapolis/St Paul audience,
research would be done via questionnaire, frequently door-to-door, in order
to instill immediacy and universality as well as local flavor and interest into
their productions. As their pieces developed through various stages, they
would have women who understood the issues come in to view the
rehearsals and gradually have small audiences critique the content and
presentation.[24]

There are different ways in which the companies get their audiences
involved in performance. Sometimes the audience is an integral part of the
performance. In the Foot of the Mountain production of Martha Boesing's
The Moon Tree, which takes place in an asylum, all the men had to come into
one area and be the visitors; the women members of the audience were
considered inmates and could move about and sit anywhere.[25] Often
productions are not done on a stage; instead they are performed in the midst
of the audience, providing a sense of actual presence in the setting and at the
event. This was done in Omaha Magic Theatre's *Babes in the Bighouse*. The
audience entered as if into the prison and the scenes were played in close
proximity to the audience. The idea was to make the audience members
feel, at one and the same time, as though they were in the prison but also
that there was a commonality between some of the prisoners' suffering and
that of the outside world.[26] Sometimes the show will even stop, as in an It's
All Right to Be a Woman production when a woman in the audience is
asked to tell a dream and the production continues, with the actors
improvising and physicalizing the dream. In a production of Martha
Boesing's *The Story of a Mother*, the audience members were periodically
called upon to provide additions or bridges of material, as when they were
asked to call out things their mothers had told them or to complete 'I Never
Said . . .' as their mother or themselves as mothers. Finally, the production
concluded with the women as daughters completing 'I Never Said . . .' as if

to their mothers.[27] In Omaha Magic Theatre's production of *100,001 Horror Stories of the Plains*, the audience was encouraged to bring a dish for a picnic in lieu of money for a ticket. Members of the audience were given a bowl of stew when they arrived and gathered more food from the donations. They were seated at picnic tables with the actors, who helped serve them and gradually got up, after getting acquainted with the persons at their table, and began to tell them the stories.[28] All productions of this type of theatre are presentational rather than representational, frankly acknowledge the presence of the audience and frequently speak directly to them or request verbal or non-verbal responses which may modify the production. Productions have opened with chants or sing-alongs, or this type of action may occur during the production. In addition, I am not aware of any such theatre which does not have discussion after performance as a regular part of the session. It is important to the companies to give their audiences, which are still largely women – in some theatres men are excluded – the opportunity to express their reactions to the pieces and to share their experiences. It is important to give the final impetus to the 'consciousness raising', and the content of these discussions adds another dimension to the production. After the Foot of the Mountain production 'in the asylum', discussions became a sometimes emotional telling of stories; the women were encouraged to 'claim their own madness', thus becoming part of the ritual which is very important to many of the women's companies.[29]

Most women's theatres adhere, with their own particular contributions and variations, to the statement of The Women's Experimental Theatre:

> Our program includes the creation and performance of collaborative works, the development of experimental methods of acting through workshops, and public research with women on themes relevant to our experience.[30]

In varied ways, then, the companies attempt, through workshops, discussions, and production experimentation, to develop a style, themes, and an audience relationship which best serve their purposes. The feminist actress does not live in a 'world of her own' but is constantly open to the suggestions of the group and the relationship with the audience. The woman in the audience comes to realize that she is the 'acting partner' of the performer on stage, a partner in forming the production and in creating the moment of performance. The Women's Experimental Theatre, like Circle of the Witch, does a very systematic research project with many productions – decides on a thematic area, prepares a questionnaire associated with key experience areas, and then goes forth to encourage women to 'challenge or corroborate' something the company has come to believe is a truth.[31]

This 'either/or' is typical of much of the work – frequently there are no absolutely right answers provided by the productions. Sometimes people are frustrated with productions which do not give answers but raise many

questions which the audience member must answer for herself. Among
their requirements for sound 'political art', Alexa Freeman and Jackie
MacMillan require the development of a 'visionary content'.[32] Today, after
a decade and a half of women's collaborative theatre, the content is still
heavily laden with consciousness-raising material and questions, rather
than 'visions of a future society'. As a recent issue of the *Foot of the Mountain
Newsletter* notes, they reject the 'One size fits all notions of feminism'.[33] Also,
as attested in the recent *Women in Theatre Festival Newsletter*,

> Many of the pieces presented problems rather than solutions; it is a sad fact
> that the position of women, the poor, persons of color, and other oppressed
> groups has not changed significantly enough in recent years to eliminate the
> need to talk about it, reveal it, and confront it. Theatre often presents the
> stimulus to thought which can lead to change.[34]

Again, full circle to Karlyn Campbell, who said each woman must decide
'whether, and if so, what action' is appropriate.

So collaboration is pervasive in such theatres – among the members and
with the audience and at every stage of the process. This mode is clearly
process-oriented throughout. Why do theatre this way? Campbell and
Gillespie have suggested that a new mode is needed for the rhetorical
emphases and for the particular audience. The theatre members' position, I
believe, is well articulated by the collective of the Women's Experimental
Theatre:

> Theatre is an inherently collaborative art form. We do not do it out of principle
> but because we love it – it is exciting, stimulating, and forces our personal and
> artistic growth at an amazing rate.[35]

This theatre process also is designed to provide the atmosphere for the
personal and political growth of the audience. Most of the theatres in the
United States which perform a feminist 'rhetoric', and I consider this to be
the majority of the women's theatres, utilize this process of collaboration
among themselves and the audience. As Dinah Luise Leavitt states:

> Although no two feminist theatres are identical, certain common character-
> istics such as collective organization, process-orientation, focus on the
> woman's experience, community involvement, lack of money, and use of
> experimental developmental techniques are discernible among them.[36]

Because of a strong political orientation, some theatres have refused to
accept any funding which may represent ties or strictures of any kind. This
disdain of funding has been a mitigating factor in the demise of some of the
theatres but others have used it to their advantage, keeping the productions
simple yet imaginatively filled with the appurtenances which speak to
women's concerns.

> Those very qualities considered by society to mark our inferiority will prove the
> source of our energy and power. . . . We will bring together all kinds of art forms

and styles to submerge the audience in our experience. Film, tapes, music, slides, sculptures, paintings etchings, actresses, dancers, puppets, masks everywhere, on top of you, below you, around you . . . Also, we must bring the environment of our lives to the stage. Cooking utensils, cosmetics, cleaning gear, underwear, hair rollers, wigs, diapers . . .[37]

Women's collaborative theatre frequently reverses the apparent problem of lack of funds to the advantage of creating a distinctive 'women's theatre' statement. The soft sculpture utilized in the Omaha Magic Theatre productions of *Goona Goona, American King's English for Queens,* and their total decor of collected quilts for *100,001 Horror Stories of the Plains* provide a striking visual statement of this distinctive women's collaborative theatre design.

The rhetorical and political bases of the theatre add complications beyond those of financial considerations. A collective and largely leaderless method of making decisions in all matters, including the script and style of production, is a time-consuming and frequently frustrating and chaotic form of decision-making, yet, when it works, there is something immensely satisfying about this process-orientation. The lack of a single, well-known playwright may mitigate against publication and lead to inconsistency of artistic merit; it may also provide more universality and variety than is possible from one vision. Because the theatres tend to be poor and engage in extensive developmental work with a collective of writers, not only is very little of the work published, but there has never developed an adequate theory of citicism to cope with the productions. Whether deliberate or coincidental, there is a method to this madness: it means we, as audience members, cannot simply read the plays, we have to go to see the productions. We have to make our own critical judgements, and, even if the productions are not artistically spectacular, it is seldom that audiences will consider the presentations to be dull. The collaborative process generally results in plays about more than one leading figure and focuses on both the notion of autonomy for the woman and solidarity among women.[38] Though numerous theatres have fallen by the wayside in the struggle to balance the political and the artistic, there have consistently been reports that the productions have succeeded in changing lives – certainly of the performers; at times of the audience members – and that is an outcome for any theatre, but especially a political theatre, devoutly to be wished.

NOTES

1 Karlyn Kors Campbell, 'The Rhetoric of Women's Liberation: An Oxymoron', *Quarterly Journal of Speech*, 59: 1 (1973), 79.

2 Ibid., p. 79.

3 Ibid., p. 80.

4 Ibid., p. 81.

5 Ibid., p. 85.

6 Patti P. Gillespie, 'Feminist Theatre: A Rhetorical Phenomenon', *Quarterly Journal of Speech*, 64: 3 (1978), 286. The emphasis in this paper is on the majority of collaborative women's theatres which are a collective of women performing for a largely or entirely female audience.

7 Eleanor Johnson, 'Notes on the Process of Art and Feminism', in *Women in Theatre: Compassion and Hope*, ed. Karen Malpede (New York: Limelight Editions, 1983), p. 247. See also, Margaret Croyden, 'Women Directors and Playwrights', *Viva*, May 1974, p. 39.

8 Dolores Brandon, 'On Acting', in *Women in Theatre: Compassion and Hope*, pp. 258; 261.

9 Gillespie, 'Feminist Theatre', p. 291.

10 Rosemary K. Curb, 'The First Decade of Feminist Theater in America', *Chrysalis, Catalog of Feminist Theater – Part 2*, #10, p. 63.

11 Mickie Massimino, 'Collectively Speaking: Part II', *Gold Flower*, May/June 1977, p. 6. See also, Dinah L. Leavitt, 'The Lavender Cellar Theatre' in *Women in American Theatre*, ed. Helen Krich Chinoy and Linda Walsh Jenkins (New York: Crown, 1981), p. 309.

12 Lucy Winer, 'Staging for Consciousness-Raising' in *Women in American Theatre*, pp. 307; 302.

13 Dinah Luise Leavitt, *Feminist Theatre Groups* (Jefferson, NC: McFarland and Co., 1980), p. 99.

14 For an interesting discussion of the complex message system involved, see, Elizabeth J. Natalle, *Feminist Theatre: A Study in Persuasion* (Metuchen, NJ: Scarecrow Press, 1985), pp. 15ff.

15 Occasionally the theatre has a leader and some groups have included men among the founders; however, the majority of collaborative theatres have been founded by groups of three to seven women.

16 Leavitt, *Feminist Theatre Groups*, p. 101.

17 Interview with Megan Terry, June 1983.

18 Leavitt, *Feminist Theatre Groups*, p. 9.

19 Ibid., p. 64.

20 Interview with Terry and participation as discussion leader for *Goona Goona*. Also, see preface of each play: Megan Terry, *American Kings English for Queens* (Omaha: Omaha Magic Theatre Press, 1978); Megan Terry, *Babes in the Bighouse* (Omaha: Omaha Magic Theatre Press, 1974); *100,001 Horror Stories of the Plains: A New Musical* (Omaha: Omaha Magic Theatre Press, 1978).

21 Jill Dolan, 'Women's Theatre Program ATA: Creating a Feminist Forum', *Women & Performance: A Journal of Feminist Theory*, 1: 2 (Winter 1984), 9.

22 Interview with Artistic Director Phyllis Jane Rose, December 1985, and *At the Foot of the Mountain Presents Newsletter* (Fall, 1985), 22 November to 22 December.

23 Leavitt, *Feminist Theatre Groups*, p. 108.

24 *Circle of the Witch Papers* (St Paul: Minnesota Historical Society), Boxes 4–5.

25 Leavitt, *Feminist Theatre Groups*, p. 74.

26 Interview with Terry and preface to the play. See also, Rosemary K. Curb, 'Re/

cognition, Re/presentation, Re/creation in Woman-Conscious Drama: The Seer, The Seen, The Scene, The Obscene', *Theatre Journal*, October 1985, p. 313.

27 Martha Boesing, 'The Story of a Mother, A Ritual Drama' in *Women in the American Theatre*, pp. 45–8.

28 Interview with Terry and preface to the play.

29 Leavitt, *Feminist Theatre Groups*, p. 76.

30 *Women in Theatre*, p. 235.

31 Clare Coss, Sondra Segal, and Roberta Sklar, 'Notes on the Women's Experimental Theatre' in *Women in Theatre* (New York: Grove Press, 1982), p. 242.

32 Alexa Freeman and Jackie MacMillan, 'Prime Time: Art and Politics', *Quest: A Feminist Quarterly* (Fall, 1975), p. 30.

33 *At the Foot of the Mountain Presents Newsletter*, (Fall, 1985).

34 *Women in Theatre Festival Newsletter*, 1 (Jamaica Plain, Mass., 1986), 2.

35 Coss, Segal, Sklar, 'Notes on the Women's Experimental Theatre', p. 238.

36 Leavitt, *Feminist Theatre Groups*, p. 17.

37 See, for example, Winer, 'Staging for Consciousness-Raising', p. 305.

38 Ibid., p. 302.

The next stage: devaluation, revaluation, and after

DIANE SPEAKMAN

PREFATORY NOTES

This account of Magdalena '86, the first international festival of women in experimental theatre, is partial in two senses: I was unable to see and so cannot write about three of the performances and I attended only one series of workshops; and in its bias, my subjectivity – everyone present would have placed emphases differently; made other connections and interpretations; been stimulated (or not) by the event to follow other paths.

I would like to express my thanks to all the practitioners who talked with me, sometimes through interpreters, sometimes when they were tired and preoccupied with the demands of their workshops and/or performances; and, particularly, to Susan Bassnett, Aileen Christodoulou and Jo Swift. Errors and inaccuracies remain, of course, my responsibility.

(Autumn 1986)

Cardiff Laboratory Theatre, the company responsible for initiating Magdalena '86, has created some seventy experimental theatre pieces for special events in and out of doors, as well as more formal productions for theatre spaces, over the past twelve years. Many of the projects have toured throughout Europe.

In common with other experimental groups, Cardiff Laboratory Theatre constructs its productions, which have a strong visual, musical and physical bias, from individual and collective experiences and observations. The process through which these are assimilated, refined, built up and expressed anew as 'the story discovered' produces the style and decides the nature of the collaboration. The 'performance' is thus a sharing with the audience of the group culture and dynamic.

Although the group's structure and permanence, and members' ways of working together, have passed through various phases, three interrelated areas of activity have remained constant over the twelve-year period and are the bases of the group's theory and practice. The first is the performance projects themselves. The second is the Centre for Performance Research

(CPR): this is the group's memory bank and educative resource, housing all kinds of material about experimental performance, theoretical, critical and actual, from previous projects, as well as information collected from audiences, other companies and individual specialists. The third area is that of collaborative projects.

As early as 1977, Cardiff Laboratory Theatre was invited to an international meeting of theatre groups in Bergamo, instigated by Eugenio Barba, the director of Odin Teatret, Holstebro, Denmark, and former disciple of Jerzy Grotowski. This was crucial to the group's development in several ways. For example, on their return, members negotiated to put down roots in an extension of Chapter Arts Centre's Edwardian school building, and the gymnasium became the group's base. Another important outcome was the growth of collaborative work with individuals and companies from at home and abroad, including Odin Teatret (1980), and Grotowski's Teatr Laboratorium from Wroclaw (1982). Their example and that of Artaud have informed the work of many of the individual women and women's groups taking part in Magdalena '86 – in the emphases on dream and trance and the creation of a special kind of energy, anthropological 'fishing' for revitalizing material with which to improvise and the dedicated training of the body and voice as instruments.

The idea of having, for the first time in Europe, an international festival of women in experimental theatre was conceived in 1983 at another festival in Trevignano by Jill Greenhalgh, who became the project's director, Julia Varley of Odin Teatret, Geddy Aniksdal of Grenland Friteater, and others. They were concerned on one hand about experimental theatre's increasing struggles to combat inertia and create and develop into the unknown, while receiving less and less funding and public interest; on the other, they were curious about the nature of women's creativity and keen that these actors, with their own artistic strengths and presence, should be given more opportunity to devise their own art, if it *is* distinct; explore their own experience, fully bring to life their own visions and culture, exert their rightful influence in male-dominated companies and open up new directions for their work. The festival's title, 'Magdalena', established early on, derived from the cult of Mary Magdalen, a powerful, independent spirit exuding sexual energy, relegated to the margins of society rather like women's art.

The festival was funded by the Welsh Arts Council, the Calouste Gulbenkian Foundation, Chapter Arts, the British Council and various private sponsors; it was organized by a team of more than twenty-eight women and men. Greenhalgh worked on the project more or less continuously for three years. Using personal contacts made during her work with Cardiff Laboratory Theatre, she invited up to thirty women, each on the basis of her contribution to experimental theatre in her own country either in a group or solo, from about fifteen countries, including South and North America, Europe, but not the Third World, to participate as workshop leaders, performers, visual artists, technical staff. Each woman invited had to find her own funding.

Magdalena was planned in two phases, covering nearly three weeks. Phase I, from 11–17 August, comprised morning workshops, afternoon discussions and other events, and at least three sequential evening performances. From 18–28 August the practitioners collaborated in an unstructured female process, and in Phase II, 29–30 August, showed their work-in-progress to the public. All the events were open to men and only two workshops – Kozana Lucca's and Maria Consagra's – were for people with previous experience of vocal or physical theatre work.

In launching this first festival in Wales the aims of the organizers were: to open up discussion of women's role in new theatre forms and to encourage the public to appreciate women's artistic power and the validity of female interpretations of life; to provide a forum for women from different cultures to exchange ideas about their work in experimental theatre in a variety of companies; to explore the nature and different aspects of women's creativity and perhaps attempt to define its components; to bring strong talented women artists together that they might share and develop their work, and to allow something to take root organically from that collaboration; to produce a record of the festival's work and process; to break down all sorts of barriers – between theatre and life, performers and designers, artists and audience – to reduce physical tensions and linguistic misunderstandings.

On the morning of 11 August, about 120 women and a handful of men crowded into Cardiff Laboratory Theatre's gym to register for workshops.

In the company of about twenty-five other women, I began working on sense-perception techniques with Graciela Serra, a Mapuche Indian from Argentina. Serra met Gerda Alexander (no relation to the Alexander of *the* Alexander technique) thirteen years ago and has been developing her own approach to body work on Alexander's principles – of, for instance, the flexible use of correct amounts of energy for each action – since then. Serra specializes in building up intuitive physical awareness and working on tensions all over the body, accumulated in daily and theatrical life: children's perception of the contradiction between their parents' words and their body language, which affects their own behaviour; relaxation techniques for pregnant women who have opted for natural childbirth; actors' chronic stress points. Her aim is to unblock, to encourage healing creative energy to flow once more, as it did in our first months of life.

At twenty, Serra had wanted to be everything – dancer, actor, journalist, musician. She had a devastating rejection at theatre school, when a famous

director told her she would never succeed in theatre because she was too
blocked. Encouraged by a female teacher there, Serra began to think of
teaching and started body expression classes at Patricia Stockoe's prestigious school in Buenos Aires. Through her, Serra got to know the
influential book, *La eutonia* [balance, tone] *de Gerda Alexander*, and ranged
widely in her reading – neurology and anthropology as well as theoretical
works on theatre. Eventually, Serra started up her own school, with a
friend. (It was while working with a class on tensions in the arms there that
Serra overheard one man, whose body had been unreceptive to all the
exercises, say, 'This one would be good for torture', and knew she was being
watched by the police.)

Serra is the embodiment of her teaching in her daily life: she moves with
flowing grace, suppleness, and *energy*. Although I, in common with other
members of her workshop, had strong physical reactions to the exercises, by
Day 4 I felt on a different plane, healed, invigorated, sharply intuitive and
creative: her techniques do work. She also embodies her teaching in her art
and, for me, Serra as shaman, conjuring by means of her spirits, scenes from
the (real) life of Facundina Mirando, a 110-year-old Chinquana Indian
woman, pushed to the very edges of society, provided the most intense and
moving experience of the festival. Using only the simplest of props – some
hats and chalk for the circles of magic – and very little text (in Spanish), she
offered us the essence of the time of youth and love-making; the experience
of childbirth; and beyond, the time of the dead. At one point in the
enactment, when Serra had just drawn a circle, the lights over her head
began to crackle and blink – spirits possess energy; power beyond science
and rationality . . .

Serra created her piece with the help of Eduardo Hall, an actor–director
(and since 1977 her husband). Eduardo's work with Barba and the Odin
Teatret in Italy in 1981 had a great influence on both of them: Serra found
herself sympathetic to Barba's and Grotowski's ideologies of theatre and
felt that she had naturally been moving in the same direction. She wanted to
do further research, and she wanted again to express herself, to perform. It
took eighteen months to construct *Facundina*. Serra immersed herself in the
culture and (lost) language of the Chinquana Indians and began to build
up scenes, deciding which and how much text to use, with Eduardo
observing and making suggestions. It is *her* show, the power of veto is hers;
but she feels his participation is vital – he helps her to be disciplined, to go
forward again. Finding funding in Argentina is extremely difficult and they
each had to have multiple jobs, working up to twelve hours a day to exist
and then find time for their son, and for *Facundina* at weekends. Exhaustion
and anxiety over personal and political issues were part of each day's diet.
When *Facundina* was first put on, some critics in Argentina said the piece
was an anthropological investigation rather than theatre; but others and

11 Graciela Serra (photo: Mary Giles)

workers in European experimental theatre came out strongly in its support. Serra is extremely interested in audience reactions and knows that in Facundina, a woman nobody in Latin America cares about, she makes some members of the audience feel guilty, that they're being attacked.

In the summer of 1985, in the period of 'democracy', Serra was perform-ing in a tourist city in Argentina, when she was told that she and Eduardo were next on the list of those to be 'disappeared'. Until then she had wanted to stay in her country, but she suddenly thought how could she live with her current level of fear in a 'democracy'? With her family, Serra now lives in Spain, continuing her teaching, research and performances.

Akne Theatre's production, in Polish, of Genet's *Maids* was disturbingly powerful. The venue, a cellar under the CPR, was an essential ingredient in the evening's success: smells of corruption, damp stone, rotting woodwork, something indefinable; thick motes of dust floating through the light beams; bench seating arranged to induce claustrophobia – truly, 'the darkness is dangerous'. In Zofia De Inez-Lewczuk's set design, Madame's bedroom was draped with black and white dresses, some upside-down like bats or hanged people. And then there were the mirrors, literal and metaphorical, layers of them. The sisters, narcissistically and incestuously reflect their own ambivalence and self-loathing (*Claire:* 'I'm sick of seeing my image thrown back at me by a mirror, like a bad smell. You're my bad smell'); through their ceremonial role reversal, mirroring the class struggle, they play out servants as 'rich people's distorting mirrors'; the text as a whole reflects the audience's, society's, secret fantasies and impulses. Appropri-ately but ironically, a large portrait of Saint Genet, actor and martyr, was triumphantly shown to the audience at the end.

The Maids was adapted and directed by Zofia Kalińska, who also played Madame. Her performance and those of her colleagues in Akne Theatre, Jolanta Biela-Jęczmyk (Claire) and Jolanta Gadaczek-Nowak (Solange), were compelling and impeccably orchestrated. In the trance-like state of expanded consciousness decreed by Artaud/Genet, the actors' destructive energy flared up and died away or was transformed into a powerful sado-masochistic eroticism.

Zofia Kalińska has been working in Polish state theatre for more than thirty years. She met Tadeusz Kantor in 1960 and joined his company. At Richard Demarco's invitation, they performed at Edinburgh Festivals in Witkiewicz plays, including *Dainty Shapes and Hairy Apes* and ten years ago, Kantor brought the avant-garde 'Theatre Hundred' of Cracow to Cardiff with his *The Dead Class*. Both Kantor and Witkiewicz have had important influence on Kalińska's work. However, the big turning-point in her life was breaking with Kantor and forming in Cracow her own company, the only women's theatre in Poland, initially without any state support. She

12 Members of Akne Theatre in Genet's *Maids* (photo: Jan Jeczmyk)

called it Akne Theatre, after the daemonic heroine of Witkiewicz's book, *622 Falls of Bungo*, a creation based on the great nineteenth-century Polish actor, Irene Solska, with whom Witkiewicz was in love. Kalińska and her colleagues began experimenting with *The Maids*, working through to their own supranatural charged state of playing. At first they performed free, for friends; then gradually they received some funding for the set and dresses; in 1985, supported by Dom Kultury Pod Baranami, they were invited by Richard Demarco to perform at the Edinburgh Festival and in Coventry, where they were received with the same enthusiasm as at Cardiff.

Akne Theatre members continue to perform in their own official theatres, so time together is limited. (Kalińska works in the Słowacki company, Cracow, and directed for the first time in 1986 – Williams's *Glass Menagerie*, also playing Amanda.) The new piece Akne plans to do, *The Sale of the Daemonic Women*, will be based on Witkiewicz's plays, which all contain female daemons to partner the male Titanic heroes, and it will again play in the womb, the unconscious, a cellar. It will be set in the present and contain perhaps males as hanging puppets or half-dressed anatomical models and female types meeting in a kind of grave after death, comparing experiences, looking back over their lives. The types will be drawn from the praying mantis, the nun, the woman who committed suicide while pregnant, a young mad woman also pregnant who wants to kill herself *again*, a mother who grows ever stronger as she ages, a nymphomaniac, a narcissistic woman who has regressed to infantilism . . . The fascination of these types for Kalińska seems to be their potential to embody daemonism rather than to make statements on sexual politics. She saw the weekend workshop she was involved in as an opportunity not to teach, for she doesn't see herself in that role, but to explore this range of types through techniques leading to the expanded consciousness of dream-state or trance.

Several members of the workshop reacted adversely either to Kalińska's work methods or to the images of women being presented, or both. Others, in the workshop and in the Phase II collaboration – including, interestingly, Brigitte Kaquet, whose work in *Hésitations 3* is at the other end of the spectrum, with mixed-media high technology – felt that the methods practised, the concentration of intensity, the improvisations, play with ritual objects, worked well for them and they wanted to continue using them in the future, possibly continuing to meet as a group.

Despite the negative and male-referring images of women she projects, Kalińska certainly believes in women's strengths in theatre; and the style of ensemble acting Akne is developing seems to me specifically a women's style, something new, powerful and exciting.

Anna Lica's *Madame Bovary – Downtown*, Netta Plotzky's *The Happiness of the Pre-form*, Lis Hughes Jones's *8961 – Caneuon Galar a Gobaith (Songs of Grief and*

Hope) and Sandra Salmaso/Cinzia Mascherin's *No Man's Land* didn't have the same degree of intensity as Serra's *Facundina* or Akne's *Maids*, but each, through dance, song, visual imagery, mask, lighting, music, snatches of text, symbolic objects, experimented, often successfully, to conjure various internal states of reality.

Anna Lica, formerly of The Theatre Marquez, Århus, Denmark, constructed her show, *Madame Bovary – Downtown* (given in English), with Tage Larsen from Odin Teatret, who also directed. Lica gave a varied and polished performance; she has a strong presence and a distinctive quality of contained stillness. She and Larsen offer Sally as a contemporary reflection of Emma Bovary's self-indulgent yearnings for that 'marvellous world where all was passion, ecstasy, delirium'; Sally is installed in poverty in a downtown Parisian garage after being spurned by her husband George. (In Lica's skilful impersonation, George is so emotionally impoverished he can only spout from the *Wall Street Journal* or *The New York Times* before sending Sally his rejection letter.) In the garage, from a crate marked 'Do not tilt', Sally flamboyantly re-runs her life, enacting the compulsive image-making of our time, always starting from a base-line of masochistic self-loathing, invalidation and distrust. So we see the woman whose husband and children have left, forced to choose between days of dutiful housework or driving maniacally round Paris, long blonde hair streaming in the wind; or, in the thick alcoholic haze of the party our culture has constructed for male heroes – Jagger, Newman, Bogart – Sally, the hostess with the leastest, feverishly welcomes guests to the ironic strains of Sinatra's 'My Way'. There were some stunning visual images: Sally winding the tape of George's rejection letter round the neck of his suit hanging from a stand; the slices of lemon the woman abandoned fitted inside her glasses before her bitter drive round Paris; Lica's dance, in a long white slipper-satin dress whose sleeves extended until they became a straitjacket into which she fastened herself (this was so powerful a climax for me that I had difficulty attending as the sequence moved on); and the last image as Sally lies dead across the crate, surrounded by blue standard lights flashing crazily.

Both Emma's and Sally's lives lacked content, contact with their own reality and worth as women; all – life, death, emotions – had been play. *Madame Bovary – Downtown* is disturbing, powerful, full of content about inflated emptiness, and therefore its style of presentation seemed, appropriately, kitschy (but I know other women thought Lica was presenting woman-as-victim essentially uncritically). The key line, for me, was Cleopatra's 'I'll set a bourn how far to be belov'd'. Or, as Mae West had it, 'Stuff heartbreak'.

Lica studied at the Århus Theatre Academy for eighteen months and between 1981 and early 1986, worked in the Theatre Marquez, particularly with Else Marie Laukvik from Odin Teatret, who encouraged her to create

13 Anna Lica impersonating George (photo: Jan Rüsz)

14 Anna Lica in *Madame Bovary – Downtown* (photo: Mary Giles)

her own piece. Some early group work was done, but at that stage the show was quite formless. Then Lica began to establish Sally's text herself, and to experiment with dance and song. She showed what she had done to Tage Larsen and together they thought of using Flaubert's text, because they wanted story. They gradually interwove more and more material from Shakespeare, Laing, journal entries and dreams, developing a novel form of direction in that they collaborated by telephone.

Lica gave the first performance of *Madame Bovary – Downtown* in April 1985 and plans to tour the show further in Europe. She has begun a second collaboration with Larsen, on a Shakespearian theme, but this time they will both be actors, taking equal responsibility for the text, movement and imagery.

Netta Plotzky, from Israel, gave a performance remarkable for its visual inventiveness, its generosity – many needs and fears are revealed – and its swiftly-flowing transformations in movement and emotion, from pathos to laughter, curiosity to menace, to sexual invitation . . . She was also the only performer to establish an explicit relationship with the audience: she started playing among us, eating an apple, tearing our tickets, making noises, evoking laughter. Thereafter, the show, *The Happiness of the Pre-form*, was split into three parts.

The first was 'Variations on Ophelia', the 'mad' woman validating the non-rational – we feel on the whole 'comfortable with her madness'. To flute music Netta, dressed in an all-embracing white plastic mac, with an umbrella that suddenly turned on her and one enormous, one normal-size shoe, that reminded me of Little Tich or Chaplin, drank from the umbrella, attempted to stuff up the flute, brought mid-stage an object wrapped in red cloth (what *was* it? a baby? a stone?) . . . A figure in black enters (Anna Lica) – Hamlet, Death, Fate – and Ophelia dons an absurd small black net hat, complete with squeaky squid attachment, to lure him. At this point she is speared by a butterfly (memories of love, happier days . . .). Squeaking, on the attack, Ophelia hesitates and then collapses into a waiting wheelbarrow (pram, coffin, refuse carrier); the mood changes yet again, and after a moving and pathetic sexual invitation, in which she opens her self, her legs, to the black unresponsive figure, mad Ophelia is wheeled off, butterfly still flapping.

Part two offered us an ageing, perhaps senile woman, a Polish Jew in wartime, wearing glasses, who mumbles, sings, potters, dreams of her youth, is suddenly distracted by the audience and goes to sit on a chair surrounded by toys on the floor. Then comes the most powerful image in the show, for me: after half-heartedly uttering '*Heil Hitler!*', she mimes eating a rose and, standing on the chair, vomits it up all over the playing area. Later, in yet another change of mood, the old woman gives us a wonderful knowing wink.

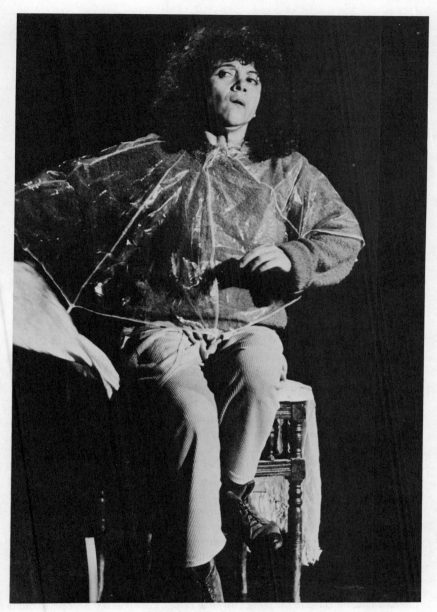

15 Netta Plotzky rehearsing (photo: Mary Giles)

The third part was called 'Young mask searching for a love' and was full of sadness and ambiguity: the woman mask becomes a young male mask; her back becomes his front; all the usual clues of facial expressiveness are lost to us and we must look afresh at the body's language and focus on the significance of the props used – here, hats.

Plotzky immigrated to Israel from Poland when she was thirteen. She graduated from Nissan Nativ Acting Studio and acted, directed, studied at the Theatre Faculty of Tel-Aviv University. She spent many years playing leading classical roles in conventional theatre and waited to be discovered. In 1980, she was invited to attend the International School of Theatre Anthropology, directed by Barba, and at the age of thirty-five she had a complete change of being and direction. She began further training at Odin Teatret. Barba took her back to nothingness and told her to get to know herself, so that, as a performer, she could start experimenting completely afresh. She was stunned by the experience, by the new freedom to be anything, by the *entelekheia*, by the necessity to adapt to being confused and blind. In her one-year stay at Odin, where actors work alone on their own projects, Plotzky did begin afresh, developing her sense perceptions, using *her* body for the first time. She subsequently extended her range of theatrical functions by adapting and directing Wilde's 'The Nightingale and the Rose', and J. D. Peretz's story, 'The Widow and the Wind'.

Plotzky has been influenced by the writings of Carlos Castenada and by Dr Yankalen Raz as well as Barba. After leaving Odin, she continued her research in Japan with Buto master Ohno Kazuo and Buyo master Katsuko Azuma; she had previously had *commedia dell'arte* training, so that when she came to work on her present piece, she had many cultural and theatrical traditions to draw on. She often builds up her work from props – for instance, she can't be angry in that dress, so what shall she be? The title, 'Happiness of the Pre-form', comes from a sculpture (and painting) exhibition in Tel-Aviv, which breathed life into form. From this, Plotzky understood that she must be a fluid, living sculpture – all the emotions are there inside her, waiting to be embodied. She believes that, certainly for her, there can be no creativity without sexuality and that if she has an inspiration for an image, a way of moving to convey emotion, and can bring it to life truthfully, she can impregnate the audience and so it will become universal, its influence will spread, its life continue.

Appropriately, the most overtly political piece in the Festival was *8961: Caneuon Galar a Gobaith (Songs of Grief and Hope)*, constructed and performed by Lis Hughes Jones and directed by Mike Pearson, both directors of Brith Gof, a theatre company dedicated to performing in a language spoken by only 500,000 people, a minority confronted by the threat of cultural takeover and suffocation.

In a scaffolded cube of light and dark, cell, cellar, square, against a 'backdrop' of corrugated iron used for the shanties in which so many of the world's poor have to exist, Hughes Jones became in turn, through her body, one of the 8961 *desaparecidos* in Argentina undergoing torture, one of the oppressors, one of the women – mother, daughter, sister, wife – waiting in dread and in hope for news, for confirmation, for the loved one.

The first part of the piece, the torture sequence, electrified me – the

16 Lis Hughes Jones in *8961* (photo: Mike Pearson)

guard's torch probing the dark cell to transfix the prisoner, the crash as the
hurtling body hit the corrugated iron . . . thereafter, I experienced a sense of
anti-climax. I don't think this was attributable to the alienation of the
video-recording of events in Santiago National Stadium in 1973, or Pearson
hanging up titles for the twelve scenes – we must feel and we must *think* – or
indeed to my ignorance of Welsh (and the key quote, from the Amnesty
International Report, 1985, was read out in English), but to my having
seen, only two weeks previously, a programme in the 'Eleventh Hour' series
of Latin American films, *Las madres de Plaza de Mayo* (directed and produced
by Susana Muñoz and Lourdes Pontillo), which had upset and angered me
deeply. Not having acted on those emotions, I seemed to be unwilling to
experience them again. *Songs of Grief and Hope* did polarize the audience's
reactions. Some were angered and moved by the material and left feeling
powerless because they didn't know what to do to help; others questioned
whether it was appropriate for non-Argentinians to do the piece at all – yet I
know that Graciela Serra, herself one of those threatened with 'disappearance', was very moved by it.

Whatever the reaction, Hughes Jones's performance was strong, haunting and powerfully imaginative. At one point, the waiting woman washes
and hangs out a shirt belonging to her lost love – and suddenly hurls blood
at it; the drips continue to punctuate the action. Victor Jara sings and
Hughes Jones sings, in a voice that comes from the belly, to John Hardy's
piano music, songs from fiesta and songs of lament; and she dances the
tango. She feels, smells, the suit of the man who has gone, places it on a
chair and sits on his 'knee', his 'arms' around her once more . . .

Hughes Jones studied literature at Exeter University and started working, alongside Pearson, at Cardiff Laboratory Theatre in the late seventies,
first as a costume designer, then gradually, as a performer. When Odin
Teatret visited Wales in 1980, she was inspired by the special transforming
energy in the performance of Iben Nagel Rasmussen, with whom she
continues to collaborate. In addition to the Odin philosophy, Grotowski's
theories of 'the body politic' have been a major influence on her work.

In 1981 Hughes Jones and Pearson left Cardiff for Aberystwyth and
formed their new group. They are the core of the company, which has
produced over twenty shows now, all in Welsh, but they collaborate with
other individuals and groups. At first Brith Gof worked solely in and for
rural Welsh communities in the west of the country – community rather
than experimental theatre – but then the company began to tour further
afield throughout Europe and to Latin America. Hughes Jones hoped to
perform *Caneuon Galar a Gobaith* for the Welsh community in Patagonia in
1987. An innovative development early on was the two-year teaching
programme, theoretical and practical, which the company undertook in the
drama department of Aberystwyth University, and they have also taught at
Bangor University.

Brith Gof (Faint Recollection) exists to make theatre to reflect the concerns of contemporary Welsh society in its traditional artistic forms to that society but not only that society: the Welsh are only one example of a minority besieged. The company has devised various kinds of theatre for different kinds of venue: street performances, like *Pedole Arian*, a celebration of Gypsy culture; more formal work like that based on the Book of Revelation presented in St David's Cathedral at the end of September 1986, with performers, narrator, a score by John Hardy and the use of professional musicians; solo performances in chapel. Hughes Jones recited the hymns and letters of Ann Griffiths, an eighteenth-century mystic and folk hero, to an elderly, largely female, congregation in about fifty chapels in Wales and also took the piece to Argentina and Patagonia.

She started work on *Caneuon Galar a Gobaith* in May 1985. There are two versions, the changes being not so much in the word structure as in the music – earlier harp music having been replaced by John Hardy's specially-composed piano score. The inspiration for the piece came from two Chileans – Pablo Neruda and Victor Jara (who died in Santiago National Stadium) – and in the absence of material from Argentina itself, until 1985, Hughes Jones used material about the technique of disappearance from other Latin American totalitarian regimes, of which there is unfortunately no lack. The roles of company members and the ways they work change from piece to piece. In this instance, Hughes Jones constructed the content – poetry, words of reportage and daily life, vocal and instrumental music, dance – performed and co-directed with Pearson; it was the first time she had worked with a recorded soundtrack and she felt she needed someone else's help. In any case, as a creator and performer, she believes it's essential to have women and men contributing to the company's work (though as the only full-time woman member at the moment, she says she misses other women).

In her creation of women, the texture of their life experience must be accurately translated into theatre – even if it means presenting them through men's eyes in traditional roles. She likes to use photographs and recordings of women from other cultures to help her build a character, and is always concerned to be precise; she uses few props but they must have significance in the daily life of the women.

Songs of Grief – and Hope? To Hughes Jones there *is* hope for the rest of the world in the spiritual, emotional, physical strength and courage of the grandmothers in the Plaza de Mayo and that hope 'deserves to be honoured'. In the last lines of Neruda's poem, 'The People' (translated by Alastair Reid):

'Everything will pass, and you will still be living.
You set fire to life.
You made what is yours.'

So let no one worry when

I seem to be alone and am not alone,
I am not with nobody and I speak for all –

Someone is listening to me and, although they do not know it,
those I sing of, those who know
go on being born and will fill up the world.

In their solo performances Sandra Salmaso and Cinzia Mascherin (Italy),
Geddy Aniksdal (Norway) and Helen Chadwick (England) all used text by
Sylvia Plath.

Created for Magdalena '86, Salmaso and Mascherin's *No Man's Land*,
directed by Alessandro Tognon, offered an unusual collaboration between
actor and sculptor respectively, and was the most densely symbolical
performance of the Festival. Several women echoed my own reactions to the
piece. We found it hard, literally, to see the many beautiful natural textures
and objects lying on the floor or at the far end of the playing area, owing to
the distance and the unraked seats, and one wondered whether the
performance should have been staged so that we could have promenaded
slowly, taking in the objects, around the action, which was mimed to pre-
recorded text. We also found it hard spontaneously to work out the layers of
meanings and had to make conscious efforts to let go of our left hemi-
sphere's pursuit of rationality and allow ourselves to experience material
from the specifically feminine unconscious – for, according to the devisers,
the key words for this piece are *flusso-lunario* (literally, 'flux-almanac'): 'the
moon lays a hand on my forehead'.

The piece was a parable of women's evolution, apart from man's literal
presence, but implicitly on debatable ground, in an interim space before
hostile relations are resumed. In the opening sequence Salmaso appeared
before us blind and in chains, 'sexily' displayed in a sort of Barbarella outfit,
maniacally struggling, to pop music relayed at deafening pitch. Mascherin
approached her on her knees and gradually felt up Salmaso's body,
smearing her with red (blood) and blue (woad). Salmaso shuddered and
started, but there was no communication between the women, no delight,
no self-love – only fear. Another 'picture' suggested Venus rising from the
waves; another, an Amazon, all passion spent, examining her bow, now
become a beautiful ritual object, a harp, hung with trophies. In a funny
concise sequence, pregnant with application, Salmaso, now in a frock of our
time, laboriously wound up a toy mouse, then stood on a stool and
screamed as it fulfilled its role. Yet another showed Salmaso ostensibly and
obsessively teaching her baby submission, how to behave on the stage of
life; but the baby had no head – and has therefore much to teach her (and
us) about instinctive behaviour and natural flowing movement.

I found *No Man's Land* strong and disturbing, innovative in content. It
encouraged the audience to *be*, and so view familiar experiences of women's
lives from a different perspective.

17 Sandra Salmaso and Cinzia Mascherin (photo: Mary Giles)

The Stars are no Nearer, 'a journey in the poetical world of Sylvia Plath', directed by Tor Arne Ursin, was Geddy Aniksdal's first solo performance and she gave (in English) a tensely dramatic and subtly expressive interpretation of five poems: 'Thalidomide', 'Mirror', 'Death & Co', 'Lady Lazarus', and 'Edge'. The recurring images of these poems are the moon and stars, flowers, mirrors and stretches of water, and the human body in various stages of corruption; the colours black, silver, shadow, ash, white – and red. Aniksdal appeared before us in a longish wine-red dress virtually concealing her pregnancy, and in 'Thalidomide', for instance, proceeded to croon and cradle her ideal baby in her arms before suddenly dashing the bundle to the floor to maniacal cackles of laughter, her shadow clawing its way down the white back wall of the play area as she slumped to her knees. Aniksdal did indeed make 'each word a physical event', and the blood run cold.

She began reading Plath's prose some time ago and then *Winter Trees*. She conceived the idea of performing a Plath text someday, but only after the birth of her first child did she buy all the poetry and begin to read through it and later, A. Alvarez's account of Plath's death. Aniksdal speaks and writes in Old Norwegian (ON) and she worked originally with Clav Hauge's translation into ON of most of the Plath poems she's using (not 'Thalidomide') only working on them in English two weeks before she arrived in Cardiff. She plans to perform them in ON again in Oslo and Scandinavia in future months.

Aniksdal belongs to Grenland Friteater (GF), the Norwegian Theatre Laboratory, established in 1976 in Porsgrunn, an industrial town south of Oslo. The company is funded annually by Porsgrunn Commune as well as the Ministry of Culture and Science, Telemark County. In 1986 the mixed group of about eleven people is to move into its own theatre, where it will continue to arrange seminars and festivals. To further the education of its members, apart from working towards performances itself, GF has absorbed the theory and practice of Barba, Grotowski and eastern dance and theatrical forms and invited individuals and companies from abroad to Porsgrunn – including Odin Teatret, Sayari (Tanzania) and Teatro Potlach (Italy). Equally, it has toured extensively throughout Europe (complete with crèche), as well as performing in the prisons, psychiatric wards, schools and streets of its own country.

The company usually works with minimal text, devising and improvising its shows from themes of ordinary life, folk tales, historical incidents. In daily body-training sessions, some inspired by Grotowski, members improvise solo or ensemble on the current show, while the director – one of three men in the company or Aniksdal herself – watches what's happening. She or he will then slowly select sequences which work and orchestrate the piece. For five years the company has collaborated with one particular

18 Geddy Aniksdal (photo: Luca Gavagna)

director, Ingemar Lindh, from the Institutet för Scenkonst, Pontreholi, Italy, in this method of working.

In 1986 GF had five group shows in its repertoire: *Fever* – inspired by the group of Scandinavian artists known as the 'Christiania Bohème', which included Munch; *Too Much of Nothing* – based on the fiction of Hammett and Chandler; *Sjakk & Ludo* – a clown show for children of all ages; *Våkenatt (The Wake)* – performed in Latin and thus distanced from us, with nineteenth-century Norwegian folk customs in part at its base, this show queries the significance for us all of formal rituals surrounding death and the dying; and *The Miserables* (again directed by Tor Arne Ursin) – who were not wretched at all, as Geddy Aniksdal, Anna Erichsen and Elin Lindberg demonstrated in a bar at Cardiff. *The Miserables* is a show based on the music of pop songs, jazz, rock and roll, soul, you name it, and the trio of women (plus the young Aniksdal) in drag and shades, singing, playing guitar and the fool gave themselves and us a lot of laughs and fun. Last but by no means least in the GF repertoire, is Aniksdal's solo performance – but she is not sure that she wants to do another show by herself; it's so exposed: she prefers to work with other people.

Helen Chadwick doesn't react in the same way; after touring with her solo recital, *A Gift for Burning: A Celebration of Women Poets*, often dealing with the theme of daughters and mothers in life and in death, she plans to create another piece about daughters and fathers.

A Gift for Burning has been constructed from poems, essays and letters by Sylvia Plath, Frances Bellerby, Stevie Smith, Anne Sexton, Marina Tsvetayeva, Susan Griffin and H.D., with additional poems and music by Chadwick herself. No fewer than three of these seven poets committed suicide. The undoubted appeal of the piece lies in its simplicity, clarity, luminosity – the 'staging' consists of a piano, several wicker chairs for the women makers and sharers, and a set of lamps – and the haunting quality of some of the melodies. Chadwick presents, in the material she has selected, a range of emotion, from rage at the rape of an eighty-three-year-old woman, to enjoyment in pointing Smith's surreal text; but for me (and the basic subject matter is near the top of my emotional agenda), the performance was curiously muted and I feel there is even more pain to find. It may be plumbed in her next solo show, for which she plans to write as well as compose her own material.

Chadwick's training was in theatre studies (at Dartington). In 1979, she co-founded Dr Foster's Travelling Theatre and worked with the company until 1982. Then she came to Cardiff Laboratory Theatre and the following year performed in *The Heart of the Mirror* as Joan of Arc: the 'flames' of her pyre were accounts of rape. The experience had a profound effect on her and out of the crisis her own creativity was born. She began writing poetry and music. Slowly, over the next year or two, she began shaping material for a show, asking her mother's opinion of thirty poems at one point; at another, working with a colleague each writing music then slotting improvised lyrics into appropriate sequences. The first performance of *A Gift for Burning* was in 1984; it was enthusiastically received and she toured with it in 1985 and 1986. Chadwick relishes the total artistic control she has, but finds the administration taxing on her own.

She has been taking voice workshops for actors and 'only-in-the-bath' singers, both at home and abroad, since 1981, and in 1985 she obtained her Advanced Diploma in Voice Studies at Central School of Speech and Drama. She is a tutor in voice and movement for British Theatre Association courses and has worked at the National Theatre with Peter Gill's group in the Studio. She has also worked with the Roy Hart Theatre, Cicely Berry, Ludwig Flaszen and Frankie Armstrong. She led a workshop at Magdalena – partly to move her own work on a stage further – and I spoke to a participant as well as to her about it. Chadwick introduced 'Praise Song for my Mother', by the Caribbean writer, Grace Nichols, to her group, with some music she'd prepared, and intended asking the eight members to describe one incident each remembered about her mother and to bring in

19 Helen Chadwick

an appropriate object, in order to develop some music. It became clear that this idea was too ambitious, however, so they did breathing and body exercises to loosen, heal and unblock and lots of vocal improvisations on the Nichols text (not using Chadwick's music), whose last line, 'Go to your wide futures, you said', resonated through the group and brought forth some very powerful creative work in drawings and writing.

Ida Kelarova, from Czechoslovakia, who formerly worked with the Divadlo Na Provazku theatre company, organized another vocal workshop. She introduced her group to Halecacky singing, a traditional calling style from the mountain regions, practised exclusively by women. Its sound was intrinsically haunting and became compelling when performed by women *en masse*, with energy and discplined timing.

Ida Kelarova and Ali Robinson also performed their stirring *Song of Celebration*. Ida sang at the piano and, with Ali on cello, they played Ida's own compositions, contemporary songs and traditional Slavonic folk music.

Akademia Ruchu Theatre (Academy of Movement), Poland's premier performance company, was founded in Warsaw by Wojciech Krukowski in 1973 and has been under his artistic direction ever since. At first Akademia Ruchu concentrated on building up its own techniques of intensive body training and developing skills of visual narration by means of signs denoting social relationships between the individual and the group. In 1975 the company began to give, for the first time in Poland, performances in all sorts of playing areas, using the city of Warsaw as a set and forging links with the community, which peaked in their establishing an innovative cultural programme in Grochow, a workers' district. From its inception, the company had taken part in international theatre festivals, colloquia, given workshops at home and abroad and collaborated with, amongst others, Cardiff Laboratory Theatre and Odin Teatret. In 1979 Akademia Ruchu evolved into a 'theatre centre', an interdisciplinary studio of artistic research, and it continues to present its own work and that of other groups and individuals from a variety of theatrical traditions all over the world.

In 1986, Jolanta Krukowska performed apart from the company for the first time in her own show 'a dance about . . .'. Unfortunately, I didn't see it, but women seemed particularly struck by one sequence, which was described to me. After 'living with' the rocks and pebbles scattered round the play area, testing their weight, moving them, Krukowska gathered a pile of smaller rounded stones between her legs outstretched on the floor. Relating to each one, which bespeak 'my marriage', 'my life', and so on, she hefted, carried and placed it in a large clear bag suspended from the ceiling – and lay beneath. As the bag filled, bulging and heaving, tension grew . . . and was only relieved by the avalanche of stones.

This intense language of signs was clarified for me a few weeks later, when I saw Krukowska perform in London with the company in *Supper.* *Good Night*, conceived and directed by Krukowski and commissioned by the Midland Group, Nottingham for the National Review of Live Art, 1986. The performance draws on stereotyped images of Polish life in the eighties acquired by people in the West from the media. So, in one sequence, all the action of ordinary daily life is broken up by black-and-white screens which, in another, placed close together lengthwise, form a Poe-ish Polish corridor, in which men are seen to be at each other's throats. Or we see, through clouds of cigarette smoke dimly, plain-clothed state police in trilbies, down on their knees from the fatigue of watching. It's 'well known' that life under communism is drab, so all five actors (three women, two men) at first wear grey or brown. Eventually even this conviction hardens: while they play at catching – and frequently drop – the burning torch of freedom, the actors encase themselves completely in black and white until, in the final sequence, we're captive in the constructed red bleeding womb of communist hell, where even apple-eating has to be synchronized, where there is no communication and, above all, no joy. Behind the bloody erected screens, as we see when one of the actors knocks one over, there is pure and simply a free figure, a woman, hair flying, smiling, glad to be alive.

What I found fascinating about *Supper. Good Night* was the tension between the stark simplicity of presentation – thanks to the actors' and directors' skills – and the rich complexity of application, social, political and psychological. Through the power of its theatrical language, the piece demands that we think about propaganda and the manufacture of stereotypes, totalitarian regimes, Polish life, our life now.

Several women led workshops but did not perform in their own shows.

Maria Consagra (USA/Italy) who teaches in New York University's Experimental Theater Wing, worked along the lines of her current research to channel energy through an 'object' to produce a piece of theatre.

Andrea Dishy and Stacy Klein (USA), the artistic director of Double Edge Theater, Boston, who has collaborated with Rena Mirecka from Grotowski's Teatr Laboratorium, led a two-day workshop using physical, psycho-physical and vocal training, texts, and musical instruments, to encourage participants to find a new source of energy and theatrical invention.

Kozana Lucca (Argentina/France), for fourteen years one of the forty members of the Roy Hart Theatre community, whose work is founded on the study of the human voice, led a workshop directed towards musical and theatrical expression.

The Theatre had its origins in the First World War, when Alfred Wolfsohn heard extraordinary energy and pain in the cry of a dying soldier in the trenches and started to research into the potential of the human voice, *in life*, including 'as a means of knowing oneself' and as 'a muscle of the soul'. He escaped from Nazi Germany in 1939, and came to London. During his teaching work with a group of students, he met Roy Hart, then at RADA, and on Wolfsohn's death in 1962, Hart took direction of the group. In 1969 the group made its debut as the Roy Hart Theatre, with a performance of *The Bacchae* by Euripides at the World Festival at Nancy, and afterwards began touring with shows (eighteen since 1969) and teaching courses all over the world.

In 1972, Jean-Louis Barrault invited the Theatre to participate in Journées du Théâtre des Nations, in Paris; this French connection resulted in the Theatre leaving London and establishing its base at the Château de Malérargues, Anduze, where the Theatre community researches ways of 'living the voice', runs courses, does domestic and restoration work on the Château in rota, and creates musical and theatrical pieces. There are other permanent centres, at Paris, Lyons, Geneva and Amsterdam. Entry to a community of individuals is usually by participating in a workshop, then staying on to share life, daily work, cleaning, training, and gradually, over years, performance. The forty equal members, twenty women, twenty men (with no overall artistic director) are drawn from seventeen nationalities, so there is a rich mixture of cultural, musical and theatrical traditions and skills to draw upon. Singing is the common denominator. It is a means of exploration, a way of inter-relating, recognizing and *changing*. It involves discipline and submission to the teacher. People don't arrive with 'good' voices; it's a matter of training and learning to embody their own voices.

Among the mixed shows the Theatre has worked on and performed, are *The Tempest* (1976–8), *Pagliacci* (1981), *Calling for Pan* (1982) and an opera, *Ani Maamin*, for which members acted as composers as well as performers at the 1984 Avignon Festival. Audience participation is an important factor in the performances: on one occasion, members were asked to draw what it felt like to be themselves and an exhibition was held of these 'soul portraits'.

When Roy Hart died, in 1975, there was a struggle for leadership among the men. Power bases are constantly shifting, but the men in the company have always been powerful; although Hart was very sympathetic to female artists, women in the group have been slow to strengthen. A rule was established long ago that members of the community should not have children, that a woman should 'grow her own baby in herself'. About three years ago, this rule was reversed, by 21 votes to 19, but the woman who went ahead and had a child changed in her attitudes towards the community and towards material rewards and lost some of her concentration. It's a continuing area of difficulty for the Theatre (as elsewhere). Lucca created, about five years ago, a solo performance called *Piantos*, from *Piano/piangere* – involving singing lessons and a mad woman, viewed with love. One of her tenets is that of 'divine gossips' – that the public act of theatre springs from our everyday private life and ordinary occupations – so she incorporated some of her experiences as an apiarist (the hive satisfactorily living out the feminine principle in nature) and also used her native dance, the tango. She started working with other women in the group on the Demeter myth, but while she was away, they asked a male member of the company to direct them . . . Lucca believes that women everywhere, but centrally in theatre, have to struggle now to be present, counted and properly valued; that they have their own sources of inspiration and creativity for theatre and have to work to make every moment richer for themselves and live in a way that is at one with that work. She herself wants to explore the areas of myth, magic, mystery, ceremonial ritual and, of course, music.

Her immediate preoccupations were the next workshop, in France in September, and the second Women's Theatre Festival, in Córdoba, Argentina, in October. At the first Festival, in 1984, women did everything together; it took even more courage and determination to initiate that event than it would ordinarily, because women until recently haven't been visible let alone spoken out in South America. More women were attending in 1986, but no sponsorship had been forthcoming and there was very little money. Lucca's sister, Elena Depelli, was organizing the festival and Lucca was going to teach, perform and direct. She also intends to work in Denmark soon on a performance of the Cinderella myth at three levels and from a femininist perspective – leaving out the Ugly Sisters, for example.

In the afternoons of the week of Phase 1, in addition to other events, there were discussions, all except the opening and closing ones suggested by participants. No product was forthcoming, as pat answers, nor was consensus arrived at, but the process of voicing questions such as these was important and may be far-reaching:
— What is the nature of women's inspiration and creativity? What do they mean? Do they differ from men's?
— Is there a feminine or feminist aesthetic? Should there be? What is it?
— Is there a feminist style of acting, directing?
— Why aren't there women theatre theorists as influential as Barba and Grotowski? Are they essential?
— Women often have to rear as well as bear children. If women feel these experiences are creative, can they be combined with their creativity as artists in processes of cross-fertilization?
— What *is* theatre? Simply 'what takes place between spectator and actor?' Every room; everywhere? What is experimental theatre?
— Have we, as spectators, the right to say a 'performance' is not theatre? Do there have to be professional standards of singing, dancing, acting, before 'theatre' can be said to take place?

— Do we have to 'understand' a performance for it to be valid? Does it
  matter to the creators that people see different meanings and significance in the same performance?
— Are collages, fragments, episodes, cycles, the natural structures for
  women?
— How can women 'go public', gain more confidence as artists in a
  patriarchal world?
— Do women speak a different language at work? Have we learned to
  speak in two modes? Can we develop our own language?
— How important are class as well as gender differences in art? Should
  women artists encourage the use of tapes rather than books and radio
  phone-ins, where possible, instead of theatre, for wider accessibility and
  participation?

The final discussion, before the performers started collaborating on their
piece, exposed some sharp divisions between women who felt too many
shows had been constructed with too many men in the traditional hierarchical patriarchal way, and that even where men weren't involved, there
had often been an 'authoritative' text – in three instances, by Plath – and an
absence of women's own truly experimental text; and those who felt that the
performers were being devalued as puppets by these remarks, that there
was no difference between male and female creativity and that more
communication was needed between the sexes, not less.

Out of the discussion emerged the concept of a ceremonial 'enactment'
rather than a conventional performance, and we were asked to help the
performers by meditating on an object or idea or feeling we'd been close to
or thought of or had during the week, and to feed our images to the group.
Among those put forward were recurring circles, broken or breaking and
rejoining; jumping butterflies (me); a volcano of tears; a flower and snake;
Mary Magdalen; fire; bronze; audience involvement; softness, sexuality,
ritual and fun. The performers had also been sent extracts from Susan
Griffin's *Woman and Nature*, as possible sources of inspiration.

Then we left the twenty or so actors, three musicians, four artists and four
technicians for ten days to their unstructured, undirected collaboration,
assailed by risk, reliant on individual strengths, skills and talent, but also
facing differences in personality, politics, religion, language, culture and
theatrical tradition.

In the mornings the performers worked in the gym, with different facilit-
ators. The rest of the day they worked in their eventual (and very cold)
playing area, entitled, rich in irony, 'Edward England's Potato Factory'. As
expected, the women ran through most of the emotional range in their
collaboration and alliances shifted, broke, got refocused. One woman left
and several, including, to my regret, Serra and Lucca, scarcely parti-

cipated. It was time that pressured content in the end – something had to be put before the public on Friday 29 August.

Because visual imagery is such a vital component of experimental theatre, involvement of visual artists throughout the Festival had been planned from the start, in contrast to conventional theatre practice. Accordingly, the four visual artists – Gerd Christiansen (Denmark/France), Kari Furre and Rona Lee (England) and Cinzia Mascherin in another role, exhibited their work during the first week and in Phase II determined the nature of some of the action by the settings they envisaged and constructed. For instance, the most varied 'happenings' were enacted in 'the river room', a long narrow space filled with sand and a channel of water running roughly through the middle: Christiansen told me the artists had finished constructing it about three days before the opening, and had then invited performers to improvise in it, alone or in groups.

Christiansen herself, Danish-born, but living in the South of France and working in a mixed group of five collaborators, directs and acts as well as envisioning and constructing settings; she also works as a designer in more conventional theatre to earn money. She has been influenced by Grotowski and Barba and is now developing her own techniques. Her particular interest lies in proposing settings – using the elements, bringing the outside inside – and images, ritual objects, sacred animals, all of natural material, with the intention of liberating performers, through the framework she has constructed, towards creating a ceremonial theatre. She feels this kind of enactment is particularly important for women, although men are interested too. She is working now on a new project involving ten people, 'I have Dreams to Remember', drawing material from the unconscious; she wants it to have the same quality as dream in performance.

I saw the work-in-progress (for which the public was not charged) on both nights and this proved to be essential, for spectators were split up and saw different things each night. I hadn't known this the first evening and had interesting if bemusing discussions with other spectators afterwards.

The area outside and the whole ground floor of the factors were given over to a promenade production in twelve scenes. The structure, particularly the first night, resembled a patchwork of different pieces of material woven – an image floated by Greenhalgh to practitioners at planning stage – into a loose whole. There were changes to the content the second night, with the result that the piece cohered much more, and was seen to be a time piece – no one actually took an alarm clock apart, but we had to wade through a sea of them on the way out . . .

Several sequences did work or begin to work, for me. The opening was haunting. Set in an industrial urban wasteland fit for washer-queens, and to bell-peal and gulls' cry, Hughes Jones and Krukowska shared a work song (if not the work), as Hughes Jones thwacked and washed and hung out sheets by the canal. Lica walked perilously along a parapet, in her potent slipper-satin dress, luna-tic, and beat the water with the long straitjacket sleeves before rescuing a baby from it (Moses? the Divine Child of Eleusis?) while the other women whispered together looking righteously askance . . .

Then, inside, the group of six daemonic women working with Kalińska, who want to continue their collaboration, in symbolic white, black and red evening dresses, circled around a clock face, looking, as women have had to, through another medium – here, a bandaged mirror/window – into worlds within and without, playing with ritual objects and fighting, loving, despairing, hating, to climax and reprieve, as Kalińska tightened one thread – 'Remember the circle' – and Susan Bassnett the other, with her improvised archetypal narrative.

The next sequence built up a lot of tension but went on too long. To the rhythmic striking, by Lica, of rock on rock, four women wound and unwound, but stayed attached to, the bed-rock of existence (childbed, marriage-bed, deathbed), the earth, Gaea. Simultaneously, Krukowska darted across the playing area and Hughes Jones and Chadwick sang in counterpoint a composition by Chadwick about our mother: 'it is a silent song . . . sing it, sing it; it is a hidden thing . . . bind it, bind it; it is a bleeding wound . . . love it, love it'.

Another sequence, woven by Alena Ambrová, influenced by (the real) Theatre on a String, Czechoslovakia, provided a rare and welcome note of surreal humour and fun. In dream-time, several diners, sitting on non-existent chairs, fenced with knives and tried to eat objects (dream ham-burgers, for instance) which arrived – or not – via the roof from which they were all suspended on string, their plight controlled by Ambrová.

Passing quickly by the Triple Goddess Fates (first night), spinning from a suspended mermaid-like figure (aspect of the White Goddess, Aphrodite, Eurynome, creator-goddess Tiamat of Sumerian myth?) we were in the room of time and the river, facing sands of time. Here, on this bank and shoal of time I thought I saw a butterfly (Hughes Jones) jump . . . certainly several performers played the fool with time and poked fun at Magdalena and themselves – for instance, Lee, visual artist, blind and dressed in a ballet skirt of Magdalena leaflets. Lindberg was, as usual very funny physically, demanding to know where the fish was (*Hésitations 3*) and then starting to swim on top of a box.

I was very shocked and moved, the first night, by Brigitte Kaquet's appearance, naked, as the mad Ophelia with weeds entangled in her hair and flowing down her (and our) beautiful and vulnerable female body. She slowly advanced along the sand, writhed, turned, and retreated, to a speech pre-recorded: 'I always thought that I loved you so much, Daddy, but sometimes I have to beg your pardon because I am so happy without you; I am so happy because you are dead.'

After a tender and farcical meeting, mid-stream, between an ageing Mary (Ambrová) and a heavily-pregnant Joseph (Aniksdal), presenting as Andy Capp at the seaside, we were ushered back into the first arena for the final re-enactment: the Last Supper. Hughes Jones sang us out, the second night, simply, fittingly, in Welsh.

So the Festival ended. For me, Magdalena '86 was a rich and varied learning process, in theatrical and personal terms. Further, it seems to me that a number of the organizers' aims have been realized, at least in part: an exchange of ideas and attitudes among participants began, albeit more often in private than in public; certainly, from what women in Serra's workshop were saying, tensions in bodies were released and creative energies set flowing, women learned important things about themselves as women and as workers in/lovers of theatre; something organic and exciting did start to emerge from the 'work-in-progress' and I think spectators recognized there, and in the Phase I shows, the validity of women's creative contribution and certainly their artistic strengths.

I believe that the source from which creativity springs and the channels through which it flows may be similar in women and men, but that women, if left alone, will engage with different content and develop distinctive techniques of theatrical expression, through a most painful learning process. It's frightening, as so many women said to me, to be thus exposed, but to build up our reserves of strength and confidence, to test our potential, to discover our feminine principle, surely we need to work alone together as well as in mixed groups? In the theatre and society balance must be restored. As Stein said, 'There is too much fathering going on just now and there is no doubt about it fathers are depressing.'

My dream-reality is that there will be (as has been discussed) future Magdalenas, annual Magdalenas circulating all around the world, organized by women and involving a wider range of cultures, races and theatrical traditions; properly funded to allow a significantly longer period of time for participants to work together on one or several pieces. The features which have come up time and time again in performance, in talking about what is important to us, what binds us (and what is also vital to our societies with their terminal industries and lifeless technologies) and which the piece(s) would probably embody, include music, dance, magic, the poetic language of myth, our own experimental text constructed from the textures and rituals of women's traditional daily lives, confronting gender roles, the unconscious and dream/trance state, sacred objects bound up with spiritual ceremonial, and the celebration of our free sexuality.

What is the next stage? We have at last to stop mourning our suicides, and solidifying our oppression, end our submission in a negative sense and, fragile though we feel, take responsibility for ourselves and jump over the edge into land unknown or forgotten, (re)constructing our own ikons and heras, speaking our own language (including one of comedy), weaving our own pattern without authority or permission; seeking, to adapt Serra's words, the occasion to lose ourselves *and* find ourselves: self-possessed.

AFTERWORD

There *will* be future Magdalenas. The Magdalena Project, as Magdalena Conferences (UK) has now been established as a permanent networking, research and work-development organization, an associated project of Chapter, Cardiff, funded by the Welsh Arts Council.

The programme for 1987 included: two weekend workshop-conferences in September and December, exploring the question, 'A Woman's Language in Theatre?' based at Chapter; two international meetings in Denmark in July and November, hosted by Odin Teatret; and the promotion of a British tour by Akne Theatre.

In 1988, Jill Greenhalgh hoped there would be a Magdalena Festival in the south of France and that a new piece of women's work would tour through Europe the following year.

'So much more than just myself': women theatre artists in the South*

CINDY LUTENBACHER

Right now, theatre women in the South are in the very thick of a theatrical vision so compelling, potent and simple that it offers nothing less hopeful than a general overhaul of theatre in the South. However, the restructuring of theatre is not the main focus of what I observe as a theatre movement and a movement within theatre; theatre of, by and for itself is too often a cause and not a cure for a 'deadly' theatre. Rather, the essence of this vision is one that profoundly bonds theatre to a community by restoring that community, be it a geographical, racial, ethnic or genderal community, to the center of the theatre's commitment and artistic expression.

History, Western and non-Western, shows us that for the most part theatre, or the performance event, has typically been placed at a community's heart, as a public recognition of the community's identity. In America today we can witness theatres with similar inception and reason in Omaha and Minneapolis, New York and San Francisco, Vermont and West Virginia. What is interesting is that this theatrical commitment seems to be spread throughout an entire region; one has the sense that wherever a non-commercial theatre has arisen, its goals and commitments have been based on the needs, issues, and inheritance of a community, and on critical social change within and through the expression of that community.

It is important to record that even in a region which unanimously denied the Equal Rights Amendment a few years ago, women are invariably either leading or participating as equal partners in ensemble companies that share this vision. As Helen Krich Chinoy observed of the tradition of women's theatrical contribution, 'one learns again and again that much of what women did was dedicated to realizing a dream of a different kind of theatre'.[1] To find where most of the women are in theatre and to find where women's voices are most profoundly heard, one should search first among the non-commercial endeavors away from the mainstream.

In this paper I offer some observations about the women theatre artists I

---

* A draft of this paper was read at the *Themes in Drama* International Conference held at the University of California, Riverside, in February 1987.

have encountered in the South, then I introduce a sampling of their work. But I must first speak of the work of Alternate ROOTS. Though not all of the women in the following pages are members of ROOTS (most are), I believe that the work of ROOTS is integral in the continuity and potency of this theatrical movement in the South; its goals represent some of the most important common bonds between the women I have observed and interviewed.

Alternate ROOTS (Regional Organization of Theatres South) is a large, deeply active, theatrical umbrella organization whose purpose, commitment and composition are of 'Southern performing artists and groups committed to the creation of an original, indigenous art.'[2] 'A community-centered vision', says Ruby Lerner, past director of ROOTS, 'is what is central.' Lerner is an arts management specialist, formerly with the Manhattan Theatre Club, and an eighteen-year veteran of teaching, acting, directing and the management of theatres.

> We're constantly bombarded with this myth of the alienated artists; it's an aesthetic of alienation. But for most of the people you see here, the focus is on the things that make a difference to a community – and I don't mean solely a geographic community, it could be a particular constituency within the larger community – women, gays, the homeless, the unemployed, etc. Their work might deal with issues that a community is currently facing, or with the community's dreams and hopes for its future, or with uncovering its buried history, its assumptions, its mythology. So the community is at the center of the vision as opposed to just the individual. It's a different way of seeing oneself as an artist, different from the views about art that are generally promulgated. We don't believe in shutting out that very personal expression at all, but I think the focus is more on the interaction between the individual and the community.

The work of ROOTS takes a multiple of forms: yearly, week-long workshops; biannual showcase festivals; resource and supporting networking for practical and economic as well as spiritual grounding. ROOTS has been in existence ten years and has a membership of several hundred theatre artists. Says Lerner:

> I think all of us here in ROOTS are really interested in being part of creating the kind of South that we want to live in. And I think the characteristic of that kind of South or any place really, is a deep respect for diversity and an ongoing commitment to working out just these problems. The problems between men and women, black and white people. There are many people here who've been active in the women's movement, the civil rights movement, the Vietnam movement, Central America, so that for many, the commitment to perform-ance has grown out of these other kinds of movement. To abolish sexism, racism, isms, isms, divisivisms. And on the other hand, I think there's also a willingness to talk about those issues when they do occur among us, which is something that often gets the tiptoe treatment in other places. We haven't solved the problem. I'd be misportraying the imperfect state we exist in if I said that. But at least I feel that here there's a general openness and a commitment to confronting our own racisms, our own sexisms, which is on of the first steps toward solving the problems.

Lerner acknowledges that this vision is not unique to the people and groups of ROOTS.

> There are other artists, companies, individuals working around the country who share some of these same values. What I don't see is any kind of organization that really tries to bring people together who are concerned about these issues, in the way that we try to bring people together, where the work is central. I don't see anywhere in the country a way for people who are doing this kind of work to get together in an atmosphere of trust and hopefully mutual respect to share that work, to get better at that work. And to talk about the ideas that propel that work. This is really about the generation, the genesis of work. It's about company development and the sharing of ideals and visions across a region. I wish I knew why there weren't more organizations like this. I can't say that I understand it and I have tried over the years to just outline what we do, for other people. It's not that difficult or even expensive and we know it works, we've been doing it for ten years now. That we're somewhat unique in this, I don't see that as something to be particularly proud of.

The impact of an organization such as ROOTS should not be overlooked in understanding the viability of such a region-wide, theatre movement. Though ROOTS did not create any of the theatre groups or artists, it has offered them a means by which to escape the artistic and personal isolation so problematic for non-mainstream, politically committed artists and groups. ROOTS has also been instrumental in gaining economic support for its members and in spreading information throughout the South and the nation. And in terms of artistic support, I would simply recommend attendance at the next ROOTS workshop or festival to witness for yourself the deepening of work, the crystallization of idea, the personal connection and profound delight that can happen when eighty or ninety people from across a region convene to share a vision through work.

Though that vision takes many individual forms, there are still a number of common threads that resurface in the weave. First, most of these women are affiliated with or are members of theatre ensemble companies who also have at heart the commitment to community. Second, all of these women wear several theatrical hats at once: writer, performer, director, teacher, manager, etc. In no instance did I find, for example, a writer alone in her tower churning out words apart from the theatrical and the larger community; she is always engaged in teaching or performing or some other participation as well.

Thirdly, there is a particular focus of intent within the work of most of these groups which, while neither new nor unique, has important implications for a potential future of theatre. For most of these artists the event of performance is in itself an event of community, of communion. This event inevitably includes the political relevance and personal empowerment which are typically individual matters, but it goes one or two steps further. The audience is not only the vital participant in the performance, it also becomes aware of itself as a community, aware of its shared experience both within and outside the performance. This awareness bespeaks a form of empowerment in which the total is far greater than the sum. The last 'act' of Pearl Cleage's and Zeke Burnett's performance is a full-audience, on-stage dancing lasting until some unordained hour of the morning; Road Company's *Echoes and Postcards* concludes with a community honoring its dead. Such visible examples are common; in other, less salient ways, the results of community union are the same. *How* this community event occurs is the subject of another inquiry, but I would suggest that it has a great deal to do with performance honesty and vulnerability, and personal, political commitment to the communities which are fundamental to the performance.

Finally, and critical to understanding the power and potential of these women and groups, their primary work is born within and grows from the indigenous language, stories, lives, issues and heritage of each individually defined community. I would find it difficult to overstress the importance of this observation in considering a future for both theatre and the body politic, for it is in the naming and claiming of experience that a community finds the capacity for both change and continuity. As Georges Gusdorf notes in *Speaking (La Parole):* 'Nothing is completely true for us as long as we cannot announce it to the world and to ourselves.'[3] Until we are performed, we do not actually exist. In the enactment of a community's own self, its own languages, issues, thoughts, mythos, texture, and self-named identity, the community finds the identification and validation necessary to criticize itself, to see from what it has come, where and how it is, where it must go, what it must change and what it must save. This commitment and consciousness of intent are the most profound themes underlying the work and reason of these groups in the South. And women are invariably leading the way.

A SAMPLER OF WOMEN THEATRE ARTISTS IN THE SOUTH

Jo Carson, a writer and performer living in Johnson City, Tennessee, writes plays, stories, essays and a blend of anecdote, tale, commentary, memory and local voices that she has named 'People Pieces'. She has performed her People Pieces over 200 times all across the United States, as well as in Nicaragua and on National Public Radio's 'All Things Considered'. Carson performs many of her works as a solo artist, as well as in collaboration with theatre groups, especially Road Company, also of Johnson City. In Road Company's 1986 work, *Echoes and Postcards*, Carson was one of the writers and a member of the ensemble. The work, revolving around the images and ideas of Tennessee life, is a collaborative collage of improvised work, theatrical story, stories from the actors' own lives, scenes, memories, songs and anecdotes. For example, Carson performed a piece, separated into two segments, about youthful attempts to sing like Patsy

Cline while atop her grandmother's coal bin, and in the family car. 'Jo, honey, *please*', says her mother. Late in the show, when Carson finally did sing with unabashed fervour, Hank Williams's 'Your Cheatin' Heart', the entire audience cheered with the shared experience of childhood wish fulfillment. Carson is intrigued with the blend of 'factual' material and imaginative creation. Not only is the blend exciting theatrically, it 'shades the distinctions between what is real and not-real, the various truths'. Her 1984 play, *Preacher with a Horse to Ride*, is based upon events in the Kentucky coalfields during the 1930s, and grapples with the pain, division and complexities of coal mining, unionization, poverty and family. Carson's work is deeply rooted in the language, images, thoughts and feelings of the mountain region because she believes in knowing the place she writes about, because otherwise, 'I suspect about the best you'll be able to do is gossip.' Carson's commitment to writing and performing is in the empowerment that people receive from the shared experience of that performance.

> I'm concerned with the greater community. Experiences are common and I don't mean everyday. I mean that most people's experiences are similar to most other people's experiences in one fashion or another – they're parallel. Their finding out of that and their realizing of that are central to what it is to be a community. And communities are what we're on the verge of losing in this country.

Carson often opens a solo performance with the following People Piece:

> Well, now I want to tell,
> a person can't help if they're not so pretty as the next
> All of us are given different things
> and the gift that God give to some of us
> ain't always looking like we just come out of the beauty shop.
> Now I don't mind, I got what I want,
> but I always told my mother that
> teasing me about always looking so awful
> was gonna make me mean.
> And it did.

Pearl Cleage of Atlanta, though not originally a Southerner, has lived in Atlanta for eight years and has spent four of them as playwright-in-residence with Just Us Theatre Company, Cleage, like Carson, writes in several genres, but always with the idea of performance. 'I don't think so much about the form, I just talk to people,' says Cleage. Cleage's plays include *Puppetplay, Good News, Essentials,* and *Hospice*, which won five AUDELCO awards in 1983. Cleage primarily writes and performs for a Black audience; her voice and concerns are from the perspective of herself as a Black woman. Her piece, 'I'm Married', deals with the dilemma of protection and independence an unattached woman faces when confronted with men whose eyes want to *know*.

Is your husband at home? And I said, 'Ah, no he's not here right now.' I toyed
with the idea of saying, 'Yeah, he's asleep in the back.' I knew immediately that
the fact that I have no husband, won't have no husband, don't want no
husband was not information needed by the heavy man at my porch railing,
leaning in bizarre imitation of the rebel soldier who asked for food at Tara's
back door and received a blessing in the form of the angelic Miss Melanie who
hustled up a plate of what looked like pinto beans and then asked sweetly about
the possible whereabouts of her husband, Ashley Too-Good-For-This-World
Wilkes.

In her piece about buying one's first 45 record – The Temptations – Cleage
writes of the desires and fears and treasures of a Black girlhood: 'I was
looking for the music that made you know something good was coming to
you in the next couple of years.' Cleage performs her own work in a variety
of places, sometimes alone, sometimes with the Just Us ensemble,
sometimes in conjunction with other writers and performers.

Linda Parris-Bailey is artistic director of Carpetbag Theatre which is one
of the oldest, continuously operating Black companies in the country.
Located in Knoxville, Tennessee, Carpetbag is widely known in the South,
and primarily tours throughout the region in the usual theatre spaces as
well as in many non-traditional places such as churches, prisons, recreation
halls and schools, 'wherever the people are', says Parris-Bailey. The
company's focus is on the development of its own original works that speak
from the heart and history of the community, in order to 'give something
back to the community – its own positive image reflected'. Carpetbag
maintains a repertory of original creations including *Red Summer*, based on
the Knoxville race riot of 1919, *Cric?Crac!*, a collage of African, Haitian and
American Southern Black folktales, and *Dark Cowgirls and Prairie Queens*,
which was originally created in part as a response to requests by teachers
and principals in Knoxville for a performance for Black History Month.
Written by Parris-Bailey in collaboration with the rest of the ensemble,
Dark Cowgirls and Prairie Queens is based upon the stories of Black women
who were part of the move west. Biddy Mason, a slave who has walked to
California behind her master's wagon pleads in a California court for her
freedom, and describes slavery:

> I heard tell of a woman who tried to go North to freedom with a little baby, but
> she got caught. They tried to take her and the baby back to her master. They
> beat her so bad nobody could hardly recognize her. Well, when they finished
> whuppin' her, they gave her baby back to her and she took a stone and bashed
> the child's skull. She tried to kill herself too, but the marshal stopped her. She
> said she would never raise another child in slavery. When massa Smith told me
> we wuz goin' to Texas, I felt that woman inside a me. I took a knife and tried to
> cut my Maggie's throat but I couldn't do it. God knows I tried, but I couldn't.
> She is here today because my hand wasn't strong. No, you don't know 'bout
> slavery.

Like nearly all of the artists and ensembles burgeoning in the non-mainstream theatres across the South, Carpetbag's commitment lies in the community from which it springs. The theatre was originally created from the belief that the 'community, being Knoxville, had the right to create and develop their own art and aesthetic values'. Though Carpetbag has changed and grown over the years from the primarily training-oriented community workshop to the professional ensemble of four women and two men that it is now, it remains committed to the ideal of the power of local artistry. 'If I have a right to do my art in Knoxville,' says Parris-Bailey, 'and people have a right to experience my art, then art becomes something that belongs to communities, and I think that's important.'

Maya Levy of Hammond, Louisiana, writes independently of a theatre company, but is beginning to see her works received. *Daughters*, a play 'for young women', was presented at the International Thespian festival in 1985 and has been published by Baker's Plays. The play is a series of nine monologues for adolescent girls and deals with a variety of difficult issues such as divorce, drug addiction, abortion, incest and beauty. The play begins with a girl who describes her own sense of worthlessness as she slowly climbs into a garbage bag. 'I think she makes me take out the trash cause that's all I'm good for. That's all I'm good for at school, too. Cleanin' erasers for the rest a my life. I'm nothin' but the garbage girl. I'm nothin' but the garbage.' The monologues reveal young women dealing with or stuck inside the various confusions and hard complexities of contemporary youth. The play concludes with a victim of incest who has decided to give herself a new name. 'My new name. The name I chose for myself. Since I named myself, that must mean I have a lot of power over me. I like that.' Though most of Levy's works are not for adolescents, she sees it as part of her mission to write for young people because 'nobody is writing for these kids, they have to do adult works'. Levy's focus in writing is on women: 'I suppose I'll be accused of just writing about women, but I'm not worried about it.' As a writer, she feels grateful to the women's movement because it 'broke open the drama'. She adds, 'and not only that, it broke open the way for all kinds of new works. There's been a huge surge of all theatrical energy because of the women's movement, and I'm grateful to be my little part of it.' Levy also sees her location in Hammond as pivotal to her work: 'It's great writing down here in the Third World, you are free of all kinds of influences.' In addition to full-time writing and the creation of award-winning silk scarves, Levy runs a summer theatre camp for young people in Hammond, where the work is a combination of dance and drama. 'It can get kind of twilight zoney, sometimes', says Levy, 'but that's okay. We work to combine the two disciplines in a meaningful way. They're growing from it.'

One of Jan Villarrubia's most recent plays, *Odd Fellows Rest*, is a funny and touching play set in a wonderful tombed cemetery that you only see in southern Louisiana; it won the New Orleans Contemporary Arts Center's New Plays Festival award in 1986 and was consequently produced at CAC. *Odd Fellows Rest* is peopled with quirky New Orleans characters who are all devoted to the cemetery not only as a place of great history but as one of great liveliness. 'It would kill Bijou', says the character, Ma, of her son. 'He *lives* for this cemetery! He grew up in here. It's all he knows, and they want to make it a parkin' lot.' 'You and your boy Bijou'd be fixed for life with the money, Ma,' says Anton. 'You don't understand. Half the tombs here was carved by his father and his grandfather. His great-grandfather was the first sexton here. They was all Odd Fellows.' Villarrubia is both playwright and poet: as Poet-in-the-School, she teaches writing in New Orleans area schools; and she is part of the Playwright's Unit at Contemporary Arts, a writing and producing workshop. Villarrubia also writes monologues and pieces which she calls her 'characters'. They are short writings similar in nature to Jo Carson's People Pieces. 'There are so many wonderful people in New Orleans', says Villarrubia, 'all around where I live, in the grocery store, in line at the movies, everywhere people with these beautiful voices. And I want to share those people with everyone else.' Occasionally a critic from elsewhere than New Orleans has complained that her works are too local, too regional, but, says Villarrubia, 'New Orleans is where I've always lived, I grew up here and I don't really want to live anywhere else. New Orleans is what I know.'

Lee Heuermann is an Atlanta Jazz performer whose cabaret act was inspired by the work of Edith Piaf and Lotte Lenya because of the strength of individual style and statement in their work, an individuality particularly potent in light of the manipulation of so many women's talents in that era. Cabaret is an especially rich form for Heuermann, who is a committed political activist, because its overtly political nature and its delight in immediate response, criticism and action are very near to her own vision of her work. 'I think that performance has such an incredible amount of power to move people. And it's a shame in our country that we've lost touch with that. We've lost touch with the audience being deeply connected to the performance, with responding to and criticizing it, and moving and acting on it.' Heuermann believes that one of the first tasks of a performer is in allowing herself to be vulnerable with an audience, which is one of the aspects she most admires in the work of Piaf and Lenya. 'You really get the sense of them being very strong women, like they're not hiding, they're not covered up with all this other stuff . . . Their voices show who they are. Incredible tone quality is secondary to being real, and letting the audience affect them.' Heuermann's own difficulty is compounded by the bias in the jazz world that female musicians are not particularly intelligent about music. 'Usually they're surprised when they find out otherwise', says Heuermann.

Angelyn DeBord is one of the mainstays of Roadside Theater, a touring, teaching, tale-telling company out of Whitesburg, Kentucky. Roadside, now entering its sixteenth year, performs stories and tales from Appalachia, as well as original, ensemble-created plays based upon characters and stories from the mountains. The company and its staff are all from the mountains; in many respects what they do is a theatricalized version of what they all grew up knowing – the power and necessity of tales, of stories. Roadside maintains a repertory including *Pretty Polly*, a play based upon the real life of Polly Branham, a mountain woman tale-teller who took her stories into the mountain schools and communities in the 1930s. As DeBord explains

> *Pretty Polly* begins with an introduction of how we are each the *history* that school history books know nothing about. Then the show commences. *Pretty Polly* is a series of stories creating one story of a woman's experiences with the dark and light sides of life through the times of her youth until her ancient years when she reaches a state of acceptance and of grace. The show ends with a lined-out hymn which the audience joins in singing: Bright mornin' stars are risin'/ Where are our dear mothers?/ They have gone to heaven a-shoutin'/ Day is a-breakin' in our souls.

DeBord is Polly; she was also one of the collaborators in the creation of the script. In addition to the position as performer–director–writer shared by the three men and two women of the company, DeBord is a Kentucky Artist-in-Residence in the public schools in eastern Kentucky's hollers and way-backs. She teaches story-telling and performance to kids of ages six to eighteen, always drawing the children to what they already know, their own heritage of stories and mountain living. DeBord began her own writing career with a play about child abuse because she believes that most people have suffered some kind of abuse; her hope is that through understanding abuse, people might find some measure of healing. 'Sometimes I think we're a wounded world', says DeBord.

> I just look at people's faces and their wrinkles become scars and their expressions are full of sorrow. And I sometimes feel that we're all just carrying around such burdens of doubt and we don't really know why we're not perfect. We think we ought to be, but we're just not sure why we aren't and I think I want people to understand that we really are. We are basically perfect. We are put into this world pretty perfect and what happens to us happens through circumstance.

DeBord maintains an optimistic commitment which carries her forward 'because there's so much that needs saying and so little time to say it. It's so much more than just myself.'

I would like to be able to tell you so much more. I would like to tell you about Rebecca Ranson in Atlanta, and Cynthia Levee writing in 'the Cajun-Jewish tradition', and Marsha Jackson and Jomandi, and Sallie Bingham in Louisville, and Rebecca Wackler with Southern Theater

Conspiracy, and Linda Gregoric of Contemporary Arts, and *Cabbagetown: 3 women . . . an Oral History Play with Music*, and *Louisville 200*, the celebration based on 250 oral history interviews and created by TriCenter Theatre Company for Louisville, Georgia's 200th celebration . . .

If, however, the material here presented has pricked the finger of your curiosity then I will consider the task at hand accomplished. I do believe that the growing movement we are observing in the South in which women are playing such pivotal roles, offers for both theatre and its community, models and cause for great hope. I do not see this movement as a peculiarly Southern phenomenon and therefore viable only in the South; the South is simply where the idea is catching on most rapidly, right now. Ruby Lerner is equally suspicious of a cultural analysis which would name ROOTS and the network of theatre artists as somehow Southern:

> A lot of people have said, 'Yes, but the South is different, you know,' but I'm Southern and I don't exactly buy that. I think a more unfortunate but plausible reason is that the incredible lack of financial resources here in the South has forced people to work together in a way that they might not have had to work together in places where there is more support.

Lerner's vision is that there would be networks of community-centered theatres all over the nation, theatres delving into their own cultural necessities for a reason to be, and 'that we will all be able to share ideas and work and resources back and forth in an atmosphere of mutual respect and exchange'. With customary optimism, Lerner goes on to cite A. B. Spellman of the NEA who believes that small, community-grounded theatres and artists like those of ROOTS are in fact the theatre of the twenty-first century.

In a time when so many are moaning the stasis of theatre, in a culture in which most of the mainstream definitions of theatre leave it so expendable that it could die and be buried without even making the obituaries, I find the energy of these theatre artists and groups particular reason for optimism. That theatre should arise from indigenous culture, life and language, should commit itself to the needs and inheritance of particular communities, should grow up within that relationship of performance to community, and should see itself operating within a definite point of view, social and political commitment, signals a necessary return to the taproots of the fact that performance has always existed in the human collective. And in a time when the loss of understanding and communion are threatened, these rejuvenated old, old thoughts of theatre speak to the most profound hope I have for the future of the polis. For me, it's all just damn good reason to cheer.

NOTES

1 Helen Krich Chinoy, introduction, *Women in American Theatre*, ed. Helen Krich Chinoy and Linda Walsh Jenkins (New York: Crown, 1981), p. 7.
2 *Alternate ROOTS newsletter*, August 1986, p. 15.
3 Georges Gusdorf, *Speaking (La Parole)* trans. Paul T. Brockelman, Northwestern University Studies in Phenomenology and Existential Philosophy (Evanston: Northwestern University Press, 1965), p. 72.

Women in the London theatre: a contemporary account

SUE JAMESON

The expected is the accepted. This would certainly account for some of the difficulties experienced by women not just in the theatre, but in a more universal way. Over a period of eight months, I interviewed women working in the theatre about current projects, backgrounds, families and aspirations. Wherever possible I have let them speak for themselves to tell their own stories, explain their anxieties and express a unanimous enthusiasm about the work they do.

ALISON CHITTY
Designer at the National Theatre in London. July 1987

There are some people who never considered for a moment that Alison Chitty would become one of the country's top theatre designers . . . the ones who failed her when she took Art O-Level twenty-five years ago. Luckily her parents and teachers had the sense to ignore the setback and encouraged Alison to take A-Level Art, which helped gain her a place at one of the first-league art schools, St Martin's.

She's now one of a handful of women designers who can be considered to have 'made the big time' insofar as designers ever find themselves in front of, rather than behind, the spotlight. She has worked closely with director Peter Gill for the last eight years at the National Theatre and they have built up what she describes as 'a rich mutual vocabulary' which eliminates at least a percentage of the pain necessary in getting the show on the road:

> I say 'More John Davies-ish?'
> 'No Darling, more Rothco-ish' he'll say and then we know where we are.
> Ultimately it's the director who has the final say.

When we spoke she was just days away from the opening night of *Mean Tears*, written and directed by Gill and being performed in the Cottesloe Theatre, the smallest of the National's auditoria. Her design was bold and blue. Rakes of boards painted in royal blue took the stage back as far as it could go, while above were canvases covered with images of the sixties and of London; a huge mug of pencils, telephones, answerphones, Balzac's *Lost Illusions*, Mozart, a jumble of atmosphere. The final images had been worked out after compiling a list ten pages long of all the cultural references and objects in the play, Alison's starting point. She's obviously pleased with the finished product:

> It's like a great plain the figures are on and, with the lighting, they're almost outlined against this very rich blue. Of course, they've got no furniture poor things! It's also got the director's nightmare of flying from location to location which writers seem very keen on nowadays and which we have to sort out.

The fact it's a new play also gives her satisfaction, because the designer's contribution 'is so powerful', an essential part of the moulding process. Not that the audience will consciously appreciate the fact, though the image of the play they take away with them will have the designer's mark indelibly printed:

> I don't think people really do recognize the contribution made by designers. Peter [Gill] often says to me, 'Don't imagine anyone is going to see that. It's got to be bright red and turned around before anyone will notice.' However I'm not going to give up! I just hope one can make a world that will make it possible for the story to be told by the actors in the best possible way.

The process itself, the steps towards that opening night, are far from trouble free, and Alison declares 'I shall go to my grave saying how awful it is to be a theatre designer'. The sharp flash of inspiration is only an occasional visitor and for the most part it's a grind, hunting and searching for the right images to do the work justice. 'It's a ridiculous torture trying to find a style,' she says, adding that for 99 per cent of the time she feels certain she won't be able to do it, that she'll be found out at last and shot at dawn! Much of her confidence comes from her collaboration with Gill. 'It's the last push that makes it work, I've never known Peter be wrong.'

When she joined the National Theatre, she wondered whether the fact she was a woman would make a difference to the treatment she received, as female designers were still an unknown quantity, particularly in the workshops. Her main worry, however, was her height: 'I'm not a terrifically tall person and I was more aware of that than being a woman. I just thought: this place is so enormous, how can I have strength in this situation because I look so small and short?' While she still has anxieties about the fact she may not know as much about the stress in timbers and metals as some male colleagues (though her expertise is very wide) she also feels that there are situations where being a woman helps. 'It's much easier to be silly and have a laugh' she says and laughter, of course, breaks down the barriers. 'You can often get people to do what you want without being devious or scheming' though she hastily adds that she doesn't believe in exploiting her femininity or using it ruthlessly. Within the world of the

20 Alison Chitty

theatre, she feels that there's generally less discrimination and male chauvinism than in 'real life', and regards herself as 'first and foremost a theatre designer'. If forced to examine the differences between male and female designers, however, she can see other advantages:

> I think there are some things that women are better at that actually help you to be a good theatre designer, like being prepared to look at someone in their shirt

for the fifteenth time. For some men, looking at it fourteen times might be enough and the thing that makes me look fifteen times is the something in me which may come in handy one day if I'm ever a mother. The rudest thing I can call it is 'nappy changing'. This has nothing to do with what finally ends up on stage as a piece of scenery, it's to do with the working process which is tricky, sensitive, difficult, and worrying and women can find a role in that with the support, encouragement and strength to give people confidence.

Despite the fact that the theatre demands so much from all those involved (the hours are longer and more insistent than many other jobs) she feels it's unlikely that she'd drop out of the profession. If she had children, she says, she would certainly take a break, feeling certain it would be near impossible to do both jobs. The business does exert a magnetic hold, however, particularly when its power is felt early on. In fact, had Alison's father not been a clergyman, her career might have taken a different course. As his job demanded weekend work, he always took Tuesday as his day off. Her Mother was 'completely crazy' about the theatre and because it was cheaper to take Alison rather than paying a babysitter, 'I was taken to the theatre every single Tuesday.' Looking back, she admitted that as a child she had found it impossible to distinguish between theatre and real life. 'I didn't ask the question. In *Ross*, Alec Guiness was really ill with malaria and I thought "This poor man is going to die!"' She doesn't, however, hold the view that theatre is in any way *magic*. That, she says, romanticizes it and the real thing is very different and rather grim. Her early theatre experiences laid the foundation stone for her career, but she didn't assume that was her ambition till later. ('I wanted to be a florist for a long time.') She began her art training, with little idea of the outcome, till her tutor suggested she went to have a look at the interesting theatre design department at the Central School of Art. There she saw

> Big rocks covered in 'Zeebrite', costumes made out of bin liners with nuts and bolts stuck all over them, and cut-off bits of foam rubber sprayed with silver and gold.

She was hooked! After her course, an Arts Council bursary took her to Stoke-on-Trent for eight years where she learned to ply her trade. She feels that her students nowadays have less scope for learning the basics that can only be absorbed 'on the job'.

> They have no real experience of just simple, simple requirements for working in the theatre. Even just six months in rep. teaches you not to walk in front of the director during rehearsals and I see it all the time. If something falls over in rehearsal, nobody springs up. I'm the one who does it because of the years at Stoke-on-Trent.

Despite all the worries and anxieties inherent in the job and her initial lack of confidence at the start of any project, she enjoys theatre, even though it impairs her social life:

I'm fortunate because I'm in this unreal world packed with caring people. I meet at least five people a day and then read in women's magazines of those who never see anyone. I can't even remember the names of those I've met. I'm sure people could hide in their work, but I'm not of that school. I want everything and that's hard!.

ELEANOR BRON
Appearing in Marivaux's *Infidelities*, directed by William Gaskill
at the Lyric Theatre in Hammersmith. July 1987.

Eleanor Bron was at the forefront of British comedy at about the time Alison Chitty was failing her Art O-Level. She was 'not just an actress' in an era when it was much harder for women to break the mould. She acquired the kind of immortality that only starring in a Beatles film could give one in the sixties, and was a constant face on television comedy shows which were heralding in the new era of bolder and satirical writing. If it's tough in the 1980s for women to 'do' comedy, it was far worse twenty years ago! I wondered if it had been easier for her to insist on presenting her own material when she became, 'Eleanor Bron; personality':

> No, I always fought against that. What I really wanted to do was to become a better actress and that was very difficult. Nowadays people like Julie Walters do comedy, drama and everything. I suppose Maggie Smith moved from revue to drama but there were very few who did and it was very tough.

Her first battles were to be given the right sort of material to present. Peter Cook and John Fortune were part of the creative team with which she worked regularly. She found they just weren't giving her enough to do, though admits part of the problem was because, 'I wasn't as clued up on political things as they were and nearly all the material was political'. Frustrated as a performer, she began to write material with John Fortune to widen her scope and the two veered away from politics and into social comment.

Comedy and confidence are inseparable, and it's often suggested that the reason that there are far fewer female comics, even now, is because women tend to lack the kind of confidence needed in the aggressive medium of comedy. Eleanor feels that she wasn't at the sharp end, because she was presenting the material as an actress. 'My main aim was simply to act', she says and most of the time she felt frustrated that she wasn't able to develop a character as much as she would like in the limited time available:

> It wasn't as direct as stand-up comedy usually is. There, you are presenting your own personality to the audience and that is an act of great courage. The things I was doing were slightly removed and oblique which is why I found the confidence to do them.

Eleanor feels as strongly about stereotyping now as she did then, realizing that it's always been easier for men because there are more jobs for men.

'The problem', she opines 'is that not enough women are writing.' She confesses to a certain amount of guilt that she's partly responsible for the dearth of women's writing but is also sure she's not capable of writing a play, 'that's a very specific gift, I think'. (She has employed her obvious writing talents in other ways recently with her *Pillow Book* which amalgamates diaries, musings and jottings over the years.) To the question of *why* more women aren't writing she points out that it's part of a long slow process, with a slight increase in the numbers but an overall imbalance with many more parts for men and the parts that there *are* for women usually being set in a man's world: 'Until women are active in the world and what makes it tick, presumably there won't be a female Corialanus.' She admits that she's turned down many roles because she felt the women were too stereotyped, particularly when she first began working in the West End. 'Probably a terrible error' she muses and brought home to her when she recently accepted a part she'd refused twenty years earlier, Lady Cynthia in Tom Stoppard's *The Real Inspector Hound*. The latest production was at the National Theatre:

> I try and make it a rule that there's got to be a good reason for doing a part. I try to do roles that I would enjoy watching myself. You can't always afford to do that, of course, but I try as much as possible.

GILLIAN DIAMOND
Casting director at the National Theatre. She has now moved to the Drama Centre in Chalk Farm, London. August 1987.

Gillian Diamond was working at the Royal Court when she finally told her employers she was pregnant. She was told not to have it in the office, informed that she wouldn't be paid and asked if two weeks was enough time off. In the end she took six weeks which was considered a little extravagant. This was in the sixties when women were often given the sack the moment they announced a 'happy event' and the theatre was probably a slightly more sympathetic employer than some. However, Gillian clung tenaciously to her theatre career, at a time when the pole was already well greased, and survived the difficulties to become one of a handful of casting directors in the country. To say 'casting director' is to summon up visions of the power of Hollywood, making and breaking the careers of the good, the bad and the beautiful, but the reality in the theatre comes without the glamour. She's the first stage for any young actors wanting to join the National, or to find out more about the profession, the vital bridge between actor and director. 'The letters we get are innumerable,' she says, 'and a lot don't get replied to. I have a drawer of fifty needing replies at the moment.'

Gillian became a casting director by accident. They didn't even exist when she began working in the business. Her love of theatre was fostered early, though she realized she wasn't going to be an actress when her sister was playing King Lear while she was Cassius in *Julius Caesar*. Being forced to play endless games of charades also helped remove any ambitions in that direction, though her sister going to RADA did afford her some rare theatrical opportunities. She went to the first night of *Look Back in Anger* with Albert Finney as her escort. Parental encouragement was pretty thin on the ground. 'It was assumed that we would not have careers but that we would make reasonable marriages. I was instructed by my parents that I wouldn't keep a man if I didn't provide a meal at night and look after him.' For her father it was the beginning of the end when he found a suspect RADA student ironing his trousers in the kitchen.

She was a model for a moment, 'It was when we wore those stiletto heels which made me 6' 6", so I kept hitting my head' and then attempted for the first and last time to be conventional by taking a shorthand and typing course, on her parents' insistence. It was not a success. 'The last thing they said to me was "Please, Miss Diamond, don't write here for a reference because we won't be able to give you one." I was the only one able to do faster typing than shorthand.'

When her sister landed a job in rep. at Canterbury, Gillian went too and met Clifford Williams who needed a 'helper'. She acknowledges it was very much a woman's role but adds,

> We were enormously humble because we were girls and had spent fourteen years in a convent. My self-discipline and humility knew no bounds. I'm so pleased with the next generation because they seem much more confident of their position in society. I think there's a completely different attitude.

Not yet hooked on theatre as a career, she made a determined effort to become a probation officer. She took two extra O-Levels, but gave up at the A-Level stage. Some time later she was accepted for training as a mature student, but had started a family by then and didn't feel she could 'drop everything and run'. When Williams joined the Royal Shakespeare Company in 1962, Gillian went too. 'It was tremendously exciting. We had the literary department and the casting department, anything – because the Aldwych was empty.' She feels that from that day to this she has been unable to break away from the strong conditioning which demands that woman 'serve'. 'I always felt a service person, I am brainwashed and I feel no hope for myself.'

While feeling that she will find it impossible to overcome a lack of confidence and strong conditioning about 'a woman's place', she is also in an excellent position to look at the status of women in the theatre generally. She remembers only one woman stage manager in the sixties but now, she says, the applications for stage management at drama schools come more from women than men.

For directors and writers the real changes are more recent. Di Trevis is the first woman to lead a group at the National. Sarah Pia Anderson is directing both at the National and the RSC. Jude Kelly directed *Sarcophagus* for the RSC. Gillian feels these firsts shouldn't make for complacency:

> I don't see the plans for it to be a continual thing, but then you'd be branded sexist if you said we must have a woman. Di and Sarah have very good careers ahead of them now and they will pave the way.

Gillian feels that lack of real confidence is still the greatest block to women's ambitions in the theatre. She is worried to see how a few women directors behave (she preferred not to put names 'on the record') surrounding themselves with other women assistants, voice teachers and so on and making a formidable defensive enclave. It creates more problems than it solves, she believes. 'They are so touchy about being women in that position that if any male did assert himself, they would immediately feel he was working against them.' Young male directors are going to make certain mistakes in their first productions – it's expected – but the women feel they are not allowed to fail at all, says Gillian. The fact that most of the theatres are run by men makes it doubly difficult to get that first job. 'The Fringe has an awful lot of women but I feel it's because they have nowhere else to go, so they make their own work in a way.' When men are interviewed for a job they are more likely to look and sound confident about running the artistic *and* financial side. Do men tend to believe men then?

> I think there's no question. We don't have authority and when we do it's called 'bossy'. Even now when I'm being continually crossed I want to say 'If I was male you would accept this!' However, it's more women who abuse their own kind. Men possibly feel there's no competition between a man and woman, which, indeed, there rarely is. They tend to be kinder and more polite.

Female writers, Gillian believes are in an even more difficult situation because they do tend to write about women. 'They are so horrendously domestic!' she says with exasperation. 'What I'd love a woman to do is write a play where all the characters are male and then just before it's printed, turn them all into women and not alter the play! Then we wouldn't have the "and then I went shopping" plays.' There are exceptions admits Gillian; Pam Gems and Caryl Churchill immediately spring to mind. However *Neaptide* by Sarah Danials made me 'so angry, I could hardly cast it. What an insult to women that play was.' (The play was on in the Cottesloe theatre in 1987.)

Having children will, of course, always make some difference to a woman's career whether in the theatre or another profession. For a start there's the guilt. 'The books said "to ensure your child is happy and confident, you should stay with him for the first five years". I was with mine for the first five minutes!' Her marriage broke up when the children were ten and twelve years old and she puts this down to an inability to look after three areas of her life: work, children *and* partner.

I was rivetted to the person who had been with my children all day. I always felt that if I could get under her skin, she would have loyalty to me and then she would care for my children. When I got home, I'd spend all the time with the kids. Then at about eight o'clock, there'd be a mournful face at the door saying 'Where's supper?'

Having children also means that you're more likely to start the working day with the disadvantage of not having read the papers, and lacking the time for advance preparations. Despite having more faith in today's young women than she has in herself (though her accomplishments are obvious to her colleagues) she still feels they must be very careful. 'It's such a fine line of survival. I'm grateful I haven't got two daughters because I don't know what I'd say to them.'

JENNY LECOAT

Comedienne, Jenny Lecoat and the Diamantes were one of the late night shows at the 1987 Edinburgh Festival. August 1987.

Jenny Lecoat doesn't deserve her reputation; at least *she* doesn't think she does! For when people mention her name, they tend also to describe her as 'outrageous' and Jenny feels there's a lot more work to do before she fits that particular mould. Not that she especially wants to. In Edinburgh her show runs after midnight and Jenny says the audiences are usually in a better mood for comedy, feeling freer and easier than at eight o'clock for instance. (Maybe a few drinks during the evening help!) The show is not just the stand-up comedy which has been earning Jenny a reputation for being fast, funny and even shocking; it includes music as well. The addition of the songs brings her full circle in her stage career because she first appeared in folk clubs, 'doing terrible songs about my boyfriend and how everything was so tragic'. Over the years she's managed to lose almost all of those early outbursts of creativity and she's secretly glad of that, displaying a keen intolerance for the material she wrote before she was twenty. (She's just reaching the end of that decade now.) One song survives called 'Brand New Car'. 'It was about buying a new car when you'd just split up with your boyfriend and then driving around and running him over. I always enjoyed singing that one!'

She's learnt more about what works for an audience and realized that some songs will stand up for years whereas others, 'you look at six months later and think "Ugh!, this is rubbish, not funny. Let's get rid of it."' Jenny's keen to inject songs with humour, moving further away from her original work laden with emotion, saying she doesn't take herself so seriously these days. Nowadays every song has at least a smile in it, if not a laugh a minute.

I think comedy is incredibly important, but having music you can do more interesting things with humour than just with stand-up. People have time to sit back and listen. You can present a different sort of humour, more satirical, more ironic.

Jenny's not sure where the 'outrageous' label has come from but now that it's stuck, she thinks people hear shocking things in her material that they wouldn't if it was being performed by someone else. She maintains there's nothing in the show she wouldn't laugh and talk about with her friends in the pub, and gave an example of the most outrageous item she could think of in her repertoire:

Everyone seems to be nervous about AIDS and new relationships, so I say that you can help by sticking instructions on your body about things you can and can't do. One up top, saying 'fine', one lower down reading 'limited access' and then one at the back saying 'You must be joking!'

Jenny believes that the fact she says these things on stage rather than in the pub makes some people nervous, both men and women. 'Culturally, comedy is a very aggressive thing to do. Telling a joke is an aggressive action and therefore for a woman to do it is a bit of a shock really.' Women like Victoria Wood have helped considerably to break down the barriers with audiences, who respond to her now as a comic rather than a woman, but Jenny senses there's still a large degree of discomfort about women trying to be funny on stage:

Part of the problem is that a lot of women comics are nervous, and that in turn makes the audience nervous. Comedy is all about confidence. You can tell a story with confidence and it will get uproarious laughter if you really go for it. If you say exactly the same lines thinking 'I'm not sure about this, I'm not really very funny at all and I want to go home and die', then it doesn't work.

She admits that she built up her own confidence by introducing chat between the songs and then making a conscious decision to lose the songs. 'It wasn't as much of a shock as saying, "Right! I'm going up on stage with twenty minutes of new material and I'm going to get up and do it." I'd have been desperately scared to do that and wouldn't have started if it hadn't been for the music.' Jenny looks forward to the day when there won't be a differentiation between male and female comedians and has made her own standards clear. She has never, she says, set out simply to shock and dislikes those who do. Finally her aim is simple. 'I just want to make people laugh.'

ANDREA BROOKS

Co-Founder and administrator of the Good Luck Theatre Company. Good Luck is presenting *True Love Romances* at the Old Red Lion Theatre. August 1987.

Andrea and the company are just getting used to nightwork. That's not unusual for any theatre group, but Good Luck has been confining its activities to a lunchtime operation in Covent Garden. The reputation has been built on lunchtime theatre but there are very good reasons for a change. Firstly, a limited number of plays to be performed in an hour, secondly, a growing number of full-length plays the company is very keen to try and lastly, a question of money. The Arts Council does not fund a company which performs lunchtimes only. The decision to change the time necessitated a change of venue as well, 'So we decided to move the company to "very cramped offices", basically the corner of a bedroom' says Andrea. Much of the conversation is about money because, for a small group, a few hundred pounds can make the difference between six weeks work and 'resting'. The actors are not paid, there's no profit-sharing because there are no profits and the most the participants can expect is a travel card. Despite these material drawbacks, Good Luck has consistently attracted 'names' – David de Keyser and Fenella Fielding have both worked with the company in the last year and Channel Four took up one of the plays, *Exclusive Yarns*.

For Andrea, the lack of money is about the only drawback to running a small but artistically-successful theatre company. 'No-one's in this business to get rich' she says ruefully, 'but we have given three years of basically unwaged work and we have to think in terms of a venue.' She's sure there's nothing she'd rather be doing and couldn't 'grit my teeth' to do a nine-to-five day for materialistic reasons. Not that *she's* always had to beg and borrow. She began her theatre career as an actress, not taking the leads but, in her early twenties, she was getting regular West End work. One contract ended early and she picked up another at once with Anthony Hopkins at the Old Vic .

> Even though I was at the Old Vic and saw the telegrams, I couldn't enjoy it. I was obsessed by the fact it was a limited run and it was the one aspect of acting I couldn't come to terms with. It wasn't that I wanted a fixed wage, but there was no 'through line' in my work. I wanted control over my Destiny (which sounds a bit grand for a lunchtime theatre company!) but that was basically it.

Andrea was also becoming disillusioned with the sort of parts her agent was sending her to audition for, and she became tired of 'trying to be deeply enthusiastic'. She felt destined to play forever 'young, pretty, blond and tarty girls', when she was keen to have a crack at Phedra or Lady Macbeth! Starting the company meant she could also fulfil an ambition to direct – the area she'd had her eye on since starting in theatre.

Andrea feels that women in theatre administration *are* discriminated against and not taken as seriously as men when they apply for jobs. 'Employers always think you've secretly got plans to act or direct and tend to be suspicious of women who want to make a career out of admin.' She runs the company with Matt Salisbury and they always attend business meetings and sponsorship negotiations together, but Andrea notices that the 'follow-ups' tend to be addressed to him. During budget meetings, she's conscious of a pervasive attitude which translates as 'Andrea can natter on about the plans and we won't let her bother her pretty little head about hard financial matters.' Those outside the company, she says, seem to talk to Matt automatically more than to her.

To the question of why there are not more top female directors, Andrea suggests that it's

> part of a much bigger problem which extends beyond the theatre. I mentioned that I wanted to direct but one of the things which went through my head was 'until I'm older and have worked with more wonderful people, I'm not going to be able to do this'. But I know some very young male directors who started at twenty-one or twenty-two and it didn't seem to occur to them to wait till they were older and more experienced.

Having said that, *she's* determined to pursue her directing career and leave the administrative side within the next five years, though she admits to a lack of confidence about how to approach companies and ask to direct! Over the years she's realized that few outsiders understand anything other than acting and fail to appreciate the amount of work that goes into producing or administrating. Most actors, she suggests, also have no conception about what the jobs involve and Andrea finds that irritating:

> The other day I bounced in and reeled off the publicity I was getting for *True Love Romances* with interviews, photos etc. 'Oh great' they said 'I hope they're not coming on the first night because I'm so nervous.' I've always been of the opinion that to act well, one has to have an enormous understanding about *everything*. People like Tony Hopkins do understand stage management and publicity, but some of the younger ones wander around being very vague. Perhaps that will change with more actors like Kenneth Branagh wanting to do everything.

VANESSA FORD

Vanessa Ford Productions. Rehearsing the autumn season of
The Lion, the Witch and the Wardrobe, The Voyage of the Dawn Treader and
Winnie the Pooh. August 1987.

Vanessa Ford turned the corner in her theatrical career when her production of *The Merchant of Venice* made a profit of £28. Work on the classics was artistically rewarding but very expensive, *any* profit being a cause for celebration. However, it was not until she began her foray into children's theatre that she found *real* success.

About four years ago the company was 'resting' over the Christmas season, yet felt unable to compete against big-budget pantomimes. 'My husband Glyn asked me what my favourite book had been as a child and I replied, *The Lion, the Witch and the Wardrobe* or *Winnie the Pooh*. "Get the rights to one of them," he said "and I'll adapt it."' The decision to play not only mornings and afternoons, but evenings as well paid off when they discovered over 50 per cent of the audience was adult. 'They'll find a child from somewhere,' says Vanessa, 'to see one of *their* childhood favourites!'

The company operates with no public subsidy and the bank manager still has a tendency to rush out of the backdoor when Ms Ford comes in through the front! In fact he's a great support for the company and is closely involved in all stages of the finance.

Vanessa's route to this position of success would make a book in itself and certainly demonstrates her great tenacity as well as talent and ambition. She had always wanted to act and after drama school worked as a dresser (between jobs) for stars like Olivier, Joan Plowright, Constance Cummings and Dennis Quilley. At that time she had no plans for anything other than acting and in her quest to avoid 'resting' she became a go-go dancer almost by accident:

> I replied to an advertisement. I always like a good bop, so I turned up at this terrifying audition and suddenly heard over the microphone '. . . and this Friday we're going to try a new go-go dancer. Miss Vanessa Ford.' Bang! After dying a thousand deaths, I got up, did a quick bop and they said, 'Do you want to work tonight, love?' It was either that or go hungry, so I said 'Yes'. That started a strange career, for about a year, of dancing in sleazy pubs and clubs around London.

She was paid £4 a session ('topless' paid more, but she always refused) and says it was the only time in her life she was very fit and thin! After this invigorating episode she found sporadic work as an actress both on stage and television but soon realized she was out of work most of the time, with the jobs she was forced to take while 'resting' less than satisfying. 'Waiting at tables and working at petrol stations wasn't what I wanted to do in life. I wanted to be in charge of my own career'. Her first attempt was an unqualified disaster and left her with huge debts to pay off while still only in her mid-twenties.

Whilst working at Yorkshire Television, she was introduced to a 'very young, very dynamic impresario, who was going to make history'. Together they planned a tour of *A Christmas Carol* with Leonard Rossiter, directed by Mike Ockrent, and it went well. The next venture was *The Merchant of Venice* and Vanessa realized far too late that her co-producer had no idea about how to handle finances. She borrowed money from her father to pay the actors' salaries, discovered it had been spent when pay day came, and took out a £2,000 loan from the bank. The tour ended badly in the red. Vanessa describes it as, 'a traumatic experience' and admits she had no understanding of how shows are sold:

I was over-kind, and didn't realize where the money was coming from, or that
the only cash that was going to come to me was from the box office, and that you
have to let people know the play is coming, or they won't buy tickets. I assumed
theatres did their own publicity. That's impossible with twenty shows coming
in every season!

It took two years to pay off the debts ('every penny of them') and Vanessa
then decided to manage the next company herself so that any failings would
be her own. She was working at Yorkshire Television as assistant floor
manager on 'sitcoms' including *How's Your Father?* with Harry Worth, when
the last penny was handed back. She formed 'Vanessa Ford Productions'
the next day and asked Harry to be the star of her first show. The tour was 'a
happy little farce' called 'Pardon Me, Prime Minister' and lost about £100:

It was quite containable and I was so determined after that because I'd
discovered it was such *fun*, terrifying but fun! The first three years were just
brute force and ignorance. If I wanted a theatre, I just used to go there and say I
wouldn't leave till I'd spoken to the manager. Eventually they'd give me the
dates I wanted.

Vanessa believes that the fact she was a woman might have helped her at
the beginning, though she's also aware theatre managers were probably
humouring her. 'They did tend to raise their eyebrows and say, "You want
to put on . . . Shakespeare?" with a slightly hysterical note in their voice'
and then ask her gently if she understood how expensive it was to tour the
classics. Within a year, the same managers were welcoming her back
having realized she *could* produce the goods. 'Slowly, slowly, one fights and
claws one's way through.' She has a total respect for the theatre public and
has learned the lesson that if they like it, they'll come again. This 'far
vision', was taught to her by her husband who was running a theatre
magazine in Eastbourne when they met. He had been involved in the
marketing of top companies such as the Oxford Playhouse and Nottingham
Playhouse and had also worked at the Arts Council. Their relationship
developed after he interviewed her. 'It was instant love as far as he was
concerned and instant *need* as far as I was concerned,' she laughs:

I kept ringing him up and saying, 'How would you do this?' and in the end he
said, 'I'd better come and do it myself.' Undaunted by my protestations that I
had no money and he could command a salary of £15,000 a year, he shrugged,
'Well I suppose you could always pay me in kind and we'll talk about it later!'

Gaining a partner who could help her fulfil her theatrical ambitions was an
immediate benefit to the company (the partner soon became a husband
too!), Glyn enjoyed the freedom of total marketing control.

Their joint freedom, particularly Vanessa's, could have been seriously
compromised by a baby but it was dealt with in the same determined way.
They had planned the pregnancy to fit in with the company's busy schedule

(luckily nature obliged) and Vanessa says she was determined it wasn't going to make any difference:

> I booked apointments at 9 a.m. every day, talked firmly to myself and told myself I couldn't possibly afford to have morning sickness. (In fact I was very lucky.) We were about to embark on an autumn classical tour and I went so far as to say, 'Right, I'm going to be in the plays.'

The plays were *A Man for all Seasons* and *Romeo and Juliet*. Vanessa also made the costumes renaissance style! She played Catherine in the first play, 'who might as well have been pregnant' and Lady Montague in the Shakespeare. 'She dies before the end, so we just reckoned she'd died in childbirth!' Her tremendous confidence and belief in her abilities were not shared by all. Their last tour date was Yorkshire, and the birth was imminent:

> The Bradford Alhambra have never quite forgotten this enormous pregnant ship that sailed into their theatre saying, 'I am the company manager, I'm also the producer, wardrobe mistress and I'm acting in it. Any questions?'

Alexander was born a few weeks later and Vanessa 'wallowed in the emotional love' for a few weeks, then it was back on the road, and 'baby came too'. She feels the future of the company is *on* the road and doesn't find the prospect of her own resident theatre alluring, preferring to concentrate on touring quality work. She has a fierce desire to succeed in her chosen field which she attributes partly to her sex:

> When women go into an area dominated by men, they're the ones who are utterly determined to make a success of it where a man may feel it's just a job. A woman is more likely to be single minded. I wish there were more, but I do think the whole theatre feeling is just changing.

Like most successful women, Vanessa appears to have bucketfuls of confidence. Again, as with most successful women, appearances can be deceiving. She knows well enough that she must present a strong outward show as one of the producer's main roles is to impart confidence to the company, but . . .

> there are nightmare moments for me, usually about six weeks before the production opens, when I wake up in the middle of the night and realize that because of what I've said, it means we *have* to open a play and people are buying tickets. If I've employed anyone who's wrong, it will show. I must have happy companies.

Vanessa believes that women are better at thinking about *everything* all at once. 'I usually have ten things in my mind and can think about them all' The office is run with a series of wallcharts detailing every aspect of the company, present and future:

> Holding the balance; that's what frightens me. We must book two years in advance and I think: 'What am I going to offer them?' That's where women are

good, because they have the capacity for an enormous amount of detail (sometimes needless details). Every morning I have to have a meeting so I can offload some of it and get on with my job of booking ahead. It's fascinating, like a wonderful crossword puzzle.

Despite her success and reputation, she's often still mistaken for the secretary, 'they assume it will be a man and if they've been silly enough not to have an open mind, I enjoy putting them right!'

GWENDA HUGHES (actress–director) and
ELAINE FEINSTEIN (poet and playwright)
Touring production of *Lear's Daughters*,
presented by the Women's Theatre Group. September 1987.

This must be the only play with the name Lear in the title which doesn't even have a walk-on part for a man. On the other hand, Regan, Goneril and Cordelia have *far* more to say than Shakespeare ever gave them. Elaine Feinstein describes her play as a 'prequel, not a sequel' and stresses that you don't need to have a working knowledge of the original to appreciate the strengths and purpose of her play. 'It's more about how women develop in society'. 'Though,' adds Gwenda, 'a lot of Shakespeare's themes are touched on in the play. Lear is more a metaphor for patriarchy and what that does to women.' In particular, the play explores the relationship between the three sisters and the contradictions in how they relate to their father. Goneril and Regan are in the 'ugly sisters' role, suggests Elaine. They are 'the most inscrutable of his major figures', she continues, 'They have enormous stage presence but we don't know much about them.' The play tries to discover *why* they turned out the way they did, and the writer has a simple answer to anyone who accuses them of a literary form of sacrilege:

> Oh yes, I should hope so, that's the idea! It wouldn't be any fun at all otherwise. We're not *reducing King Lear,* but I hope my play makes it impossible for anyone to view the opening scenes of the original in the same way again.

Lear's Daughters typifies the plays presented by the Women's Theatre Group. The company has a policy of employing women only and was set up because of a dirth of women's writing, plays and parts. Opportunities are given to both new and established writers – such as Elaine – with some plays being given rehearsed readings, whilst others have full productions. This all-women policy also leads to accusations that the company is therefore as unbalanced as a predominantly male company:

> *Gwenda.* I don't think it is. There has been very little work done predominantly for women and it's just trying to redress something that's very imbalanced. It also means that, because of work done by the Women's Theatre Group and others, there's now a good body of work by women, so the excuse that the plays don't exist is no longer true.

Presumably the nature of the group leads to a different working environment

> *Elaine.* I didn't notice it actually. You know, I forgot it almost at once. I just felt everyone was doing their job. Didn't you feel that?
>
> *Gwenda.* Yes I did. I've worked with other all-female groups and the make-up of the company is absolutely dependent on the individuals involved. What is very strong, when working with women, is a common language which makes it more direct. On this play we did a certain amount of work on personal experiences of families, and I think the fact it was all women made it possible for a lot of good, sensitive material to emerge. In a peer group you feel it's safer to be vulnerable.

As to discimination, Elaine feels more protected as a writer and has long been used to being the only woman on trips with groups of poets to such places as Australia and Russia. 'Women have had an honorable position in the novel for a long time.' Gwenda feels there's no point moaning about the situation. 'My personal response when I decided to direct was to stop complaining and do something about it.' She has felt at some job interviews that being a *small* woman hasn't impressed the board but it's nothing on which she has hard evidence. 'The statistics do speak for themselves,' she says, 'in the number of directors there are in the country and the percentage of them that are women.'

CARMEN MONROE

Actress making West End directing debut with *Remembrance* in the Black Theatre Season at the Arts Theatre. September 1987.

Carmen Monroe used to tiptoe around school and proudly tell her friends that she was taking ballet lessons. This was not, in fact, true but Carmen says she remembers a *need* to perform. She doesn't believe it was merely showing off, but she knew she wanted to be an actress from the age of eight. It took her a while to achieve her ambition and the route was not an obvious one. After a stint as a librarian, she worked at the Ministry of Fuel and Power, in a typing pool, and in the control room of what was then Associated Redifusion. However, she eventually fulfilled her ambition. This year she collected marvellous reviews for her central performance in James Baldwin's *The Amen Corner*. So why does an established actress develop the urge to direct?

> I fell into it! It thought a few years ago that I'd like to direct, but didn't know how to go about it; how to push myself into that place or create the circumstances. In a way it's confidence, but I also had to be sure it wasn't just because I saw *other* actors directing. It was more that I wanted to explore my potential. I might have decided, 'Right! I'm going to produce a play' or have decided to be a lighting technician.

With experience of both jobs, she feels the director's role is the harder one and is having to learn how to stand back and let the actors create, explore and expand. 'It takes a very large person to let it go and make the space for the actors,' she says. Carmen's main difficulty for the first few weeks was to quash the urge to get up on stage and do it herself. She still feels that, watching the play. As an actress she was part of 'delivering the baby each night':

> . . . as a director, you're totally out of it watching this baby and realizing it's not *your* baby and it never was! There's also frustration when it goes to a certain point and it's not going over, the brilliance isn't happening. That takes time and I have to be patient. Now I realize directors need an immense amount of patience and trust. You must have respect for the actors, you don't have to *love* them but respect you must have.

She was asked to direct the play by Yvonne Brewster (incidentally the only women director with whom Carmen has worked) and said yes only to panic afterwards. She's determined that the experience will lead her into more directing jobs, but is also aware that a cast may initially react differently towards a female director. 'There is a moment of uncertainty facing her', Carmen believes 'She wonders if it will be all right and the cast knows the job is usually done by a man.' She understands, too, that there can be a 'double questioning' when the female director is also black, but feels those worries subside almost instantly. 'I couldn't be doing with that,' she says, 'it would get in my way as an artist.'

JANE ASHER
Actress and writer. October 1987.

Jane Asher's other career is almost in danger of swamping the original one. She's becoming almost as well known for her cookery books as she is for acting. Her latest, *Easy Entertaining*, has just been published, as have two children's stories, illustrated by her husband, Gerald Scarfe.

She started the cookery to add another dimension to her life rather than just fill in the gaps when there was no acting work, though originally the idea was almost a joke. She sent polaroid photographs of her intricate and humorous cakes (they come in all shapes and sizes from a grand Piano, to a tennis raquet or newspaper) to a publisher who replied in strongly negative vein. After another six similar replies the idea was accepted and there was an encouraging response from readers. She says her perseverance has been developed as an actress. 'We need it just to continue in such a difficult profession. Every "last night" you think you'll never work again!' Her reasons for wanting to do something else are honest:

> There's a side to me that thinks acting is a bit silly, if I'm truthful. Much as I love it and would never want to give it up, you sometimes think, 'What am I doing dressed up pretending to be someone else, saying these silly lines?' There's something a little more grown up about having words in print.

She has never felt affected by the stereotyping of actresses (particularly pretty ones) as having less brains than the average carpet. She's been more wary of the stereotype of actresses 'doing books', and she put off writing the children's books for a long time because of her unease. She went ahead because she was determined to do something more creative.

> Acting is creative in a secondary way because, finally, you're always interpreting someone else's work. With my books, it's all from me, which is nice.

Jane sees a difference in the approach of male and female actors in theatres and says it comes down to a very mundane level. 'Women tend to rush into rehearsals with bags from Waitrose and say they have to fetch the children', but she thinks that living in this way brings what she describes as 'a healthy realism' to acting. Male colleagues, she surmises, are more likely to have risen late, had a leisurely lunch and strolled to the theatre. 'It's dangerous when actors have no life outside their own world. You need to keep observing and being part of life to keep your acting fresh.' She's turned down work because of family ties, has felt a pang of regret, but known it's worth it.

Jane has considered directing, and not yet ruled out the possibility, though the change would not be because she finds acting unsatisfying all the time.

> A lot of it is, yes, but there are such moments of satisfaction. Every night there'll be something to interest, or amuse and it's extraordinary how you can be in a long run and lose something, maybe for weeks, and suddenly one night it all clicks back into place. That can be magic.

Jane feels lucky that she has played a variety of roles. She admits there was a time when she was offered a lot of 'slightly cool, English, acerbic characters', but she enjoyed playing them anyway. She nurses a small ambition to be allowed to do more comedy.

FRAN THOMPSON

Designer at the Young Vic Theatre. Designed *Comedians* by Trevor Griffiths for both male and female casts. October 1987.

Fran Thompson describes herself as 'a vocal designer who hates to be ignored'. She's also keen to be involved with all stages of a production. Hence she found herself frequenting Working Men's clubs this year to find the right tone for the production of *Comedians*. She admits the production team looked completely out of place but word soon went around that they were from the BBC. After that, every joke was aimed directly at their table! Possibly the entertainers also cleaned up their acts because Fran says she was able to restrain herself: 'The feminist in me didn't feel wild at any time. There were a few dodgy jokes, but it was mostly OK.'

The greatest challenge, and the most interesting aspect of her involve-

ment with both productions, was to study the differences between the two
casts, male and female. The basic design didn't alter much (an adult
education class in a post-war school and then a club) but it was the
costumes which highlighted the change, 'because the way *women* present
themselves in a club is totally different from the way men would'. She
noticed that one of the main characters used sexuality far more in the female
version. Many of the acts were rewritten by the actresses in consultation
with Griffiths, and Fran found that watching all parts of the production
process gave her 'an excellent input into the play'.

She says *Comedians* was 'a more complete play for the men' and was
interested to observe how aggressive the women were with the comedy:

> I don't think it's defensive – it's almost that they're trying to prove they can tell
> as *sexist* or as *racist* a joke [as the men]. The quality of humour did surprise me
> because it seemed more like imitation than having any kind of progressive
> quality.

Fran feels strongly that designers are too often ignored by the audience,
which takes away the image of the play without ever considering where it
came from. 'People think costumes arrive because you've gone down to the
nearest shop and bought them!' She thinks the theatres are at fault for
assuming women want to restrict themselves to costumes. She finds the job
description 'wardrobe mistress' demeaning, and makes an effort to call
them 'wardrobe supervisors'. 'It may sound like a haranguing feminist
stand to take, but it is important. The equality isn't here yet.' There are
plenty of potential designers in the wardrobe departments, she says:

> Women tend to be seen as the people who go out and dress the actors. It's seen
> as a more feminine role to play, whereas doing a set, talking about mechanics
> and saying, 'This is the shape I want' is something people still find hard to
> accept in a woman.

The resistance is also present at production management level and she's
worked for some companies (not the Young Vic!) where there's been a
suggestion of 'you don't know what you're talking about' because she's
female. She has one advantage: her height.

> It *does* make a difference when you look a carpenter in the eye, or even down
> your nose at him, wielding a hammer at the same time! I think some *directors*
> also have a problem with women designers. It's something women suffer from
> generally and we're fighting hard against it. It's to do with women being
> allowed to be academic, intellectual, being able to analyse a play and put that
> into reality. Expectations do seem to be low, with women underestimated.

While Fran loves working in the theatre and intends to stay in the
profession, she can see that women have far more cause for frustration than
their male counterparts. 'Women have got so much to contribute to the
theatre and they're unable to do that because of traditional views. It's
extremely frustrating!'

JILL TREVELLICK
Administrative director of the Young Vic Theatre. January 1988.

Jill Trevellick admits one has to be 'tactfully persuasive' in her line of work. When you suggest that 'bossy' might be another way of describing it, she grins and admits that it's not a job to suit a shrinking violet, because colleagues *have* to listen to your advice. At the age of thirty-two, Jill has already run the Liverpool Everyman, been the first and only female front of house manager at the National Theatre and is now the well-respected administrative director at the Young Vic. We were talking just after the announcement had been made that David Thacker would be directing Eugene O'Neill's *A Touch of the Poet*, with Vanessa Redgrave and Timothy Dalton. It would transfer to the West End after the Young Vic showing and was a tremendous coup for the theatre. For Jill it's one of the main reasons she's in the job; to be a part of the process of bringing such drama to the public, even if she also has to be responsible for floor cleaners, contracts, licences and actors' salaries along the way.

Unlike the administrators of commercial companies, Jill says the theatrical administrator's job is all about 'trying to reconcile things which are irreconcilable'. Her most important function, she believes, is to provide the director with the information he needs to make sensible artistic judgements; to run the business, so that the director can get on with casting and directing. In theory, the director has the final say on everything, though in practice most are more than happy to leave some of the more mundane paper work to the administrator:

> My *raison d'être* is that I really want David to do *A Touch of the Poet* or *Comedians*. That's my motivation, though day-to-day work can be the same as a manager in many other spheres. However, there's no market value on the commodity, so you have to be sensitive to the creativity as well as looking at the bottom line.

Jill first became an administrator when she was 'absurdly young' and did encounter many difficulties. She's not sure if that was because she was a woman, or because she was twenty-three. Councillors and the public tended to be the worst:

> I felt that people weren't used to being confronted by a woman in a position of authority and certainly not one who looked so young. I tried to make myself look older by having my hair cut. Also I had to get used to *thinking* of myself as someone in this position and that's quite difficult when you only left university two years ago.

The green room of Liverpool University's Dramsoc was the scene of a chance remark when a fellow student (whose father ran a theatre) mentioned that it was apparently hard to find really good theatre administrators. Jill says she never plans her life much in advance, had been worrying about what to do after a degree, and so was heartened to find a gap in the

21 Jill Trevellick (photo: Gordon Rainsford)

market. (At least her law degree came in handy for the contracts!) She
started almost immediately as the box office manager of the Liverpool
Everyman with absolutely no experience. She was called 'manager'
because she was the only full-time employee in that department. She joined
at a time when the theatre was being rebuilt. Not ìdeal working conditions:

Very often I had to disappear into a cupboard to answer the phones because I couldn't hear anything, but the workmen brought me strong cups of tea to keep me going. I was lucky to be *in* the theatre at all. They had me sitting outside the theatre in a transit van at first. I thought *no one* would ever give me money so I made signs saying 'This really is the Everyman Box Office!'

After a year working in the box office (not all of the time in a van) Jill took on the post of 'publicity manager' for a further twelve months. She didn't apply for the job of administrator. In fact, she was on the interviewing panel! When the board asked her to consider the job herself, she said no, believing she didn't have the weight or experience to tackle a business with a £350,000 turnover. (She admits now, a man in her position would probably have said yes.) She was finally persuaded by the man who was leaving the job to go for the interview, and decided she would have to take it, if the board considered her the right candidate. She finally accepted, and describes the next year as 'a baptism by fire with a totally inadequate apprenticeship'. She survived the accounting side by having many chats with the local, sympathetic bank manager.

The fact she was a woman had a direct influence on her next job. The obvious move would have been to one of the regional reps:

I felt they wouldn't take me seriously because I was then a 26-year-old woman and still felt I wasn't the ideal role model. When I looked around at who *was* doing the jobs, they were basically men who had been in the business at least fifteen years, so I didn't pursue that.

She applied for the post of theatre manager at the National Theatre. At the final interview, Sir Peter Hall said 'You are a very young woman to be taking on this responsibility' then immediately checked himself, adding 'No, I shouldn't say that because people used to say that to *me!*' The main difference in the job was having a staff of 150 instead of twenty and she's certain they were expecting a man to be in charge of them:

Out of all the jobs I've done, that was the one where I least fitted the role model people must have had in their minds. The idea of a theatre manager is someone in a dinner suit and all *I* had was a bow tie!

In fact, the raised eyebrows she encountered when she began her duties were, she feels, more because she'd come from the Liverpool Everyman than because she was young and female. With hindsight, Jill can see it took her at least a year to acclimatize and that she frequently found herself saying 'Well, at the Everyman we used to . . .'

At the Young Vic, she is in charge of twenty-five regular staff as well as the acting company and has the responsibility to step in and help any department she feels is particularly under pressure. Jill freely acknowledges that *her* pressures are greatly helped by her partner, Bob!

I would find this job much more difficult to do if I wasn't able to go home and say, 'Do you know what happened today?' He's unfailingly supportive. Women do need a lot of emotional support and I think they're more able to ask for it.

Though she would like to have children she can't see an easy way they'd fit into her working schedule, which has her at her desk by ten and not usually leaving it till after 6pm on a good day. 'Everyone demands some of your time – that's the great difficulty in being an administrator. It's all over the place and you have to be careful not to be disorganized.'

Her next career move wouldn't, for example, take her to the National or the RSC as administrator. There is a dislocation in the larger organizations, she feels, betwen what happens on stage and what goes on in the administrative offices. 'All the problems and less contact' she suggests.

'Are you ambitious?' I ask,

No, I worked it out of my system! The experience of all that responsibility so early in my career made me realize there was something much more important than having your name on a letter heading.

NANCY MECKLER (director) and CLARE MACINTYRE (writer)
Low Level Panic at the Royal Court, a collaboration with the
Women's Playhouse Trust. February 1988.

Clare Macintyre is an established actress though a new playwright and she noticed a degree of undermining went on as soon as word passed around she was writing a play. The feedback (always safely indirect) asked 'What's she got to say? What's she writing about anyway?' Clare has the perfect answer: '*Low Level Panic* is about women's sexual fantasies.' That usually stops further comment for a while!

Director Nancy Meckler is not phased so easily, nor did she think about the play itself at first:

When you're sent plays, you know nothing. You just open them and usually realize within a few pages that it doesn't grab you, the person can't write. Frankly it was just *such* a surprise to open it up and discover someone who *could* write, that I didn't look at the play. I just wanted to make contact.

When asked what attracted her the most, Nancy describes the play as being 'startlingly honest'. The 'honesty is probably there because Clare wanted to write about something she *felt* rather than go in search of an interesting topic and research a subject. It's not though,' she adds, 'autobiographical!' The play was given a reading in June 1987 and she was then commissioned by the Women's Playhouse Trust to develop it. The final go-ahead for the Royal Court showing was in December:

Clare. I went completely berserk because I thought 'I'll never do it, I'll never cope' but here we are all in one piece.

22 Clare McIntyre

Not only in one piece, but with a commission for a further play. *Low Level Panic* has three female characters: Jo, Mary and Celia who share a flat and battle over the bathroom. Clare thinks her student experiences probably shaped the play, though says she wasn't aware of that as she wrote. 'Setting the play in a bathroom just seemed right, and I'm still sure it's right, though I can't explain why.' Nancy also felt it was a world she could believe in, though she doesn't always understand what a play is *about* from the beginning. 'It's more to do with whether the writing is alive and whether there are real characters there. It becomes a journey of discovery to see what it's about.'

Clare took a drama degree at Manchester University. She had originally gone to study sociology, but only lasted one week. After attending a lecture on 'The Methodology of Research', she realized her maths were not sufficient to last the course and switched to general arts. A year later she'd changed to a drama course and found she was an actress. Writing, however took more confidence. She doesn't see a clear motivation, ony a clear circumstance that made her branch out:

> I did a film (*The Pirates of Penzance*) and earned lots of money. For the first time I had a little stash, and started writing because I was relaxed enough to do it and didn't have this great burden of having to get a job. It was not so much motivation as getting the confidence to do it. I just wanted to find my own voice and what was truthful for me. I think you then come up with better work because you're not trying to fit in with other people's plans.

Clare describes her reaction to the news that this 'truthful' work was to receive a wider public as, 'not so much surprise as total shock horror and, yes, delight!' For Nancy, as director, it's a happy production on which to work – particularly for a female director. The situation isn't always as pleasant:

> If you're very upset at what's happening (like if you feel the people producing the play aren't behind you), I think it's a lot easier for a man to shout and for everyone to go running, saying 'He's upset.' If a woman shouts, people roll their eyes and say, 'She's becoming a bit hysterical,' and you feel awful because you know it's happening! A woman's voice *does* tend to get shriller and if you get *really* angry, you might even cry which is the worst thing you can possibly do.

Nancy adds that she's managed to avoid tears for a long time, but she's also tried to work more in places where she's felt supported. At the Royal Court, for example, she's impressed that, on very low budgets, everyone is 100 per cent behind the production.

Like Clare, Nancy began as an actress and says she 'fell into directing'. During her acting training she was required to direct and then started to acquire a reputation as someone who *could*. Suddenly she was directing all the time, was not getting much work as an actress so she 'just let it go' realizing she didn't have the 'courage' to act. When you ask if a director doesn't need *more* courage, she laughs and says you only have to inspire *others* with courage. 'It's much easier to say "I believe in you" than to say it to yourself, let me tell you!' Nancy quotes Peter Brook who says there are two types of directors. The first goes in with an amazing concept, explains it and inspires the cast to make the vision come true. 'The other type goes into the rehearsal room on a voyage of discovery when you don't know where you're going to end up. I put myself in the latter class,' she says. She only gains confidence during the rehearsal process when the choices she's making no longer seem arbitrary. Clare interjects to say she doesn't care if a director is male or female just so long as they 'don't go on about how clever they are with the play – particularly if it's *your* play!'

Both have noticed more female directors emerging during the last few years, perhaps because they've been more in evidence at the major houses:

> *Nancy.* I think these things have to be done quite self-consciously at first and I'm sure the RSC and the National felt embarrassed and shamed into having women directors. That doesn't matter because after a while it just becomes a question of whether it was good or not. I think it *does* have to be artificial at first; it doesn't happen naturally, does it?

Nancy should know. She's saddled with the unenviable label of 'The First Woman Director at the National Theatre', though it's not something she's unduly concerned about. 'If you've got very blue eyes, you don't go around talking about it the whole time, only when it comes up.' She's keen to fight the feeling she's been discriminated against. However, she has a nagging suspicion it has happened. Ten years ago she directed *Uncle Vanya* and had the kind of reviews that materialize once in a career. She never received a further offer to direct Chekhov and says she's sure that had she been a man the offers would have filtered through.

Clare became aware of discrimination on a different level when she spent three years with the Women's Theatre group as an actress, also commissioning and working with women writers. There was certainly evidence that if a play was 'feminist' it stood far less chance of being put on by male-dominated companies (in other words most of them). It hasn't however, made a difference to the way *she* writes:

> I'm not going to be writing like a man, because I'm not a man, but because most playwrights to date have been men. The way men write is what people tend to think plays are. *Low Level Panic* couldn't have been written by a man. And it's not the answer to have male playwrights doing good parts for women (David Hare's *Plenty*, Tom Kempinski's *Duet for One*). It goes deeper.

She does have to reassure people she's still acting. 'I'm starting to be known as someone who *used to* act. I had to tell my agent I haven't retired!' At the moment she's enjoying her solitude which makes it easier to write. She says she hates anyone around her while she's working.

Nancy has a husband 'in the business' (David Aukin at the National Theatre) and two children. She suffers the usual guilt of working mothers that neither role is being fulfilled perfectly but says she was lucky not having a great deal of work when the children were small. She doesn't think she could ever have pursued her career had she not had a husband who could offer financial support. She remembers a friend saying to her, 'Nancy, you just have to assume your career is ten years behind that of any man.'

> Actually it made me feel more comfortable because instead of thinking 'Oh God, I'm thirty-two and I still haven't done this', I could suddenly think if I was twenty-two, then it would be all right. The trouble is that you haven't as much energy as you get older, so there is a problem about it all happening ten years late! It will always be a problem unless a woman is very good at handing her children over *completely* to a nanny.

Index